CHRISTMAS PAST

It was time to look to the future...

When seventeen-year-old Mary O'Connor collapses in church she is taken to live with Dr Roberts and his wife in a beautiful Yorkshire village, where she becomes the daughter they were never able to have. With Britain at war, she works in the local steel works but when her fiancé Tom Downing is killed, a grief-stricken Mary is convinced it is retribution for their night of sin during Tom's Christmas leave. Eventually Mary marries local miner Jack Holmes, and sets up her own dressmaking business, but the business starts to dominate her life until tragedy once more threatens to destroy all she most cherishes.

CHRISTMAS PAST

CHRISTMAS PAST

by

Glenice Crossland

Magna Large Print Books
Long Preston, North Yorkshire,
BD23 4ND, England.

British Library Cataloguing in Publication Data.

Crossland, Glenice
    Christmas past.

    A catalogue record of this book is
    available from the British Library

    ISBN   978-0-7505-2856-6

First published in Great Britain in 2007 by William Heinemann

Published in Large Print 2008 by arrangement with
William Heinemann,
one of the publishers in Random House Group Ltd.

Magna Large Print is an imprint of Library Magna Books Ltd.

Printed and bound in Great Britain by
T.J. (International) Ltd., Cornwall, PL28 8RW

For my brother Bernard,
Dorothy and Simon.
With love.

Acknowledgements

With thanks once again to Georgina Hawtrey-Woore and all the Random House team for their continuing support. Also to Rob Hindle and the members of the WEA Creative Writing class at Stocksbridge, for their encouragement and friendship.

Special thanks to Maggie Caine for patiently struggling through my first draft. And to Maureen Hall for taking the trouble to read my finished script.

Chapter One

'Michael, you must let her go. It will be the making of the girl.'

Mick O'Connor made no response and the priest tapped his fingers on the oilcloth-covered table in frustration. He tried again. 'It's just what Mary needs. The finest fresh air, nourishing food and most of all the treatment for her TB glands. Rowland Roberts is a fine doctor,' he stressed.

'She should be getting the treatment she needs here, from our own doctor, in her own home,' Mick O'Connor said.

Mariah O'Connor gave her husband a look which spoke volumes. 'Yes, we know she should be having treatment here, Mick, and we all know why she isn't getting it: because nothing's been paid off the doctor's bill since our Michael was born.' She broddled the poker through the shining, blackleaded bars and riddled the ashes vigorously into the pan below. 'A shilling a week is all it would take.'

'Just as I was saying,' the priest continued, 'Rowland Roberts will give Mary a course of injections which will put her right in no time. Besides, she'll have a room of her own.'

Young Mary O'Connor had been supposedly engrossed in a library book but she gave Father Flynn her full attention at the mention of her own room.

11

'After all, the boys ought not to be in with the girls for much longer.'

Mick O'Connor shuffled nervously in the straight-backed chair. Father Flynn was right as usual. Although his sons Bill, Jimmy and Michael were younger than their three sisters it wouldn't be long before the sleeping arrangements would have to be looked at. Mariah had told him often enough, not that she nagged though the Lord knew she had good reason to do so. Oh no, she wasn't the type of woman to nag. Too good for the likes of him was Mariah. He would have to mend his ways, keep off the beer and move them out to somewhere better.

If he had but known it the same thought was going through the mind of every other person in the room. His wife Mariah was mentally exhausted by trying to make ends meet and had been driven to waiting at the pit gates on a Friday in order to get her hands on the housekeeping money before the nearest pub landlord did so. Even so, if Mick had run short of beer money by Monday he would help himself to anything left in her purse, in order to finance another day's drinking. A collier's Monday they called it, and it was rare for some of the miners to turn in for work on the first day of the week. God only knew how Mick had kept his job. Still, he was said to be the hardest grafter in the pit on the days he did turn in. It made Mariah seethe inside to think of the money wasted on beer when they could have moved out of the row and into somewhere large enough to house them all comfortably.

Young Mary at the tender age of sixteen and a

12

few years older than Norah and Kathleen was having visions of a room of her own. To begin with she hadn't really wanted to go and live with the doctor friend of Father Flynn and his wife in a village somewhere in Yorkshire. She had begun to panic at the thought of leaving home and travelling halfway across the country. Admittedly the thought of leaving the employment of the awful Mrs Brown and her two pampered daughters had been tempting, but not tempting enough to persuade her. The promise of a room of her own was another matter. Mary had begun to dread the time of the month when her periods began. Smuggling the blanket squares in and out of the bedroom was difficult enough, but if the bleeding started unexpectedly during the night, hiding the bloodstained sheets and nightie was virtually impossible. In fact only last week young Michael had asked if she had cut herself and sent his older brothers off into a fit of giggles.

Another thing Mary hated was the thin wall against which she slept. When her da had been drinking he never cared how much noise he made, or how the bedhead knocked against the wall when he did things to her ma. Mary would draw the blanket over her ears and pray that her ma wouldn't become pregnant again and overcrowd the house even more. Then she would have to go to confession and tell Father Flynn about her sinful thoughts. She blushed when she remembered some of the things she had revealed to the good father about her family.

Oh, she did wish her da would keep off the beer. She loved him dearly from Tuesday to

Friday when he had no money left and came straight home from the pit. Black as hell's kettle was how her ma would describe him. There he would sit in the old tin bath in front of the fire whilst her ma scrubbed him with the hard brush, but even the scrubbing brush and carbolic never managed to remove the blue slivers of coal embedded in his flesh.

Father Flynn's thoughts were taking a similar turn. 'They're a good couple, Michael.' He was still bent on persuasion. 'They were never blessed with children of their own; Mary will be treated like their own daughter.'

'Aye, don't you see, man, that's the trouble? She isn't theirs. She's mine, my Mary, and I love her.'

Mary was shocked to see that her da looked close to tears.

'It's all right, Da, I won't go,' she said. 'I don't want to leave Newcastle anyway.' But she did. The idea of going on a train and out of Newcastle for the first time in her life had begun to seem like an adventure.

Father Flynn ignored her. 'Yes, Michael, you love Mary, you love all your offspring. The trouble is you love the drink more.'

The living kitchen suddenly became deathly silent. Michael O'Connor sat with his head in his hands, for once lost for words.

'I'll make a pot of tea,' Mariah muttered, and filled the kettle at the low stone sink.

'I'll help you, Ma,' Mary said, lifting the cups from the hooks beneath the shelf in the corner.

Father Flynn realised he had overstepped the

mark. He wasn't an interfering man, nor did he usually moralise. Besides, he felt immense pity for the man across the table, who hadn't been a drinking man at all until a few years ago. It was the explosion at the pit that had begun his downfall. The priest couldn't condemn him, not after what had happened: it had been enough to drive any man to drink. Michael O'Connor had dug, sometimes with his bare hands, to free the trapped men. And then to find his twin brother almost sliced down the middle would have landed many a man in the asylum; in Michael's case it had sent him to the bottle.

The four of them sat, Mary and her mother clutching their hot teacups between their hands, the men facing each other with the steaming brew in front of them, all lost for words. It was Mariah who finally broke the silence.

'You're sure they would look after her, Father? If she went, I mean.'

'Ma, I'm sixteen,' Mary pointed out. 'I can look after myself.'

'Do you think I'd let her go otherwise, Mariah? A lassie I've watched blossom since the day she was born?'

'And she'd get the course of injections the doctor says she needs?'

'She would.'

'And she wouldn't be worked to death like she is at the Browns'?'

'A few light duties is all that would be required of her. Why, if I know Gladys Roberts, Mary will be the one who's waited on hand and foot.'

Father Flynn knew all about the longing Gladys

15

had harboured for many years, the yearning for a child of her own. He considered it a tragedy, a couple with so much love to give and no child to lavish it upon. When he had written to Rowland asking for advice on how to treat TB glands, he hadn't really been surprised when his friend replied with an invitation for Mary to go and stay with them, and he hadn't been fooled for a second by the explanation that they were in need of a maid.

Mick O'Connor spoke at last. 'She shouldn't have been at the Browns'. A bloody slave-driver, that woman – I never could abide her. The hours she worked, no wonder she's suffering. I should never have let her go.'

'It's all right, Da – she's not all that bad. I get paid regularly, and look at the clothes she gives me.'

'Aye, so she can brag about what a charitable woman she is.'

'More like it's an excuse to buy more finery for her two horsey-looking daughters. Dress them in as many fancy ribbons as she likes and they'll still look as though they ought to be pulling a plough.'

Mary giggled, pleased that Father Flynn was back to his normal jovial self.

'Ten hours a day my lass worked for that woman, and I let her carry on. If she hadn't collapsed in church she'd still have been doing it. What sort of father does that make me?'

'Now then, Michael, you weren't to know the girl was ill. It was nobody's fault.'

'Would she...' Mick looked embarrassed at his sudden thought, 'would she be able to come

16

home? If she didn't like it, I mean.'

'She'll have a return ticket if and when she needs one. The Robertses promised me that.'

'What do you say, lass? Do you want to go or not?'

Mary felt a surge of excitement wash over her but tried not to appear too eager. 'Only if you think I should, Da,' she said. 'And only if I can come home if I don't like it.'

'You'll like it, Mary, I promise.' Father Flynn was almost as excited as if he was going with her. 'Wait till you see the place. I won't tell you any more. Let it be as much of a surprise as it was for me the first time I visited my old friend. The best friend I've ever had, even if he is a blooming Protestant.'

The priest thought back to when he and Rowland Roberts had first met on their arrival at university. He chuckled to himself as he remembered some of the antics they'd got up to in those carefree days.

Mary grinned. She had known Father Flynn would persuade them. He could get blood out of a stone, that man; her da had always said so.

Torn between excitement and anxiety, Mary had worried all the way from Newcastle about what she would do if no one should be at the station to meet her. However, Father Flynn had arranged everything to perfection, and she had spotted the chauffeur even before the train had drawn to a halt at Sheffield.

She was soon settled nervously in the back seat of the gleaming black Morris and for the rest of

17

the journey sat feeling somewhat in awe of the dark-haired driver, who didn't look much older than herself. Fortunately, he whistled cheerfully most of the way so conversation was unnecessary. Instead she found herself relaxing and marvelling at the comfort of the soft leather seats, in the first car she had travelled in throughout her uneventful life.

It was only as they approached the drive that Mary became aware of her surroundings. Green lawns, still sparkling from an earlier shower, spread out before her, lined by rhododendron bushes and disappearing to the rear of a beautiful old house.

'Holy mackerel,' she exclaimed, using one of her mother's habitual expressions, 'I must have arrived in heaven.'

She scrambled out of the car, completely unaware that the young driver was being given an equally interesting view of brown lisle stocking tops. Remembering his manners he turned away, but not before he had managed a good eyeful of shapely white thigh.

Mary gathered her few pieces of luggage together, mesmerised by the glory of the scene. The large, stone-gabled house; the miles of purple-heathered moorland stretching to left and right and down to the long valley below them, then up the hill beyond; the looming grey crags in the distance; and everywhere green meadows, like a patchwork quilt, dotted here and there with stone farmhouses. To the left two tiny hamlets nestled, one deep in the valley, the other high on the opposite hill.

Mary's wide brown eyes travelled downwards to the valley and the large, pear-shaped reservoir that had been created there. She could see smoke rising to the right, a looming grey cloud of it.

'Is something on fire over there?' she enquired of the rather handsome young man beside her.

'No, that's Sheffield yer can see. Spoils the view a bit, doesn't it? Still, it's handy for the shopping and not too far for the doctor to travel to the hospital. He lends me the car sometimes, to take my young brothers to the park. A right good sort is Dr Roberts. Yer mustn't take advantage of 'im, mind. He's not daft and he'll soon 'ave yer weighed up.'

'Oh, I would never do that,' Mary assured him. 'But why would anyone want to visit a park when they've all this countryside here?'

'Yer'll be surprised. When you've been here a week or two yer'll be longing to get back to civilisation, especially in't winter when snow blocks road to Longfield. Yer'll wish yer'd never set eyes on't place. If yer look over t'other way that's Lower Longfield in the bottom and up the hill is Upper Longfield. Doesn't the church stand well? I suppose yer'll be going there on Sunday. Even if yer not religious it meks a change.'

'Is it Catholic?' Mary asked doubtfully.

'No. We don't have a Catholic church in Longfield. I expect yer'd 'ave to go into Sheffield for the nearest, although there is one over in Millington where some of the lads go on St Patrick's night, but that's only to the dance – yer'd be as bad burned as scalded trying to get over there every Sunday. By the way, I'm Tom Downing. I hope yer like it here and stay a bit longer than the others. Like I said, it isn't much of a place for young folk. I'm used to the quiet, being born down in the village, but for someone from town it takes some getting used to. Can't seem to keep a maid at all. Can't think why, with a good boss like doctor. Where are yer from, anyway? Obviously not Yorkshire with an accent like that.'

'Newcastle.' Mary smiled and clasped Tom's outstretched hand, then grabbed her bags and hurried up the steps towards the large panelled door. It opened even before she reached it, revealing a rather buxom, grey-haired lady who looked immaculate in a black skirt and crisp white blouse, the sight of which made Mary feel even more bedraggled. She should have brushed her hair in the car, and someone should have warned her not to stand near the edge of the platform. She had been speckled with soot even before leaving Newcastle.

She patted her beautiful chestnut hair back into the tortoiseshell comb behind her head. Then her hand was clasped in a warm welcoming one and she was drawn into the hall, from which a staircase curved upwards. Mary had seen a picture of one like it once, in a book at Father Flynn's, but imagined they only existed in the homes of film stars and royalty.

Gladys Roberts not only fussed like a mother hen, she looked quite like one too. Her head jutted forward when she walked and her nose had a little bump on it making it rather beak-like in the middle of her ruddy face. Despite her fifty years her eyes had not yet lost their healthy shine, and her whole appearance seemed to ooze energy. She had been up since six this morning cooking and baking. The windows had been polished to a high shine with crumpled newspaper and the large range in the kitchen blackleaded until it gleamed. Despite the warm August day she had built up a fire to give the kitchen a cosy glow, and all for the new maid. Dr Roberts had pointed out to his wife that Mary was not to be treated like a hotel guest but as the girl appointed to do all the tiresome jobs Gladys was now doing herself, thus leaving her time for the leisurely pursuits befitting a doctor's wife. But Gladys Roberts had no more intention of taking to her sofa with a piece of fancy, useless embroidery than the doctor had of neglecting his patients.

Truth to tell it wasn't a maid Gladys needed but someone on whom to lavish the deep maternal love which had grown in her heart from the day she was first married. Not once in all the years had she voiced her disappointment at her childless state but inside she had grieved continuously, as much for her husband's sake as for her own. She had never suspected it to be his fault, nor he hers. They had come together from the first with an earthy passion, never forced but exchanged spontaneously, whenever and wherever the urge came over them. Yet for all the love they had to give she had remained barren.

Gradually the pain had subsided but she still continued to lavish her pent-up affection on any young person available. If only the house had been nearer to town she would possibly have considered adoption, but, being an unselfish soul, by the time she realised it was too late for motherhood she considered herself too old to be a suitable companion for a child out here at the back of beyond.

So a series of maids came and went again after a few months, and now another. Perhaps this one would be different. She certainly looked less flighty than the previous ones. Father Flynn had pointed out in his letter that Mary was hard-working and eager to be taught, but in the end what had persuaded Mrs Roberts to take her on instead of one of the local girls was the fact that Mary had been diagnosed as suffering from TB glands. Newcastle and the lack of nourishment endemic among miners' families there could only restrict her recovery, so here she was, to be filled with as much food as could be stuffed inside her and more fresh air than she had breathed in her entire life.

'Come in, come in. Whatever is Tom thinking of letting you carry those bags? You must be exhausted after your journey. Here, let me take your coat. We usually leave our outer wear down here in the hall – it saves so many journeys up and down stairs when we're in and out of the garden or the outbuildings. The wind's cutting up here in winter so don't you be running around without a coat.'

Mary's coat was placed carefully on the hall stand along with the more expensive garments belonging to the Robertses. She felt her face burning at the sight of the threadbare sleeves, but Mrs Roberts didn't seem to notice. She guided Mary by the elbow through the first door on the right. 'This is the dining room. Don't you think it's lovely?'

Mary managed to suppress the words 'Holy mackerel'. Instead she stood there open-mouthed. The rectangular room seemed enormous, with a large marble fireplace furnishing one wall and three tall windows along the opposite one. A long table in the centre was surrounded by eight velvet-bottomed chairs and everything in the room seemed to shine like the new pennies in a Christmas stocking.

Dumbfounded, Mary followed Mrs Roberts back into the hall and towards the door opposite.

'This is the lounge, smaller but much more comfortable, I think.'

'A piano!' Mary couldn't conceal her excitement. For years she had been fascinated with the school piano, pomming out 'Chopsticks' with one finger whenever Miss Williams happened to leave the room and receiving a crack across the knuckles with a ruler on numerous occasions for her efforts. Of course she would never be allowed to touch this one either, but she might hear someone else playing it.

Mrs Roberts was flicking an imaginary fleck of dust from its lid.

'Yes, and doesn't it take up some space? Still, my husband loves his music. He's the choirmaster, you know,' she told Mary with pride. 'We usually retire in here after supper. He's obsessed with the wireless at present. World affairs, you know.'

Mary didn't know, but she wasn't going to admit it.

Apart from the piano – a baby grand which really did take up some room – and a wireless set on a small table, all the room contained were two large leather straight-backed easy chairs and a long low sofa. Not one like Father Flynn's with worn upholstery and a wobbly leg, but a beautiful, padded, leather one with two curved arms and a buttoned back. The leather matched the wooden floor and the walls which weren't lined with books were also of panelled wood. The curtains and central carpet square were a warm honey beige. Mary wondered how she would keep a carpet of such a pale shade clean.

'And now the scullery, my favourite room.'

Mary loved it on sight. The long, white, scrubbed table, with chairs to match, was laid at one end with a folded checked cloth and a china tea set. The fire cast a glow on to the brass fender surrounding the nasturtium-patterned hearth tin, and the copper kettle, saucepans and bellows hanging on the wall. Two spindle-backed chairs were set in front of the fire, and long wooden cupboards lined the back wall. A side dresser was stacked with willow-patterned crockery, and shelves were crammed with colourful chutneys, jams and preserves. The alcove by the fire was brightened by gingham curtains, under which was a sparkling white ceramic sink.

Mary had never seen anything like it. The contrast with the living kitchen back home was unbelievable. If only her ma could have a kitchen like this – no, a scullery. She must remember to call it a scullery from now on.

She never thought she would be grateful for the elocution lessons Father Flynn had encouraged her to have, but she was glad of them now. At least Mrs Roberts could understand what she was talking about. Her Newcastle accent was not nearly as pronounced as it used to be, and anyway Mrs Roberts had a slight Yorkshire accent herself, although it was a lovely voice all the same.

'Come and sit down, Mary,' she was saying. 'We'll have a cup of tea. You must be parched. Or would you prefer nettle beer?'

'Oh, tea please,' said Mary, not sure what nettle beer tasted like, or if it would have the same effect on her as the beer had on her da.

A slice of parkin was placed in front of her, sticky and hot with spices, almost as good as her ma's.

'Eat as much as you like. We really must fatten you up a bit and get some roses in your cheeks. We grow all our own fruit and vegetables, thanks to Tom. I really don't know what we'd do without that boy. I do hope we aren't going to lose him to the war service but Dr Roberts can see it happening soon. Still, I hope you'll be a help to me when you become accustomed to things. Then I should have more time to spend in the garden. If there's one thing I enjoy it's my garden. Are you used to housework, Mary?'

'Oh, yes, ma'am. I've been in service since I was fourteen, and learned from my mother long before that. My mother's the best cook in our street: everyone comes to her for help at weddings and funerals. The trouble is she's hard up most of the time so can't afford the ingredients, but I can cook almost as good as she can. Even Mrs Brown who I worked for admitted that and she never says anything good about anyone.'

Mary blushed as she realised she was rambling on but Mrs Roberts laughed and poured another cup of tea.

'I think we're going to get along fine, Mary,' she said. 'But now you must be tired. Come, let me show you to your room. We have supper in here at seven thirty, but don't bother coming down tonight. I'll bring you a tray and you can have an early night. We'll discuss your duties in the morning.'

Mary marvelled at her room. At home, the only privacy she ever had was in the lavatory and even there she'd rush in and out again, panic-stricken at the sound of scurrying rats from the midden round the back. And now, here she was, in this beautiful room.

Though the sun had disappeared the room seemed to be filled with light. The yellow curtains were matched with the bed covers and the lino on the floor. A carpet square of green reminded Mary of the velvety lawns outside. She looked out of the window, unable to believe anything could be so glorious.

If only their Norah and Kathleen could see her now, and her ma and da. Oh, she was going to miss them. She felt the tears prickling her eyes, but she mustn't cry. Mrs Roberts might think she didn't like her room and she seemed such a kind woman, it would be dreadful to disappoint her.

Mary unbuttoned her dress and stepped out of it. Then she poured water from the jug into the basin and began to wash, finally stepping out of her undergarments and washing her whole body, revelling in the silky feel of the water, softened by the scented soap and the fluffiness of the towel, yellow to match the furnishings. How lovely to smell of lemon instead of carbolic.

The knock on the door startled her.

'Can I come in? What was I thinking of, not showing you the bathroom? Slip on your dressing gown and I'll take you now. Then you can eat your supper.'

Mary blushed. She had never had a dressing gown; indeed, it was only thanks to Mrs Brown that she had a couple of presentable nighties. She slipped one over her head and stood waiting.

Gladys Roberts suddenly realised the girl's plight. Wishing she could recall her words, she left the room and was back immediately with a dressing gown of her own.

'I wonder if you would like this?' she said. 'It's far too small for me. Come along, the bathroom is just along the corridor. Don't worry if you hear a banging in the night, it's only the air in the water pipes. If you want a bath this is the best time – the water has time to heat up again then for the doctor. I usually take mine in the afternoon, when I've finished in the garden.' She smiled.

The bath was unlike anything Mary had ever seen, long enough to lie down in and decorated with a blue floral pattern. The water closet stood beside it. Mary was speechless.

'Well, I'll leave you now, but don't be too long or your cocoa will be cold. Goodnight, Mary. I'll see you at breakfast.'

Then Mary was alone, more alone than she'd ever been in her life, and she didn't care at all.

Chapter Two

During the months that followed only three things worried Mary. One was the electricity. For the first few days she managed to avoid switching the contraptions on and off by busying herself with other things until Mrs Roberts did it for her. Finally she had to tackle the frightening thing herself, and was surprised to find it quite painless. After that she was delighted to use the huge, noisy vacuum cleaner which made the carpets look almost new again, and she always made sure the lounge was bathed in light by the time the doctor and his wife retired there in the evening after supper.

The second thing she worried about was the injections. The doctor had given her two so far, and even though they didn't hurt she felt quite sick at the thought of them. Dr Roberts had examined her carefully and gently, given her a large bottle of Scotts Emulsion with which she was to dose herself every night, and done her more good than all the medicine in Sheffield by telling her she was like a ray of sunshine flitting about the house with her freckled face and shimmering hair. She was still rather scared of him, with his booming voice and his infectious laughter.

'Hello,' he would bellow every time he passed her as she went about her work. 'And what has my little town mouse been up to today then?'

At first Mary had blushed and stood there

tongue-tied, but gradually she had found herself beginning to enthuse over the day's activities: how she'd dared to feed the hens without Tom's assistance, or had made five pounds of bilberry jam, learning quickly from Mrs Roberts how to test the fruit – which had cropped late this year – for setting.

After a while the doctor sought Mary out most evenings for a chat, on the pretext of asking if she was feeling better, an unnecessary question, for Mary was blooming like the beautiful bronze chrysanthemums which were at present growing in profusion in the glass lean-to round the back of the house. She gradually overcame her shyness and chatted away as though she'd known him for ever. His little goat's beard and curled moustache fascinated her, and once she had grown accustomed to the volume she found his deep voice beautiful. Once she heard him singing to his wife's accompaniment on the piano and she opened her bedroom door to hear more clearly, overcome by the deep bass rendering of 'Linden Lea', and other songs she had never heard before.

The third worry, which Mary harboured long after the others had been solved, was what to do about her religion. She had written a carefully worded letter to Father Flynn, along with one to her mother, giving them to Tom to post in Longfield. She had explained how she had not been to Mass since leaving home as the only church within reach was Protestant, and it was time she went to confession. So far the only reply had been from her mother, and that was no help at all. Ma assured Mary that the family were all well, and then went on to tell her about Joyce Bailey, who had been her best friend. Joyce, to everyone's dismay, was expecting. The young man, who had been in Newcastle looking for work, had moved on before Joyce had realised the plight she was in, and her father had thrown her out on to the street. Joyce had been taken in by One Shilling Lil and everyone knew how she'd turn out living with a woman like that. Everybody was sorry for the girl's ma, being shamed like that, and Mary must remember not to do anything which would put her in the same position.

Mary, who had been looking forward to her first letter, felt quite depressed after reading it. Poor Joyce. All her life she had been deprived of affection. Her parents had been even worse than her da for the drink, and Joyce had been brought up hanging around pub doorways waiting for closing time. Maybe she'd be better off with One Shilling Lil. At least Lil's house was clean, and she had often given Mary and the other children a penny or a slice of bread and jam when they were little. Then her ma had found out and forbidden her to go there again. Mary had learned later that Lil had come by her name by entertaining men during the evenings, but she still liked her. She was a kind woman. Maybe that's why the men liked her, too: because she was kind and laughed a lot. Besides, she was ever so pretty. Yes, Joyce would be all right with Lil. Mary knew she shouldn't be thinking such things and felt ashamed. She really ought to go to confession, but she couldn't ask Mrs Roberts, her being Church of England.

Suddenly, Mary's worry was resolved by Dr

Roberts. Once a month he visited the orphanage at Upper Longfield. His duty was to keep an eye on the children, treating any colds, tummy upsets or more serious complaints which affected them from time to time. The orphanage was run by nuns from the convent, a dark dismal place hidden completely by trees so that passers-by rarely noticed it, and even if they did they were deterred from exploring further by the locked iron gates.

The young novices' only worldly pleasure was working at the orphanage, when at least they were allowed to speak freely and enjoy caring for the children, who would have been in a sorry state without them. Dr Roberts was the only male, apart from the priest, they were allowed contact with and they had even been known to laugh on occasions during his visits, as he narrated anecdotes to them from the outside world. He knew he was their only link with it and made sure he passed on any items of local gossip, feeling pity for the poor girls cooped up away from reality.

It was on one of his visits to the orphanage that he mentioned Mary, and was told she might attend Mass in the chapel once a week. Tom was to take her every Wednesday, when she could also make confession. Dr Roberts found it difficult to imagine what she could possibly have to confess, but he knew from a letter he had received from Father Flynn that she was worrying about it. Why in God's name hadn't the girl told him? And there was he thinking she was nicely settled in and able to talk to him without reservation now. Well, at least she didn't hide away from him any more, or blush crimson at the sight of him.

31

Besides, she had certainly done Gladys a world of good. He hadn't seen her so animated in years; teaching the girl to dressmake now by the looks of things. He must arrange with Tom to take them into town next week when he dropped him off at the hospital.

Gladys could buy some material then and have the girl make herself some pretty dresses, instead of the dismal things she was wearing now, even when off duty.

Mary was in seventh heaven. They had set off at eight o'clock along the road to Sheffield. The moors resembled a large golden-brown carpet, and the hedgerows were a mass of scarlet rose hips and luscious juicy blackberries. Hazelnuts clustered together on branches overhead.

She spoke not one word on the journey to the infirmary. Dr Roberts had to be dropped off at eight thirty and had promised to show them the new operating theatre block before Tom took them into town.

Mary, who had never been in a hospital before, would rather have stayed in the car, but had to admit the place was impressive. Mrs Roberts left Mary alone and went off to chat with her husband's colleagues, and when Mary caught a glimpse inside an opened door she felt quite faint at the sight of a small boy lying on a rubber sheet on the floor. A nurse, seeing her scared white face, assured her that he was only recovering from having his tonsils out.

'The recovery room will be full before the day is out,' she said. Even so, Mary hoped she would never need a tonsillectomy herself, and was most relieved when they were on their way again.

Tom weaved his way in and out amongst the tram-cars. He seemed to know exactly where he was going and pointed out various landmarks as they passed them by. He knew just where preparations were being made in case of attack. The announcement that Britain was at war had been made a few days ago. Dr Roberts had come sadly home from church and told them the news, his eyes filling with tears as he did so. By now most of the halls throughout the town had been either closed or taken over for military recruiting and other purposes. Tom seemed to know all about it, and told Mary how the city had undergone a trial blackout as long ago as last year, so that things would be in order when the war finally came.

Now the worst had happened. Everybody was living in fear and a kind of panic had set in. Children were being sent to schools out in Derbyshire, and some had already been evacuated. However, Sheffield seemed not the least bit frightening to Mary, and when Tom dropped them off at the market she almost skipped with excitement by the side of Mrs Roberts.

Gladys Roberts didn't usually shop in Castle Market, but today was Mary's day. If she was to settle in Sheffield, as Gladys hoped she would, she would need to know her way about. They bought a few yards of fine material, which Gladys let Mary choose herself. She didn't interfere except to suggest that Mary would look lovely in green or lemon, which would bring out the colour of her hair. Mary took her advice and left the stall thrilled with the chosen fabric.

They also found fresh herrings for tea, and Mrs Roberts bought some extra for Tom to take home for his family. Mary was fascinated by the fish market, and Gladys bought her a tiny plate of cockles to eat at the stall. She thought they were delicious.

Afterwards they walked up town and Gladys showed Mary the City Hall. They wandered round the gardens and visited the Graves Art Gallery. When Tom returned with the grocery order they went to Gladys's favourite restaurant for lunch together, and the coffee was so delicious that Gladys bought some beans to take home. Mary loved Sheffield and thought it was the happiest day she had ever spent. Even so, she couldn't wait to get home and begin work on her new dresses.

As she tacked the dress material ready for Mrs Roberts to sew, however, she began to feel a little guilty. Her sisters would be wearing the same old dresses they had had when she left, some of them cast-offs of her own. She felt the warmth and comfort of the scullery around her and tears pricked her eyes as she recalled the shabbiness of the kitchen back home. Suddenly she needed her mother's smile and the sound of her sisters and brothers, laughing or even arguing. For all the luxury of Moorland House, nothing could make up for home. Then Mrs Roberts smiled across the table and Mary cast aside her homesickness and the feeling of guilt. This was her home now. Even so, she vowed to write to her parents regularly and make sure none of her family forgot her.

She handed the tacked bodice to Mrs Roberts

and excitement overcame her sadness. She was to have a new dress to go with her new life, a life she could never have imagined until she came to Longfield. She vowed that if she ever had children of her own she would do everything within her power to protect them from poverty and instil in them the importance of working hard to keep to the standard she was determined to set for them.

Chapter Three

It was Mary's big night. Tom was to take her to the Harvest Ball in Longfield School. Dr Roberts was lending him the car and had given Mary permission to stay until eleven thirty. He didn't know who was the more excited, Mary or Gladys. Mary looked a picture in the dark green crêpe de Chine dress. The bodice fitted like a second skin, emphasising her high firm breasts, and the skirt flared out over her slim hips. Mary had thought the pattern much too plain but could now see Mrs Roberts's reason for choosing it.

'What did I tell you?' Gladys said. 'You don't need frills and flounces with hair like yours.' She was right: Mary's hair shone like polished copper. Gladys had tied it back loosely with a ribbon the colour of her dress. Round her neck she placed a single strand of pearls. Mary had protested, afraid she might lose them, but Mrs Roberts insisted, saying pearls needed to be worn otherwise they would lose their lustre. Dr Roberts had arrived home the previous evening with a pair of satin shoes, with a dainty heel and a strap fastened with a satin-covered button. Mary had almost hugged him and he had been touched by her gratitude. He knew he was a fool treating the girl like one of the family, but the pleasure he gained from having her around the house was a reward in itself.

When the door bell rang Mary's heart almost skipped a beat. She hadn't been able to help wondering if Tom had invited her to the dance out of sympathy. Still, his two sisters were joining them, so he needn't feel tied to her for the night.

If only she'd known it, her worries were groundless. Tom liked Mary. She didn't throw herself at him as the last maid had, nor did she shirk her work or become hysterical at the sight of a few hens. Even so, he wasn't prepared for the sight of her standing there in the hall. Like a vision she was. None of the other lasses would hold a candle to her. By, he'd have to keep an eye on her where the lads were concerned. They'd be round her like flies round a jam pot.

'It's only Prince Charming come to escort Cinders to the ball,' he joked, trying hard not to stare at her.

Mary laughed and blushed, her eyes shining. She would have liked to tell him how handsome he looked in his dark blue suit and stiff-collared white shirt, but it wouldn't be right. She suddenly realised he might not be here for much longer. He had confided to her a few days before that he would soon be joining up, and it was only then that she had realised how fond of him she had become.

'Come on then,' he said, 'the coach awaits yer.'

She looked at Gladys and the doctor. 'I shan't be late,' she said, then suddenly she gave them both a quick hug. 'Thanks for everything,' she whispered and hurried out, before they could notice the tears in her eyes.

'Well,' said the doctor, 'let's hope they enjoy themselves. I almost wish we were going with them.'

Tom parked the car outside the school. The music reached them as he opened the car door, and Mary began to wish she hadn't come. Everybody would stare when she walked in. What if she couldn't dance and made a fool of herself in front of everyone? She had found the steps easy in the scullery. Mrs Roberts had brought down the gramophone from the spare room, a lovely polished cabinet affair with two doors at the front and a picture of a little dog inside. Dr Roberts had taught her the waltz, the foxtrot and the veleta, and had told her about the Paul Jones, when everyone swapped partners – she would sit that one out. That was if anyone asked her to dance in the first place. Mrs Roberts had changed the records and kept the gramophone wound up, and they'd all laughed when he had bowed and thanked her at the end of each dance. Mary had been touched when he had asked his wife for the last waltz, and had made herself scarce, leaving the couple alone.

In the schoolroom a four-piece band was playing but no one was dancing. Mary almost fainted when she realised she had to cross the large expanse of wooden floor to reach the cloakroom, but Tom's sisters Bessie and Lucy linked arms with her and marched her across. Every eye in the room followed the trio and Bessie giggled as they heard two old dears mutter to each other about how disgraceful her backless dress was. They patted their hair into place and Lucy lent Mary a lipstick.

'Remind me to wipe it off before we go home,' Bessie said. 'Me dad'll have a fit if he sees us caked up in lipstick.'

Mary grinned and relaxed now she knew Bessie and Lucy were just as friendly as their brother. She just wished her own sisters weren't so far away.

Satisfied with their appearance at last, they marched out of the cloakroom to join the other dancers, finding seats amongst the rows of chairs lining three sides of the room. The band was on a raised platform taking up nearly the whole of the other wall, and in the corner stood a trestle table filled with cups and saucers, and a tea urn larger than anything Mary had seen before. Also on the table were plates already containing two sandwiches and a bun. Every so often someone would trundle a pram across the floor, some-times containing two babies who couldn't have been born more than nine months apart.

The two old dears got up to dance. The band was playing 'Daisy Daisy' with a few wrong notes, and soon several couples had taken to the floor, most of them women dancing together, or little girls dragging boy cousins or playmates, much to their chagrin.

Mary asked her friends where all the men were.

'They'll be here when the pub closes at ten,' said Lucy. 'You won't get the lads dancing until they've had a pint or two.'

'Then they'll expect to walk us home.' Bessie laughed. 'They're in for a disappointment tonight, though. We'll be riding home in style.'

'Just depends who asks us,' said Lucy. 'I quite fancy Harry Holmes from Millington.'

'Yer'd better not let me dad know,' Bessie said. 'The Millington gang have quite a reputation.'

Tom had not come in with them, disappearing in the direction of the pub, but now he walked in and came over to them.

'Well, Cinders, how about a dance with Prince Charming?'

'What's up wi' you then, coming in before closing time? Wonders'll never cease.'

Tom took no notice of Lucy. After one pint he had for some reason become rather bored with the same old jokes, and decided Mary would make better company.

She wished he hadn't asked her to dance yet. The floor was still rather empty and everybody would see if she stumbled. Luckily her long dress covered her ankles and as Tom swept her into a foxtrot she was surprised how easy he was to dance with. Still, she suspected he had had plenty of experience; she could see the envy in some of the girls' eyes as they twirled past.

The next two dances he had with Bessie and Lucy but after that he never left Mary's side. The floor became crowded as the men and youths filed in when the pub closed, red-faced, jovial and laughing far too loudly. When the band struck up the Paul Jones, Tom persuaded her on to the floor despite her protests, and she wondered nervously which of them would be her next partner.

Jack Holmes couldn't believe his luck when he found himself with Mary in his arms. He could feel the swell of her breasts through his shirt and pressed his body a little closer into hers. Mary blushed and tried to loosen his grasp. She could feel his manliness and even though she was embarrassed it excited her too, to be held like this.

'I shall have to come here more often,' Jack said. 'I never knew Longfield possessed such beautiful partners.'

Mary smiled nervously, keeping quiet instead of saying something stupid.

'I'm Jack Holmes,' he offered. Mary still said nothing. 'Well, what should I call you? I can't just say hey you all the time.'

Mary smiled. 'Mary O'Connor,' she said.

'I might have known it. The only girl in the room to steal my heart and she turns out to be a foreigner, a real Irish colleen.'

'I'm not Irish. My grandparents were, but my parents were born in Newcastle, and so was I.'

'Well, at least we have one thing in common – we were both brought up amongst the coal dust.'

Mary noticed everyone had changed partners again but Jack had kept a tight hold on her.

'My da works in the pit,' Mary volunteered.

'So do I.'

The music finished with a roll of drums. Jack bowed slightly, surprising Mary, and thanked her before leading her back to her chair.

'Trust you to get the pick of the bunch,' said

Bessie. 'Every girl in the room fancies Jack Holmes.'

''Cept me,' Lucy said. 'It's his brother I fancy.'

'You just keep away from that one,' said Tom. 'I'll guarantee there'll be a fight before the night is out. He's been making up to young Saunders's wife all night, and Saunders'll not put up with that. He always gets a bit nasty after a drink or two.'

Tom queued for refreshments in the interval and claimed every dance afterwards. Suddenly Mary realised it was time to leave.

Lucy had at last been asked to dance by Harry Holmes. She began to sulk at having to leave, but as no one had offered to walk her home she had no option but to go with them.

Mary was on cloud seven. Not only had she been to her first dance, but she'd enjoyed every moment, hadn't made a fool of herself, and had danced with the two best-looking men in the room.

As they drove down the hill along the side of the reservoir and up the other side, Tom held her hand in between changing gears. He considered his feelings carefully. He believed he had fallen in love tonight. Well, not just tonight – he supposed it had happened the day he first set eyes on her at the station. There wasn't much he could do about it, though. Mary was too young to be tied down, especially to a soldier, and that's what he'd be in a few weeks' time. Still, she was worth waiting for, and if she felt the same as he did when he came back he would marry her. In the meantime he didn't know how he was going to live without seeing her, touching her, just being near her.

41

God, it was going to be slow torture.

Mary gazed up at the moon. It seemed to be smiling down at her through the dark looming tree branches, hanging like a balloon, as though she could catch it by its string before it floated away. She returned its smile. She too felt as if she was in love, but the trouble was she didn't know whether it was with Tom or Jack Holmes. She hadn't thought about loving anyone until tonight. Tom had started it by looking so handsome, by caring for her and looking after her. But then the feeling she'd experienced with Jack had been different altogether: more exciting, more sinful somehow.

Maybe she loved both of them. Anyway, tonight she had enough love for everybody. She was overflowing with it, and she had never been so happy in her life.

Chapter Four

It was one of those days when nothing went right. Tom had called his employer a bloody idiot, and although he had apologised immediately Rowland Roberts had stormed out of the car and slammed the door, leaving Tom to assess the damage. Tom, who was trying to teach the doctor to drive in the few days left before his departure, couldn't understand the man's inability to turn left. He had almost demolished the gatepost at the bottom of the drive, and Tom, who had tended the motor as though it was a baby, had become incensed at the sight of the dented mudguard.

The doctor slammed every door in the house, shouted at Mary and ignored his wife. The truth was he actually felt a bloody idiot; Tom had taken to the wheel like a duck to water and the older man had expected to do the same. After cooling down he realised he would either have to get back in the driving seat or employ another driver, though where he could hope to find one with all the young men joining up God only knew. In any case, now Mary had taken over most of the outside work he doubted if he really needed another handyman. The lass was worth her weight in gold. Amazingly, she never seemed to run out of energy, and actually appeared to enjoy all the work.

Mary was feeling hot and miserable, even before the doctor snapped at her. She had just finished pegging out three lines of washing when the heavens opened and it poured with rain, so she had brought the whole lot in again and heaved it up on to the rack over the fire. Now the kitchen was filled with steam, not only from the damp washing but also from the plum puddings boiling away over the fire in readiness for Christmas. The condensation ran down the windows, dulled the brassware, and moistened Mary's hair so that it curled up the wrong way over her forehead, just when she wanted to look nice for Tom tonight.

On Mondays she usually paid an evening visit to Tom's family, enjoying the chattering of Bessie and Lucy, and playing a game of Shop Missis with his young brothers Cyril and Douglas, but tonight she was staying in to keep an eye on the

Christmas cakes in the oven. Dr Roberts had a choir practice in the schoolroom and he was taking his wife with him to do the refreshments, so Tom would more than likely be coming to the house to keep her company. It had been taken for granted since the dance that Tom and Mary were courting. Everybody seemed delighted, but a cloud hung over the couple as the day of Tom's departure drew near. Although Tom hadn't discussed the war with Mary, she had started listening to the wireless and knew he would probably be sent to France, and France to Mary sounded like the other side of the world.

Over the past few weeks Mary had changed. She had always liked Tom, but now when he kissed her he awakened feelings in her she hadn't known she possessed. She knew now that it was Tom she loved and she couldn't bear the thought of his going, worse still the possibility of his never coming back. Yet he had to go, along with all the other young men who had received their call-up papers.

The doctor was in a more amiable frame of mind when he came in for tea. He seemed to be getting the hang of steering at last and he always felt happier on practice night, especially when they were rehearsing carols. Dr Roberts loved carols and looked forward to leading the choir not only at the charity concert in the school, but also in the run-up to Christmas when they visited the local pubs and collected donations for the orphanage. Gladys used the money to buy a present for each child and a few luxuries so that the nuns could organise a party. Dr Roberts guessed

44

the young novices gained as much pleasure out of the event as the children.

Mary chopped vigorously at the dried chives, then beat them into the bowl of eggs and cheese ready to make omelettes. She always did a light meal on rehearsal nights so as not to upset the doctor's digestion. She had made a junket to follow, so she wouldn't need to open the oven door and spoil the dark rich Christmas cakes.

The table was already set, and Mary marvelled as usual that she should be sharing the meal with her employers. The fact was she was treated almost like a daughter, and she never failed to be grateful. She wondered what to wear tonight and couldn't wait to soak herself in the long bathtub. At least with the fire roaring away to keep the oven hot there would be no shortage of hot water.

She decided on her brown dress. Fashioned in lovely soft shantung, it was supposed to be worn at Christmas, but as Tom wouldn't be here then she would wear it tonight. She wanted him to remember her looking her best. She slipped into the satin panties and brassiere she had bought on her last trip to Sheffield. It was the first time Mary had ever spent anything on herself apart from essentials. She had spent the rest of her accumulated wages on presents: warm stockings for her ma, Norah and Kathleen, socks for her da, a dictionary for Bill – the only studious one – a book about animals for Jimmy and for little Michael a brightly illustrated nursery rhyme book. A handkerchief for Father Flynn, and a pretty lace one for Joyce Bailey, which she sent direct to Lil's house in case her ma refused to deliver it on her behalf.

Dr Roberts had offered to pay for Mary to travel home for Christmas, and longing to see her family she had almost accepted his offer. Then, realising how much the Robertses would miss her help in the house over the busy period, she had decided to stay here. Besides, although she loved and missed her family, Moorland House had worked its magic on Mary so that she now felt as much at home here as she had in Newcastle.

Gladys's relief at her decision was well worth forsaking the Christmas visit for. She was promised the fare to go as soon afterwards as she wished, and made up her mind to take advantage of the offer the moment the worst of the weather had passed, secretly dreading being stranded up in Newcastle by snow. A visit was one thing, but Mary couldn't face the thought of not coming back to Longfield.

Tom tapped on the kitchen window for Mary to let him in. The doors were always kept bolted after dark, even though passers-by were few and far between up here in winter.

She threw her arms about his neck before she realised how wet he was, then helped him off with his overcoat. He watched her hang it on the cupboard door handle near the fire to dry, drinking in the beauty of her as he would wine. God, if it wasn't for the bloody war he would marry her tomorrow.

Mary poured the tea, strong and thick, into the two cups, then added milk and sugar and stirred it sitting at the table. Tom stood with his back to the fire. He remained silent for what seemed ages, until Mary felt herself blushing beneath his gaze.

'Well, have you lost your tongue?' She smiled.

'To tell yer the truth I've so much to say to yer I don't know where to start.'

'Well, start somewhere.'

'I love yer, Mary, so much it hurts just to look at yer, knowing that tomorrow I shall be leaving yer.'

'Tomorrow? I thought we'd two more days? You said you were going on Thursday.'

'I know, love. I didn't want to upset yer more than I had to. It would only have spoiled yer weekend, and it wouldn't have altered owt.'

Mary felt her eyes fill with tears, so she jumped up and busied herself raking down the fire so that Tom wouldn't notice. He reached out and ran his fingers through her hair. She straightened up and moved closer to him, and he drew her into his arms, seeking her lips hungrily. Mary pressed closer. She would have got inside him if it had been possible. She felt him harden and her own body responded in a way she had never even dreamed of. She felt his hand stroking her neck, then moving to her breast, and starting to undo the tiny buttons on her dress. Impatiently she helped him until she could slip it down over her shoulders and let it fall to the floor. Tom felt the warm slippery satin covering her body and slowly guided her hand downwards towards him, hoping for relief. Mary felt the warm hardness in her hand, and was overwhelmed by her need of him. Then, suddenly, Tom pushed her from him. Bewildered, Mary wondered what had happened.

Surely that wasn't all there was to it?

Tom cradled her in his arms.

'I'm sorry, Mary. I shouldn't have done that – getting worked up like that, I mean, and you too. It wasn't fair.'

'Didn't you want me, Tom?'

'Want yer? I was going mad for yer, but I won't spoil yer, Mary. It wouldn't be fair – yer might regret it once I've gone. Yer could meet someone else, love. Yer only young, Mary, an' I'm going to be gone a long time.'

Mary began to cry. 'I don't think you love me at all. If you did you'd have wanted me just like I wanted you.'

'Don't let's quarrel, not tonight. Let's have something happy to remember when I'm gone, and something to look forward to when I come back. That's if yer still want me.'

'Oh, Tom, I love you. I'll always want you, even if I've to wait for ever.'

She suddenly realised she was undressed and reached down for her dress. He pulled her back. ''Ere, let me look at yer. I'll never see pink satin again without thinkin' of you. Still, I can't wait to see yer without 'em.'

Mary giggled. 'I'll look forward to that,' she said, thinking suddenly about Joyce Bailey and feeling grateful to Tom for not putting her in the same position.

'Hey,' he said. 'Have yer got something in the oven?'

Mary jumped up and flew to the oven. 'The cakes,' she shrieked, praying they wouldn't be ruined. She lifted them out, noticing the currants were rather black on the top. 'Just in time,' she said. 'Another few minutes and they'd have been ruined. It's a good job the fire had burned low.'

'Who needs a fire with you around?' he said. 'You'd melt a bloody igloo.'

'Just wait till you get to know me better.' She settled on his knee, looking at him with adoration. 'I love you, Tom Downing, and I'll wait for ever if necessary.'

The preparations for Christmas kept Mary occupied during the days, but nights were a different matter. Thoughts of Tom filled her with longing and disturbed her sleep, so that Dr Roberts became concerned at the dark circles beneath her eyes.

'It's only natural she looks peaky,' said Gladys. 'The girl's in love. What's more, she's never stopped working since Tom left. Still, it may be the best thing for her.'

Mary had filled the cellar with pepper cakes, mince pies, cooked hams and Christmas bread, enough to feed all Longfield. The house had been scrubbed and polished from top to bottom, and decorated with coloured paper trimmings from the attic, and holly laden with scarlet berries from the garden. The spare rooms had been prepared for Rowland's nephew, his wife and their two little boys. Christmas cards filled every available shelf and window ledge, and now on Christmas Eve Mary was trying to pluck the chickens while rising the Yule cake for tomorrow's breakfast.

Gladys had disappeared upstairs on the pretence of resting, intent upon finishing the costume she was to give to Mary on Christmas day. Only the buttons needed to be sewn on and it was ready. She hoped it would cheer the girl up. It wasn't like Mary to be so subdued. Still she was missing not only Tom but her family too. Perhaps she should have gone home after all in the circumstances.

The knock on the door caused Mary to swear to herself. What a mess she was in, with feathers clinging to her fingers and apron. Shaking her hands to be rid of the down, she reluctantly opened the door. Her shriek brought Gladys hurrying downstairs, but seeing Mary enfolded in Tom's arms she climbed silently back up again, leaving them to get on with whatever the young lovers felt like doing. Gladys might be fifty but she wasn't yet past enjoying a bit of hanky panky herself, nor one to deny anyone else the pleasure.

Tom had almost let the cat out of the bag in his letter to Mary. He knew he was entitled to leave after six weeks but he hadn't been certain it would fall at Christmas, so he had kept silent rather than disappoint her. Now he knew he had been right to surprise her.

Dr Roberts invited Tom to spend Christmas day with them at Moorland House, but considerate as usual Tom thought about his mother's delight at having him home and compromised, accepting the invitation to dinner, which was to be at two o'clock, and determining to go home afterwards to tea with his family. Gladys insisted Mary take the afternoon off so she could go with him.

At dinner Gladys enjoyed spoiling their nephew's children, who were in high spirits, and

Mary was reminded of her brothers, though it saddened her that they would never know a Christmas such as this. Afterwards they opened presents round the fire in the lounge, encouraging the little ones to sing for them the carols they had learned at school. Mary excused herself to reset the table for tea, slice up the hams and ensure Gladys had little to do later. Satisfied with her preparations, she slipped upstairs to change, impatient to try on the costume which had been hanging behind her door when she awoke that morning. At first she had felt ashamed that all she had for the Robertses were carpet slippers, but they had been as thrilled as if she had given them the crown jewels.

The costume fitted like a second skin, and the soft brown checks brought out the warmth of her eyes. Rowland had bought her a cream satin blouse to go with it. Mary hardly recognised herself in the wardrobe mirror and hoped she didn't look too posh to fit in with the Downings. Still, she knew Tom liked her in satin. She giggled to herself as she remembered their last meeting, then hurried downstairs.

Yesterday's rain had changed to a light sprinkling of snow during the night, and now the flakes were large and feathery, covering the countryside with a white blanket. Tom held her hand and they walked round the house, making footmarks in the virginal carpet. Old Pepper neighed a welcome even before Tom unlatched the stable door.

'Happy Christmas, old boy,' he said as the horse nuzzled his nose into Tom's shoulder. 'And happy Christmas to you an' all, love,' he said, drawing her inside the rough warmth of his greatcoat and wrapping it round her. He knew that, for all his good intentions, nothing except resistance from Mary would prevent his giving way to the burning passion she roused within him.

It did not come. He kissed her slowly, removing her jacket, and then her skirt, folding them carefully, thoughtful even in his eagerness. Gently, he undid the tiny buttons of her blouse and slipped it from her.

He removed his coat and spread it on the hay, and as though in a dream Mary lay down. He lay beside her, caressing her sensuously, while she fumbled with the broad webbing of his belt.

And then, in the stable, sheltered from the cold Christmas afternoon, Mary discovered the miracle, the fulfilment of love.

Chapter Five

The snow continued well into the new year. Mary had thought the house beautiful in the August sun and the autumn mists, but now the sight of it snug in its snowy blanket filled her heart with an unbelievable serenity. Every morning a robin waited for the scraps she brought out. At first it grabbed its fill and escaped to a nearby rhododendron shrub; later, gaining confidence, it remained close by, so that by now it was almost meeting Mary on the doorstep. Icicles hung like crystal chandeliers on the laburnum tree, dripping in the weak midday sun only to freeze again in the late afternoon.

Mary was at peace at Moorland House. To her it was home now, and she knew that whenever or wherever she travelled in the future, this house, this winter, would remain vividly in her memory – the time when she had emerged from girl to womanhood. She thought of Tom every waking hour but now she could bear the separation, knowing she belonged to him and he to her. She dismissed from her mind the thought of what would happen once his training finished, thinking only of his next leave, praying the weather would mellow and make the village accessible before he was due to arrive.

Gladys had guessed immediately that the couple had made love. She had noticed the footprints leading to the stable whilst taking the little boys to see Pepper on Boxing Day morning, and even without that evidence she would have guessed anyway by the look on Mary's face. Gladys remembered only too well the change she herself had experienced after her first sexual encounter with Rowland, the difference being that she and Rowland had waited until their wedding night. Still, things were different in wartime; no one knew what would happen from one day to the next. Gladys, more knowledgeable than Mary about the progress of the war, decided to say nothing. Soldiers were being shipped out every day to various destinations, and only God knew what horrors were awaiting them on their arrival. It was better for Mary to remain in ignorance of what Tom might have to face.

Tom's next leave was spent quietly. The snow had been thawed temporarily to a squelchy mess by incessant rain, and this time, without the Christmas celebrations to distract them, the only thing on their minds was the uncertainty of when they would next be together. Everyone was unnaturally cheerful and only Tom's mother showed her true feelings, starting to cry when little Douglas asked Tom, 'Have yer killed anybody yet, Tom?'

'Not yet.' Tom laughed. 'But just you wait. As soon as I see one of our enemies he'll have a bullet up his arse and no mistake.' A game of soldiers then began, with Tom chasing his little brothers round the table, drawing his mother's attention away from her sadness at his approaching departure. Had it not been for the youngsters, Mary had the feeling that everyone would have just hung around waiting for Tom's leave to end.

They didn't make love again. It was as though something special had occurred, something too precious to spoil. Instead they held each other, touching, kissing, gaining satisfaction just from being together.

When the time came for Tom to return to his unit, Rowland took them into Sheffield in the car, driving erratically once he got amongst the other traffic, although he doubted if they noticed. He left them with a couple of hours to spare, promising to pick Mary up when it was time for Tom's train. Then he drove to the infirmary, concerned about a patient who had been injured by a roof which had collapsed under the weight of the snow.

The couple strolled round the shops, laughingly choosing furniture, optimistic that it wouldn't be long before they would be buying. Mary promised to fill her bottom drawer ready for Tom's return.

'And don't forget the pink satin,' Tom warned. Then he led her to Brown's the jewellers, where instead of window shopping he took her inside. 'I didn't get chance to buy you a Christmas present,' he said.

'We'd like to see an engagement ring,' he told the assistant who approached them.

Mary almost fainted, wondering what obligations went with becoming engaged. She'd never known anyone in real life who had done so, and she had no idea.

'I don't know,' she stammered. 'I ought to ask my ma or somebody.'

'Yer don't need consent to become engaged. It's just a belated Christmas present, and a promise that I'm going to marry yer. Or don't yer want to marry me? Is that it?'

The assistant watched, hoping they weren't going to walk out without buying. Trade had been quiet since Christmas and an engagement ring would boost her commission. She wanted her hair cutting in the new style and she would be able to afford it if they bought a ring. She glanced at Mary's hand, guessing the size from experience, and plucked a sparkling ring from the tray.

'Perhaps Madam would try this for size?' She offered the ring to Tom. The realisation that she was being addressed as Madam so shocked Mary that she let him slip the ring on to her finger. It was a perfect fit.

'Oh, Tom, it's beautiful. But I can't let you buy it – you can't afford it.'

'Who says I can't? I've never been one to throw my money around, and anyway there'll be nothing else to spend it on where I'm going. We'll take it.' He turned to the assistant, who visibly relaxed then uncertainly told him the price.

Tom fished for his wallet and counted out the money, then placed his arm round Mary's waist and led her outside. He drew her towards him and searched her face closely, hoping to imprint the loveliness of her deep within his memory, knowing it would be a long time before he saw her again.

'I love yer, Mary, never forget that. Whatever happens, however long I'm away, I love yer.'

Then he kissed her, right there in the street.

Suddenly she wanted to cry. Sadness swept over her, and than a sudden coldness, as though something terrible was about to happen. She clung to Tom, unwilling to release him. He gave her a final squeeze and then smiled down at her.

'Come on, love,' he said. 'We should be celebrating instead of standing here with faces as long as fiddles.' He threw his kitbag on his back. 'We've just time for a cup of tea.'

They set off in search of the station refreshment room. 'We should be drinking champagne instead of this stuff,' he joked, when they were finally sitting at a table. 'It tastes more like washing-up water than tea.'

Mary forced herself to smile, weeping inside, knowing that in another twenty minutes he would be on the train. How long would it be before she saw this beloved man again?

Chapter Six

Longfield might have been immune from the war. Only Tom and one other young man had been of an age to enlist. The older men were either working their own land or holding key positions in the steel mills and could not be spared. In Sheffield, women were recruited by the hospital to replace the men who had joined up, and the doctor was full of praise for them as they learned to drive vans and ambulances in preparation for the inevitable attack. Dr Roberts was rarely home now until late and to Mary the atmosphere of the house seemed to have changed.

At first Tom's letters came frequently and then in April they suddenly ceased, leaving Mary anxiously awaiting news. She redoubled her efforts both indoors and out. The garden was turned over, the outbuildings whitewashed and the house spring-cleaned, and still Mary was left with a useless feeling. In the end she reluctantly revealed to Gladys her need to be doing something worthwhile.

'Perhaps I ought to go home and find a job there,' she said. 'I know I've been treated like a daughter by you and Dr Roberts, but I don't feel it would be right for me to take an outside job whilst I'm living here. After all, you only took me in in the first place as a servant.'

Gladys, who had half expected something like

this to happen after Tom's departure, chose her words with care.

'Look, my love,' she said, 'maybe we did take you on to help in the house, but that's all changed now. To us you are a daughter, and this is your home for as long as you want it. If you'd be happier doing some kind of war work then go ahead, so long as you come home each night. There's not a lot to do in the house at present. You've kept it like a new pin, and now young Cyril Downing's helping out a bit after school with the poultry and the garden we're well organised, as you know. Why don't you ask Rowland about doing something at the hospital?'

Mary considered that possibility, but found herself cringing at the thought of the hospital atmosphere. Instead, she discussed with Bessie the idea of going into the steel works at Millington; both Tom's sisters worked there and apart from the five-mile bicycle ride there and back they seemed happy enough.

Gladys didn't much care for the idea. She would hardly see Mary if they put her on shift work, and the long journey would mean a ten-hour day. She discussed Mary's plan with Rowland, anxious that the closed-in factory atmosphere might not be good for her.

Rowland had been worried about Mary for some weeks. The girl hadn't been herself since Tom's departure. He had found her at the station buffet sobbing her heart out and although she had bravely tried to hide her tears he had taken her in his arms, and just like a father encouraged her to cry out her grief. Afterwards she had seemed calm enough, but he thought now it might be a good thing for her to get amongst some young company.

'Well, I don't like it at all,' Gladys fretted. 'What if her health deteriorates again?'

'We can keep an eye on her,' Rowland said. 'Better a bit of hard work than a nervous condition. Besides, I have a notion that if she doesn't do something to occupy her mind she might take it into her head to go home.'

Gladys had also been afraid that that might happen, feeling that if she did she might decide to stay now that Tom wasn't here. The offer of the fare to Newcastle was still open, but Gladys silently prayed that she wouldn't accept.

Going home was the last thing Mary wanted. Not only did she consider Moorland House her home now, but she needed to be near Tom's family, on hand in case any news arrived. Even so she missed her own family and felt rather guilty that she hadn't written for some weeks, so she decided to make up for it with a long letter.

Moorland House
Long Lee Lane
Longfield
Near Sheffield
April 1940

Dear Ma and Da,
I'm sorry I haven't written sooner but I have been rather busy spring-cleaning, and getting the garden ready for planting out. I hope you are all well and not in any danger from the war. Dr Roberts doesn't think

much is going to happen, but there are a lot of preparations going on in Sheffield anyway. He says they are fitting people up with gas masks, and Anderson shelters, though only as a precaution. How is Joyce getting on? Has she had the baby yet, and is Father Flynn all right? I miss you all very much. Has our Norah started working yet? If so not at Mrs Brown's, I hope. I've decided to get a job in the works at Millington. It's five miles away but I have Tom's bike to go on so it won't be too bad.

By the way I have a surprise for you all. Tom and I have got engaged. I have a beautiful ring – I wish I could show it to you. I was going to come home for a holiday but what with the war I should only feel guilty. Still, I will come soon, once I hear from Tom and know he's all right. Write and let me know the news. I worry about you all, with the war and everything.

Love from Mary.

PS Thanks for the Christmas card and the apron – I wear it every Sunday. Tell our Michael thanks for the picture he drew, and give him a kiss from me, and one for the others too, and you.

Mary finished off with a row of kisses and placed a ten shilling note inside the letter. She addressed the envelope to her mother, knowing that if her father opened it the hard-earned money would be handed over the bar of the nearest public house.

The next day Mary posted her letter in Lower Longfield. Since rationing had begun she had been collecting the groceries from the village shop, enjoying the walk when the weather was fine. It had been a hard winter but now the trees were in bud and fluffy pussy willows flourished in the hedgerow. Broken reflections danced on the reservoir and daffodils waved in the spring breeze.

Mary loved this place where Tom and she had walked, huddled together from the biting wind, singing in harmony and laughing when a huge brown cow had startled them with a long loud moooo. She also loved the village shop, where Mrs Poppleton weighed up the sugar into blue bags, twelve ounces a person, and cut butter from a large round block, twelve ounces for the three of them.

Mary handed over the basket of eggs she had brought and the bill was adjusted accordingly. In summer Gladys would supply Mrs Poppleton with vegetables too but at present most of the buying was done by Mary, glad of the opportunity to exchange gossip with the village wives who had watched her arrive from behind immaculate white net curtains and found some excuse to join her in the shop.

'Bad job about owd Joss Shepherd,' said one of them now.

'What's up wi' 'im this time?' asked Mrs Poppleton. 'Got canned up again and fallen down the Plough steps, has he?'

'Not this time.' The other laughed. 'Their Annie 'ad sneaked out ladding when she was supposed to be in bed, an' left the cellar grate off so she could sneak back in again. Well, what wi' the blackout and the drink, owd Joss staggering home never noticed, an' next thing he knew he was down in't cellar, one foot straight into't heap of coal only delivered yesterday. Twisted 'is leg under 'im.

Black and blue he is, what wi' bruises an' coal dust.' She finished the story almost hysterical with laughter, and then her face straightened again as she added, 'Eeh, it's their Annie I feel sorry for. She din't 'alf cop it when she came 'ome. He took 'is belt off to 'er by all accounts – I'll bet she doesn't leave grate off again in a hurry. Eeh, I'd 'ave given owt to see 'is face though when he disappeared dahn that cellar.'

Mary almost wet her knickers laughing and had to ask Mrs Poppleton if she could use her lavatory out round the back.

After handing out a bit of news in exchange, about what was happening in Sheffield, Mary left for a visit to Tom's mother, knowing that the kettle would be singing a welcome on the black-leaded range and the brown teapot warming in the hearth. Mary loved the gentle woman, and enjoyed the quiet chat on a Friday morning whilst the girls were at work and Cyril was at school, and only little Douglas was at home, playing with a small ginger kitten. Mr Downing was always busy outside on the farm, ploughing, milking or mucking out, helped by his old friend Sid who should have retired years ago. From what Tom had told Mary his father made more out of the farm than he would admit, and the farmhouse was warm and comfortably furnished. In fact, the family didn't seem to want for anything.

Mrs Downing met Mary in the yard, asking immediately, 'Any news, love?' Her face fell when Mary shook her head. 'Oh, well, no news is good news. I expect there's a letter on its way some-where.' She smiled at Mary. 'Come in, love, and

62

have a cup of tea.' The aroma of baking bread greeted them as they entered the kitchen. 'How about a warm oven bottom cake with a spreading of rendered lard?'

Mary was almost tempted but declined the offer, knowing Gladys would have dinner ready on her return. 'I really came to leave a message for Bessie and Lucy. I've decided to go after a job in the works. I'll ride over with them on Monday and see if they've anything to offer me.'

'I'll tell them to wait for you, then. At least it's light in a morning, though it'll not be very nice for you in winter coming round the reservoir on yer own.'

'I'll be all right. I think I know the road blind-fold by now, and anyway I can't go on hiding myself away up at the house, not now there's a war on.'

'You'll need some thick trousers to protect yer legs. One of the girls lost a leg only last week on a length of steel strip so just you be prepared, and be careful.'

'I'll be all right.' Mary smiled. 'Anyway, I must be going. I'll see you on Monday then. Bye bye, Douglas. He's a lovely little boy, Mrs Downing.'

'Aye. Came as a shock, he did, at my time of life, and so long after the others. Like a belated gift, yer might say, and he brought love with 'im just the same as the others did. Ta-ra then, love. Take care.'

As Mary carried the groceries up the hill she marvelled at the friendliness of the people in this beautiful Yorkshire village, and thought she could quite happily stay here for ever. How Tom must be missing it all. She prayed silently that he would return safely, and her stomach turned over as she remembered she hadn't attended Mass since Christmas. Somehow she couldn't bring herself to confess a sin that didn't seem like a sin at all.

If only Father Flynn was here. She thought she could have made him understand. Oh, well, perhaps she would ride up to the convent next week. There again, she might not have time if she began her new job.

She started to sing to herself as she walked along the lane, a hymn she'd heard on the wireless, and somehow she gained comfort from the words.

Chapter Seven

By the time Mary saw Millington for the first time she thought her legs didn't belong to her. The journey had consisted of the hill down into Longfield, then up past the convent and down into the next valley, which Mary learned was called Cowholes. Then, they had yet another hill to climb and she found it impossible to pedal more than halfway up.

'Come on, buck up, we're going to be late,' Bessie called. 'It won't be so bad after today, it's just that you haven't had enough practise on yer bike.'

'I feel as though I've walked five hundred miles,' said Mary. 'I'm beginning to hope I don't get the job if it's going to be like this every day.'

Lucy laughed. 'Never mind, it's all downhill from now on. Can you see the works down in the bottom?'

The road wound down past a church and through street after street of grey stone houses. In the bottom a row of stark black chimneys belched out smoke from the steelworks, which stretched the length of the valley, separated from the main street by the river. Mary's stomach churned nervously. She hadn't realised how vast the factory would be. Crowds of workers made their way silently in the direction of the entrance.

Bessie told Mary where to go and whom to ask for, and then she and Lucy hurried away through a pair of swing doors. Mary parked her bike, walked across some railway lines and knocked on a door marked PERSONNEL. A voice boomed out for her to enter and her stomach gave another lurch.

'Well?' said the voice, its owner not looking up from the desk.

'I – I'd like a job,' Mary faltered.

'What can yer do?' asked the balding head.

'I don't know. I haven't worked in a factory before.'

The man looked up at last, appraising her as though she had been dragged in by the cat. 'Been mollycoddled, have yer? How old are yer?'

Mary felt the blood rush to her face.

'I've been in service and I'm seventeen. I'm here because there's a war on, but if you don't want me then I'll be going.' She turned on her heel and reached the door.

'Here, hold yer horses. Come back here. Don't

yer know it's Monday morning, and I'm not in the best of moods on a Monday. Anyway, yer look like a lass with a bit of spirit, and we can do with a few like you. Did yer have owt in mind? I mean, do you know anyone who works here?'

'I know Bessie and Lucy Downing in the spring shop.'

'Oh, well, if yer pull yer weight like those two yer'll not go far wrong.' He reached out and opened a book, scanning the pages. 'Hmm, I don't know about the spring shop – set a bunch on only last week. We're desperate in the strip department, though. I'll give yer a try in there.'

He wrote something on a card and asked her name and address, raising an eyebrow when she mentioned Moorland House. 'Take this to the strip across the lines, third door on the left, and watch the locos.'

When Mary found the place she opened the door to a dazzle of artificial light, the smell of paraffin and the noise of at least a dozen slitting machines all working at once. A young lad whistled at her even though she felt like a frump in the brown melton trousers and overall which showed inches below her coat. Another man in a brown overall came and took the card, beckoning for her to follow him. She walked up the aisle between the machines until he stopped and spoke to a woman quite a bit older than Mary.

'Yer've got a new mate, Madge,' he said. 'Show her how to go on, will yer, an' fit her up with an apron and some gloves.'

Madge showed Mary where the stores were and Mary went in search of gloves and an apron which seemed to be made of cardboard rather than cloth. She returned to the bench in front of one of the machines and Madge explained how it worked.

'What's yer name, love?' she asked.

'Mary O'Connor.'

'Right then, I'm the pairer, you're the packer. I cut the coil into strips and your job is to lift the coiled strips off the machine and secure them with pieces of flat band ready for the inspector,' Madge said, demonstrating as she spoke. 'Then they'll be taken to the warehouse. All right? Now you have a go.'

Mary lifted the next coil off the machine and began to spin it to remove the centre.

'Now then.' Madge put out a hand. 'Never do that without gloves or you'll cut your hands to smithereens.'

Mary donned her gloves and had another go, fastening up the coil with flat band.

'Good,' said Madge. 'Now see how fast you can do it. More tonnage we get out, more money we take home on a Friday.'

Mary liked Madge. Not only did she work with her, helping her to pack, but she explained what the different-sized coils were to be used for. Most of them would go through to the spring shop; some would be made into razor blades and watch springs but most would end up as cartridge clips for machine guns.

'It was mainly umbrella strip before the war started,' Madge explained. 'Now I suppose the poor buggers'll just have to get wet.' Mary smiled, grateful to have found a mate like Madge.

At one o'clock Madge asked, 'Did you bring some snap?'

Mary looked at her blankly.

'Sandwiches. Snap,' Madge said.

'Oh, yes. On the table with my coat.'

'We'll find a locker for you tomorrow to put them in.'

Suddenly the buzzer went and everybody downed tools and made for the end of the mill.

'Bring your snap,' Madge said.

They all went into a room which Madge said was the canteen. Pots of tea stood on a metal table and everybody grabbed one and found a chair.

'Have you a spare pot, Doris?' Madge enquired of a small plump woman. 'We've a new lass here.'

Doris produced a huge pint pot and slammed it in front of Mary. 'Here you are, love. Pay on Friday when yer get yer money.'

The tea was strong and delicious and Mary enjoyed listening to the chat of the girls and a couple of young lads.

After snap time she quite enjoyed her new job, but she didn't know how she was going to pedal her bike up those hills after standing for an eight-hour shift.

The first week Mary wanted nothing on her return from work other than a hot meal and bed, and she thought she would never become accustomed to the long daily routine. But gradually she found the energy to resume some of the household tasks, insisting on doing the washing on a Saturday instead of the usual Monday. Gladys quite enjoyed pampering Mary by preparing a lovely hot meal on her arrival home in the evening, relieved to see her back to her normal cheerful self.

By the end of the second week Mary had got to know all the slitting shop girls by name, and some of the mill men as well. She had also discovered that Madge wasn't only money-mad but man-mad too. If she was to be believed she had been with quite a few of the mill men, regardless of whether they were married or single.

'I could tell you stories that'd make yer hair curl, if it wasn't curly already,' she said proudly.

'I don't doubt it.' Mary laughed.

Madge also tried to draw Mary into telling her if she had had any sexual experiences herself, but Mary simply kept quiet, though she did ask once, 'Is that all you can talk about? I think you're man-mad. No wonder they call you the merry widow.'

'Jealousy, love, that's all it is. Take that Doris on the oiling machine. Never had a man in her life, wouldn't know what to do with one if she got chance, so she simply makes out she doesn't want one. No, lass, you're only young once; enjoy yerself while yer can, that's what I say. Mind you, when my Walt was alive it was a different matter.'

Madge's face clouded over for a second and suddenly Mary realised that the brittle exterior was actually a sham to disguise the sadness at the loss of her husband. After a moment Madge continued, once more her cheerful self. 'Now, when my Walt was alive I would never have looked at another man – never needed to. A lovelier man you couldn't wish to meet, nor a better one in bed. Still, you can't bring them back, and if you do right by them while they're here you've nothing to

69

reproach yourself for when they've gone, that's what my mother told me after he'd died, and nobody can say I didn't do right by Walt. Never left his side at the end only to wash the dirty linen, and though I say it myself his bed was kept spotless. I was right relieved when he finally went, poor soul, nothing but skin and bone. They wouldn't let a dog suffer like he did. They'd have had it put down. Oh, well, you can't live in the past. Like I said, enjoy yerself while you're young, love.'

Mary thought she was lucky to be working with Madge, but the other girls didn't like it when they earned more bonus than anyone else in the shop, and Mary soon realised that she would have to work full tilt to keep up with her mate. Instead of using the small portable crane which had to be brought from one machine to the other, Mary felt obliged to lift the heavy coils manually in order to work at twice the speed. She soon got the knack of supporting the weight on her stomach and swinging the coils from machine to bench, though it was heavy work and according to the other girls it was against the rules. Madge told her to use the crane if any of the bosses were about and they'd be all right.

It was during the third week on her new job that Mary made friends with one of the other packers, a girl named Theresa Murphy, who invited Mary to go with her to the Saturday night dance in Millington. Although she was tempted, she declined on the grounds of not being able to get home, knowing she wouldn't enjoy it without Tom anyway.

'You could stay at our house. My mother won't

mind, and you could go to church with us on Sunday morning before you went home.'

'Got to go in the sin bin to confess after Saturday night, have yer?' Madge laughed.

'Don't class everybody with yerself,' Theresa retorted, to much laughter.

Mary said she would think about it, but that was as far as it went. She mentioned Theresa's invitation over dinner on Sunday.

'You ought to go out more often,' said Dr Roberts. 'It would do you good.'

'It wouldn't be right, not while Tom's away. I wouldn't mind going to church, though. It isn't the same at the convent, which is why I don't go very often.'

'Then go you shall. I shall take you over in the car next week. A visit to my friend Ernest is long overdue. I need some sheet music for the choir, though when we'll get round to practising I don't know, since they're all occupied with this home guard business at present. I know we ought to be grateful, but I'll be darned if I can see the need for it out here. So you arrange it with your friend, and I'll visit Ernest and pick you up when the service is over.'

St Catherine's was packed to capacity. Nowhere near as large as the Protestant church which dominated the main street, St Catherine's was situated halfway up the hill. Theresa's large and friendly family accepted Mary into their midst and made her promise to stay to lunch next time. Mary felt at home immediately in the church, though she left feeling more sinful than ever, having shirked

71

confessing what she privately thought of as the Christmas sin.

Dr Roberts had a brainwave on the way home. 'You can learn to drive the car and then I can lend it to you on a Sunday. That way you won't be so tied, and what's more you can go into Sheffield with Gladys on a Saturday. She needs to get out more and I must confess I'm really not up to town driving.'

'You're surely not serious?' said Mary. 'Why, I don't know one end of a motor from the other. We're likely to end up in the reservoir with me behind the wheel.'

'If the girls at the ambulance station can drive then so can you. I'm sure you've more brains than the giggly lot of them put together, and they've taken to the wheel as though they were born to it.'

'I wouldn't dare.'

'Well, we'll see. You can have a go after dinner.'

Mary couldn't help feeling excited. Tom had once suggested letting her take the wheel but it hadn't seemed right without the doctor's permission. The image of Tom warmed her heart and as always when she thought of him she prayed that he was safe. She suddenly realised that her job had diverted her mind from the desolation and doom that had occupied it after Tom's departure, and she was thinking about the future more positively. Suddenly she felt fulfilled. She was doing a worthwhile job, even if it was only cutting steel strips to make cartridge clips.

Mary made up her mind she would learn to drive. After all, how many girls were given a chance like that, especially in wartime? Besides, it would provide a way of paying back the doctor for everything. She knew how much he hated driving, so now she could take them out at weekends. That was one thing about being a doctor: he was allowed a fair amount of petrol. Another incentive was the thought of Tom's face when she picked him up at the station in the car. She would wear her pink satin on that occasion.

Oh, it had done her good to go to church again, even though she hadn't confessed her Christmas sin.

Chapter Eight

Robert Scott crumpled up yet another sheet of paper and gave a deep sigh. How the hell was he expected to write a letter of such importance when he was in this state of physical and mental exhaustion?

He had thought the horror was over once he was picked up on the boat. How bloody wrong could a man be? That had just been the beginning of the nightmare.

The nights were the worst: the cold sweats, the trembling, the palpitations and the churning pain in the region of the solar plexus. Worst of all the constant reliving of the train of events from the time Tom and he had arrived at Cherbourg. The first week hadn't been too bad; in fact the only thing to spoil the peace of the farm buildings they had taken residence in had been the bloody church clock which had struck every quarter-hour day and night. They had laughed then and sung. That was before they moved to Armentiers. It was there that all hell broke loose; things happened so fast then that they hadn't known where they were. He picked up the pen once more.

Darlington, June 1940. Dear Mr Downing…

He paused, head in hands, unable to go on. How the hell could he be expected to write such a letter? They should never have made each other such a promise. Yet he knew if the boot had been on the other foot Tom would have kept his word and written to Robert's parents.

He would make it easy for them, distort the truth; in fact it would have to be a bloody great bare-faced lie. He began to tremble as another panic attack began.

He covered his ears as he heard once again the sound of Messerschmitts above him, and saw again in his mind's eye the Hurricane as it came down at what must have been about three hundred miles an hour. He smelled again the blood of the young pilot, whose head had been completely severed by a piece of propeller blade.

Robert cried out in agony at the memory. He could hear Tom's voice again, singing as they drove towards the Dunkirk road, trying to shut out the sound of dive-bombers overhead. He tried again to write, something to soften the news, but all he could think of was the truck suddenly caught by the Jerries, the shells shooting through the roof within inches of their heads, the whistling of MG bullets and a hand grenade which seemed to come suddenly from underneath. The panic to abandon truck, only to find themselves prisoners, completely surrounded by tanks and armoured vehicles, unable to do anything for Tom and Jocky Johnson still trapped inside the blazing truck.

It was the French who had given the prisoners the chance to escape to a nearby ditch, by opening fire on the Jerries. Robert had stayed knee deep in water for what seemed like hours until it was safe to return to the truck, only to find it completely burned out. He had sheltered, soaked to the skin, in a wood near Dunkirk, watching as sixty or seventy bombers worked at finishing off what was left of the docks, and then he joined the mass of men thronging the beaches, shuffling slowly forward, carrying injured and dying covered by greatcoats. Shell-shocked men wandered about, wondering what on earth they were doing there; others, dispirited by the surrender of the Belgians, marched half asleep, following the crowd.

Robert started to write again, but the rows of words before his eyes became rows of men, long organised rows, silently waiting, moving gradually towards the calm dark water's edge, and then into it.

The panic came again. He couldn't swim; the water was chin high. Petrified, he moved on. Soon he would be out of this bloody world, soon he would be with Tom and Jocky Johnson – then suddenly he was heaved upwards into the boat, and he heard again the cry of, 'That's enough.

Another boat's on its way, lads. Keep yer chins up.'

He was sweating now and wanted to vomit as he relived again the rise and fall of the small boat, and then the relief as sleep overcame him and the ship carried them home.

He would write the letter another day; he was too tired tonight. Robert sank into another sleep, a fitful sleep in which another nightmare awaited him.

Mary knew something was wrong as they cycled down the lane. Mr Downing was leaning on the gate with an arm round his wife, and the boys were sitting on the wall swinging their legs in a woebegone manner.

'Oh, no,' groaned Bessie. 'Don't tell me they've lost Honeysuckle. She seemed much better last night. I hope to God it isn't foot and mouth. Me dad thought it might be.'

'What's up, Mam?' Lucy asked anxiously.

Mrs Downing handed her a letter, breaking into sobs as she did so. Mary suddenly realised it was about Tom. Her hair seemed to stand away from her scalp and she felt cold, despite the warm evening.

Lucy read the letter aloud slowly.

Darlington, June 1940

Dear Mr and Mrs Downing,

I suppose by now you will have heard the news from the War Office, but being Tom's best mate from the day we both joined up I always promised Tom if anything should happen I would write to you.

First of all I would like to reassure you that Tom was

laughing and singing right up to when the accident in the truck occurred. It was all over so quickly that he wouldn't have been aware of what was happening.

Tom talked about you all constantly during our nights together, especially Mary, so that I now feel I know you all personally. I would like to visit you sometime in the future. We always told each other that's what we'd do, if it's OK by you.

As for Tom, you can be proud of him. He was a brave man to the end. I for one am proud to have been his friend.

From his best mate,
Robert Scott

Mary seemed oddly detached from the scene before her, as though she was accepting the inevitable, and had already lived through the shock and grief even before it happened.

Lucy crumpled the letter viciously.

'It's all lies,' she cried. 'He's got a cheek scaring us like that. We'd have heard by now from the War Office. He can't be dead.' Then she broke into deep, heart-rending sobs. Mrs Downing drew her daughter into her arms in an effort to comfort her, silently suffering herself even more than the grieving girl.

Little Douglas kicked his clogged feet rhythmically on the drystone wall, too young to know anything unusual had happened. Cyril, unable to stem the tears, jumped down and ran to the closet, slamming the door behind him, ashamed of showing his feelings in public.

It was Tom's father for whom Mary felt the most sympathy. He seemed to have shrunk since

77

she had ridden past him that morning. His brown work-worn wrists were thrust deep into the pockets of his corduroy breeches, stretching the braces to their limits. His shoulders, usually squared and jaunty, were slumped, causing him to look inches shorter in his distress. Only Bessie seemed unaffected. Then she began to laugh, at first softly and then louder.

'It's all a joke,' she cried. 'Our Tom's not dead.'

Her laughter turned to hysteria, which held them all in frozen distress until Mary remembered how her mother had dealt with Auntie Norah after the pit accident. She slapped Bessie's face sharply, shocking her into silence. Then she said softly, calmly, 'Come on, let's go inside.'

She had known all along that he wouldn't come back. Something had told her outside the jeweller's. She hadn't been able to stop staring at him, knowing it would be for the last time.

She must take after her grandmother. The same thing had happened to her on occasions, like the day before Mary's uncle had been killed in the pit. She had begged him not to go to work the next day but he had laughed. They had all laughed but she had been right. Now it had happened to her. Her da always said she had her grandmother's ways, and now it seemed he was right.

'I'll go and make some tea if that's all right?' she said. Mrs Downing nodded, and she set off into the house. The family followed her, slowly, silently, as though in a funeral procession. To a funeral without a body.

Chapter Nine

For a change Rowland Roberts showed his authority and insisted Mary take a holiday. The day after the letter arrived at the Downings' he went to the station and bought a ticket to Newcastle. Then he wrote out a sick note and delivered it personally to the steel works, along with others for Bessie and Lucy, who were in a far more obvious state of shock than Mary.

'She's too calm,' he said to Gladys after they had seen Mary off to bed with a mug of hot milk. 'I don't like it when they don't show any emotion. It causes nothing but trouble in the long term.'

'She'll be all right,' Gladys said. 'She did all her grieving after Tom went back from leave. It was as though she knew he wouldn't return. Didn't I tell you at the time, about the premonition? It seems she takes after her grandmother, knew in advance what was going to happen, though I can't say I ever believed in such things until now. Still, my mother always said there's something strange about Catholics.'

'It's nothing at all to do with religion. I've seen stranger things happen at the hospital on more than one occasion – patients claiming to have left their bodies during surgery and watched the whole operation being performed. At first we put it down to vivid dreams caused by the ether, until one patient accurately described the layout of the theatre and the surgical team, all of which she'd never set eyes on. Oh, there're some strange forces at work which none of us understand. Still, if it's softened the shock for Mary it can only be for the good.'

'Even so, I think you've done the right thing by insisting on her going home for a while,' Gladys said. 'There's nothing you want more than your own flesh and blood in times of trouble, though this place'll be like a morgue without her and I shall be counting the hours until she comes back. Oh, when I think about Tom I can't believe we shall never see him again. What his poor parents must be going through, not knowing officially one way or the other. I'll go down as soon as I've seen Mary off and find out if there's anything I can do.'

'Yes, you do that, dear. All this bloodshed, I can't for the life of me see what good can possibly come out of it all. Still, we mustn't be downhearted. There's work to be done, not only on the front lines but here in the hospitals. I'm beginning to think our city will be a target before long. Better for Mary to go now before things begin to hot up. Though I shan't rest until she gets back. I only hope I'm doing the right thing by sending her.'

'You are, Rowland, I'm sure of it. If she stays here she'll be going off to work as usual, and I'm sure a change can only be for the good. Oh, but I'm going to miss her so much.'

'I know, dear; God knows I couldn't think more of the girl if she were our own daughter. I only hope she doesn't decide to stay with her family, but that's a risk we have to take. Oh, well, shall

80

we be going up? Somehow I don't feel like listening to the radio tonight.'

Mary had boarded the train with the feeling of a lead weight in her stomach, but by the time she reached Newcastle she couldn't fail to be uplifted by the anticipation of seeing her family again. Besides, a crowd of airmen had piled into the compartment and sung for most of the journey, trying to persuade her to join in. She hadn't done that, but instead she had taken out the enormous packed lunch Gladys had made and handed round the oven bottom cakes filled with eggs and salad from the garden, and by the time the sandwiches had been eagerly devoured Mary had confided the reason for her journey and been offered consolation and inundated with requests for her address. One of the airmen lifted her bags from the rack for her and she left the train feeling much more cheerful. She could just imagine her ma's face when she walked into the house.

The cheer vanished as she dismissed the taxi two streets from home and walked the rest of the way, not wishing to attract the attention of the neighbours. Even so she noticed the curtains shifting at a number of windows as she passed by, and was filled with disgust at the squalor of some of the houses. Surely the area hadn't been so bad when she lived here, or was it just that she was spoiled now by her present environment? She pressed the brass sneck, relieved to see that it was newly Brasso'd, and walked into the living kitchen, welcomed by the smell of frying onions and potatoes.

Kathleen saw her first. She was setting the table

and squealed with delight as Mary walked in. Dropping the cutlery, she ran to throw her arms round her sister, then stood back and looked down at Mary's best costume, as though afraid of soiling it.

'Ma,' she called, 'our Mary's come home. She looks lovely.'

The scuffle on the stairs announced the entry of her mother. 'Holy mackerel,' she exclaimed, and Mary went into her arms, weeping for the first time since Tom's departure, inconsolable as she gave way to the pent-up feelings of the past months. She closed her eyes and for a moment felt like a child again, comforted as she once was by the special warmth and devotion that only a mother and child can exchange. She realised at that moment that, much as she loved Gladys, it had been worth the long, uncomfortable journey to be here in her mother's arms at this time of grief.

'Nay, bonny lass,' said her mother wiping her own eyes, 'you should be laughing to be home, not turning the tap on and almost wetting me through.'

Mary smiled through her tears and said simply, 'Tom's dead.'

'Oh, God, no,' Mrs O'Connor said softly. 'Oh, you poor lass, have a good cry then.' And she gathered Mary into her arms again, rocking her right and left as though soothing a child to sleep.

'Do you want to talk aboot it?' she asked after a while. 'Tell us what happened. It's better oot than in. Or shall we have a cup of tea and talk later?'

'Yes, let's do that,' said Mary. 'I feel better

already – it was just seeing you again after all this time. Anyway, I'm dying for a drink. Where are the others?'

'Oor Norah's at work – she'll be home aboot six – an' yer da's on afternoon shift, finishes at ten. Eeh, I can't wait to see his face when he knows you're home. I think he's the one who has missed you the most. Blamed himself for you gooan', said if he hadn't spent so much on the beer we shouldn't have been living here amongst the grime and smoke and you wouldn't have been ill and had to go convalescing halfway across the country. Well, I'll say one thing: he's a cheeanged man, determined to shift us all out of here as soon as he's able.'

'Well, I'm glad some good came of my leaving.'

'Why are you talking different, our Mary?' asked Kathleen.

'I'm not,' said Mary, shocked.

'Yes you are. Isn't she, Ma?'

'Well, I suppose she's just picked up a different accent.'

'I never noticed. It must have rubbed off on me from the doctor and Mrs Roberts. Oh, Ma, they are lovely – I'm ever so lucky to be living there. I wish you could visit the house some day.'

'That'll be the day when I go anywhere further than the shops.' Mrs O'Connor laughed. 'Are those stovies ready yet, Kathleen? I bet our Mary's starving. I'd have done another panful if I'd known you were coming, lass, not that there's many onions amongst the taties. Who'd have ever believed there could be a shortage of onions?'

'Perhaps this chicken will make them go further,'

said Mary, opening one of her bags and taking out a brown paper parcel. 'It was only cooked last night, in fact the poor thing was strutting around the garden yesterday afternoon.'

'Eeh, lass, are you sure they can spare it? I mean with all the rationing and everything?'

'I didn't have chance to refuse. It was killed, cleaned and cooked before I knew anything about it. I told you how good Mrs Roberts is.'

'Look out, the camels are coming.'

The door burst open and in rushed Jimmy and Michael, stopping dead in their tracks when they noticed Mary, to stand shyly in the doorway.

'Well,' she said, 'aren't you going to say hello or something?'

'Hello,' said Jimmy. 'Have you come home?'

'Well, what does it look like?' said Kathleen.

Mary laughed. 'Oh, you haven't half grown.'

''Ave I grown?' asked Michael.

'You certainly have. Why, I don't think I'd have recognised the pair of you if I'd seen you outside. Where's our Bill, then?'

'Gone to the allotment.'

'I didn't know you had an allotment, Ma!'

'It's not ours, it belongs to the school, but anyone would think it belonged to our Bill, the way he's taken over the running of it. Oh, well, let's get out the stovies. Have you cut the bread, Kathleen?'

'I'll do it,' said Mary.

'Oh no you won't, not in those clothes,' said her mother.

'Well, give us a pinny, then. Oh, it's lovely to be home again.' But Mary couldn't help wondering how long it would be before she was yearning to be back amongst the green hills and valleys of Yorkshire.

As it happened it wasn't the yearning for the countryside which forced Mary to return at the end of the week but the guilt of being away from work. The first few days had been made up of visits to Joyce, Father Flynn, and the shops, where she bought a new dress for her mother and shoes for her father, brothers and sisters, not caring that her precious savings would all be gone. After all, what could she possibly want, now that she wouldn't have Tom to share it with? She also bought a white frilly pram set for Joyce's new baby boy, crying bitter tears as she held the warm cuddly form in her arms.

'It's all right,' she said when Joyce became alarmed. 'It's just that I could have ended up having a baby too. Sometimes I wish it was me who had got caught instead of you, then at least I'd have had something belonging to Tom. I loved him so much, Joycey. I don't think I can bear it knowing I shall never see him again.'

Breaking into more sobs Mary set the baby off crying too, and then turning red in the face he suddenly gave a huge thrust and filled his nappy. The girls began to laugh and Mary handed him back to his mother.

'I've changed my mind,' she announced. 'I'm relieved I didn't get caught after all.'

It was Father Flynn who offered her the most consolation. The relief of confessing the Christmas sin was tremendous, and afterwards she poured out her heart to him, anxiously questioning him about what would happen to the soul of a Protestant, and one who hadn't attended church very often at that.

'Well, didn't you always have a good judgement of character, my child?' he said to Mary as they sat by the fire in his cosy sitting room, he in the old horsehair chair and she on the floor at his feet, her head resting on his knee, the way she had on so many occasions as a little girl. 'I can't think for a moment that you would ever give your heart to one who wasn't a good man and worthy of it, regardless of his beliefs. Surely he will not remain in limbo for long if you pray hard enough for the gates of Heaven to open for him. Besides, there's far too many of our own faith with a multitude of sins behind them for there to be room for every Protestant outside. Sure Tom will be accepted without delay if he was as good a man as you say he was.'

Father Flynn always had the knack of cheering Mary up, and he couldn't for the life of him see what good it would do to keep the girl in a state of unhappiness for the sake of a few kind words. Even so, he couldn't help feeling rather relieved that she hadn't landed herself for good with a member of a different faith.

On the Saturday before Mary's departure a charity concert had been organised to be held in the British Hall at the end of the street, and of course the whole family had tickets. Mick O'Connor scrubbed away the coal dust with extra zest and donned his best white shirt and navy blue suit; he couldn't remember the last time he'd worn it or had a pair of brand new shoes. He would never forget old Nesbitt the clog-maker's face when Mary had produced the money and ordered shoes for the lot of them. 'She's a right good lass, oor Mary,' he said to himself in the mirror as he brushed his thinning hair, noticing how much healthier he looked since he'd cut down on the drinking, determined the rest of the family wouldn't leave home if he could help it. Still, he was proud of his eldest daughter, who had the face of an angel, marred only by the sadness in her huge brown eyes. He prayed that time would heal her hurt, but at the same time he knew she would never regain the carefree innocence she had possessed before she had loved and lost.

The audience were all assembled by half past seven. Mrs Cree from number ten struck up on the piano with 'There'll Always be an England' though it took some recognising with all the wrong notes. After three more tunes, and umpteen anxious glances offstage, she suddenly scurried off behind the curtain. The youngsters in the audience began to stamp their feet, then one young lad at the back of the room began to chant 'Mrs Cree's gone for a pee' and soon a whole bunch of them were chanting with him. Mary couldn't help giggling, although she gave their Jimmy a good-natured clout when he joined in.

With a face the colour of strawberry jam Mrs Cree tottered back on stage and sat at the piano, her hands poised two feet above the keys, waiting to begin. Suddenly two little girls dressed in red and waving what were supposed to be a ship's scarlet sails glided from behind the scenes with a small boy in a sailor suit between them. He came to the front of the stage and began to sing 'Red Sails in the Sunset', gesticulating in an exaggerated manner as he pretended to peer out to sea for the ship. Fortunately the child's tuneless warbling was almost drowned by Mrs Cree's bashing at the keys, the scraping of chairs and coughing in the audience. Nevertheless, wild applause brought smiles to the young performers' faces at the end of the song.

Next on the programme was a large lady in a purple taffeta gown, which was at least two sizes too small and some twenty years out of date. Mrs Cree began the introduction and then, in a tremulous voice which seemed to flit from contralto to soprano, the lady gave her rendering of 'Cherry Ripe'. Every time she reached for a high note her enormous bosom heaved, fighting for release from the tight low-cut neckline. The audience were spellbound and Mary glanced around at the men, who were open-mouthed with anticipation, and the waiting wide-eyed women.

'Ripe I cry.' Reaching the end of the song, the singer took a deep breath and gave her all, flinging her arms into the air. 'Come and buy!' she cried, and out of her dress burst one heaving pendulous breast.

The hall was silent as a tomb and then, as the poor woman bowed low and realised what had happened, the whole audience began to stamp and cheer. The same young lad who'd begun the previous chant suddenly shouted, 'I'll buy a pound of those any day.'

The unfortunate performer, hastily covering

herself, hurried off behind the curtain, whilst Mrs Cree, oblivious of what had taken place, stood and bowed happily, wallowing in her first ever standing ovation.

The laughter rang along the street as the crowd spilled out of the British Hall and made their way home.

'We'll have oor own sing-song,' Mick O'Connor promised as he invited the neighbours from both sides in for a bite of supper. Mary's mother had left the oven full of roasting potatoes and the aroma met them as they opened the door. Young Jimmy was sent to the back door of the Hart with the large water jug to be filled with beer. Mary was pleasantly surprised at the change in her da, who seemed to have deserted the Hart and hadn't been there at all since her arrival. Intent now on working to move the family into a larger house, he hadn't had a collier's Monday since the day Mary left.

Old Jimmy Reed from next door had called in home to fetch his melodeon, and now he was entertaining them with his jaunty version of 'Blaydon Races'. Soon the singing could be heard at the bottom of the street, and one or two of Mick's work-mates had sidled in to join them.

The highlight of the night was when Mary amazed not only her family but herself as well by singing 'Linden Lea' in front of them all, bringing tears to the eyes of her parents, who were sad that their daughter would be leaving tomorrow, but oh so proud of the beautiful young woman she had blossomed into.

Chapter Ten

After hearing the news of Tom's death Jack Holmes had loitered by the smithy every night for a week. The news had spread rapidly when the Downing girls had failed to turn in for work, and Jack, who had been taken with Mary from the night he had held her close at the dance, thought it only right that he should offer his condolences. It was Madge who noticed him standing by the smithy, watching eagerly as the day shift left the strip department. Never one to miss the chance of chatting up a handsome young man, she asked him if he was waiting for someone.

'Mary O'Connor,' he said. 'My sister told me about her fiancé, and I thought it only right that I should – er...' He paused, not really knowing what it was he should do.

'Oh aye,' grinned Madge, never one to mince words. 'Fancy her yerself, do yer? Well, lad, I can't say I blame yer, but if yer want my advice you won't rush things. Grief is a nasty thing and has to have its time. Still, I'll tell her you've asked about her when she comes back. Yer'll have a long wait if you intend standing here every night. She's gone home to Newcastle for a holiday – the best thing for 'er in my opinion.'

'Will yer tell her, then? That I asked, I mean?'

'Aye, lad, I'll tell her. Now I should get off home if I were you. On nights, are yer?'

'Mornings,' he said as they set off up the hill. 'I finished at two, only I shall be on two to ten next week, so it'll be awkward to see her then.'

'Give it a week or two, lad. Like I said, there's no point in rushing things. Mind you, if yer feeling in need of a bit of female company in the meantime...'

Jack gave her a grin. 'Well, what a shame my heart's already spoken for, otherwise I might 'ave taken you up on that.'

Madge gave him a shove. 'Get away with yer,' she said with a grin. 'I'm old enough to be yer mother. Mind you, I'm not dead yet by a long chalk.'

They were still laughing when they parted company at the top of the hill, but as they went their separate ways both hearts were heavy at the thought of what Mary and the Downing family must be suffering after the loss of the young soldier.

Jack walked on thoughtfully. He had been tempted to seek out Mary after the dance. After all, his brother's favourite saying was 'All's fair in love and war'. Usually he would have taken his chance against young Downing but somehow it wouldn't have been right, not with him being a soldier. Now he thanked God that he had kept his distance. At least the poor young bugger had known Mary was waiting for him. That must have sustained him whilst he was over there in the thick of the action.

He passed the Catholic church. That was another thing. He had seen her going in there one Sunday with Theresa Murphy. What would happen when his family knew he was knocking about with a Catholic? He smiled to himself; he wasn't knocking about with anybody yet. Mary might not even entertain the idea of going out with him, especially if she knew about his brother's reputation with the lasses, and who could blame her? She was so lovely – he could see her now in the green dress she had worn to the dance. Well, he'd never been religious, but he swore to God that if Mary O'Connor gave him a chance, he'd never look at another woman as long as he lived.

Mary's stomach gave a lurch as she stepped down from the train and she half expected to see Tom waiting at the ticket barrier the way he had been on her arrival last summer. She mentally prepared herself for all the familiar things which were sure to remind her of him at every turn, telling herself it was time she pulled herself together. What was it Tom had said? 'You're young, Mary; you could meet someone else.' Well, she didn't want anyone else, but he was right, she was young, too young to walk around with a face as long as a fiddle. Besides, she had to think about Tom's family. They needed cheering up, especially the little boys.

She deliberately fixed a smile on her face, surprised at how much better it made her feel, and walked through the barrier, bags in hand.

The station clock told her it was almost four. If she walked briskly she could be home by half past five. She wasn't sure, on this return journey, that she could afford the cost of a taxi.

She felt the familiar pang of grief as she glimpsed and turned away from the jeweller's where Tom had bought her ring, then she straightened her shoulders and set off towards the outskirts of town.

She was almost on the Longfield road when the rag and bone man drew his horse to a halt.

'Want a ride, missis?' he called.

Mary didn't know whether to laugh or cry at the greeting. She knew she'd aged considerably inwardly, during the past months, but she still didn't feel like a missis. She smiled. 'Thanks. My feet are killing me.'

'Jump on then, if yer don't mind sitting on top o't pig fodder.'

Mary looked in dismay at the rotting vegetables and potato peelings. The man found an old coat and made room for her to sit on it.

'I expect yer surprised to see this lot.' He laughed. 'It's from pig bins down in't city. I can give yer a lift as far as Hedge Farm at Cowholes.'

'I'm not going quite so far. Longfield will be fine.'

'Just tell me where yer want dropping off then, bottom or top,' he said. 'Makes no difference to me, except that it livens up the journey having somebody to talk to.'

Mary smiled. It was cheering her no end being jolted along in a cart full of pig food. Wait till she told the girls at work tomorrow. Why, it might even put a smile on the faces of Bessie and Lucy.

A little while later Mary opened the door of a silent Moorland House. She called out to Mrs Roberts but received no reply; then she heard the clatter from the direction of the cellar.

'Mrs Roberts.' Mary hurried down the steps to

find Gladys surrounded by old pans, kettles and utensils of all descriptions, and stood there open-mouthed. 'What on earth are you doing?'

Gladys beamed at the sight of Mary. What a miserable week it had been without her. She clambered noisily out of the mess and hugged the girl to her.

'Oh, I am glad you're back, Mary. You'll never know how much we've missed you. If only I'd known you were coming back today I'd have had something special ready for you.' She laughed as Mary stared at the tranklements littering the cellar floor. 'Well, I had to do something to occupy me whilst you were away, so I've been colecting old aluminium for the war effort. There's a collection being organised in town. I've done quite well considering the size of the village, don't you think?'

Mary laughed. 'Very well. How are you getting them all to town?'

'Rowland's taking them on Saturday morning. He'll be so pleased you're back; you'll be able to go with him and practise your driving.'

'With this lot in the car I'll be lucky if there's room for me.' She suddenly began to giggle.

Gladys smiled. 'What's so funny?' she asked, pleased to see Mary like her old self again.

'I'm just thinking, I ride into Longfield on a cart full of pig food and out again in a car full of old tin cans. Oh, Mrs Roberts, I am glad to be back.'

'And I'm glad to have you back. Come on, let's go and see about dinner. The doctor will be home soon.'

Mrs Holmes sat in her usual place by the fire, rocking rhythmically in the old wooden chair.

'Aren't yer going out tonight, Jack?' she asked inquisitively.

'No.'

'It's not like you to stay in on a Friday.'

'No.'

'Are yer spent up? Yer can always 'ave a couple of bob if yer are.'

'Mother, it's pay day. How can I be spent up on a Friday?'

She gave it up as a bad job; she knew she would get nothing out of her lads if they didn't want her to know anything.

'I'm off to bed, Mother,' Jack said.

'At this time, when yer haven't to be up in the morning? Are yer sickening for something, lad?'

'No, I'm just tired, that's all. Don't forget I've been up at five all week.'

'Aye, lad. Well, as long as yer not badly, I don't suppose an early night'll do yer any harm.'

'I'll fetch coal up for morning, then I'll be going to bed then.' He went to the cellar door, picking up the coal bucket on the way.

Mrs Holmes watched him out of her eye corners. He was a good lad, their Jack, not as headstrong as Harry, and thoughtful. It wasn't like him not to confide in her if anything was bothering him. Perhaps she was just imagining things.

'Goodnight then, Mother. Tell our Harry not to make a noise when he comes in.'

'Nay, lad, I shall be in bed mesen by the time he comes home. Yer might as well lock door – whoever's next in knows key's on't string through't letter box. Knowing our Harry, yer dad might well be in off night shift by the time he comes rolling home. Where he finds to go till all hours o't morning I'd like to know.'

Oh, no, she wouldn't like to know, Jack thought. In fact she'd have a seizure if she knew he was down at Ada Banwell's whilst her old man was away in the Navy. It was a miracle his brother hadn't been caught before now, with all the married women he seemed to become involved with.

If it wasn't one of the husbands it would be his dad who found out one of these days, and despite his age he wouldn't put it beyond the old man's capability to give his brother a damned good hiding.

Oh, well, he couldn't say he hadn't been warned.

Jack couldn't sleep. In fact he wasn't at all tired; he just wanted to be able to think about Mary O'Connor without interruption. He wondered if he had waited a reasonable length of time before approaching her, and if Madge had mentioned to her that he had been thinking about her. If he weren't on afters next week he could have gone to meet her out of work; now it would be another ten days before he could see her.

He wondered what she did at the weekends. She certainly never came over to the pictures or the dances at the Victoria Hall. If only she didn't live miles from anywhere it would be easier. Anyway, he made up his mind that a week on Monday he would meet her from work. He hadn't considered yet what he would say to her, but he would come up with something before then. He felt a stirring in his loins and turned on his stomach, aiming to

96

relieve himself just by thinking of Mary O'Connor. He hoped Ada Banwell kept their Harry occupied for a while. He wanted the bed to himself.

Madge had warned Mary that Jack Holmes meant to look out for her, but she was unprepared all the same when she came out of work on the Monday. She found herself blushing as he came across the road.

'Hello,' he said, cap in hand. 'I'm, er, sorry about the bad news.'

'Oh,' said Mary, staring at the ground.

'I wondered – well, I know it's a bit soon and I don't want to rush things, but I wondered if you'd like to go to the pictures one night?'

'Well, it's a bit awkward. I mean, it would mean me walking back to Longfield on my own.'

'Oh, I'd see you home all right.' He laughed nervously. 'Why, you don't think I'd let you walk all that way on yer own, surely?'

'Well, I don't know. I couldn't let you walk all that way and then have to come back again.'

He laughed. 'Don't worry about that. I must walk so far every day of the week, once I get underground. All the way to the pit, and then all the way back again underground. Daft, isn't it?'

Mary laughed. As they set off walking up the hill, he took hold of her bike and wheeled it for her.

'You'll have to get a bike like me,' she said.

'Aye. We could go a ride together,' he said, looking at her hopefully.

'Well, you could come over to Longfield then,'

she said.

'I could come over anyway,' he said eagerly. 'I can easily borrow a bike, that's no problem at all.'

Mary smiled. She couldn't help liking Jack. She had liked him since the dance – her face changed suddenly as she began to feel guilty – but not as much as Tom. She'd never like anyone as much as Tom. Even so, Jack was well mannered and nice. Besides, she couldn't shut herself away like the nuns in the orphanage. As Tom said, she was young.

'I shall be going bilberrying on Saturday afternoon if it's fine. You could come with me if you like.'

'It's a date,' Jack said, his pleasure showing on his face. 'What time?'

'How about two? I'll meet you outside the school and we'll walk along the lane to the moor.'

'I'll be there,' he said, grinning like a half-moon.

Bessie and Lucy appeared from the works yard.

'Are yer coming, Mary?' Bessie called.

'Yes, I'm coming,' she replied. 'Well, I'll see you Saturday then.'

'Yes. I won't be late.'

Mary joined the sisters as they set off pedalling along the main road.

'What did Jack Holmes want?' Bessie asked.

'He just wanted to say how sorry he was about Tom.'

'I bet he wanted to go out with yer,' Lucy said.

Mary felt her face growing hot.

'It's OK, you've no need to feel uncomfortable. Nobody expects you to live in misery for ever,'

Bessie said. 'Besides, he's nice is Jack Holmes.'

'I know,' said Mary. 'It's just that I keep thinking about Tom all the time. I'll never feel the way I did about Tom with anyone else, so perhaps I shouldn't see Jack Holmes after all.'

'Don't be daft,' said Lucy. 'Our Tom wouldn't expect any of us to turn all morbid and miserable. Besides, you might be able to put me a good word in with his brother.'

'Oh no she won't,' retorted Bessie. 'You'd be the talk of Millington going out with him. They're as different as chalk and cheese are Harry and Jack. He'll fall over anything in a skirt will Harry Holmes, and he seems to prefer the married ones from what the girls at work say.'

'So he should be more experienced then.' Lucy grinned cheekily.

Bessie almost fell off her bike as she turned the corner up the hill. 'Lucy Downing, just you be careful of your reputation.'

Mary felt a weight lift from her. She hadn't known how Tom's sisters would react to the news of her seeing Jack, but she should have known she could count on them remaining friends. That was the way the people of Longfield were. It must be the result of living in such a clean, beautiful village; it seemed to make them less small-minded than city people, or perhaps she was just lucky in her choice of friends. She began to look forward to Saturday and said a silent prayer that it wouldn't rain.

Mary's prayer was answered. She dressed carefully in a thin cotton dress and set off at quarter to two for Longfield school. Jack was already waiting and she couldn't help thinking how handsome he was in slacks and white cricket shirt open at the neck. A little on the lean side, perhaps, and rather pale, but she supposed that was the result of working in the pit away from the sunlight. Well, today he could make up for it. The sun was hot on her arms and Jack marvelled at the brilliance of her hair as she approached him.

'Have you been waiting long?' she asked, unable to think of anything else to say.

'About ten minutes,' he said, taking from her the basket which Gladys had insisted on her bringing.

It was filled to the brim with a selection of sandwiches, a fruit pie, a tin box in which to collect the bilberries and a bottle of nettle beer, which Mary had found quite pleasant once she could be persuaded to sample it.

They walked in silence along the lane, past the church and old stone cottages and out on to the moor. There was a slight breeze which swayed the bracken and a lone oak sapling; one day it would lend shade to weary walkers, but now it struggled bravely to survive out here in the elements. The heather was young and vivid purple and the bilberry bushes hung with lush, juicy berries. Mary climbed a path away from the lane towards the shade of a row of rocks where, out of breath, she flopped down on the grass with Jack beside her.

'This is absolutely my favourite place,' she said, looking out over the valley to the distant hills. 'I don't think anywhere in the world could be more glorious.'

'It's certainly beautiful,' Jack said. He stretched

out his hand and broke off a sprig of heather and, stroking Mary's hair away from her face, placed it behind her ear. 'But not as beautiful as your hair. It makes me want to run my fingers through it.'

Mary felt her face colouring. She hated it when she blushed, and turned away embarrassed.

'We'd better start bilberrying,' she muttered.

'I bet I can pick the most.' Laughing, Jack rose to his feet, taking a blue two pound sugar bag from his pocket.

They picked steadily for about an hour, until the bag and the tin box were almost full, and their hands stained almost black from the juices.

'How many do you reckon we've picked?' asked Mary as they walked back to the basket.

'At least enough for a couple of jars of jam,' Jack estimated.

'I'll make you one, and give it to you next time...' She paused mid-sentence. Perhaps there wouldn't be a next time.

'That'll be something to look forward to.' He grinned, relieved that he would be seeing her again.

Mary unwrapped the sandwiches and a couple of hard boiled eggs.

'Hey, you certainly eat well out here,' he said. 'Are you immune from rationing in Longfield?'

'Of course not,' said Mary. 'It's just that Mrs Roberts grows all her own salad stuff, and the chickens reward me for feeding them every day, with a good supply of eggs.'

'Well, now I know why you've got skin like a peach. It's all the fresh food you eat.' Jack ran his fingers along her arm, causing a sensation Mary had only experienced with one man before. She drew away. It was too soon; it was unfair to Tom.

Jack knew he was going too fast. He hadn't intended to, it was just that he couldn't keep his hands off her. He picked up the nettle beer and took a drink, then lay back in the sun, unbuttoning his shirt to allow the sun to reach his chest. A covering of dark curly hair glistened in the sunlight, which Mary had an urge to reach out and caress. What was wrong with her? It must be the nettle beer. She ought to have provided some less potent refreshment.

She lay down beside Jack, feeling drowsy in the heat. A lazy moth landed on her face and she brushed it away, returning her hand to her side, where it touched Jack's. He entwined his fingers in hers and they lay as one, joined by a current too strong for either of them to resist. Jack rolled towards her and, leaning over, kissed her, tenderly at first; then, feeling her respond, more fiercely, until their passion threatened to overcome them and they broke apart, content to wait until another day, confident that this special thing between them was worth waiting for, and must be allowed to grow in its own time.

Mary heard a grouse calling. 'Go back, go back,' it seemed to say. She knew she couldn't go back but it was also too soon to go forward. She was confused about her feelings for Jack. Her feelings for Tom were still paramount. She had thought Jack could be a friend but it was obvious things were moving beyond friendship and she was not ready. She released her hand from his. 'Jack,' she said, 'I like you a lot but I need some time to think about Tom, just to remember our time together. So I won't see you for a few weeks.' She blushed. 'Well, you might not want to see me again anyway.'

'Of course I do, but I understand. Just don't make me wait too long, that's all I ask.'

'I won't.' Then she took his hand again and they walked together along the lane.

Chapter Eleven

Jack was waiting outside the sweet shop opposite the cinema. His face lit up when Rowland and Gladys dropped Mary off on their way to spend Saturday evening with their friends Ernest and his wife Celia.

They always enjoyed what usually turned out to be a musical evening, during which Ernest would play the violin accompanied by Celia on the piano. Then Rowland would sing, after which he would look through any new sheet music available and see if any of it was suitable for the choir. Tonight however both he and Gladys were rather uneasy, troubled that Mary seemed to have fallen hook line and sinker for the lad Jack Holmes. Not that they disapproved of the friendship, just that she seemed to have rushed into it rather suddenly after Tom's death. Rowland said it would blow over and she would probably have a number of romantic encounters before settling down, but Gladys could recognise a love affair when she saw one, and dreaded the day when Mary would break the news that she and Jack were considering marriage.

With Tom it hadn't bothered her; the chances of his ever taking Mary away from Longfield had been virtually nil. But if Mary married Jack, Gladys knew she would settle down over in Millington, which might as well be a hundred miles away as far as Gladys was concerned. Oh, well, all they could do was welcome the boy into their home and that wasn't difficult to do, seeing as he was such a likeable lad.

Mary smiled radiantly as Jack handed her a box of Black Magic. They crossed the main road and joined the queue which stretched halfway round the cinema just as the first house was beginning to trickle out. The ones who were too impatient to stand for the National Anthem came first, and then the rush.

Mary was excited. On the rare occasions she had set foot inside a cinema it had been for the afternoon matinee and she had been lumbered with Kathleen and Norah, not like tonight when Jack was buying tickets for the circle. He led her up the marble staircase with the brass handrail, and on to the back row. Mary felt slightly embarrassed when she realised the seats were double ones with no armrest in the middle, obviously designed with amorous couples in mind. She saw the funny side and began to giggle.

'You're a sly one, Jack Holmes,' she said. 'I wonder how many girls you've snuggled up to in these seats before tonight.'

'Hundreds,' Jack teased, then added seriously,

'but not one of them as nice as you.'

'Nice? What a romantic man you are. Not beautiful, not even pretty, just nice.'

Jack coloured. 'Well, I'm not very good with words,' he mumbled. 'You are – beautiful, I mean – only I'm not good at fancy speeches. If you want all that flattery you should be going out with our Harry.'

'No thanks.' Mary laughed. 'I've heard about him at work. Mind you, all the girls seem to fancy him.'

'Don't you dare tell him that; he's big-headed enough already. Besides, he seems to prefer the married ones, unfortunately.'

Mary didn't know what to say to that so she opened the chocolates. 'Come on,' she said, 'I can't eat all these myself or I'll be as fat as one of Tom's pigs.' She experienced the familiar churning in her stomach as she realised what she had said.

Jack put an arm round her shoulders, glad of the excuse. 'It's OK,' he said, 'I don't mind you talking about him. It wouldn't be right to shut him out, and it wouldn't be good for you either. I know you were engaged; we can't pretend it never happened.'

Mary smiled up at him, relieved now that she had mentioned Tom and so discovered that Jack wasn't going to be jealous; little did she know what an effort it was for Jack not to show his true feelings.

He looked down into the sun-freckled face and their eyes met. She reached her mouth up to his and Tom was forgotten along with the chocolates

105

and the film.

'I love you, Mary O'Connor,' he mumbled between kisses.

'And I love you, Jack Holmes,' she said, thinking there was no need of fancy speeches from a man as lovely as this one.

Thankful for the blackout Jack paused at intervals to kiss Mary as they walked to the music shop at the top of Hawley's Hill, which Ernest Sessions ran in between giving music lessons and leading a small local orchestra.

Unlike Rowland he had not lost many musicians to the Local Defence Volunteer force, despite an average age somewhere in the mid-fifties, but the undoubted star of the orchestra was a nine-year-old pupil of his who was doing so well he had been given a place in the first violins, much to the delight of audiences, who had taken the boy to their hearts. Actually, Gladys was becoming rather bored by Ernest's enthusiastic account of how brilliant the boy was, and she sighed with relief when Mary rang the bell on the door of the shop, in front of the living quarters.

'Well,' she said, rising to her feet and looking round for her coat, 'that sounds like Mary. We'd better be on our way.'

'Why don't you invite her in for a cup of tea?' said Celia in her usual friendly manner.

'Thanks all the same, but she's rather shy,' said Gladys, unable to face yet another account of young what's-his-name's talents.

'Yes, we'd better be off,' said Rowland. 'It's slow going on the narrow lanes with the reduced lighting on the car. Luckily there's a moon tonight, but even so we'll be on our way. How much am I in your debt for the sheet music?'

'Get away with you,' said Ernest. 'What's a few shillings between friends?' His words made Gladys feel terribly guilty about being in such a hurry to leave. She knew that the real cause of her uncharacteristic irritability was nothing to do with Ernest, and everything to do with Jack Holmes.

Nevertheless, she was amiable enough towards him when they got outside, inviting him to tea a week on Sunday, and offering him a lift home, which he politely refused, saying he didn't live a cock stride away, and the air would do him good anyway.

'Nice boy that,' commented Rowland rather grudgingly, as they drove through the countryside back to Longfield.

'Yes,' said Gladys simply, thinking what an understatement that was. She could well understand what had attracted Mary to the tall, dark-haired young man, and spent the rest of the journey wishing dreamily that she was thirty years younger.

'I wish I wasn't going,' said Mary. 'What if they don't like me.'

'If they don't like yer they must be daft,' Madge grunted whilst lifting a hundredweight coil from the machine.

'What shall I wear?'

'I don't know as it matters. If Jack likes yer it doesn't matter about anybody else.'

'I'll go in my brown costume seeing as I'm

going to church the next morning.'

Madge looked at the girl sharply. 'Has he told them you're a Catholic?' she asked.

'I think so. Anyway, Jack doesn't care what they say. Still, I do hope they like me.'

'Well, there's one who certainly will,' said Madge. 'He'll have yer knickers off before yer know what's hit yer will that brother of his.'

Mary laughed. 'Oh no he won't because I don't wear 'em, didn't you know?'

Madge laughed affectionately with Mary. It was nice to know she was back to normal after the tragedy. In fact she hadn't half come out of her shell this past few weeks. Oh well, that's what love did for you.

'How're yer getting home, tomorrow night I mean?' she asked.

'I'm not. I'm staying at Theresa Murphy's, going to church Sunday morning, then Jack's walking back with me and staying for tea.'

'I'm going to church tonight,' Madge said softly.

'You?' said Mary incredulously. 'Going to church, and on a Friday night? You're joking.'

'I'm not,' the woman said. 'I sometimes go to the Spiritual Church in Darnall.'

Mary didn't know what to say, and just repeated Madge's words parrot fashion. 'Spiritual Church in Darnall? Where's that?'

'Other side Sheffield. It takes two buses to get there, but it's worth the journey. I don't know why, but I feel like I've gone home when I walk into that church.'

'What do they do? I mean, is it weird? I always

imagined it would be frightening with all those seances and things.'

Madge laughed. 'There aren't any seances. It's just a church, but a lot more cheerful than the ones here. All they do at the one I got married at is talk about everybody and their grandmothers, and I've heard tell it's worse still at the chapel. Like my mother used to say, yer don't need to attend places of worship in order to do Christian deeds, but I must admit I've gained a lot of comfort from that little church in Darnall.'

Mary would have liked to ask further questions but just then the buzzer went.

'Hey, come on,' said Madge, 'home time. Look, don't say anything to the others, about me going to Darnall, I mean. They'd only ridicule me if they knew.'

'Of course I won't. In fact I'd like to know more about it when we have more time.'

Madge's face lit up. 'Yer don't think I'm daft, then?'

'No. My grandmother had too many strange things happen to her for me to think it's daft.'

Madge linked arms with Mary as they walked down the gangway. 'Yer could come with me if yer liked.'

Mary blushed. 'I couldn't. It's not allowed in our Church.'

'Oh, no, I forgot. Oh well, let me know if yer change yer mind.'

And with that they parted company, both anticipating what the weekend would bring.

Mary was scared stiff when Rowland waved

goodbye from the car in Millington. He had dropped her off near the clock, and she moved nervously from one foot to the other as she waited for Jack. She saw him hurrying down the hill towards her and set off to meet him. She wondered if he was nervous too about taking her to meet his family. They walked back in the direction of five long rows of brick houses.

'We live on the top row,' he said. 'That's why I'm so thin, trudging up this hill every time I go anywhere.'

Mary smiled, knowing his lean frame was the result of working like a horse in the pit at the far end of Millington.

They reached the top row, and turned to walk on to number forty. It was the middle house Jack said. Despite the cool of the day men and women were sitting outside, watching the children play; some on doorsteps, others on straight-backed kitchen chairs and one young man even reclining on an upturned zinc bath, straightening to stare at Mary and muttering to Jack as they passed.

A small boy in patched trousers came running towards them. 'Will yer play footy with me Jack?' he called.

'Not today, Robby,' Jack answered, ruffling the already tousled hair.

'Aah, come on, you allus play footy on a Saturday.'

'Not this Saturday. Go find yer pals.'

A disappointed Robby continued to try to coax Jack into changing his mind, until Mary was led over a newly whitened step into the house.

Mrs Holmes was in her usual chair. She had

changed her all-round pinafore for a clean apron and rocked gently as she weighed Mary up. Mary was suddenly filled with a longing for her own mother and the little house in Newcastle which was so similar to this one.

'This is Mary, Mother,' Jack announced. 'Mary, this is my mother.'

'Pleased to meet you, lass. Come in and sit yerself down. We don't stand on ceremony in this house – yer'll 'ave to take us as yer find us if yer going to join't family.'

Mary coloured, embarrassed at Mrs Holmes's assumption when Jack hadn't even asked her yet. Jack winked at Mary, putting her at ease. 'Where's the clan?' he asked.

'Eeh, yer might know, lad. Yer dad's gone to bed for an hour. Said he'd be down before you arrived but yer know what he is after he's had a pint at dinner time.'

Jack grinned. 'Where are the others?'

'In't room. Carding, I expect. It's to be hoped yer know how to play cards, lass; it's like a gambling den in our room when the family gets together.'

'Gambling den, she says. Pennies, that's all we play for, and then me mother forgets to put in half the time.' He laughed and dodged his mother's hand as she aimed a good-natured blow at him. 'You should feel honoured, Mary. If you hadn't been coming she'd have been in the game herself by now. Let's go in and meet the clan.' He led Mary out of the kitchen, past the bottom of the stairs, and into the other room. The smell of Mansion polish and smoke met Mary as she entered. Harry Holmes – whom she recognised from the farmers' ball – sat shuffling cards at a round polished table, then began to deal them to his sister Marjory, her husband Bill Bacon, and Margaret, his other sister, who looked about Mary's age. A little girl of about four was counting an enormous pile of pennies and broke off to run into Jack's arms, laughing as he threw her up into the air and caught her again.

'Say hello to yer Auntie Mary, Una,' he said.

Una muttered 'Hello' before stuffing her thumb in her mouth and turning all shy. Mary guessed the pretty curly-haired child would be jealous of her and opened her handbag to find the bag of toffee Gladys had made that morning.

'Here,' she whispered. 'I've brought you some toffee.'

The little girl beamed, struggled free of Jack's hold and ran into the kitchen, where Mary heard her showing off the sweets to her grandmother. Jack fetched a stool from the kitchen and she sat nervously, wondering whether she ought to go back and keep Jack's mother company. Mrs Holmes made up her mind for her by bringing another chair and joining the family at the table.

'Fancy a game, love?' Bill Bacon asked as he began to shuffle the cards.

'I don't think I know how to play,' said Mary.

'We'll show yer. Come on, put yer money in. Halfpenny in the middle and halfpenny in the kitty,' Bill said, not giving her chance to refuse.

Margaret volunteered to show Mary how to play, and before she knew it she was on a winning streak.

She had an idea she was going to like this family, probably because they reminded her of her own back in Newcastle. She suddenly wondered what her parents would think of Jack, and had the feeling they would love him as much as she did.

After tea Mary had a wash in the sink in the corner of the kitchen, combed her hair and put on a dab of Phul Nana, then set off with Jack for Theresa Murphy's house a few doors away. The little lad who had approached them earlier turned out to be the youngest of her nine brothers and sisters. Mary wasn't sure if everybody in the house belonged there or if they were just friends or relations. Mrs Murphy didn't seem to take much notice of anybody. Fat and jolly, she just sat near the fire with half a dozen Lady Jane curlers fighting a losing battle against her straight wispy hair. She prised herself to her feet at intervals to mash another pot of tea, which she poured pale and watery into an assortment of cups and pint pots, mostly without handles. A loaf of bread stood on the bare tabletop with a large jar of jam keeping it company.

'Has everybody had their teas?' she finally called at the top of her voice, and as nobody bothered to answer she covered the bread with a newspaper, scooped all the pots with a clatter into the smelly stone sink in the corner, and wiped the spill stains off the table with what looked like a floor cloth. Mary decided there and then that she wouldn't bother with breakfast in the morning.

Theresa, Mary and Jack set off eventually for the dance hall. It was a massive place with a large stage at one end. Mary couldn't help but compare it favourably with the schoolroom at Longfield.

Throughout the evening she was introduced to a succession of Jack's mining friends. Everybody in the room seemed to know him. Also present were many of the girls from the strip department. The small band was excellent and their repertoire included everything from the hokey-cokey to the tango. Mary loved to dance and found Jack an easy partner, and was really sorry when the National Anthem was played.

Jack had been hoping that Theresa would walk home with one of the lads she had been dancing with, and he was slightly put out when she tagged on with Mary and himself, so that all he got from Mary was a quick goodnight peck on the cheek before she had to follow Theresa into the house.

Mrs Murphy was still sitting by the fire reading the *Woman's Companion* and Mary wondered if she would be staying there all night; maybe she was too fat to climb the stairs, or, worse still, perhaps there was no vacant bed for her to go to, what with the ten of them and Mary besides.

'Come on,' said Theresa. 'We're sleeping with our Laura. Do you want to go across the yard before we go up?'

Mary thought she'd better, and they went fumbling hand in hand in the darkness towards a long dark passage with half a dozen lavatories inside. Theresa, always game for a laugh, began making ghostly noises whilst Mary was inside and she ended up running back to the house with her knickers only half pulled up.

The laughter continued well into the night, as

114

Laura told them smutty jokes which she picked up from the canteen at the bottling company where she worked. Then, just as they were settling down to sleep, one of the young brothers came gliding into the room with a sheet over his head pretending to be a ghost. Mary wondered if she had landed herself in a madhouse and giggled with the others until it was almost daylight.

It was only when she began itching in church the next morning and discovered the bug bites that she decided she would have to be really desperate before she would ever spend another night in Theresa Murphy's bed.

Chapter Twelve

Old Toothy Benson was on his last legs, and had been for at least three months. Jack enquired after his health daily at the pit, secretly hoping there would be no improvement. Old Toothy must be ninety if he was a day and was still hanging on in the house Jack had been promised when it became vacant, which Jack was beginning to think would never happen.

The end one in a red brick row overlooking the fields of Barker's Farm, it seemed a bargain at only ten shillings a week rent. Actually it would need a miracle to bring it up to a comfortable standard after years of neglect, but Jack was blind to its faults and saw it only as a means of persuading Mary to arrange the wedding.

Much as Mary loved Jack, she was in no hurry to marry. She would never forget Tom, but she was coming to terms with his death, and the sweet memories were beginning to outweigh the painful ones. In many ways the last few months had been the happiest of her life and she was in no rush to change things. In fact, she was dreading having to leave Moorland House and the Robertses.

For Gladys the ideal solution would be for the couple to live permanently with her and the doctor, but she knew that that was impossible, and was resigning herself to the fact that Mary would be leaving them any time now. She was reconciled to Mary's choice of a future husband. Jack had taken to spending Sundays with them, making himself useful round the house whilst Mary busied herself cooking the dinner. He had built up the fence round the chicken coop, swept the kitchen chimney with a minimum of mess and was learning to drive the car.

After dinner the four of them would go for a ride, sometimes over to Castleton or Bakewell, where they would walk by the river wrapped up in warm scarves and gloves against the cold, driving slowly over carpets of soggy brown leaves, along lanes overhung with bare grey branches, ghostly in the late autumn mists.

Jack had been introduced to a new way of life, a life of luxury compared to the one he had been used to, yet he was in no way envious of the Robertses. On the contrary, he was full of admiration for Rowland, talking to him at length about his work, and worldly affairs neither Gladys nor Mary had the slightest knowledge of. In return

Rowland would question Jack about his work at the mine, interested to learn that he was working a new piece of machinery, and roping him in to search out a fault on the car.

Jack wondered anxiously if Mary would settle in a house with no bathroom or other comforts, and he made up his mind that he would work his fingers to the bone to provide her with the best, determined that if she married him she would never regret doing so.

It was a fortnight before Christmas and a party of strip workers were on their way to the city hall in Sheffield for their annual night out. A charabanc had been booked to take them, and most had managed a new outfit of some kind despite the war. Mary had made herself a skirt of grey crêpe de Chine and was wearing the satin blouse for the first time since last Christmas. Her heart skipped a beat as she slipped it on and Tom's face invaded her thoughts. She wondered if she would ever be completely free of the painful memories. She shook herself and placed Tom's engagement ring on her finger, then took it off again. She couldn't wear it; it wouldn't be fair to Jack. She put it back in its box. It would be a beautiful keepsake, a treasure.

Most of the party had never set foot in the city hall before and Mary felt she was dancing on air as she took to the beautiful sprung floor.

They were in the middle of a foxtrot when the siren sounded. No one took much notice at first; warnings had been given many times in the past and nothing had happened, so why should it now? Only the party from Millington became alarmed. They didn't fancy becoming involved in the action here in the city when they were used to the peace of their small town. There were discussions as to whether they should make their way home, but at eight o'clock the argument ended when the building was evacuated.

Mary was all for taking to the shelter with the rest of the dancers, but the bus driver had other ideas.

'You lot please yerselves,' he said, 'but I'm taking my bus home. That bus is my livelihood and I'm not having it blown to smithereens by the bloody Jerries, so you either get yerselves on board now or I'm slinging my hook without yer.'

Mary had no time to think. The lot of them piled into the bus and were soon on their way home. The driver made good time, stopping only once outside the infirmary to have a word with the Home Guard, and slowing down only when he was safely away from the city.

Even in Millington the fires of Sheffield could be seen. It was after midnight when the raids began, and none of the city escaped the high explosives except the Brightside and Darnall areas, which happened to be shrouded by a blanket of fog.

Dr Roberts told them that Graves Park and Crookes had been devastated and a number of civilians killed, but that was many days afterwards when he managed to leave the overcrowded hospital and the many injured for a short visit home. He and Gladys even missed the performance of *The Messiah*, which went ahead as planned at the

Victoria Hall in Sheffield on the Sunday afternoon after the raid. Tragically, a second raid took place that night, increasing the numbers of homeless throughout the city, and this time Darnall was in the thick of it all.

Mary worried about Gladys, who became more and more anxious when her husband was away at the hospital. She tried to calm her by pointing out how lucky he was to be working here, instead of somewhere on the front lines. Gladys appreciated that, and cheered up a little. 'Yes, you're quite right. Do you know, it's the first time I've ever been grateful for the fact that my Rowland's getting on in years.'

Everybody agreed that the works outing had been a washout, but they were so thankful to have escaped the blitz that no one complained.

'Oh well,' said Madge, 'I'm just praying my church has been spared.'

Mary didn't answer. She was busy reflecting on the fact that until a few months ago she had never even heard of Darnall, and now it had been brought to her attention again. She wondered if it was an omen, indicating that she should attend the Spiritual Church with Madge. Jack had laughed when she had mentioned it, but hadn't been against her going.

'You go wherever you like,' he said. 'So long as you don't expect me to go with you. I'm not one for religion in any shape or form.'

'You're a heathen, Jack Holmes,' Mary said. 'Don't you ever fear for your soul?'

Jack began to laugh. 'You know what our old

man always says?' he asked.

'I wouldn't be surprised at anything he says.' Mary smiled. She and Jack's father had been taken with each other from their first meeting. He was called Our Old Man by everyone in the family except Mary and little Una, but it was said in an affectionate way and everybody loved the work-worn middle-aged chap, who looked much older than his years. His back was hunched from working in the pit, due, according to Jack, to working in seams not much more than three feet high. He had a racking bronchial cough which worried the family, but he never complained and refused to see a doctor, or take time off work. Mary thought he was the most generous man she knew. Not only did he worship the ground his family walked on, but he went out of his way to assist any neighbour in times of trouble. He was a man of few words, refusing to join in any gossip, and one of his sayings was, 'If tha can't say owt good about anybody, keep thi mouth shut!' His one fault as far as Mary could see was that he swore like a trooper, but his wife had long since given up trying to change him and idolised him despite the swearing.

'I'll tell you what our old man says,' said Jack. '"I've only got one soul and that's my arse 'ole."'

Mary paled with shock, but then she began to chuckle. In fact, they laughed so much they ended up in a passionate embrace, which wasn't unusual these days. Indeed even Mary had begun to enquire about the health of old Toothy Benson.

After much discussion and many tears the wedding was finally arranged. The tears stemmed from Mary's longing to be married back home in the heart of her family. She realised, however, that transporting all Jack's family and their many friends to Newcastle would be difficult, so she kept her disappointment hidden and the tears for the privacy of her room. The arguments stemmed from Jack's refusing to promise that any children of the marriage would be brought up in the Catholic faith.

'I've seen enough of their brainwashing,' he said. 'You've seen for yourself the poverty caused by the Catholic Church.'

'Whatever has the Church got to do with poverty?' Mary's temper always rose to simmering point when her religion was condemned.

'You know very well what it has to do with it; one bairn after another. Take the Murphys, for instance. The poor woman has bred like a rabbit for at least twenty years, just because they cling to the idea that contraception is sinful. I doubt she's finished yet, and not two pennies to rub together between them.'

Mary looked down, her eyes filling with tears. She knew in her heart that Jack was right.

'I don't want a life like theirs for you, or for our kids. I've seen the Murphys filled with the fear of Hell on occasions. I tell you, Mary, it isn't natural.'

'It isn't like that.'

'Maybe not where you come from, but I'm telling you I've seen it with my own eyes.'

The arguments were long and unsolvable, and it was only Mary's determination that forced Jack to relent and take the necessary instruction so that the wedding could take place at St Catherine's. He knew he would lose Mary otherwise and stubborn as he was he knew life without her would be purgatory here on earth, let alone in death.

Perversely she wasn't altogether happy about St Catherine's. Although she had been welcomed by the congregation, she didn't feel the same devotion as she had in Father Flynn's church back home. Perhaps the trouble was that she couldn't help but compare the dour, grey-faced priest with the rosy, smiling moon face of Father Flynn. Besides, she was feeling rather guilty about the time she had accompanied Madge to the little church in Darnall, where she had found herself warmly received into the loving atmosphere Madge had previously described. The disappointment that no message had come through for her during the service had been utterly dispelled when Madge had received convincing evidence that her late husband was present. The medium had passed on amusing messages and an atmosphere of hilarity had pervaded the hall. Mary had never known laughter in a church before and was most impressed by the medium, who brought joy and also tears to the congregation.

Afterwards she had described the incident to Gladys, who couldn't help wondering if Mary was as dedicated a Catholic as she made herself out to be.

'Are you sure you want to be married at St Catherine's?' she enquired.

Mary coloured. 'Of course,' she said. 'I wouldn't feel properly married otherwise. Besides, what would I tell my parents? Why, they'd never forgive me, even though they won't be at the wedding.'

'No, that's true,' Gladys said thoughtfully. 'Don't you think it might be possible for them to come down?'

'Not all of them,' said Mary sadly. 'I'm afraid it would cost too much, and my mother wouldn't come on her own.'

'No, I suppose not,' said Gladys.

So it was arranged for Rowland to give Mary away and for Gladys to provide the dress.

'I intended wearing my brown costume. After all, there is a war on.'

'What, and deprive me of seeing my wedding dress given a new lease of life?' said Gladys wistfully. 'Come upstairs.'

She led Mary up into the bedroom she shared with Rowland and opened the door of the large wardrobe, taking out a hanger completely covered by a large white sheet, and smelling strongly of mothballs. Mary gasped as the sheet was removed to reveal a gown of ivory silk.

'It's beautiful,' she sighed.

'It was, thirty years ago. Now it's terribly old-fashioned, but that won't take long to remedy. Now let's see. There's enough material to lift the drop waist a couple of inches, and add a few darts here and there. Why, no one will recognise it when I've finished.'

'Oh, you can't! Alter your wedding dress, I mean. What would Dr Roberts say?'

'Between you and me,' Gladys laughed, 'I don't think he even noticed it. The only thing on his mind on our wedding day was the anticipation of seeing me without it.'

Mary giggled and the two of them sat down on the pink satin eiderdown.

Gladys's eyes filled with tears. 'I've never had children of my own, so please let me enjoy the privilege of acting mother, just for the one day. After that you'll be gone, but for the time being please let me be a mother.'

Mary threw her arms round the weeping woman's neck.

'You are a mother. You're my second mother, and not just for the wedding. I'll never go, Mrs Roberts, not in my heart. I couldn't. I'll never love another house like this one, and not just the house, but you and the doctor. You've been like parents to me, and I won't forget you just because I'm moving away. I'll come back every weekend, we both will. Jack's already said so.'

Gladys took out a pretty embroidered handkerchief and blew her nose loudly. 'Right then,' she said. 'Take off the dress and let's get started on the alterations. Goodness, who would believe I ever had a waist so slender?'

'Lucky I take after my second mother, then.' Mary laughed. 'Otherwise it wouldn't fit.'

Chapter Thirteen

The wedding day arrived at last, sunny and warm considering it was early February. Gladys would have preferred the reception to take place at Moorland House but the number of guests from

Millington had risen, making it awkward to transport them all to Longfield and back. Instead a small catering firm had been given the order for salad teas in the hall behind the church. Gladys had run up a pink bridesmaid's dress for Una Bacon, with a matching muff and headdress. The child had stayed at Moorland House overnight and was overcome with excitement at the thought of the day ahead. Mary would have liked to ask Margaret to be a bridesmaid too, but couldn't bring herself to do so when her own sisters wouldn't even be attending the wedding. Besides, Margaret seemed to prefer an outfit she could wear afterwards, rather than some frivolous creation.

Gladys never ceased to amaze Mary with her many talents. She had wired together an assortment of snowdrops and evergreen from the garden into a small bouquet, and it would have been a day of complete happiness for Mary if only her family had been able to come down for the ceremony. She had written as soon as the date was decided, but a short note was returned apologising for not being able to attend. She had cried herself to sleep for a few nights afterwards, but knew the cost of the journey would have been too much for her parents even to consider.

At twelve o'clock Rowland Roberts disappeared in the car with a warning from Gladys to be back in good time, although the wedding wasn't until half past three. Mary hoped he would hurry back, especially as he had promised to transport the Downings to the church before returning for Mary. By two o'clock she was beginning to panic, but with his usual hearty laugh he bounced into the kitchen.

'Well then, are we all ready?' he asked, pinning a flower on to his lapel. 'I thought I'd got to the palace by mistake when I saw a little princess in a pink dress.'

Una danced with delight and Gladys had to adjust her headdress for the umpteenth time.

Mary appeared in the doorway to a stunned silence. The ivory dress was a perfect shade to complement the glory of her hair, which shone through the intricate lace of the thirty-year-old veil.

'Oh, Auntie Mary, you look just like Cinderella,' sighed Una.

'Thanks to Auntie Gladys,' Mary said softly. 'I'll never forget what you've done for me today. Nobody would think we were in the middle of a war. I must be the most pampered bride in the whole of England.'

'And the most lovely,' said Rowland. 'And let's not think of the war today of all days.' He turned to his wife as she placed a large blue hat upon her head. 'But I'll tell you something, Mary, my wife looked just as beautiful thirty years ago, though I don't suppose I bothered to tell her so.' He coughed self-consciously. 'Well, come on, or that young man of yours will think you've jilted him.'

When they got to the church, Rowland asked Mary to wait in the porch while he showed Gladys to her place. Mary straightened Una's headdress once again and lowered the veil over her face. She heard the strains of Handel's *Largo* change to the Wedding March, and then, instead of Dr Roberts, there walking towards her was her father, white-faced, nervous, but grinning from ear to ear. Lost for words, Mary placed her arm through his and they set off in a daze towards the altar.

'You might have given me a heart attack,' Mary said after the ceremony. 'In fact I thought I was seeing things.'

'You surely didn't think I'd let my daughter marry withoot being there.' Mick O'Connor laughed, relaxing now his duty was done and his daughter had been given into matrimony. He only hoped the lad was worthy of her, but the doctor seemed to think highly of him, according to all the letters and phone calls to Father Flynn which had been necessary to arrange it all.

'Why didn't someone tell me?'

'What, and spoil the surprise?' Jack laughed. 'It was all Mrs Roberts's idea. Blame her.'

'And Rowland,' said Gladys. 'As soon as your father told Father Flynn they were going to make the journey after all, I thought how lovely it would be to surprise you.'

'I might have known you would be in on it.' Mary chuckled as she planted a kiss on Father Flynn's bulbous red nose. She caught a glimpse of the local priest watching disapprovingly and wanted to giggle. In fact she wanted to laugh and dance and show everyone how happy she was.

'Oh, Ma, you do look bonny, and me da too in his new suit.' She reverted back unknowingly to her Geordie accent.

'What about me?' said Michael, as usual fishing for compliments.

'You too. In fact you all look so smart, I don't think I'd have recognised our Bill.'

'He's got a girl,' said Jimmy.

'No wonder,' said Jack. 'A big smart lad like him, I'll bet all the girls are after him.'

Norah stood looking at Jack in admiration, and wondered if he had a younger brother, but Kathleen had already become acquainted with one of the Murphy boys.

'Would the wedding party like to follow me down to the studio where the photographer is waiting.' Rowland was busy rounding up the parents, brothers and sisters, and was having trouble persuading Jack's father to join them.

'I reckon nowt to folks gawping at my face,' he grumbled but his wife placed her arm through his and almost dragged him with the joyous crowd in the direction of the studio. There they were placed in order of precedence, standing to attention like two rows of dominoes, except for the two mothers and Gladys who were seated on chairs at the front. Mrs Holmes amused them by asking if she could take off her shoes as her corns were killing her.

Gladys had at first refused to be in the photographs, saying she wasn't family, until Mary's mother pointed out that if it wasn't for her none of this would have been taking place anyway.

The celebrations were soon in full swing. A gramophone had been brought in after the meal and except for the elderly guests most people were joining in the fun. A game of King William was in progress where someone in the centre of a large ring had to choose a partner to kiss and change places. By the evening the number of guests had risen to about eighty, since workmates, neighbours and a number of cousins had joined the already assembled guests. By nine most of the men had dwindled off to the Rising Sun for liquid refreshment which wasn't allowed in the church hall, and by ten the immediate families were wending their way to the Holmes household where a few crates of beer were waiting. Mary wondered where everyone was going to sleep, but apparently Jack's parents had joined in the conspiracy and arranged accommodation for her brothers and sisters, the boys in Harry's room and the girls up in the attic with Margaret. Her parents were to stay with the Robertses along with Father Flynn, though Heaven knew how the five of them would fit into the Morris.

The only moment to mar Mary's day had been when Mr and Mrs Downing had announced they would like to be getting home. Though they had tried to cover up their sadness Mary had seen the anguish in their eyes as the three of them had fleetingly pondered on what might have been if it hadn't been for the bloody war.

Mary was ready for home. It had been a long day and looked like being a longer night. Someone had foolishly built up the fire and with about two dozen people crammed into the two small rooms the heat was becoming unbearable, so the door had been wedged open to let in the cool night air. Gladys noticed the harmonium on entering the room, and after a couple of glasses of rhubarb wine found courage to ask if she might play.

'If you can get a tune out of it you're welcome,' said Mrs Holmes, underestimating Gladys's ability to make music out of any old thing. In a few minutes she began to get the hang of it, and though the pedals squeaked in time with the music nobody cared. In honour of Mary and Jack she began with 'If You Were The Only Girl In The World', and Rowland brought the room to silence as he sang. Then Mick O'Connor, not to be outdone, sang his favourite 'Blaydon Races'. Soon the celebrations could be heard from one end of the row to the other, interrupted suddenly when a knock silenced the party. Jack went to the door, surprised to see three burly sailors on the step.

'Are you Harry Holmes?'

'No, but I'll get him,' Jack answered amiably. 'Harry, somebody for you.'

Harry Holmes was on the stairs, enjoying the embraces of Lucy Downing, who had persuaded her father to let her stay for the celebrations. He left her with a smile.

'Well?' he said. 'I'm Harry.'

'Aye, and I'm Ada Banwell's husband.' The speaker's fist hit Harry flat on the jaw, knocking him backwards into the dresser. He regained his balance and grabbed the legs of his opponent, throwing him backwards in the doorway, then saw the second man coming towards him. Jack rushed forward and planted a blow in the sailor's face.

'We fight man to man in this house,' he said.

Harry pushed Jack aside. 'Get out of it, man. This is my fight, not yours.'

Mr Holmes walked unsteadily towards the trouble. 'What's all this about?' he enquired. 'We don't fight at all in this house without good reason. Besides' – he glared at his sons – 'you ought to be ashamed of yerselves spoiling your lass's wedding day.'

'It's reason enough, you old fool, when a bloke's helping himself to me wife while I'm away fighting his bloody war for him.'

Mr Holmes seemed to sober instantly. 'What's 'e on about, lad? Is it true what 'e's saying?'

Harry paled beneath the blood. 'If it wasn't me it'd be somebody else. She's not particular who she sleeps with.'

'No, she can't be very particular if she'll sleep with a bugger like thee,' Mr Holmes snarled as he lifted Harry up by his shirt front and carried him outside, followed by Mick O'Connor and Dr Roberts.

'You come back here, Rowland,' Gladys called. 'I won't have you upsetting your blood pressure again.' Rowland took no notice.

Mr Holmes planted his son on the pavement and brought his fist up under his chin with such force it sent him backwards to land in an empty beer crate underneath the window.

'You can go home to yer wife now, lad. He'll not be causing any more trouble, yer can take my word for it.'

The sailor set off reluctantly along the row with the others.

'Oh, by the way, sailor,' said Mick O'Connor. 'Before you go...' and he gave the man a thump in the chest which sent him reeling backwards gasping for breath.

'That's for calling my friend an old fool.'

He rubbed his hands together and walked jauntily back into the house, stepping over Father Flynn who was fast asleep on the floor by the dresser. Mick grinned. 'Do you know, this is the best wedding I've been to in years.'

Aye, thought Mary, he's really enjoying himself, and throughout it all only one glass of beer has passed his lips and he's remained stone cold sober.

'Well if you don't mind, I think Mary and me will be on our way. We've got a home to go to now, you know.' Jack couldn't conceal the pride in his voice.

'Perhaps we should be going too,' Rowland said.

'Not yet,' said Gladys. 'Like Mr O'Connor, I haven't enjoyed myself so much in years. Do you mind if I have another glass of that delicious rhubarb wine?'

She topped up the glasses of Mrs Holmes and Mrs O'Connor and then refilled her own.

'Let's drink to Mary and Jack,' Mary's mother said.

'And to our new-found friends,' said Gladys. Then she made her way unsteadily back to the old harmonium.

The newly-weds took a short cut up through the gardens and over Barker's Fields. Had it been light Mary would have looked an odd sight with Jack's jacket covering her wedding dress as protection from the cold night air.

'Shall we light the gas or are we going straight up?' Jack asked.

'We'll go straight to bed,' said Mary, relieved that the darkness would hide her embarrassment.

Jack lit the candle and they climbed the stairs. They began to undress and Mary reached for her nightdress. She struggled with the garment for a moment and then burst into laughter. The bottom and sleeves had been stitched up.

'Who was it borrowed the key to bring up the wedding presents?' she asked.

'Our Harry and Bill.'

'I might have known. You'll just have to make do with me and my skin.'

Jack reached for her. 'Looks like they've done me a favour,' he said huskily. 'I should only have had the bother of taking it off again.' He pulled her close and backed towards the bed. She felt him hardening against her and the ache in her loins grew stronger. They fell together on to the new satin quilt and the whole bed collapsed beneath them.

'What the hell?' Jack jumped up.

'Your Harry and Bill.' Mary couldn't keep a straight face.

Jack was on his hands and knees fumbling to inspect the bed in the darkness. 'They've undone the bloody legs,' he said seriously.

Mary reached out and placed her hand between his legs. 'Like you said, they were only doing you a favour.' She began to giggle and pulled him on to the mattress. They lay face to face and the laughter ceased as they kissed, tenderly at first and then fiercely, as the months of waiting came to an end and their passion was sated not once but over and over again. It was only when the pale light of dawn showed round the edges of the blacked-out window that Jack finally got round to rectifying the dismantled bed.

Mary knew she had made a mistake when she refused to let Jack buy the chamber pot, but was too proud to admit it. The stallholder in the rag market had been not only a first class salesman but also a born comedian. There he had posed wearing a chamber pot for a hat, cracking jokes about the bloody Jerries. The crowd, some hoping for a bargain and others just passing away the Saturday afternoon, had laughed and returned the bantering.

Mary and Jack were there to buy a dinner service with the money Father Flynn had given them for a wedding gift. The one Mary liked was set out in a washing basket, but Jack warned her to bide her time, guessing the price would be reduced later in the afternoon. He had been right. Not only did they get the lovely rose-patterned set for half the starting price but the washing basket to carry it home in was thrown in, and a chamber pot at half price if required. Mary had stated indignantly that she would never use another chamber pot as long as she lived; she'd had enough of emptying the things at Mrs Brown's back in Newcastle.

Now, bursting for relief at three in the morning and with Jack on nights, she realised her mistake. It wasn't the walk round the corner in the dark she was afraid of, but the old washhouses she had to pass on the way. She didn't much like them in daylight but at night there was something really weird about them. She would have to use the bucket – there was nothing else for it. Then she realised it was catching the rain in the back bedroom fireplace, so she made her way downstairs for a saucepan to put in its place, vowing to let Jack buy a chamber pot at the first opportunity.

Back in bed she suddenly wondered what she had let herself in for, leaving Moorland House with all its modern conveniences for Barker's Row. Eager to find a place to settle down in as Jack's wife, she had closed her eyes to the fact that smoke from the kitchen fire billowed down the front-room chimney; that the back wall was so damp that a mushroom-like fungus was growing on the skirting board; and that water for the tin bath had to be ladled from the fireside boiler. She stopped thinking about the house's drawbacks, and thought about Jack and his ability to make the best of everything; he even joked that she should have brought the bike from Moorland House to travel on to the lavatory.

She peered in the darkness to the alcoves, trying to make out the dressing table and wardrobe which Jack had presented her with a few days before. Though they had been reclaimed by the furniture shop from a non-paying customer, Jack had been unable to find so much as a blemish on them, and was proud to have found such an immaculate bargain. Mary had polished them inside and out before hanging Jack's clothing in a quarter of the space, and cramming her own including her wedding dress into the remainder. Without Gladys's expert tuition in dressmaking she would never have accumulated such an extensive wardrobe. Oh, she was lucky. She relived the past few weeks, and knew that much as she missed the Robertses and the luxury of Moorland House she wouldn't swap Jack and this little two up two down for anything. This was her home now, and Jack was her life.

She looked at the alarm clock in the lightening dawn. He would be home soon, ridding himself of the coal dust with a quick scrub down, and forgoing breakfast in his eagerness to join her in the warmth of their bed, and she couldn't wait to welcome him into her arms.

Chapter Fourteen

Jacqueline Mary Holmes decided to enter the world two weeks early, a few days before Christmas. Mary was in the fish and chip shop when her waters broke, and as she was fourth from the front and had already waited a full twenty minutes, she decided to stick it out and make sure Jack had a decent supper on returning from afternoon shift.

It never entered her head that the birth was imminent and she thought it was a weakness of the bladder which caused the flow of liquid to wet her stockings and fill her shoes. Luckily the tiled floor was already a wet slippery mess from the customers' rain-soaked boots and wellingtons, so that no one was aware of her predicament.

'You shouldn't be standing in your condition, Mrs Holmes,' said Mrs Palmer as she came out from the back with a pile of clean newspapers. 'If you'd come to the front we would've served you before the others.'

'That's all right,' Mary said. 'Jack won't be in just yet and I timed it so they'd be nice and hot when he came home.'

'Yes well, think on and come to the front next time,' the kindly shopkeeper insisted.

Mary thanked her and paid for her fish and twopennyworth of chips twice, and had just left the shop when the pain gripped her. The climb up to Barker's Row seemed never-ending, and Mary had to pause twice when the pains almost brought her to her knees. Nevertheless, she managed to reach Marjory's house two doors away from her own, relieved that Bill was in and could go on his bike for the midwife, whilst Marjory took Mary home.

Mary had disliked the midwife from the first visit to the clinic. The woman not only looked like a man, she also sported a man's short back and sides haircut and had a deep gruff voice, which she delighted in using to scare the living daylights out of her already nervous patients. On Mary's first visit the woman had clumsily stumbled over a little boy, quietly playing on the floor whilst his mother was being examined, and the poor little mite had sobbed uncontrollably when the nurse had boomed out, 'Who the devil does that kid belong to?'

Mary had picked up the little boy and angrily pointed out that he was a child not a kid, and that the midwife should look where she was going in future. After that Mary had dreaded her monthly visits to the clinic, and the nurse had made her life a misery in any way she could think of.

Even so it was a relief when the woman bustled

through the door and up the stairs, grumbling as she entered the bedroom.

'What the devil do you mean by fetching me out on a wild-goose chase? The bairn isn't due for another two weeks.'

'I know,' said Mary, 'but something's happening. It feels as if the baby's coming.'

'Rubbish. You'll go the clock round with a first baby, they always do.'

Mary was too agonised to answer back as another pain gripped her loins. She felt the woman lift her nightdress and then her legs.

'Good God,' she exclaimed, and hurried out to the top of the stairs calling loudly, 'Get me some hot water and Dettol, and don't be all night about it.'

Mary vaguely heard Marjory's reply before experiencing the need to bear down.

'Hold on to the bed rail,' the midwife ordered and Mary thought momentarily what a perfect sergeant major she would have made.

Jack took the stairs two at a time to be stopped short on the small landing by the glowering nurse.

'She won't be long now,' the woman roared, and pressed a bucket of hideous-looking afterbirth into Jack's arms. The sight sent the contents of his stomach shooting upwards, so that he almost vomited on the narrow Jacobean carpet he had laid only two mornings previously. He turned and staggered weakly down to the kitchen before realising that his child must already be delivered. Then he thrust the bucket at his sister and raced back up the stairs and into the bedroom, where

Mary looking flushed and beautiful cradled the tiny form in her arms. He approached the bed slowly, ignoring the large restraining hand of the midwife, and gently kissed his wife, before lifting aside the white towel in which the infant had been wrapped, so tightly that only her nose and eyes could be seen. He looked questioningly at Mary.

'We've got a daughter,' she said. 'Isn't she beautiful?'

Jack thought the baby resembled one of the rabbits that young Cyril Downing caught on the moors for Gladys to skin and hang in one of the outhouses at Moorland House, but he thought he'd better agree with Mary.

'Oh aye, she's beautiful. A bit on the small side, but beautiful.' He grinned, then looked concerned. 'How are you feeling, love?'

'Never better. There was nothing to it.' Mary smiled, staring defiantly at the midwife, who had repeatedly warned her that she was too small round the pelvis to have a baby, and could expect the worst.

'Is she all right, the baby?' asked Jack. 'Being premature, I mean.'

'Only four and a quarter pounds, but she'll grow,' said the nurse, eager now to get home to bed. 'Keep a good fire day and night; you can't be too careful with a premature child.'

She stared at the empty fireplace, and Jack, taking the hint, raced out of the room and downstairs, coming back with a shovelful of glowing coals which he placed carefully in the grate.

'I'll be back to bath her in the morning, so see there's plenty of hot water ready.' The woman glanced at Mary. 'Oh, and get plenty of milk down you. Your breasts might be a while filling, but I'll take a look in the morning. Meanwhile a good cup of gruel won't go amiss. The little mite will need looking after and no mistake.'

For the first time Mary noticed a look of tenderness flit across the face of the nurse, only to be replaced by her usual frown as she gathered up her bag and coat, and made her way noisily downstairs.

Jack sat on the bed and Mary placed the tiny bundle in his long awkward arms.

'What shall we call her?' He touched the red wrinkled face gently.

'Jacqueline Mary.'

He grinned. 'After us both.'

'Well it's got to be Mary seeing as it's almost Christmas.' Mary couldn't help thinking that all the important events in her life seemed to happen at Christmas.

Jack opened the towel and took a tiny hand into his own coal-encrusted one. 'She hasn't any nails,' he said, alarmed.

'Well, what do you expect? She shouldn't be here for another two weeks.' Mary looked concerned.

Jack covered the baby gently. 'She'll need a lot of looking after but we'll rear her,' he said. 'And nothing will be too good for Jacqueline Mary Holmes, I'll be buggered if it will.' He started suddenly and placed the baby at Mary's side. 'I'd better go and let my mother know,' he said, 'and I'd better get a message over to Gladys and a telegram to Newcastle first thing in the morning.'

'And don't you think you'd better have a wash?'

Mary laughed. 'The bedding won't be fit to be seen.'

Jack moved from the bed quickly. 'Do you know,' he said, 'only one thing's bothering me.'

'What's that?'

'The thought of that bloody nurse taking a look at your breasts.'

Mary giggled, then sobered again as Jack left the room. She wasn't much looking forward to that herself. She sighed and wished her mother was here, then looked down at her daughter, like a little doll beside her. She was worth all the worrying, was Jacqueline Mary Holmes.

A few yards from Mary's house Barker's Row ended with double wrought-iron gates leading into a driveway at the end of which stood a garage. One side of the drive was dense with conifers and laurel bushes; on the other stood the large red brick Belvedere House. The only way in was through a wooden door built into the high wall which completely surrounded the house and garden. No one could see in, and the inhabitants could not see the washhouses and lavatories which stood between the secluded residence and lowly Barker's Row.

Mr and Mrs James Davenport were rarely seen by the residents of the row. An ex-schoolmistress, the lady was rich enough to have a cleaning lady, a hairdresser and a grocer, all of whom visited the house at regular intervals. On rare occasions Mary had seen her, dressed in an expensive-looking grey coat and hat, with grey leather accessories, making her way carefully down the stony unadopted row, probably on an afternoon visit to friends, or on the way to some kind of meeting. Sometimes if Mary was outside Mrs Davenport would nod, smile and wish her a good afternoon, but that was all. Mary always felt in awe of the woman, probably because she reminded her of Mrs Brown back in Newcastle.

Jack, on the other hand, pointed out that they were probably no more wealthy than Gladys and Rowland, and had certainly no reason to think themselves superior to everyone else. Mr Davenport, according to Marjory, was a managing director somewhere in the city, and he could be seen every weekday leaving the house in his immaculately kept saloon car at exactly half past eight. He looked and dressed like Winston Churchill, even sporting a large cigar, but always doffed his hat and commented on the weather to anyone he saw when he opened the creaky gates.

A few weeks before, when a sudden snowstorm had caused drifting during the night, Jack had left his task of clearing a path round to the lavs and helped Mr Davenport clear his drive, enabling him to leave for work not much later than usual. Now Jack was wondering if the man would repay his kindness by letting him use his telephone.

'Oh, you can't ask them,' said Mary. 'What would they think?'

'Who cares?' said Jack. 'They'll either say yes or no. It isn't as though I'm going to make a habit of it. After all, it isn't every day we have a baby.'

'But it'll cost a fortune to ring Newcastle.'

'I don't intend ringing Father Flynn – Gladys will do that. All I want is to let her know. Surely they won't object if I offer to pay for the call.'

'You could go to the gatehouse at the works. The works bobby would let Lucy know.'

'But that would mean it will be teatime before Gladys hears the news. I can but ask, Mary – there's no harm in asking.' Jack looked at the clock on the dressing table. 'If I go about quarter past eight I won't be disturbing them.'

Mary snuggled the tiny babe into her warm body, opening her nightdress and offering her erect nipple to the tiny mouth. It opened wide, reminding Mary of a newly hatched bird she had once found in a grouse's nest amongst the heather. She squeezed her breast and a squirt of fluid covered the baby's face. The child found the source of its nourishment and began to suck, choking on the first mouthful, then settling down for her first feed.

Mary could feel the warmth drawing upwards from the depths of her body, and she revelled in the experience, not caring about Jack, or the Davenports or anything else. For the time being her daughter was the most important thing in the world.

Jack knocked at the door before noticing the bell, and stood nervously waiting. The door opened to reveal Mrs Davenport in a red quilted dressing gown. Her eyes widened at the sight of Jack; then she recognised him as the man who had shovelled the snow. She had been impressed by his deft use of the shovel and the speed at which he had cleared the drive.

'I'm sorry to bother you, but I wondered if I

might use your telephone. It wouldn't be a long call, and I'll pay for it.' He paused. 'Only my wife's had a baby and I'd like to let her folks know the news.'

Mrs Davenport's face seemed to take on a glow, and she stood aside, ushering Jack into the hall. 'How exciting for you,' she enthused. 'What did you get, a daughter?'

'Yes,' said Jack, rather taken aback.

Mr Davenport gathered his coat and hat from the hall stand, smiling as Jack passed. 'My wife considers herself something of an expert in that field,' he said. 'Reckons she can tell the baby's sex by the way the mother carries it. Only said last week she thought your child would be a girl.'

Jack entered the room indicated by Mrs Davenport. The telephone stood on a highly polished occasional table alongside a box of cigars and a box of chocolates. A pink squashy three-piece suite cheerily crowded the room, and a large roaring fire filled the fireplace, casting a glow on the display of Christmas cards arranged on the mantelpiece. He tried not to stare round the room, but couldn't help himself. Gazing down at him from a narrow shelf all round the walls were dozens of Toby jugs; a cabinet close to him was also filled with laughing, frowning and curious porcelain faces.

He found a scrap of paper on which he had scribbled Gladys's number, and dialled it with trembling fingers. Unused to the contraption, he felt relief when it rang and Gladys's voice answered.

On hearing the news she bombarded him with questions as to health, weight and time of the baby's birth. As Jack answered the Toby jugs seemed to smile their congratulations, and the warmth of the cosy room filled him with a feeling of well-being.

Gladys promised to ring Father Flynn immediately and send him to give the news to Mary's family.

'I'll be over the moment Rowland can bring me,' she said, and Jack knew it would be no use telling her there was no need.

'You're welcome any time you need a telephone.' Mrs Davenport was in her element. She was actually a kind woman, but probably because of her former profession she was also a rather bossy one and tended to order people about. She pressed two paper bags into Jack's hands. 'Here's a little something for the baby, and this is for your wife.'

Jack was speechless.

'And if she needs anything you must let us know. Not that we neighbour, you understand, but we are here if we're needed.' She glanced at her husband. 'Isn't that correct, James?'

'That's right Mr...'

'Holmes, Jack Holmes.' Jack fumbled in his pocket for some change. 'How much do I owe you?'

'Oh, we wouldn't hear of it,' Mr Davenport said. 'One good turn deserves another, that's what I always say. Well, you must excuse me, Mr Holmes – duty calls and all that.' He bent to kiss his wife, missing by a couple of inches, and picked up a brown leather briefcase as he made his way to the door. 'My regards to your wife, young man.'

Jack turned to Mrs Davenport. 'Thank you for the, er, presents,' he said, not knowing what was inside the brown paper bags.

'Don't mention it. I always keep a stock of knitted garments, in case one of my husband's employees leaves to begin a family. Besides, the knitting prevents my fingers stiffening, from the rheumatism, you understand.'

'Oh, and thanks for the phone call. I won't bother you again.'

'Don't mention it, Mr Holmes, you're most welcome. Perhaps your wife will bring your daughter to see me, when she's up and about again of course.'

'I'm sure she will,' Jack said, grinning as he wondered what Mary would say when she knew how well he'd been received by the posh folks.

He hurried home, easier in his mind now the news was on its way to Mary's family.

Mary was touched when she saw the tiny knitted matinee coat threaded with pink ribbon, and a pretty pink bed-jacket for herself.

'But I hardly know the woman,' she said, almost in tears at the kind gesture.

'Well, she's obviously had her eye on you. She's been taking notice of the way you've been carrying the baby ... our Jacqueline.' He grinned. 'It takes some getting used to, doesn't it? Having a new member of the family, I mean.'

Mary smiled, looking over the side of the second-hand cot which had been used for Una a few years ago. 'Isn't she like you?'

'Like me? Oh, no, you can't be serious,' he said,

looking down at the wrinkled face.

'But she is. She has your hair.'

'Oh aye, she's going to be dark, I'll grant you that, but as for her being like me...'

'She will be, I have a feeling. It's the shape of her chin and her nose.'

'Oh, you're imagining things. Anyway, who cares who she's like so long as she's healthy and happy.'

The knock on the door startled the pair of them, and even the baby started, her tiny hands opening wide.

'Oh, no,' Jack said. 'It'll be that bloody woman again – that's if she is a woman. I have my doubts.'

Mary giggled and then sobered as the clomping feet climbed the stairs. Jack rushed to the door, hoping the water in the boiler was hot. He escaped downstairs and filled the little zinc baby bath with water, adding a few drops of Dettol. Cotton wool, baby powder, clean binder, vest, nightgown, nappy. He hoped he'd remembered everything. He didn't fancy a reprimand from that woman. She ought to be on the front lines, he thought. She wouldn't half make the bloody Jerries run.

Mrs Holmes arrived in time for Jack to go on the afternoon shift, knowing that if he didn't complete the full week he would lose his bonus. Besides, it was two days before Christmas and the day the Christmas club money was to be paid out. After seeing to her daughter-in-law and fussing over her second granddaughter she took it upon herself to bake a batch of mince pies to add to the fruit loaves Mary had already made. Then she washed the soiled bedding and dirty nappies, popping them in the copper to boil. By the time Gladys and Rowland arrived the wet things were already drying on the rack over the fire.

Gladys promised to prepare supper and stay with Mary until Jack returned from work, allowing Mrs Holmes to go home with an easy mind, knowing mother and baby were in excellent hands. Marjory popped in and out at intervals, and Margaret arrived after work, intent upon spoiling her new niece. Little Una gazed at the baby with large round eyes and told her mother she hoped Father Christmas would be bringing her one just like it.

Mary worried that everyone seemed to be caring for her when they must have loads to do at home with the Christmas festivities almost upon them, but nobody seemed to mind. They organised the shopping, cooking and cleaning between them, and refused to let Mary have her own way and come downstairs.

'Everything's under control, lass,' said Mrs Holmes. 'There's not a thing for you to do except see to yer bairn. She's more important than all the feckling and fussing, just for the sake of a couple of days' holiday.'

Rowland also put his oar in. 'You must rest now. You'll only suffer in years to come if you get up too soon. Ten days in bed now will prevent trouble later.'

So Mary stayed in bed, and Jack, on holiday on Christmas Day and Boxing Day, revelled in the task of spoiling his wife and daughter, and playing Santa Claus for the first time. And although

148

he would never admit to harbouring religious thoughts, he couldn't help comparing Mary and Jacqueline to the Madonna and Child on the Christmas card sent to them by Father Flynn.

On Boxing Day Mary insisted on Jack's joining his father and brother for a drink at the Rising Sun. Gladys and Rowland had come over for the day, and Rowland had joined the Holmes men for the annual afternoon get-together. Though the doctor wasn't a beer drinker Jack knew he would enjoy the gathering, which would undoubtedly develop into a hearty sing of all the local carols.

This year the taproom was less crowded than usual owing to the number of regulars away fighting for their country, but despite their depleted strength those present raised their voices in all the old favourites, as if to make up for their absent friends.

Rowland was in his element, his fine voice leading the men in 'Hail Smiling Morn', and 'Hark Hark What News Those Angels Bring'. By closing time he had downed quite a few whiskies, not realising that Dolly the landlady, fascinated by the stranger, who was quite obviously class, was topping up his glass in an effort to keep him singing until closing time.

Mary was glad of a respite from Jack's spoiling and was enjoying the cosy togetherness she and Gladys were once used to. Gladys was rocking Jacqueline in the chair by the bedroom fire, her thoughts travelling far away to some unknown place where her nephew Richard, now a sailor, was spending his Christmas. She thought back to last year when the family were together, and even further back to the Christmas before Tom was killed. She prayed her nephew would return safely after the war was over.

She hugged Jacqueline closer. A new life, a new generation, and what was it all for? Surely not to be blown to kingdom come, or to be left fatherless, just because certain statesmen had decided to play a game of soldiers. She sighed.

'You're deep in thought.' Mary smiled between counting her rows of knitting. 'A penny for them.'

'Oh, just feeling a little sentimental, that's all. I always do at Christmas. I was just wondering about Ruth and the boys.'

'Oh, they must be missing Richard terribly, especially yesterday.'

'Perhaps I should have insisted they come to us as usual, keep to the normal routine. But I suppose Ruth was right: her parents would need them this year, what with her brothers being overseas too. Besides, it worked out for the best, really. I wouldn't have missed playing nursemaid to this little angel for anything.'

'Well, I'm certainly glad you're here,' said Mary. 'I don't know what I'd have done without you all.'

'You'd have managed. You've got a good man to look after you.'

'I know, but I wanted my mother just the same, and you were here to take her place.'

Gladys beamed. 'It's a pleasure, and now I'm a granny too.'

When Jacqueline Mary Holmes was baptised Millington was cold, white and beautiful. At the beginning of 1942 twelve inches of snow covered the town in a few hours. However, the weather seemed of little importance compared to other incidents taking place in the area. In February fourteen soldiers were tragically killed when a steel plate ripped through a passing troop train; thirty-five more were injured and taken to hospitals in Sheffield. In the same month an explosion at Barnsley Main Colliery caused the deaths of fourteen miners. Millington colliers were amongst those who volunteered to be part of the rescue team.

One of the happier occasions was the Princess Royal's visit to Sheffield, helping to boost the morale of various organisations throughout the city. Mary wished she could have gone to join the cheering crowds who turned out to see her, but very soon realised she would rather be with her husband and daughter than with all the royal families in the world.

Chapter Fifteen

Mary hardly knew she had the baby for six weeks. The little one did not do much but sleep, and Dr Roberts said she was thriving well, but for the last two days she had cried continuously, and Mary was at her wit's end to know how to console her.

She lifted the baby from the pram in the kitchen and rocked her gently, supporting the dark little head with her left hand. She felt how hot the head was, and when she laid Jacqueline down she noticed the hoarseness of her cry. Alarmed, she ran upstairs to where Jack was trying to sleep after the night shift.

'Jack!' She pulled down the covers from over his head. 'Jack, get up. It's our Jacqueline, I think we ought to have the doctor.'

Jack was out of bed, struggling with his trousers, before Mary had finished explaining. 'What's wrong?' he enquired anxiously.

'I don't know. Perhaps it's only a chill, but we'd better be on the safe side.' She ran quickly down the stairs, Jack following behind. He picked up his daughter and held her close. He could feel that her breathing was causing her distress.

'Get the doctor.' He went towards the fire as Mary almost flew out of the door. 'Oh God,' he whispered. 'Don't let her die, please God don't let her die.'

Within minutes Dr Sellers was with them. 'We must get her temperature down.' She grabbed a sponge from the sink and poured the water from the kettle into the washing-up bowl. Wringing out the sponge, she placed it behind the neck of the tiny baby. 'Try to get her to drink some water,' she said. 'That's all I can suggest in a child so young.'

'What is it?' Jack asked, touching his daughter's cheek gently. The tiny face had turned white, but her pulse was slower and her head cooler. She coughed a wheezing cough and began to cry fitfully.

'Pneumonia, as far as I can tell. It's always difficult to diagnose in one so young, but it certainly looks like it to me.'

'Oh, God,' Mary said. 'What can we do?'

'Keep her warm. Her temperature will fluctuate, so use a hot water bottle if she seems chilled, and on no account move her. Can you bring her cot downstairs?'

'Yes,' said Jack. 'I'll do it now. Will she be all right, doctor?'

'I don't know. I won't pretend it isn't serious – with a premature child any infection is serious – but we'll do our best. I'll be back in the morning; in the meantime watch her constantly, and call me if you're worried.'

Jack saw her out. 'Thanks for coming, doctor, so quickly I mean.'

'Not at all, that's what I'm here for,' she called as she reversed her car down the bumpy street.

Jack stayed at his daughter's side all day and all night. It never entered his head to go off to work. He told Mary to go to bed. 'You'll need all your strength tomorrow, love.'

'I shan't be able to sleep. What if you drop off? What if she takes a turn for the worse and you've dropped off?'

'I won't, I'm not so daft,' he snapped.

'I know.' Mary burst into tears.

'Now now, come on, love. I'm sorry, I didn't mean to sound irritable. Come on, there's nothing to cry for. She'll be all right. Let's try some more water in the feeding bottle.'

'How do you know? Even Dr Sellers doesn't know.'

Jack looked down at his daughter. 'I have a

feeling. Besides, there's no point in looking on the black side.'

'It's all my fault. I've never set foot in church since the wedding, except for the christening. I should have gone.'

'Don't talk daft.'

'It's God's way of punishing me.'

'Then He's a bloody cruel God, that's all I can say, to punish an innocent child.'

Mary started to cry again. It wasn't so much her failure to attend church which was preying on her conscience, as the sin she had committed with Tom the Christmas before he died. God had given him the ultimate punishment; now she prayed it wasn't to be her daughter who was to suffer, instead of her.

'Don't cry, Mary.' Jack took her hand in his. 'I understand how you feel, but you must keep up for our Jacqueline's sake.'

She wanted to scream out that he didn't understand, couldn't, because he didn't know, would never know, because to know would cause him sadness, and she would never knowingly hurt this man, this husband, this father whom she loved so much. She prayed then, her head in her hands, that if the sin was to be paid for, she alone would pay the penalty. She prayed for forgiveness and that her daughter would recover, but felt only a grain of comfort at the end of it.

'Come on, love. I'll mash a pot of tea, and then you get yourself off to bed. I promise I won't take my eyes off her all night.' He lifted the kettle off the fire and emptied it into the teapot.

'I'll get your supper ready.' Mary got up to go

to the cellar head, but Jack sat her down again.

'No, I'll get yours,' he said.

'I don't want any.'

'No, neither do I.' Jack sat beside her. She looked at his face, all white and drawn, and placed her hand in his. He searched her haunted face, then they came together, clutching at each other, each intent on comforting the other, and finding solace in the closeness.

Jack murmured, 'She'll recover, love. She's too precious to be taken from us.' His voice broke over the words and they clung tearfully together, even closer in their anxiety.

Jacqueline Mary Holmes did recover, but it was a harrowing several weeks before her parents ceased to worry. After that she went from strength to strength and by Easter she was blooming like the daffodils in the front garden.

It was also Easter when Mary realised she was pregnant again. The realisation was met with mixed feelings, but after the initial shock they became resigned to the idea. Besides, they might as well raise two as one, and it would be good for Jacqueline to have a sister or brother.

Chapter Sixteen

Jacqueline stood up in the cot. She could hear her father's raised voice through the wall, and although she was too young to understand she didn't like it and could hear a pounding in her ears. Perhaps it was the sound of soldiers marching across the field. She had never seen any soldiers except for the set of lead ones in the toy cupboard at Grandma Holmes's house, but somehow she connected them with the thudding sound and the feeling of fear.

She felt hot and the throbbing increased. Perhaps the soldiers were in the garden, or even coming up the stairs. She screamed in desperation.

Mary ran into the room, taking up her daughter in her arms, relieved that her cries hadn't disturbed her little brother, but then nothing seemed to disturb Alan, who at two and a half was fair, placid and cuddly. In fact the exact opposite of Jacqueline, who although twelve months his senior tipped the scales at only a couple of pounds more. Jacqueline was a strange child and far too old for her years. Despite their differences Jacqueline adored her baby brother, and he in his quiet manner idolised his sister. Mary loved her children dearly and equally but wished sometimes that her daughter was easier to understand.

She rocked her gently in her arms, soothing away her fears, until the rapid beating of the

156

child's heart slowed to normal. Mary placed her back in the cot, taking her time, subconsciously delaying her return to her husband. Why couldn't he use a little restraint; try to understand? Didn't he realise it was just as difficult for her to resist the closeness of his body? After all, in a few more days she would be safe again, but no, instead of delaying their coming together he insisted on using one of those nasty contraceptives he had taken to buying since Alan was born. In the stark light of day she knew Jack was only thinking of her, of them all as a family, wanting the best for them. It was only after their lovemaking was over and she was lying in the darkness that the guilt descended on her, filling her with shame, and fear of what would happen to the children if she defied the teachings of the church. Since Jacqueline's illness she had looked upon that time as a punishment for her lapse, and had attended St Catherine's regularly ever since.

Jack damned the church as he lay waiting for Mary to return to her place in the marriage bed, knowing there would be no lovemaking tonight. He failed to see what could possibly be sinful about limiting one's family. He supposed it was all a ploy to keep the Catholic congregation rising in number and he knew his wife had been brainwashed from an early age. Even so, he didn't trust the so-called safe time of the month and didn't intend risking another child yet, much as he loved his children. At the same time he couldn't understand how his wife could possibly love him, and expect him to love her, to order. He turned over, pulled up the bedclothes and attempted to sleep, lying stiff and wide awake as Mary returned to the bed. He ignored her proffered hand, knowing that if he turned to face her, pressed himself against the softness of her slim, youthful body, he would be unable to resist the feelings she would arouse in him, and he couldn't bear a further rejection.

Neither his body nor his pride could stand the strain.

Marjory Bacon counted the rent money and placed it inside the rent book, ready for collection first thing in the morning. Then she placed a few shillings in the savings tin in the top shelf in the cupboard, and a pile of pennies in the window bottom to cover the gas meter. The doctor's money had already been collected and she sighed contentedly. Bill had been promoted to pit deputy with a substantial rise in wages, but her thrifty upbringing still meant she couldn't rest until all the week's payments had been accounted for.

Now she felt free to spend a little on new socks for Una and any small luxury available, such as biscuits or sweets. She liked Fridays; they meant she and Mary could get dolled up a bit and take Jacqueline and Alan to the weekly market. It was the meeting place for all the young mothers to compare babies and pass on any morsel of local gossip. She would miss the weekly jaunts when she began work the following Monday; she was to start in the canteen at the steel works, serving the dinners. It was an ideal job as she would be home before Una and it would relieve the feeling of guilt she had been experiencing at not doing something useful with her life. She and Mary had become close friends, and it was nice to have her brother and his family for neighbours. Just lately, though, she had begun to worry about Mary. She wasn't the same happy-go-lucky girl she used to be, and Marjory had decided to question her, try to get her to confide in her. It was Bill who had made her mind up, by mentioning a change in Jack too. Marjory wasn't going to stand by and watch a perfect marriage fall apart, not if she could help it.

The kettle was singing on the gas ring. She warmed the pot and mashed a pot of tea just as Jacqueline pressed the brass sneck and opened the door.

'Are you ready, Auntie Marjory?' she called.

'Nearly. We'll have a cup of tea first, love.'

Jacqueline noticed the tray of newly baked biscuits. 'I'm going to ask my mam to make some biscuits like yours,' she said.

'Oh,' said Marjory, trying not to smile. 'Why, would you like one?'

'Yes please, but will you tell my mam I didn't ask? She says I haven't got to ask.'

'But you didn't ask, did you?'

'No, but will you tell my mam?'

'OK. Is she nearly ready?'

'She's just changing our Alan's cardy, then she's coming.'

The squeaking of the pushchair along the flags heralded their arrival and Marjory poured the tea.

The pile of biscuits soon diminished in size and Marjory wondered how to get Mary on her own for a heart to heart. She knew Jacqueline never missed a thing and didn't want her niece to hear the conversation. 'Do you want to feed the

159

chickens while we finish our tea?' she said, handing the little girl a newspaper containing some scraps. Jacqueline took the parcel eagerly and made her way out through the front room to the garden beyond.

Each of the houses in Barker's Row had a neatly kept garden, divided by pathways edged by brown glazed tiles. Along the bottom was an iron railing dividing the gardens from Barker's Fields. Across the meadow stood the farm, with one corner of the grass partitioned off for the chicken houses, the rest being pastureland for the large herd of cattle. Higher up the fields were already sprouting oats, barley and root vegetables.

Jacqueline squeezed herself through the railings, not flinching at all when a number of cows, heavy with milk, ambled towards her. She trod carefully, avoiding the large sloppy cowpats, and made her way to the chicken run. Farmer Barker had told her the names of all the clucking creatures and she lifted the latch of the wooden door in the netting and stepped inside. The birds, some running, others flapping their large white wings in an attempt to fly, almost knocked her off her feet, pecking at her coat bottom and devouring the scraps before she could even let go of them. Jacqueline chided the birds and laughed with glee.

'Get away, Cissy, you silly old hen,' she shouted, backing out of the coop and closing the door carefully behind her. She decided to gather a bunch of daisies for Auntie Marjory.

Taking advantage of Jacqueline's absence, Marjory poured two more cups of tea and mentioned that Mary looked rather pale.

'You are OK, aren't you? I mean you're not poorly or anything?'

Mary made an effort to smile. 'Course I'm not ill. Why do you ask?' She settled Alan more comfortably, sleeping soundly in his pushchair.

'Well, I don't know, you've been looking rather miserable lately and you used to be so cheerful. You know, Mary, if anything's bothering you, I'd like to think I'm a good enough friend for you to confide in, especially as your own sisters are so far away.'

Mary got up and carried the empty cups to the sink, placing them in the enamel bowl. She kept her back to Marjory, and suddenly her sister-in-law realised that her visitor was in tears. She walked over and placed her hand tenderly on Mary's arm, leading her back to her chair by the table.

'Come on, love, let's get it out in the open. There's no good comes of bottling things up.' It suddenly occurred to her what might be wrong. 'You're not expecting again, are you?'

Mary was hardly able to speak for the choking tears. 'Not much chance of that,' she managed.

Marjory misunderstood. 'But surely that's not the trouble? You're not trying for another baby, are you?'

'No, it's not that, it's just that Jack doesn't make love to me any more.'

'What? Oh, come on, our Jack idolises you.' Marjory stared at Mary in disbelief.

'He did, but not any more. All he does is ignore me. He doesn't even talk about it any more, and

161

it's been three months now.'

'Well.' Marjory looked perplexed. 'Is he ill or what?'

Mary thought she might as well come out with it straight. 'It's all my fault. I won't let him take precautions, so he doesn't do anything.'

Marjory almost laughed. 'Is that all?'

'Isn't it enough?'

'But everyone uses something these days, unless they want a houseful of kids, and who can afford that?' She suddenly tumbled to what the problem was. 'Oh, I see. Of course, you're a Catholic.'

'And Jack isn't,' said Mary glumly.

'So you're going to ruin a perfectly good marriage for the sake of the Church. It's our Jack who cares for you, not the bloody priest.'

'Marjory!' Mary sounded shocked.

'Well, sorry about that, but I'm right, you know I am. Who was it went without sleep for weeks on end, caring for our Jacqueline when she was ill? Not the priest. Not once did he come near, give you a bit of comfort or hope. In fact, the only Catholic to come and offer you any help at all was Theresa Murphy, and she'd be the last one to advise you to have a houseful of kids. You didn't see that family when they were all small, Mary, but I did. I remember when the walls in their house were down to the bare brick, and the only drinking utensils they owned were jam jars.

'Our Jack says your family didn't have much back in Newcastle, but I'm telling you, Mary, the Murphys weren't just poor, they were destitute. The old man out every day looking for work – that was before the poor old soul had his heart attack, and then they had to go on relief, and that desperate woman had to trek a good eight miles to be means-tested. Many a day the poor thing's feet were so swollen she couldn't get her shoes off when she got home, and it was only for half a crown.'

Mary looked subdued as Marjory continued. 'I'm telling you, Mary, even though the family was starving the priest still called for the church collection every week, virtually taking the food out of the kids' mouths.'

Mary blinked hard and blew her nose loudly. 'But Father Flynn wasn't like that.'

'Maybe not, but I'm telling you, you should think yourself fortunate our Jack has the common sense to want to use contraceptives.'

'You don't think our Jacqueline's illness could have been a judgement then, for me not keeping up with the faith?'

'Now that's the daftest thing I've ever heard. Do what you think is right, go to church if you like, but don't for God's sake let it ruin your love life and your marriage, love.'

'You don't think it's wrong then, using contraceptives?'

'Well, Bill and me have been using them ever since our Una was born and nothing bad has befallen her.'

Mary began to look more cheerful, just as Jacqueline came running in asking if they were ready. Mary put the flower heads to float in a glass of water.

'Can Alan and me buy a windwill?' the little girl asked.

'Windmill,' corrected Mary. 'I'll see, if you behave.'

'Win win, win win,' Alan chanted.

'All right, all right, you can have one too.'

'And a windmill for Una,' Jacqueline insisted.

'And one for Una.' Mary laughed. 'I think Jack's right,' she said. 'I don't think we could keep the kids in windmills if I had my way.'

'Thank God for that,' said Marjory. 'Come on, or our Una'll be home from school whilst we're still at the market.'

St George's Road ran for about half a mile along the bottom of Barker's Row, curving down at both ends to join the main road deep in the valley. Though the road was lined with houses, some terraced and some large semis, the hillside lower down was tree-covered, known as the Donkey Wood. It was through the Donkey Wood that Mary, Marjory and the children took a short cut, through a turnstile gate and down a steep cobbled path.

No one was certain how the name of the wood originated. Some said it was because of the stream which ran underneath the cellars of Barker's Row, emerging in the wood to meet other streams and form the shape of a key before gushing down the hillside to join the River Don down by the works. But Jacqueline chose to believe that a donkey lived in the wood, and hoped some day it would appear. Until then, she was content, as today, to run on ahead down the Donkey Path, searching for the Donkey Stone, a flat square stone on which some unknown person had carved a donkey many years ago.

When they reached the market the queue at the biscuit stall stretched almost to the gate. Mary joined it, hoping the square tins containing wafer, arrowroot and other tempting varieties would not be empty by the time her turn came. Marjory took her place at the sweet stall, where she intended to buy a bag of mixed boiled sweets, pear drops, humbugs and mint rock, which she would make last until next month's ration.

Jacqueline waited patiently, watching the comings and goings of the market traders. She was fascinated by the greengrocer juggling with four large potatoes, even as she tried to keep her eyes on the corner stall where brightly coloured windmills spun gaily on their sticks, fearful lest they should all be sold before her mother was served at the biscuit counter.

She could see old Misery's stall at the far side where socks of all sizes hung on the wooden canopy, alongside pants and stockings. Old Misery, according to Auntie Marjory, had a face as long as Woodhead tunnel and Jacqueline watched to see if he knew how to smile. She also hung on to Alan's pushchair, fearful lest old Misery's wife should come and try to buy her brother again. She would never forget the first time they wheeled him here in his pram and the woman came to look at him. 'Now then,' she had said, 'how about selling me your new baby? I'll give you a silver sixpence for him.' She had laughed loudly when Jacqueline started to cry, and the little girl had never liked the woman since. She supposed old Misery didn't have much to smile

165

about married to her.

She looked up to where her mam was laughing at a joke made by the biscuit man. For the first time in ages her mam looked happy. Jacqueline gave Alan a kiss and knew that all was well with her world.

Apart from the time a doodlebug swooped down low over the hillside with a screech almost loud enough to awaken the dead, causing Grandma Holmes to jump out of bed and stub her toe on the warming brick, and the time the row of old stone cottages was bombed early in 1941, Millington didn't fare too badly in the war. There was an attempt to destroy the reservoir at Longfield which caused havoc in the village, not that there were any casualties, but most of the dwellings suffered broken windows and a fall of soot, which meant that an extra spring-clean had been necessary. Not a welcome disruption except to the children who embraced any occurrence which meant a holiday from school.

It was, however, with even greater joy that the announcement of Victory in Europe was received, and on Barker's Row it was decided that a street party would be arranged as part of the celebrations. It was to be held in the old washhouses, which Mary and Marjory began to clean out without delay. Rations were pooled and some of the people in St George's Road were invited to join in. Even the staid middle-aged couple in the house between Mary and Marjory offered to contribute a few goodies and the use of their crockery, and astounded everyone by turning up with a couple of chairs to join in the revelry. Mrs Broomsgrove suffered from a phobia which caused her to spend all her days cleaning everything over and over again. Sometimes her doorstep would have been scrubbed two or three times by breakfast time, and it was washed again each time anyone walked across the flags. After that the yard broom and bucket would have to be scoured, and lastly even the scrubbing brush. It was rumoured that even the coal scuttle was rinsed every time it was emptied, and even Mr Broomsgrove looked scrubbed almost to the bone, poor man. Nevertheless, they attended the party without a tablet of soap in sight.

When darkness descended on the town the menfolk, who had been far from idle during the day, set alight a magnificent bonfire on the spare ground adjoining Barker's Row. None of the children had ever seen a bonfire and the little ones had no idea what to expect, but as the flames reached upwards to join the rose-tinged glow from other fires across the valley they were caught up in the excitement and danced with merriment, joining in the games of the older children. A bull-rope was brought out and the parents skipped alongside their offspring, to the accompanying strains of 'Roll Out The Barrel', and 'Pack Up Your Troubles'.

It was almost midnight when the news reached Barker's Row that celebrations were in full swing down in the yard at the steel works, and the whole party made their way in a long line of the conga down the Donkey Path.

Little Alan, high on his father's shoulders,

watched the festivities wide-eyed, and Mary and Jacqueline joined the line which was wending its way, like a trail of ants, laughing and singing, down to the works.

The music could be heard across the valley, and everyone who possessed a musical instrument of any description seemed to be part of the entertainment. The Lord Mayor, high on a makeshift platform, was organising everyone willing to do a turn, and a number of would-be comedians who had already consumed a great deal of liquid refreshment were taking the stage. Una nudged Jacqueline and giggled at some of the jokes, which were rather crude, but Jacqueline didn't understand most of them. She did however laugh at the man in the lady's dress and make-up. He had a pair of balloons pushed down his bodice, and she thought it hilarious when his partner burst them one at a time.

The show seemed to go on for hours, and finished off with the vicar leading hymn-singing, a prayer of thanksgiving, and finally a rousing rendition of 'Land Of Hope And Glory' and 'God Save The King'.

Jacqueline couldn't understand why her mother was crying, but when she looked round she noticed that many others in the crowd were crying too. She couldn't know of the many men and boys who would never come home. She couldn't know that until there was peace in the Pacific tears would continue to be shed, and she knew nothing of Tom Downing.

She watched her father shift the weight of her sleeping brother, and circle her mother with his free arm in an effort to comfort her. She thought how silly grown-ups were, to be crying on such a happy night as this, and she knew that even if she lived to be as old as Grandad Holmes she would remember this night for ever.

George and Millie Barker, up at the farm, took a liking to the little Holmes girl, with her large brown eyes and shock of dark bouncing curls. She was all they would have wished for in a daughter. Sadly, their only child Charles, who was now ten, was what the locals described as not a full shilling. Some said the child had been a victim of complications at birth, and blamed the midwife for refusing to call the doctor, but others old enough to remember the boy's grandparents said the condition ran in the family. Nevertheless Charles was a happy child, strong as a horse and worth his weight in gold to his parents. He could lift a hundredweight sack of potatoes on to the cart with no trouble at all, and seemed to be almost able to communicate with the livestock, knowing instinctively when one of the horses was under the weather, and proving to be the only one able to control the bad-tempered old boar. Yet the child could neither read, write, nor even speak in proper sentences. Until Jacqueline Holmes came along, only one other child had ever been able to make sense of anything Charlie was trying to say, a young girl on Potter's Row. Jacqueline didn't seem to notice anything different about the boy. It was the older children who upset him, delighting in calling after him whenever they passed the farm, 'Charlie Charlie chuck chuck chuck, went to bed with three white ducks.'

Charles would naturally lose his temper, and on one occasion he retaliated by throwing a stone which gashed the head of a departing youth. When the local bobby was called all hell broke loose between George Barker and the lad's father – until little Jacqueline intervened.

'It was his fault,' she shouted, 'he was tormenting Charlie. You ought to smack his bottom, didn't he, Mr Barker?'

The sight of the skinny little girl with the flashing eyes waving her fist at the scowling, bandaged youth stopped the men in their tracks, and suddenly Constable Jones started to laugh. This only made Jacqueline even more angry. She stamped her foot in its black shiny wellington boot, turned red in the face, and, sounding exactly like Grandad Holmes, cried 'if he was my little boy he would get his arse tanned.'

This was too much for the feuding men, who suddenly began to roar with laughter. The policeman, almost overcome by hysterics by this time, controlled himself for a moment and stood to attention. He looked at the little girl and said seriously, 'Madam, I'm inclined to agree with you.'

The boy with the gashed head backed away from the glowering bobby and began to howl loudly, 'My head hurts, my head hurts.'

His father, now in control of himself, took him by the collar and lifted him off his feet. 'It'll not be the only thing that hurts when I get you home, yer mardy bugger. Yon little lass has more guts in her little finger than you have in yer whole bloody body.' Then he marched his son through the yard, out of the gate and down the lane.

The policeman rocked back on his heels and looked at Charlie, cowering behind his father. 'I don't think you'll have any more bother from that quarter, Charlie lad, my owd son,' he said. His face broke into a grin. 'Eeh, George lad, I don't know about thee but that's the best laugh I've had for ages.'

'Aye,' said George Barker. 'To look at her you wouldn't think candyfloss'd melt in her mouth, would yer?' He started to chuckle again. 'Come inside,' he said. 'I've a bit of 'ome-fed bacon tha can 'ave, providing tha doesn't let on to anybody.'

'Yer can count on me, George.' The bobby smiled. 'But I don't know about this little miss.' But Jacqueline was already busy collecting the eggs with a smiling Charlie.

Mary was none too pleased when she heard about the incident across at the farm. Jacqueline was the centre of attention for a few days and though Mary admired her kindness to Charlie, she was determined her children would grow up speaking correctly, and was furious when she heard about the language. She knew where Jacqueline had picked it up, and much as she loved her father-in-law she didn't like him swearing in front of the children. Jack on the other hand thought it was hilarious. 'Even Constable Jones couldn't help laughing,' he pointed out. 'In fact he congratulated me on having such a bonny little lass.'

'He would,' retorted Mary. 'By what I've heard he can swear like a trooper himself.'

'Oh, come on, love, there are worse things in

171

life than a bit of bad language.'

'Maybe, but my kids are not going to use it. There's enough cursing going on in the family with your father.'

'All right, all right, I'll have a word with him,' Jack said. But they both knew it would be a waste of time, and it wasn't until Jack had gone on night shift and Mary was alone in the privacy of their bed that she began to chuckle to herself, as she imagined her slip of a daughter standing up to three burly men. For someone not yet five Jacqueline was certainly a character, and Mary couldn't help thinking that she and Jack were going to have their work cut out if they were to keep their daughter under control. Oh well, they could only do their best, and she was damned if she was going to upset Grandad Holmes, who idolised his grandchildren, just for the sake of a few swear words.

Grandma Holmes pegged the last bit into the canvas and twisted the wooden cog on the frame, turning the half-finished rug on to the next row. The room was cosy with the glow from the fire and the flicker of gas light.

'Can we start the diamond in the middle now, Grandma?' Una asked as she worked at the other end of the frame.

'Not quite, love. Another three rows and then we can.' Mrs Holmes looked round at her grand-children, all so beautiful yet so different. Una, tall for her age and blossoming already into a little beauty, was the lively one, forever contorting her body into the splits, doing handstands, or showing off the steps from her dancing lessons. She was the one who always came first in the school sports, landed the lead in the Christmas play, and was invited to every birthday party because she was such fun to have around.

Then there was Jacqueline, so much like her father in looks that each time the child gazed at her with her large brown eyes her grandmother was reminded of the years when her own children were small. Jacqueline was a character and no mistake, and seemed happier in the company of animals than humans. She could occupy herself for hours on end with a drawing book and a tin of paints. The magic paint books she had enjoyed colouring in with water when she was Alan's age were now considered babyish, and she preferred drawing her own pictures and colouring them in herself.

'What are you painting, love?'

'I'm painting Jenny.'

'Who's Jenny?'

'Jenny Hen,' Jacqueline answered with a sigh, as though it should have been perfectly obvious to anyone who Jenny was.

'Can I have a look?'

Jacqueline showed her the picture.

'Why, that's very good.' Her grandmother was surprised. It really did look like a hen, with vivid shades of brown and red.

Una turned to look at the picture. 'Hey, that's good, Jacqui. If you were at school you'd get ten out of ten for that.'

Jacqueline flushed and her little face became animated as she smiled with pleasure. 'Caroline

173

likes it too,' she said.

Grandma Holmes's stomach seemed to turn a somersault. She had heard about the imaginary friend Jacqueline talked to sometimes, and didn't quite know how to handle the situation. Mary had thought it best to ignore it, but Mrs Holmes knew she worried about the little girl's claims that her friend Caroline, who had pigtails and a white apron, was a real person.

Una giggled and her grandmother nudged her. 'Who'd like a drink of lemonade?' she asked, changing the subject.

'Me, me.' Alan, who never missed an opportunity to eat or drink, crawled out from under the table, which tonight was supposed to be a submarine, though he didn't actually know what a submarine was; he had heard Uncle Harry talking about them and he liked new words.

Underneath Grandma's table was Alan's favourite place. Sometimes it was a castle, or a bus, or an air-raid shelter; all the things the little boy thought mysterious. Besides, it was dark and warm, enclosed by the red plush cloth with the tassels almost reaching the floor, and particularly comfy tonight, on the huge pile of rug bits which had been cut from old coats: red, and black, and various shades of green. Alan had emptied them into his submarine from the old wicker basket, knowing Grandma Holmes never cared how much he untidied the kitchen, so long as he was content at his play.

Mrs Holmes lifted her grandson on to her knee. 'Una, will you get the biscuits?' she said, and drew the little boy's fair head into her ample bosom, rocking him vigorously. How like his Uncle Harry he was in looks, she sighed, hoping he wouldn't turn out to be as headstrong as her second son. Frowning, she wondered what Harry was up to now, staying out till early this morning. She prayed he wasn't still carrying on with the Banwell woman, but the rumours were circulating again. She would ask Jack to make some enquiries before Ada's husband began causing more trouble.

Una poured the drinks and got out the biscuit barrel. The clock chimed ten, which meant the family would be home from the pictures soon to collect the children. It wasn't often the men took out their wives, and she wished they would do so more frequently, giving her the opportunity to enjoy her grandchildren. It reminded her so much of the old days.

She cuddled Alan closer and his eyelids began to droop. It was way past his bedtime. She decided to put him to bed. No point in trailing him out in the cold night air; besides, it was Sunday tomorrow and his grandad would enjoy some time with the little lad.

She closed her eyes, thinking back through the years, the good and the not so good, and knew she had no cause to grumble. All her family had survived the war and were in work. Oh, but time was passing so swiftly and she wanted to see her grandchildren grow up.

She didn't doubt that she was good for a number of years yet, but as for her husband, she didn't dare to think. His retching cough was worsening rapidly, particularly in the mornings; it was as if his dust-worn lungs would be coughed up altogether one of these days. She couldn't bear to contemplate life without her dear, gentle, cursing old man, but she feared it was coming to that, and soon.

Then there was Harry. She wouldn't rest in her grave until her son was settled, though what type of girl would want him with his wild reputation she dreaded to think. She wondered about Margaret, her youngest, who until recently had never caused her the slightest concern. Now she too had taken to staying out until all hours of the night. And she'd become secretive, never letting on where she was off to, or with whom. Oh well, they were young and must learn from their own mistakes. She had brought them up to the best of her ability; no mother could be expected to do more.

She slipped off little Alan's socks. 'Go upstairs, Una love,' she said. 'Fetch one of Grandad's shirts out of the top drawer.'

'Is our Alan going to sleep here, then?' asked Jacqueline.

'He may as well, seeing as he's fast asleep.'

'Can I sleep here too?'

'I don't see why not.'

'Caroline likes sleeping in Auntie Margaret's bed.'

Una giggled as she helped her grandmother dress her sleeping cousin in the far too large white shirt. 'It's going to be a bit crowded, Jacqui, with you, Alan, Auntie Margaret and your friend all in one bed.'

Mrs Holmes wondered how long the friendship between Jacqueline and the make-believe Caroline would last. The child really seemed to be able to communicate with Caroline, offering her sweets, talking to her, even asking her opinions on the drawings she did. It really gave her the shivers sometimes.

'Can I have a shirt, too?' Jacqueline said. 'I like Grandad's shirts, they tuck right in under my feet.' She began to get undressed, then beamed as she said, 'Caroline likes Grandad's shirts too.'

Chapter Seventeen

Mary was rapidly losing patience with her daughter, who had been in one of her sulks all morning. Mary didn't believe in bribery in any shape or form but as a last resort she said, 'Well, I can't see Father Christmas coming to our house this year, what with our Alan refusing to eat his dinner and our Jacqueline refusing to speak to anyone.'

'I want Father Christmas to come,' Alan whined. 'I want him to bring me a puffer twain.'

'Ah, but Father Christmas knows when you don't eat your dinner,' said Mary.

'I don't like turnip, it's howible.'

'Well, I don't care if he doesn't come,' said Jacqueline. 'I want to go to Grandma Roberts's today. We always go on Sundays.'

'Not this Sunday. I've told you, Grandma Roberts is having visitors. Besides, the weather isn't fit.'

'Grandad Roberts would fetch us in the car if I asked him,' Jacqueline mumbled sullenly.

Jack had been trying to read the *News Of The World* for the last half-hour and decided to put a stop to the bickering once and for all.

'No doubt Grandad Roberts would, seeing as he thinks the sun shines out of your backside, but we're not going so that's the end of it.'

'Nobody will take Pepper a walk along the lane, or brush him.' Jacqueline began to cry.

'Ah, so it's Pepper you're worried about, not Grandma and Grandad,' Mary said. 'Well, you know Cyril looks after Pepper perfectly well, so you needn't concern yourself about that.'

'For heaven's sake, can't we have a bit of peace on a Sunday afternoon?' Jack, who rarely lost his temper, had heard enough on the subject. 'One more word out of you, young lady, and I shall personally write a letter to Father Christmas cancelling his visit this year.'

Alan began to wail, and Jack folded the newspaper and went out, slamming the door behind him. What with the kids playing up, and the uneasiness filling his mind about his brother, he couldn't concentrate on the paper even in the peace and solitude of the lavatory.

It was Friday morning when the rumours reached him. He had been drinking cold tea from the bottle and eating his snap of bread and jam, and the new boy, one of the Murphy lads, had been eager to join in the conversation. 'Our Theresa says Mr Banwell is going to beat your Harry up,' he said.

'Oh, and how does your Theresa know that?'

'She was talking to 'is mate who's come 'ome.'

The conversation had ended abruptly at that

point when a rat had scurried close to young Tony, who had shrieked in horror, 'It's after me sandwiches!'

'I told you, lad, never leave the lid off your snap tin or the rats will beat you to it.'

Young Tony moved in closer to Jack. 'I don't think I'm going to like working dahn't pit. Me mother said I wouldn't.'

'Well, now yer know your mother was right. You'll find she usually is.'

'She wanted me to go to't pipe works,' Tony said.

'Why didn't yer?'

'It weren't as much money, and me mother needs more money.'

'Money isn't everything, lad.'

'It is when you 'aven't got any.'

'Aye, I suppose you're right there.'

But Jack's mind had been on the business of his brother and that low-living Ada Banwell. He would see Harry after work and warn him off, though he doubted he would listen.

Jack wondered how it was that with half the lasses in Millington running after his brother he had needed to become involved with a woman like that. She didn't even look attractive with her peroxide-blonde hair and half her flesh hanging out of low-cut dresses. Not that the woman's appearance mattered one way or the other; she was married and that was that.

Harry hadn't liked it when Jack had sought him out in the queue at the wages office and asked for an explanation as to what was going on.

'What's it got to do with you?' he asked. 'I don't

come interfering with you and Mary, do I?'

'I'm trying to prevent you getting a hammering, that's all.'

'I can look after myself, man. I'm not a bairn.'

'Then perhaps you should stop behaving like one, taking things that don't belong to you, like another man's wife for instance. Don't forget what Banwell did last time.'

'Oh, leave it out, man. I'll sort myself out, don't you worry.'

'And don't forget how our old man reacted either.'

'All right, I'll sort it.'

'Well, I only hope you do before our old man hears about what's going on. He's too old to be coping with upsets like that.' But Jack found he was talking to the back of his brother's head as he stormed out of the pit yard, intent as usual on carrying on in his own carefree way.

If Jack had but known, Harry was far from carefree. He had landed himself in a situation from which there seemed to be no escape, and it was all because of a bet amongst the lads one New Year's Eve. It was Lanky Harvey who had started it by remarking on how Ada Banwell was only hot for foreigners.

'She won't even entertain the idea of going with any of the local lads. Even the bloke she married comes from Southampton or some such place.'

Harry had laughed. 'A Southampton man isn't a foreigner, Lanky.'

'I know that – I'm on about the rest of 'em. I reckon she's been through the lot of 'em over at

180

the Polish camp, before she even started on the Americans.'

'Maybe it's all them nylon stockings she's after,' said one of the others.

'More like what they've got in their trousers,' Lanky said.

The others had laughed, but Harry's curiosity had got the better of him. 'I'll bet you ten bob I can take her home tonight.'

'Mek it half a crown and you're on.'

Harry had won his half-crown, and Ada Banwell, just like a queen bee, had drawn him into her hive.

The affair had lasted until the night of his brother's wedding, and ended with the beating. He had resolved to have nothing more to do with the woman, but Ada had other ideas. Harry had proved to be more than just a good bedmate. She had fallen for the young, good-looking miner, and, fed up to the teeth of being married to an ever absent regular marine, she was determined that Harry was for her. Besides, Harry was generous with his money, so Ada made sure the affair flared again by giving him a flash of a shapely white thigh after his resistance had been lowered by a few pints of best bitter at the Rising Sun.

Now Harry was regretting his involvement, recognising Ada for the empty-headed, loose-living woman she was. He had begun to feel envious of his brother's wife and two lovely kids, and thought it was time he put an end to an affair which could not possibly have any future.

It was then that Ada had played her ace card, informing Harry that she was pregnant.

So far Harry had managed to convince himself it was all a hideous mistake. Maybe she was lying, or her monthlies were late. At any rate, the problem could be shelved for a few weeks thanks to the arrival of her sailor husband, home for Christmas leave, and for that few weeks he intended to forget his troubles and enjoy himself. It was almost Christmas and he had presents to buy.

He called in at the Miners' Club, whistling as he stripped off to use the slipper baths. He scrubbed the coal dust from his pores and rubbed soap into his crinkly blond hair. He wanted to look his best; he had his eye on the classy little girl who worked in the Co-op. She was playing hard to get, but that was to be expected. She really was worth pursuing, different altogether from Ada Banwell. Oh, God, if only he had never set eyes on the bloody woman.

Christmas Eve was here at last. There had been no further talk of cancelling Father Christmas's visit, and the youngsters were filled with anticipation about what they would find in the morning, excited to the point of giddiness as the party at Grandma Holmes's grew more and more lively. There had been pork sandwiches and pickles, home-made brawn, jelly and custard and Grandma Holmes's special dark sticky Christmas cake. After tea the men had gone to the Rising Sun, bringing back drinks for the women, a crate of Nut Brown Ale, and pop and crisps for the little ones. Nobody had asked from where the pork had originated. Only Harry knew, and as he said, 'Ask no questions, receive no lies.'

As the night wore on the house became more and more crammed, with neighbours, friends, cousins, and others who called Mrs Holmes Auntie Lizzie, even though she had no idea to which relatives they belonged. They were all made welcome at Grandma Holmes's. A game of postman's knock was in progress, with young girls and boys from the row giggling and blushing as they emerged from the bottom of the stairs.

The highlight of the evening came with the singing of all the local carols. Una did her best to coax a tune out of the old harmonium despite her limited number of music lessons, the result causing Mary to wish Gladys was here. Nevertheless the hearty voices soon drowned the tuneless accompaniment and filled the house, and indeed the whole row, with seasonal cheer. Alan was asleep in his favourite sanctuary under the table but Jacqueline joined in the singing as she bounced up and down on Uncle Harry's knee. Then, as the night wore on, she began to worry. 'What if Father Christmas comes and we're still here, Uncle Harry?' She stood up on his knee and looked deep into his eyes.

'Don't you worry about that, sweetheart,' he assured the little girl. 'Father Christmas never comes until the children are asleep. It's part of his magical abilities to know which one is in bed and which one isn't.' He looked at the clock. 'Hey, I've got to be going,' he said.

Jacqueline wound her arms tightly round his neck. 'I don't want you to go,' she said.

'No choice, sweetheart, but I'll tell you what, I'll be up at your house first thing in the morning

183

to see what Santa's brought.'

Jacqueline clung tighter to Harry. 'Caroline doesn't want you to go either.'

Harry laughed, stood up and lifted his niece up towards the ceiling, then pretended to drop her. She usually squealed with delight, but tonight her little face puckered and she looked near to tears.

'Hey, what's to do little one?' Harry looked concerned.

'I love you, Uncle Harry,' Jacqueline whispered.

'And I love you too angel, but I've got to go just the same.' He placed her down on the new rag rug and plonked a kiss on her forehead. 'A Merry Christmas, everybody,' he called, and went over to where his mother rocked slowly. 'And a special one to you, Mother.' He hugged Grandma Holmes tightly.

'And to you, son,' she said.

He went to his father. 'A Happy Christmas, Dad,' he said, shaking him by the hand.

'And to you, yer young bugger, and don't go getting thisen into any bother. There'll be a lot o' drunkards about tonight.'

'I won't. In fact I might bring someone to meet you later on, somebody yer'll approve of for a change.'

He went out laughing as his mother called, 'And not afore time either.'

The clock struck ten thirty as Jack carried Jacqueline high on his shoulders up Barker's Row. She clung tighter here, pressing her face into her dad's flat cap. She had suffered too many bleeding knees by running and falling on the stony ground just here, and she mustn't fall and make holes in her new stockings. Not only new stockings but brown ones just like Una's instead of horrible black. Mary grumbled as she trundled Alan in his outgrown pushchair, fetched out of the loft for the late night transportation home.

'You're in no fit state to carry her,' she said as Jack stumbled, but Jacqueline knew she could trust her father with her life.

'It's Christmas Eve,' Jack said. 'If I can't have one over the eight tonight I never can. And what about Bill?' He laughed. 'Our Marj'll be lucky to get him home at all tonight.'

Bill had certainly had enough to drink. He had swayed on the three-legged stool and sung his heart out before suddenly hurrying out of the house and across the yard, to return white-faced and somewhat sobered fifteen minutes later. Jack had helped him upstairs and laid him on the bed, where he could be heard snoring even before Jack reached the bottom of the stairs again.

Jack suddenly bent down, sending Jacqueline's stomach surging upwards, and placed his sleepy daughter on the step. She could hear her mother dragging the large, heavy key up on its string and through the letter box. They fumbled their way in and Jack lit the gas.

'I hope he hasn't been,' said Jacqueline.

'He won't have,' Mary consoled her. 'But if you aren't undressed and in bed in a flash, he might.'

Jacqueline already had her coat and dress off, and was shivering as she struggled with the buttons fastening her lovely woollen stockings to her liberty bodice.

Mary undressed Alan, and Jack raked down the

few red cinders into the ash pan below.

'Mustn't have Father Christmas burning himself.' He opened the oven door, taking out the oven plate and wrapping it in a piece of blanket. 'That'll soon have you warm,' he said as he opened the stairs door and led his daughter up into the dark. He lit the candle at her bedside, sending the shadows looming tall, to shrink again as the flame settled down.

Jacqueline jumped on to the high bed and there, one on each of the brass knobs, were two freshly ironed pillow cases. She snuggled down as Mary placed her sleeping brother beside her, and pressed her feet, cold from the lino'd floor, on to the oven plate.

'Goodnight and God bless,' Mary said. 'Fast asleep now or he won't come.'

Jacqueline screwed her eyes up tight as Jack blew out the candle, remembering too late that she hadn't looked at the clothes closet door to make sure it was closed, keeping any bogey men or other horrible things inside. Anyway, she didn't care tonight. Father Christmas was on his way. She pressed her hands together.

'Gentle Jesus, please let Father Christmas bring me a desk to draw my pictures on, and if he can spare one a black dolly too, and a train for our Alan. And please could he bring some tap dancing shoes for our Una. God bless Mam and Dad and our Alan. God bless Grandma and Grandad Holmes and Grandma and Grandad O'Connor, and Grandma and Grandad Roberts. Oh, and God bless Uncle Harry.' The last bit was added as an afterthought, then Jacqueline snuggled closer to her brother, determined to stay awake to catch a glimpse of Father Christmas.

The streets were alive with party revellers, some returning home with tired children, for once eager to be abed, or others just setting out to friends for night visits. The atmosphere of Christmas seemed heightened this year, probably because eighteen months after the war most families were together again at last. Street lamps and open-curtained windows cast a glow on to the street, and bestowed an atmosphere of warmth upon the groups of carol singers, spreading the message of Christmas around the town. Harry, generous as usual, dug deep into the pocket of his Crombie overcoat and was rewarded with smiles from the grateful youngsters.

'Thanks, mister. Have a Merry Christmas.'

'I will, and the same to you.'

He hurried on to the west end of town, the area he had always labelled in the past as the posh end. He was eager to see if Sally Anderson had kept her promise to be waiting near the bus terminus. He had known Sally to speak to for some time, having danced with her at the schoolroom dances, but she had always refused his offers to see her home. He had worried that his reputation might be the reason, so it had been a surprise when she had accepted his invitation to go for a drink with him tonight.

He had been buying fur-backed gloves as a gift for Una when Sally had served him in the Co-op, looking smart and efficient as she asked his check number and placed his money in the tube and sent it off to the office. Whilst they waited for the change, Harry had chatted, and encouraged by her smile he had invited her for the drink.

'So long as it's not too early,' she said. 'I need to visit my sister after work, to deliver gifts for the children's stockings and things.'

'Any time you like.' Harry didn't care about the drink. 'If we're too late for the pub we can go up to our house. There'll be a party in progress until the early hours, I expect.'

Sally flashed him one of her ravishing smiles. 'That will be fine, then. I'll see you at the terminus at half past nine, if you can make it. I don't want to keep you from your family.'

'I'll be there.' Harry had accepted his change unseeingly and left the shop in a daze. He had never experienced feelings like these before. Now he could understand how his brother had felt about Mary.

The Co-op girls had bombarded Sally with questions. One was envious and thought Harry Holmes looked exactly like Alan Ladd only more manly. One or two warned Sally off.

'He goes for the married ones. You want your brain seeing to if you go out with Harry Holmes.'

Sally had shrugged her shoulders. She knew all about Harry's reputation; she also knew she wanted him, and was sure he wanted her. Sally couldn't wait for Christmas to see him again, no matter what her friends said.

Harry was just arriving when she reached the terminus, both of them early. They began to speak simultaneously and broke off, laughing. He took her arm. 'Where would you like to go? I thought we could have a drink at the Golden Ball.' He glanced at his watch. 'We've only half an hour and it's the nearest.'

'That'll be lovely.'

He led her to the pub, one of the better-class places where a woman could drink without being leered at by the local louts. 'What would you like?' he asked.

'A port and lemon, please.'

He made his way through the crowd at the bar, most of whom knew Harry and greeted him jovially. One of his old mates bought the drinks; Harry had treated him on many occasions when he had been out of work due to a chronic lung complaint.

'By, you've come up in the world there, Hal,' he said, nodding towards Sally, who had found a quiet corner seat.

'Aye, and my intentions are entirely honourable on this occasion.'

His mate laughed. 'I doubt you'll have much option there. She looks like a discerning young miss to me does that one.'

'That's what I like about her. I've done with the riff-raff from now on. If I don't marry Sally Anderson I'll never marry anybody.'

His mate stared open-mouthed.

'Thanks for the drinks, and compliments of the season.'

Harry took the drinks back to Sally. He had plucked a twig of mistletoe from a holly bough on the bar, and he held it over her head and tilted her head up towards him. Her lips opened and met his in a long, lingering kiss. They parted reluctantly.

'Happy Christmas, Sally,' he whispered.

'Happy Christmas, Harry.'

Then his arms were round her and they both knew this was no casual affair, but one that would last for ever.

At closing time Harry persuaded Sally to go and meet his parents. She argued that it was a bit too soon, but he ignored her protests and led her up the hill, stopping once or twice for a kiss along the way. Not that he had any unseemly thoughts as far as Sally was concerned. He was content to hold her hand, to talk about their families, their jobs, and even her concern over the atom bomb tests which had taken place at Bikini earlier in the year. He wanted to talk to her for ever, and regretted their arrival at his house.

Lizzie Holmes still sat rocking beside the fire. Jack and Mary had left with their weary offspring, Bill was asleep upstairs, and only Marjory, Una, Margaret and Mr Holmes still remained amongst the party leftovers. Lizzie looked approvingly at the smartly dressed young woman, deciding there and then that she liked her. She hoped her son wasn't messing her about. Still, she looked the type who could look after herself. Besides, she must be a sensible lass to have landed a job at the Co-op.

Harry made some tea and poured it into the best china cups. Margaret cut the fruit cake and Sally pronounced it the best she'd ever tasted.

After a while she said she must be going as her parents would be waiting up. Marjory invited them all to tea on Boxing Day and sent Una to

190

wake her father. It was then that Harry remembered he had to collect Jacqueline's present from Tommy Murphy. 'I hope our Jack's not locked up and in bed,' he said. 'I shouldn't like our Jacqueline to be left without a present.'

'Not much chance of that. He'll be making sure the kids are asleep before playing Santa Claus,' Mr Holmes said, trying hard not to swear in front of Harry's young lady. Lizzie had warned him in advance, just as she had when Jack had brought Mary home for the first time. The trouble was his good intention never lasted, but he did try.

Margaret asked Harry why he'd left the present until the last minute but he only smiled, said goodnight and led Sally outside and on to the Murphys'.

The present was all ready, complete with wicker basket and covered by a cardboard box.

'Do you mind if we go the long way round and call at our Jack's?' he asked Sally.

'Of course not, there's no rush. I just didn't want to outstay my welcome, that's all.'

'No chance of that at our house.' Harry laughed. 'Me mother loves visitors. It might not be posh but everybody's welcome.'

'I know, I noticed.' Sally snuggled up closer to Harry's side.

'Are you cold?' he asked, concerned.

'I won't be by the time we reach your brother's. He lives at the top of the hill, doesn't he?'

'Almost. Number ten Barker's Row.'

'I know. I used to see him sometimes when I delivered groceries to the Davenports' when I first started work.'

They turned the corner on to St George's Road. It was there that the figures came up behind them in the darkness.

Sally was grabbed from behind, dragged backwards and pushed into the drystone wall. She screamed as a hand, large, rough and smelly, pressed itself over her mouth, and she fell, twisting her leg beneath her and grazing the side of her face on the protruding stones. She tried to call Harry's name but the hand gagged her into silence.

Harry was momentarily shocked but soon recovered and fended off the other two men, raining blows right and left in the darkness. But one of them held him, flattening him to the gravelly ground, and then he blacked out as a fist struck him powerfully between the eyes.

Sally could hear the punches and was on the verge of passing out when she was released and the men made off, down towards the Donkey Wood.

As she groped in the darkness Sally heard a noise and suddenly remembered the basket. She found the source of the whimpering, and brought the basket to Harry's side. She found his wrist, feeling for his pulse. She panicked for a moment, then she felt around for her shoes and began to run, on up the road towards Jack's house, where she knocked frantically at the door.

Jack thought it was the carollers. 'Good, someone's come to let Christmas in,' he said.

'Well, I just hope they don't wake the children,' Mary said. 'They'll be awake soon enough as it is.'

Sally fell into the house. 'Sorry,' she stammered. 'It's Harry. He ... he's been hurt. Can you come?'

Jack grabbed his coat and set off with Sally into the darkness.

'Oh, God,' Mary murmured into the night, 'not the Banwell man again.'

She filled the kettle and placed it over the fire, wondering if she would ever have a Christmas without something disastrous happening. Last year the holiday had been spoiled by Rowland's having to rush Mr Broomsgrove into hospital, after he suffered a perforated ulcer. It had been almost midnight when Rowland had returned, having attended to the patient himself, administering blood transfusions and helping console Mrs Broomsgrove, who had probably caused the ulcer in the first place by subjecting the poor man to her phobia over the years.

Her thoughts went back to the Christmas afternoon when she and Tom had made love in the stable. Though in her heart she had no regrets, her conscience would give her no peace. She blamed herself for Tom's having been taken from her, and now it seemed her Christmases were to be haunted for ever by the Christmas sin.

It wasn't until Jack was returning home in the taxi that it occurred to him that Harry probably owed his life to Bill Bacon, and he wondered what the outcome would have been if his brother-in-law hadn't arrived on the scene at the same time as Sally and himself. Bill had sobered instantly, and his first-aid training as a pit deputy had enabled him to set about stemming the bleeding from his brother-in-law's wounds, and turning the injured man into a position which

193

allowed him to breathe freely again.

Dr Sellers had been summoned and immediately called for an ambulance. She congratulated Bill on his action, and, dedicated as she was, had stayed with the patient until the ambulance arrived, despite the fact that she had been just about to start out for Midnight Mass.

When the ambulance had gone, Bill took Sally to Mary's, where Marjory had decided the Bacons would stay in an effort to divert Una's thoughts from the sight of her uncle lying in the road. Mary calmed Sally with a cup of tea, and then the girl insisted on going home, knowing her parents would be anxious, even though it was Christmas.

Bill walked her to her door before making his way back up the hill to break the news of Harry's whereabouts to his parents. He did his utmost to reassure them, playing down the incident and stressing that Harry was in no way to blame for the attack. Then he left Margaret to comfort the worried couple. Bill thought the world of his in-laws and would have done anything to spare them the worry, but knew they would never have rested if their son had not arrived home and sent no word. Besides, everyone in the locality would have heard the news by morning, since Constable Jones had arrived at the scene at the same time as the ambulance.

The man had persisted in probing into who was responsible for the assault, but Sally had denied any knowledge of the identities of the men, knowing instinctively that Harry would wish to let the incident die down without any publicity, if only for his parents' sake. She wondered if they would let her know how he was, but doubted that they would even remember her name in their distress. After all, it was the first time Harry and she had been out together. Yet it seemed she had known him for ever. Already he seemed part of her. Sally was suddenly afraid. What if he didn't recover? She didn't think she could bear never to see him again. She didn't care about his affair with the Banwell woman. That was all in the past, before Harry and she had met, and now she loved him, and Sally Anderson wasn't a fine weather girl: she would love Harry Holmes through the bad times. She would love him back to good health. Even so, she prayed that night as she had never prayed before.

It was almost morning when Bill reached Mary's house. Marjory wanted to know how her parents had taken the news.

'They were a bit shocked, of course, but they'll be all right. It's a good thing your Margaret's with them.'

'Thank heavens she was home. It's a miracle she was, with the hours she's been keeping lately.'

When Jack arrived, white-faced, shaken and lighter of pocket from paying a taxi driver who demanded double fare seeing as it was Christmas Day, Mary gave the two men a brandy, a remedy recommended by Dr Roberts for situations such as this.

'Well,' said Jack. 'Though I don't like saying so, our Harry's only got what he's deserved for a long time.'

'But not to such an extent,' said Marjory, the sight of her brother's unrecognisable face still

195

vivid in her mind. 'And especially now when he's just found himself a nice girl like Sally.'

'But he'd been warned often enough,' Jack said. 'If somebody was messing around with Mary I should probably feel like murdering him too.'

'But Ada Banwell isn't like Mary. She's no better than a prostitute,' Marjory retorted.

'She's still the man's wife,' Jack persisted. 'Anyway, are we going to have some breakfast while it's still quiet? I don't suppose we'll get chance when the kids wake up. I thought they might have been up by now. You did do the pillow cases, love?'

Mary nodded. 'Oh, I almost forgot. Sally brought a present for our Jacqueline. I told her to put it in the front room. She said it was from Harry.'

At the mention of Harry's name, Marjory began to weep.

'Come on, love, he'll be all right.' Bill drew his wife into his arms, where she continued to sob. 'Come on, love. I know it was a shock seeing him like that, but he was recovering by the time the ambulance arrived.'

Mary placed a slice of bread on the toasting fork, just as a cry came from upstairs.

'Mammy, mammy, Father Christmas has been.'

'Oh-oh, I knew our Jacqueline would be the first,' Jack said.

Marjory recovered from her weeping. By this time Alan and Una were also awake.

'Well,' said Mary, 'no point in making the children miserable. We'd better go up – we don't want to miss the fun.'

'If that's what I think it is,' Jack said, looking at

the covered basket and correctly interpreting the stream of liquid which was flowing from between the wickerwork, 'we'd better leave it downstairs.'

'Oh, come on,' said Mary. 'I can't wait to see our Jacqueline's face when she sees Uncle Harry's present.' And the four of them trooped upstairs to join the children, Mary carrying the basket just like one of the wise men, on the very first Christmas of all.

The desk and chair caused a stir for the first few minutes, along with the black doll beautifully dressed in a red knitted outfit by Gladys, but when Mary produced Uncle Harry's present all else was forgotten.

Jacqueline removed the cardboard box to reveal a shivering brown and white cocker spaniel puppy, and from that moment a lifelong relationship was formed.

Alan didn't care about anything but his train set, a clockwork, wind-up affair, with a home-made bridge and platform on which a set of lead soldiers and farm animals were already being arranged.

The bedroom reeked of June perfume which Una had received in a box which also contained talcum powder and a large fluffy powder puff. The bed was piled high with books, coloured pencils, gloves and board games. Una was flaunting her new charm bracelet, but Jacqueline, oblivious of everything but her new pet, was already skipping downstairs in search of a dish in which to give her pup something to drink.

Mary and Jack followed their daughter and Jack

disappeared into the front room, returning with a huge parcel which he placed on the kitchen table. 'Merry Christmas, love.' He drew Mary towards him and kissed her tenderly.

'What is it?' she asked.

'Open it and see,' he said, smiling.

Mary undid the mass of brown paper, to reveal a gleaming black and gold sewing machine. 'Oh!' she exclaimed. 'I've always wanted one. All my life I've wanted a sewing machine. Oh, Jack, thank you.' She kissed him and began examining the workings of shuttle and cotton holders, before she suddenly remembered. 'I've got something for you too, but it looks so paltry compared to this.'

She opened the cupboard in the recess by the fire and climbed up on to the chair-arm so she could reach the third shelf. 'Here you are,' she said. 'It's not much,' Jack tore at the wrappings as Mary continued, 'And it's only second hand.'

Jack lifted the plane out of the paper and grinned. 'Well, it looks like new to me. Thanks, love.'

Mary had been on the look-out for a plane for months, knowing of Jack's love of working with wood. He had made a perfect job of Jacqueline's desk, but a plane would have saved him a lot of time.

Jacqueline was examining the puppy's long floppy ears with wonderment. 'Isn't he the best-est dog you've ever seen? Why isn't Uncle Harry here? He said he'd be here this morning.'

Jack looked for guidance to Mary, wondering whether to tell the child the truth and risk upsetting her.

'Uncle Harry's not very well,' Mary said, knowing her daughter was perceptive enough to see through any excuses. 'He's had to go to hospital, but he will come as soon as he's better.'

'I knew he wouldn't be well. I didn't want him to go out. I told him, and Caroline knew too, but he wouldn't take any notice.'

Mary suddenly felt a shiver down her spine. It was true: her daughter had known. She had begged her uncle to stay but to no avail. And the look in her eyes had reminded Mary of the day Tom had left her for the last time. She realised at that moment how wrong she had been to dismiss Caroline as a figment of her daughter's imagination. It had never occurred to her that her grandmother's gift of seeing the future had emerged once again. Mary hoped that history wouldn't repeat itself, and that it had not been the last time Jacqueline would see her uncle alive.

'I'm going to call him Little Harry,' the girl suddenly announced. 'That's Caroline's favourite name.'

Alan padded downstairs in his bare feet, his face and pyjamas covered in chocolate, a half-eaten apple in his hand.

'*You* are going to be sick,' Mary scolded her son half-heartedly. After all it was Christmas morning.

Bill trundled downstairs with Una's pillow case, followed by his wife and daughter, and Mary buttered the toast and poured the tea.

'Little Harry's hungry,' Jacqueline declared.

Jack set about putting together some bread soaked in milk for the new arrival. If only Harry had warned him they would have been better prepared, but then his brother always was one to do things on impulse. He hoped his wounds would prove less serious than they looked, for though he and his brother were very different they loved each other dearly.

'I love Tittle Harry,' said Alan, intent on feeding the puppy a chocolate penny.

'So do I,' said Jacqueline, 'and so does Caroline.'

Chapter Eighteen

The month of January 1947 was an eventful one for the Holmeses, to say the least. Most important was that Harry began his slow painful progress on the road to recovery. His broken nose, when it began to heal slightly out of shape only seemed to add to his handsome looks, but an operation was necessary to remove a splinter from his fractured ribs, which had punctured a lung. Sally, a constant visitor, was the inspiration he needed, strengthening his will to regain his health.

Jack told him on one of his frequent visits that the house had been taken over by Tittle Harry, with whom Alan's mispronounced name had stayed, and Mary's sewing machine, which was never still from morning till night.

One consolation for Mrs Holmes throughout the long worrying period was that Margaret seemed to have settled down again, had ceased staying out until all hours and seemed content to spend more time at home. Lizzie thought it was Harry's accident which had brought her to her senses, and couldn't help feeling relieved, despite her daughter's prolonged silences and subdued attitude. If she had but known, the heartbreak her daughter was living through had nothing at all to do with Harry, but was due to the departure of dark-haired, brown-eyed Adam, the most gentle man Margaret had ever met; Adam also happened to be Polish.

It had all begun innocently enough when Margaret had agreed to make up a foursome to go dancing. It had taken no more than one waltz for Margaret and Adam to fall passionately and completely in love. They had known the affair was doomed from the beginning. It was only a matter of time before he must leave, and leave he did. To be back in Poland in time for Christmas, where his wife and two beautiful children were waiting.

They had agreed there was no alternative, and parted bravely, both hiding their heartache and desolation.

'Don't write,' Margaret told him. 'Your future is with your family. Besides, I need to forget you.'

But they both knew they would never forget. A love like theirs was a rare and wondrous thing, and without each other life would never be the same again. Besides, Margaret knew she would strive to remember every touch, the way he walked, the mispronounced words which made her laugh. But she had no regrets, for she had known love, and no one could take that away.

Another major event was Jacqueline's starting school, after the first day of which she announced she wouldn't be going any more as she didn't think much to it.

On that first morning she had walked hand in hand with Una, full of anticipation as to what new delights she would find. By the first playtime break she already knew the horrors of a detestable teacher and the claustrophobic atmosphere of a room filled with forty-three other children. Her hatred of Miss Robinson, the middle-aged teacher, was sealed when the woman refused to set a place at the table for Caroline. Her requests for a chalk and slate for Caroline were met at first with an embarrassed silence and, later, by anger and the threat of a rap over the knuckles with a ruler if the name was mentioned again.

Jacqueline didn't mention Caroline again. Instead she worked diligently, repeating her letters parrot-fashion along with her classmates: A for apple, B for ball, C for cat and so on, becoming bored after a while doing things she had already been taught over a year ago.

After lunch she enjoyed crayoning a pattern on a square of paper, and was pleased when Miss Robinson chose it to hang on the wall, but the woman's stern looks still made her nervous and she decided school wasn't at all what she had expected.

She was shocked on the second day to discover that school wasn't voluntary and everybody had to go, like it or not. The only good thing she could think of was that she had acquired a new friend, whom everyone except Miss Robinson called Pam, short for Pamela. Pam was a freckle-faced girl with straight ginger hair held out of her eyes by a slide which Jacqueline had to replace every couple of hours, due to the slippery straightness of Pam's hair. Jacqueline saw this as a means of repayment for Pam's offer to eat all the grey, mashed, lumpy potatoes off Jacqueline's plate at lunchtime. At home time the two friends realised they lived no more than two streets apart and walked home with arms wound firmly round each other's waist, and Jacqueline promising to call for her new pal at quarter to nine in the morning. From that day on Jacqueline and Pam were inseparable, and woe betide anyone who attempted to separate them. Jacqueline even shared Caroline with her new friend, and if Pam offered a stick of liquorice root or a bag of lemon crystals to Jacqueline, she always asked if Caroline would like one too. Jacqueline on the other hand was the first person ever to admire Pam's freckles and wish she had ginger hair, for which the little girl would be eternally grateful.

After a few weeks, in which Miss Robinson realised the little Holmes girl's potential, it was decided that all the girls would knit a dishcloth and the boys make objects with cardboard and glue. Most of the girls, after being shown how to cast on the stitches by winding the thick cotton yarn round their thumbs, soon got the hang of it, and were knitting away after one or two lessons. Unfortunately knitting to Jacqueline was a nightmare, owing mainly to the fact that she was left-handed. Pam, seeing her friend attempt the task, decided to help whilst Miss Robinson's attention was elsewhere, and soon the wool was in a hopeless tangle.

Jacqueline became more and more panic-stricken as the dishcloth, nothing more than a mass of dropped stitches and knots, became impossible to untangle, and at the end of the lesson she smuggled the whole miserable mess into her shoulder bag, which normally contained nothing except a clean hanky and her dinner money on a Monday morning. She whispered to Pam that her mammy would make it right, but Pam began to wish her friend had let Miss Robinson sort out the mess. Miss Robinson would have had to be blind not to have noticed the two pairs of huge wooden needles protruding from the shoulder bag.

'Jacqueline Holmes, come back here,' she roared, as the two girls sneaked guiltily past her desk. The whole class came back, inquisitive to find out if cleverdick Jacqueline had at last done something wrong.

'Open your bag,' Miss Robinson snapped, and Jacqueline felt the blood rush to her face.

'Please Miss,' she stammered, 'I want to leave the room.' It was the expression everyone used for going to the lavatory.

'You'll go when I say so.' Miss Robinson came down from her desk, looming like a menacing monster over the scared little girl. Pam clung tighter to her friend's hand.

'Please Miss,' she volunteered, 'our knitting's all tangled up.'

'You speak when you're spoken to. Give me the dishcloth,' she demanded. Jacqueline handed over the knitting to the woman, the work slipping from the needles as she did so.

'And what, may I ask, do you call this, girl?' Miss Robinson's eyes blazed with anger and Jacqueline could see a mass of pimples and a few black hairs on the woman's chin as the face came closer. She began to cry and suddenly a warm stream of urine began to seep from her navy blue knickers and run down her legs to the floor.

'I couldn't help it. I told you I wanted to leave the room,' she sobbed. 'Besides, I was only taking our knitting home for my mammy to mend.'

A small boy in the watching crowd suddenly said in a whisper loud enough for the whole class to hear, 'Jacqueline Holmes has peed her knickers.'

Miss Robinson, exasperated now beyond all reason, screamed, 'Get out the lot of you this minute.'

Pam began to cry too, and then tried to explain. 'She can't help it. It's not her fault her hands are back to front.'

Miss Robinson suddenly saw the funny side of the child's remark. She pursed her lips in an effort to stifle the laughter which was threatening to crack her normally dour countenance, then said, 'Go home, both of you. I'll begin a new dishcloth for you, Pamela, in the next handicraft lesson, and you, Jacqueline, if you find the knitting too difficult, may join the boys with their modelling.'

Jacqueline felt a wave of relief wash over her and stared open mouthed.

'Well, go home then, child, and don't wait until the last minute in future before asking to leave the room.'

The two girls scurried out and rushed to the cloakroom before the woman changed her mind and brought out the ruler, or worse still the cane from behind her desk.

Miss Robinson found a cloth to remove all traces of the accident and suddenly admitted to herself that she would have objected to the child's being excused anyway, so close to home time. She really must try to be more tolerant, especially of the little Holmes girl who had the makings of a scholar, while her friend seemed to have the makings of a comedienne. She chuckled to herself and popped the hopelessly tangled knitting in the waste-paper basket, guessing the cleaning woman would probably retrieve it, being blessed no doubt with enough patience to unwind and reuse the yarn. That was unless the woman was unfortunate enough to have hands which were back to front.

The headmistress was passing Miss Robinson's room on the way from her office when she heard a sound she had never heard before. She came back, unable to believe her ears. It was true. Miss Robinson was actually laughing.

Mary decided it was time to discuss Caroline with her daughter and did so the next time Jacqueline asked Caroline which bedtime story she would like.

'Jacqueline, I know Caroline has chosen you for her very best friend and you can see her. That's because you're a very special little girl, but no one else can see her. You might see more people like Caroline one day. I've seen some myself. But as it's a special thing it's nice to keep it just between the two of you and not share her with anybody else. They might think it's strange if you're speaking to someone they can't see.'

'All right. She gets me in trouble with Miss Robinson anyway. You can go away, Caroline, if you like. I've got Pam for a friend now.'

Mary smiled. 'Don't forget, only special people have friends no one else can see.' She sighed with relief. She didn't expect Caroline to be banished immediately, but it was a start. Jacqueline yawned and closed her eyes, bedtime story forgotten.

Chapter Nineteen

Ada Banwell inspected her reflection in the dressing-table mirror. The bruise on her cheekbone had faded from an angry reddish purple to a jaundiced yellow, and her lip was almost down to its normal size. Considering the injuries her husband had inflicted on Harry Holmes she knew she was fortunate to have escaped so lightly.

She was growing her hair back to its original colour and at present it was an assortment of shades, ranging from grey at the temples to brown roots and blonde ends. No wonder Harry had found himself a new girl, twenty years younger than herself. He deserved the chance of a good marriage and Ada had no regrets. The affair had been sensational while it lasted, and besides, he had given her the child she had longed for throughout her marriage.

After her husband's drunken attack on her, Ada had managed to lure the sailor back into her bed, and all that remained to be done now was to post off a letter containing news of the forthcoming event, to the man whose already inflated ego would no doubt swell to bursting point as he boasted of his wife's condition. Ada herself was elated. After all the years of hoping, and suffering the accusations of being the barren one, she now knew it was her husband's fault that their dreams of a child had for so long been unfulfilled. Not that he would ever know. It was a secret only she and Harry Holmes would share, and though rumours would no doubt spread, and the gossips would have a field day, no one would ever be able to prove that the child was not a premature result of the Christmas leave.

Ada was content at last. No more brash clothing or frequenting the Sun – from now on she was a respectable married mother-to-be, and the years of loneliness as a regular marine's wife were almost at an end. She patted her bloated stomach. All the gossipmongers in the world weren't going to be allowed to destroy the joy her child would bring. She smiled as she slipped into her nightie. Ada had been a perfect lover over the years; now she was about to become a perfect mother.

St George's Road boasted only three shops, the fish shop, the off-licence and Baraclough's, which was supposed to be a butcher's and grocer's, but sold almost everything under the sun. Mr Baraclough was his own perfect advert, having at least three chins and a rosy full-moon face. His blue and white butcher's smock was clean on each morning, and the bench in the corner where he cut the meat was scrubbed every evening so the wood was almost white.

Mr Baraclough could change character at the drop of a hat, or the swing of a cleaver to be more precise, adopting a posh accent for customers such as Mrs Davenport or Dr Sellers, dropping everything to give them his full attention so they were made to feel like VIPs. They were always served the crustiest loaf of bread or the tenderest joint and so charming was his manner that they never noticed the knack he had of throwing the merchandise on to the scale with enough force to weigh it down to the bottom, lifting it off, and wrapping it all in one action. It would often be a couple of ounces light, but his rich customers never questioned the jovial shopkeeper.

On the other hand Mr Baraclough was never happier than when he could be his normal self, and then his broad Yorkshire accent would surface, so that his poorest customers could enjoy a good gossip and a risqué joke or two. He was always good for a bit of credit towards the end of the week, when the bill would be entered in a tattered old accounts book which was kept beneath the counter. Being something of a Robin Hood, he would pop a free cow heel, a bacon hock which was beginning to turn or a bag of day or two old fancy cakes in with the orders for his worst-off customers, and many a good meal would be enjoyed by the poorest families thanks to his generosity.

Just inside the shop door, next to the Rinso and

the Lifebuoy, was a noticeboard on which customers could display small adverts free of charge. Mr Baraclough found a drawing pin as Mary produced a small slip of paper.

'What are we selling today then, Mary lass?' he enquired.

'Only my services, Mr Baraclough.' Mary smiled.

'Oh, taking up in business, are yer, lass? Don't let my missus see this or she'll be wanting another new frock.' He laughed.

Mrs Baraclough came out from the back. 'Is he talking about me again?' she said, smiling at Mary.

'Mary's taking up dressmaking, love,' he said.

'Well, if the dresses yon little lass wears are anything to go by she should do very well,' his wife said.

'I'm not doing too badly already,' Mary said proudly. 'I've even made curtains for Mrs Davenport this week. The trouble is I've no idea what to charge.'

'Aye, well, don't go underselling yerself. Start as yer mean to go on. An hour's work deserves an hour's pay, and don't you forget it.'

'That's what Jack says.' Mary helped herself to a bottle of dandelion and burdock. 'Can I have half an ounce of thin twist, please?' She placed the bottle on the counter.

'By, but it must be heartbreaking going down the pit this weather. We don't get many days like this.' Mr Baraclough looked out at the bright sunshine.

'I know,' said Mary. 'Our Jacqueline's changed into white ankle socks, though I think it's a bit early yet.'

210

'They're all alike. The first warm day and they think it's summer. Well, let's hope they're right and it keeps like this for Whitsuntide.'

Mrs Baraclough was weighing up two pound bags of sugar, meticulously placing an empty bag on the scale with the weights, so making sure that the bags contained exactly the right amount. One never knew when the weights and measures man was going to pop in, and unlike her husband she wasn't willing to take any risks.

Mary paid her bill and went home, wondering if she'd done the right thing by starting to advertise. It had been Gladys's suggestion, after Mary had run up a pair of pillow cases for one of her neighbours.

'You should start up in business, Mary. Your needlework is first class and there are always people wanting good quality garments, particularly for weddings.'

Mary had laughed but had thought about it afterwards, then decided nothing ventured nothing gained.

Jack wished secretly that Gladys had kept her mouth shut. The confounded machine had already taken over the front room, and the continuous droning noise was beginning to affect his nerves. Besides, until he had bought the thing Mary had always been eager to join him in bed for an hour when he was on night shift, if Alan happened to have an afternoon nap. Now he was lucky if he got chance of a quick cuddle in the mornings, before Jacqueline had to be woken for school.

There was no doubt about it, the bloody

machine was coming between him and his love life. He thought about what his father was always threatening. 'I'm going to put my foot down with a firm hand.' He grinned to himself. The old man had about as much chance of laying down the law to his wife as Jack had to Mary, for if she made up her mind to do something neither Jack nor the devil himself would stop her doing it. Still, he did miss a bit of a cuddle in the afternoon, and now she had gone and bloody advertised.

Fine quality dressmaking and alterations
undertaken at reasonable cost.

Aye, thought Jack, reasonable to the customer perhaps, but what about me?

Mary was quite oblivious of Jack's inner thoughts and only conscious that the biscuit barrel used as her piggy bank was becoming heavier. Every penny she earned from her sewing went into the barrel, and her aim was to save for a holiday with her parents. Jack was also halfway towards being able to afford the holiday and was already planning things for the last week in July and the first in August.

At first it had been meant to be a surprise for Mary and the children, who had never seen their maternal grandparents or aunts and uncles, though the wedding day photographs had familiarised the children with Mary's family, and presents were exchanged regularly. Jack had booked two caravans for the works holiday weeks on the east coast, after arranging with Mick O'Connor by letter that the two families would meet at the coast. But Mary, becoming suspicious of the communication, had wheedled out the secret, and was now working harder than ever, intent upon making the holiday a memorable one for all concerned.

But first there was Whitsuntide, and that in itself was a source of excitement for Jacqueline and Alan.

Jacqueline was sitting high on the counter in Miss Judith McCall's, which was the most exclusive ladies' shop outside the city. The little girl had often pressed her nose up to the glass, admiring the display of ladies' wear in one window and children's in the other. She was fascinated, not so much by the garments as by the colour schemes. She had already noticed there were never more than two colours in the displays at any one time, and had noted mentally how this added to the effect, rather than the hotch-potch of colours mixed together in the Co-op.

Now she was actually sitting on the counter trying on bonnets which tied under the chin with pretty satin ribbons, and were trimmed with rosebuds in contrasting colours.

'What do you think?' Mary asked the elegantly dressed middle-aged proprietress.

'With her dark curls I would definitely say the pink,' said Miss McCall, to Jacqueline's dismay.

Mary had brought with her a sample of the organdie which was to be made into the Whitsuntide dress. It was the most delicate shade of blue with tiny sprigs of white flowers.

'Ah,' said Judith McCall. 'Then I would suggest the blue.'

'I like that one.' Jacqueline pointed to a lemon one sitting on top of a hat box.

'Oh, I don't really think so, dear, not with blue.'

'But I like it. That's Caroline's favourite colour.'

The woman glanced at Mary, who changed the subject abruptly. 'We shall need two pairs of socks. Plain white, I think.'

'Oh, definitely.' Miss McCall went to a drawer and brought out two pairs of snowy white cotton socks.

'Thank you,' said Mary. 'And we'll take the blue bonnet.'

Jacqueline opened her mouth to protest but closed it again when she saw the look on her mother's face. Mary lifted her daughter down.

'And now it's Alan's turn.' Alan, unlike his sister, hated new clothes. Mary had already made up a pair of green trousers and intended to buy a green and white checked shirt which had caught her eye in the window. She knew she could have run one up more cheaply at home but she had been unable to find a similar pattern. She would be able to use this one to cut out another couple for Alan for when he began school after Christmas. Miss McCall suspected what Mary was up to but was biding her time. Mrs Holmes was making quite a name for herself amongst the locals, and having inspected some of her handiwork Miss McCall was considering offering to sell some of Mary's garments for her. Of course, they would have to be one-off designs – Miss McCall would never risk her reputation for exclusivity – but she prided herself on recognising good work when she saw it.

'I'll take this,' her customer was saying now. 'And socks for Alan too.'

'I've just the thing.' This time the socks Miss McCall brought out were white but with green stripes round the top.

'There you are,' Mary said to her son. 'Now you'll be all posh for the procession.' Alan was unimpressed.

'I do hope the weather holds,' Miss McCall said.

Mary paid for her goods, which were placed in bags bearing Judith McCall's name, and Alan skipped out of the door with relief.

'Caroline doesn't like blue,' said Jacqueline, but Mary noticed she opened the bag to peep at the bonnet at least four times before they reached the top of the Donkey Path.

Whit Monday dawned with the sun already warm and the sky clear and cloudless. The children couldn't wait to be dressed and Jacqueline refused to eat breakfast in her excitement, although nothing would put Alan off his food. The children were to gather at the various churches throughout the area, and then the procession would set off, each church joining in on the way, to assemble at the sports field where the singing would take place. St Catherine's was the exception: the Catholic children walked alone, along the road and back again. Una said the large communal procession was far more exciting. But first they were to go along Barker's Row showing off their new clothes to the neighbours, who would admire the children's apparel and place a few coppers in any available pockets. Mary had been embarrassed last year when Una had introduced the children to the ritual but Jack did not agree that it was tantamount to begging, and pointed out that the tradition was as old as the hills themselves.

Alan, who could now count up to five, sat down on the doorstep outside Mrs Broomsgrove's and became more and more confused as his pennies amounted to more than he could tally. He consoled himself by counting the threepenny bits, knowing that each of those would buy one large cornet from the ice-cream man.

Jacqueline held her pennies tightly in her hand and wondered where Tittle Harry was wandering off to, down in the direction of St George's Road. She called his name but he trotted determinedly on his way. Jacqueline went after him. He had been lost once before and the whole family had spent a couple of hours searching for him until he was found sleeping inside Mrs Broomsgrove's washing basket, curled up amongst the newly laundered sheets. The woman had almost suffered a seizure at the thought of a few dog hairs and had washed the whole lot again.

Tittle Harry wandered across the road and climbed on to the low drystone wall overlooking the river, where it emerged from beneath the wall to flow in the direction of the Donkey Wood.

When Jacqueline reached the wall and looked over, she saw that the spaniel had jumped down and was on his way to the water. Jacqueline called his name, afraid he would drown if he reached the river. She wondered what to do. The wall was far too deep for her to get down. Then she noticed the heap of black pebbles piled against the wall, and lowered herself over the topping stones before letting herself fall the last few feet.

Then, horror of horrors, she found herself sinking down until she was waist high in the pile, which was not pebbles but soot from a newly swept chimney. The soot rose in a cloud, covering her dress, her face and catastrophically her lovely new bonnet. She began to wail and Tittle Harry ran in her direction, barking as he came face to face with the black figure. Jacqueline didn't go over the wall this time but followed the path to the turnstile. Up Barker's Row she went, the dog circling her then backing away, not sure that he liked this screaming, soot-coated Jacqueline. Everyone in Barker's Row came out to stare, unable to believe the immaculate little girl could have changed into the grotesque object which was yelling now fit to awaken the dead.

Mary didn't know whether to laugh or cry, or where to begin cleaning up her daughter. She untied the bonnet and took off the once beautiful dress. Even the underclothes were black, so she removed them too, then lifted her naked daughter up into the stone sink in the corner of the kitchen, and began to scrub the yelling child as best she could. Jack watched helplessly, then went upstairs for a clean dress and underwear. Jacqueline cried louder at the sight of them.

'I don't want to wear them old things. I want my new dress and my new bonnet and my new shiny shoes.'

'You'll have to wear your pink dress,' Mary stated. 'It's almost new; nobody will know.'

Jack got out the blacking and brushes and

cleaned up the shoes.

'I don't want to go in the parade in these old things.'

'It's too late for the parade. They'll have set off from St Catherine's ten minutes ago,' Mary said.

Jacqueline seemed to cheer up at that. 'I didn't want to walk with them anyway,' she said. 'I wanted to walk with Pam.'

Jack began to grin. 'I don't think Father would like that,' he said. 'A Catholic marching with the Sally Army.' He lifted his daughter down and wrapped her in a towel, warm from the fire guard. 'Never mind, sweetheart, you'll look just as good in your pink, and we'll go and stand at the bottom of the Donkey Path. From there you'll be able to wave to our Una, and Pam, and everybody else in the procession. Besides, if you're not in the parade we'll be first at the ice-cream cart.'

Alan's face lit up. He hadn't fancied marching anywhere, and besides, now he would be able to see the band. 'But what about our dinner?' he worried.

'Well, I'm sure you won't starve, just because you can't go to Sunday school for a potted meat sandwich and a bun. I'll tell you what, we'll all go to Grandma Holmes's for our dinners. And up to the cricket field afterwards for the games as usual.' He caught sight of Mary, adjusting her new hat in the mirror, and at the sight of her thanked God that he wasn't on night shift for another two weeks.

Tittle Harry chewed another flower off the blue bonnet.

'Oh, you naughty boy,' Jacqueline cried as he

218

tussled with it under the table.

'Never mind,' Jack said. 'I'll buy you a new one when the shop opens after the holiday.'

'Can I have a yellow one?'

'Any colour you like,' Jack said. Jacqueline jumped with delight.

He's going to spoil that child, Mary thought. It's a good thing it's Whitsuntide or she'd have had a jolly good hiding. Then they set off down the Donkey Path to watch the Whit Monday walk.

The pile of cold meat sandwiches was colossal and the jar of pickled onions opened ready for the makeshift dinner. Most of the men had called at the miners' club for a couple of drinks and the wives and children were already gathered round the table. Grandma Holmes had pulled out a couple of drawers in the dresser and placed a cushion on top of each to create two extra seats for the little ones. She mashed the tea and poured it thick and strong into the best china cups. There was nothing she enjoyed more than seeing all her family together, and this was an extra special occasion because Harry was back amongst them, and almost his old self again. Sally was now a regular visitor and although the Holmeses suspected he wasn't quite what her parents had hoped for, Sally had given them no option but to accept him. At least they admitted he was a likeable chap, and seemed to be good for their daughter.

At the table Great-aunt Edie and Great-aunt Nellie, who had walked several miles with the great-uncles for their annual visit, were already tucking into the sandwiches. Jacqueline couldn't help but laugh as Auntie Edie sweetened her tea with salt from the huge open salt pot instead of sugar. Then Auntie Nellie stabbed a pickled onion and sent it flying into the air, to land with a plop in Auntie Margaret's tea. Jacqueline liked the great-aunts, who reminded her of Cissie and Susie, two of Farmer Barker's hens, mainly because they always wore brown hats trimmed with feathers, and seemed to nod their heads each time they spoke. Alan was also glad to see the great-aunts, who seemed to have a never-ending supply of mint humbugs in their large, closely guarded handbags. Grandma Holmes said Great-aunt Nellie always carried her last will and testament in her bag, and never let it out of her sight for a minute, but Jacqueline didn't know what a last will and testament was. She would ask her dad when they got home. If it was something very special perhaps they could buy Mammy one for Christmas.

The men could be heard long before they came into view. Grandma Holmes said they were hypocrites to be singing 'Onward Christian Soldiers' when everyone knew what their views on religion were, but seeing as it was Whit Monday she didn't intend risking a discussion on the clergy and the afterlife, so she let their hymn singing pass without comment.

After dinner the whole family made their way up to the field, which was already crowded in anticipation of the races and games. Jack was chosen for the cricket team and Mary organised a game of skipping for the women and children.

Others were lining up for the obstacle race and the older folk made themselves comfortable on the grandstand to watch the fun and wish they were twenty years younger.

It wasn't until much later that Mary noticed that Jack was out of the game and went in search of him.

'Have you seen your brother, Harry?' she called.

Harry looked a little uncomfortable as he denied having done so. 'Er, not for some time,' he said. 'He was bowled out early on.'

Mary smiled and circled the field in search of her husband. Perhaps he had taken the children for refreshments. She went towards the pavilion, then stopped. There, stretched out on the grass, was Jack. By his side was a young woman. Mary couldn't quite place her, but had seen her before, noticing how attractive the girl was, and today with the sun playing in her long fair hair she looked even more beautiful. She was holding a buttercup beneath Jack's chin and the pair were laughing, with eyes only for each other. Mary was at a loss what to do. Should she go to them, break up the conversation, or walk away? Her stomach was churning. Had it been Harry she could have understood it, but not Jack, please God, not Jack. She looked round for the children. They were watching the Punch and Judy show; she heard their cries 'He's behind you' as if in a daze.

Please not Jack. Then she questioned herself, 'Why not Jack?' He was a hot-blooded man, wasn't he, a highly sexed man, until recently. She was shocked when she realised it had been a couple of weeks now. Last week had been the morning shift but even then she had stayed up till all hours finishing off the orders for Whitsuntide, children's dresses, a suit for Mrs Baraclough; it had been early morning by the time she crept into bed beside her sound asleep husband. And the week before he had been on the afternoon shift. Why, she couldn't remember the last time she'd snuggled up with Jack for a cuddle. What a fool she had been. She felt a stirring in her loins and turned in the direction of Jack and the girl. He sat up in a rush as she approached.

'Oh, there you are.' Mary fixed a smile on her face. 'Do you mind if I reclaim my husband?' she said pleasantly to the girl. 'I think it's time for tea.'

Jack jumped up and brushed the grass from his best suit. 'I was just coming, love,' he stammered.

'Good,' said Mary, taking his hand. 'The fresh air has made me quite hungry, and all that skipping seems to have been good for me. I'm quite looking forward to an early night. How about you?'

Jack grinned. 'Ready when you are,' he said. Then they went hand in hand to find the children.

It was only after the early night that Jack began to analyse Mary's lack of concern at discovering him and Joan Edwards frolicking on the grass. The flirting had all been on Joan's part and meant nothing to Jack, he being a little tipsy after a few beers, but Mary hadn't been aware of that. If only she'd looked slightly upset, or ranted and raved at him afterwards. He told himself it was good that his wife trusted him, but that gave him

222

little consolation. In fact for someone who was supposed to love him, he considered it bloody unnatural not to be just a tiny little bit jealous.

Chapter Twenty

Clutching a brightly coloured sand bucket and a long-handled wooden spade Alan skipped ahead as they approached the station. He was going on a train, a real train, with a real steam engine. In fact he was going on three trains. Daddy had shown him and Jacqueline on a thing called a map. First they would change at Sheffield and then at York. He had never been so excited and had eaten no breakfast at all in his eagerness to be off.

Jacqueline walked more sedately and was rather subdued at the thought of leaving Tittle Harry behind, though Auntie Marjory and Una had promised to take care of him, and he was already firmly established in his basket under the table in Auntie Marjory's kitchen. She carried a little leather attaché case in which she had packed a new box of crayons, a drawing book, her favourite Milly Molly Mandy stories and a brand new bathing costume bought for her from Old Misery's stall. She felt grown up with the case and walked beside her parents wondering how much further it was to the station. Her legs were beginning to ache, but Alan, usually the one to lag behind and beg to be carried, for once danced happily ahead, stopping at intervals to call for the others to hurry.

The small station was already quite crowded with families and luggage, everyone eager to be off for the annual holiday. Because of the war this was the first time many children had been away and their anticipation of their first glimpse of the sea filled children and parents alike with excitement. The bucket and spade were still clutched in Alan's plump, hot little hands when they changed trains at Sheffield. He had reclined mesmerised in the corner seat as bridges and signal boxes were left behind. The roll of the train and the steady da da da dum, da da da dum filled him with exhilaration, and now the huge bustling platform with its guards, porters and muffled announcements seemed awe-inspiring to so small a boy.

'Cawwy my spade, Jacqween,' he said, handing it to his sister so that he could cling tightly to his mother's skirt. The bustling crowd was overwhelming, and to lose himself and miss the train was unthinkable. He heard the announcer's voice, 'The train for York is now standing at platform two.' Jack trundled the luggage across the platform, with Mary and the children following closely, and Alan sighed with relief when his father threw the cases up on to the rack and the guard slammed the compartment door closed.

Jacqueline was already colouring a picture of a vivid blue sea, like one she had seen in a picture book. A golden beach and an even more golden sun completed the scene. Then she settled down to watch the colours rolling by. Vivid greens of hills and woodland, reds and slate greys of houses and churches. Cottages each with its own pocket handkerchief vegetable patch or flower bed. Cattle and sheep grazing and looking up as the train disturbed their peace. Sometimes the countryside was obliterated by high bankings strewn with wild flowers, or thick clouds of smoke from the engine. She picked up a crayon, her mind unable to rest, her fingers itching to transfer the beauty of the passing scenery on to the pages. She would make a picture for Grandma O'Connor, and another for Grandad. She forgot about Tittle Harry for the moment. She was on her way to the sea, and her grandparents, and to live in a caravan. The excitement poured out on to the pages, and best of all there was no school for six whole weeks, and no more Miss Robinson; she would be moving up to another class and another teacher.

Sunny Cliff Camp spread along the cliff top, just a short walk from the town, a spreading mass of caravans and wooden bungalows. It was a well-kept camp, with water taps and lavatories at regular intervals. The children were fascinated by the cream and green trailer, and by the fact that they would be sleeping in a bed which folded up during the day to make a sofa.

A few tears were shed by Mary and her mother at their first meeting since the wedding. Before long the children and their grandparents became inseparable and after the first night Mary and Jack had the caravan to themselves as the children crammed into the beds of Jimmy and Michael and Norah and Kathleen. Only Mary's eldest brother Bill was missing, as he was in the middle of training for a new job and unable to take leave. Jimmy said it was a girl who was the main reason for his absence.

At the first sight of the sea Jacqueline had looked down from the cliff top and burst into tears. Mick O'Connor had been most concerned and unable to fathom out what was bothering his granddaughter.

'I don't like the sea. It isn't blue and it hasn't any waves. It isn't a proper sea at all,' she cried.

'Is that all?' Mick laughed. 'Why I admit it isn't blue today, but that's oonly because the sky's so grey. Just you watch it cheange when the sun comes oot. And as for the weaves, oh, they're there all right. It's just that we can't see them from way up here. Come on doon and I'll show you.'

The pair had slid down the cliff path to the sands, kicked off their shoes and socks, and paddled through the rocky pools to the edge of the sea, where the waves tumbled gently, breaking into white foam around their feet. Jacqueline looked up at her grandfather, her face filled with delight, as she felt the rippled sand beneath her toes. He lifted her high and let her slip down into the water, so that it splashed their bare arms and faces, and they laughed, and made up for the irreclaimable years, a little girl and her grandfather together at last.

Alan was soon following Michael about like a shadow, and Michael at the age of eleven and normally ignored by his older brothers was made to feel important and flattered by his nephew's attention. After a few days on the beach they found themselves a far more interesting pastime, in the shape of a battered old bus. It had been used at one time as a caravan but now stood derelict in the

226

corner of the field. Only the engine was missing, and in their imagination the two youngsters drove to many mysterious places, working the controls and steering in turn. It was only at mealtimes and during the evenings when a visit was made to the amusement arcades that the two friends could be coaxed away from the rusty, dusty old bus.

Most of the other campers seemed to be Scots. They were a lively bunch and each night one of the party would bring out an accordion, supplying the accompaniment for singing and even dancing. Mary's sisters pronounced themselves madly in love with a couple of youths from Glasgow, and Jimmy spent each day of the holiday in the camp snack bar, waiting for the pretty blue-eyed assistant to finish work, when they would go off hand in hand in the direction of Sewerby or Flamborough Head. Grandma O'Connor seemed to spend all her days resting her swollen, blue-veined legs in a deckchair on the beach and all her nights worrying about her wayward offspring, but by the end of the holiday the tension had left her. Her nose became tinged with the sun, and her husband brought a flush to her cheeks by declaring she looked as beautiful as the day he married her all those years ago.

On the last day Mary and Jack managed to bribe Alan and Michael away from their imaginary travels with the offer of a boat trip. As they all sailed out on the *Yorkshire Man*, leaving the harbour walls behind, Jack placed an arm round his wife's waist. 'Oh well, it's nearly over, love,' he sighed. 'It'll soon be back to the black hole.'

'Oh, Jack,' Mary said. 'I'd give anything for you

not to have to go back to the pit.'

'It's not all that bad. They're a grand bunch of lads – nobody could have better mates.'

'It's not that, it's just that after all this – the fresh salt air, the sunshine – to leave all the long light days and go back to the darkness, it's just not natural.'

His arm tightened round her slim waist and he smiled down at his wife. Her hair shone like burnished copper in the sun and her freckles seemed more pronounced than ever, and he couldn't resist kissing her. Giggling, she pulled away and he said, 'So long as I've you and the kids to come home to I'm content.'

'Yes, well, we'll just keep on sending in the pools, and when our eight draws come up the pit won't see you for coal dust.' She laughed.

'What would we do then?' he asked wistfully.

'We'd come back here, and buy the house up there at the edge of the cliffs, the one with the veranda, and each night we'd sit there and watch the sun go down.'

'And then we'd go in,' he said, 'to our four-poster bed and make love until the sun came up again.'

'You know something, Jack Holmes, you're nothing but a randy old man.'

'I may be randy, but less of the old.' He laughed and kissed her again.

Young Michael turned at that moment and whispered to Jacqueline. 'Hey, look at yer ma and da, kissing right here on the booat where everybody can see them.'

Jacqueline smiled happily. She liked her mammy and daddy to kiss each other: it gave her a safe

228

happy feeling inside. She liked the seaside and she loved her grandma and grandad but she would like to get home to see Tittle Harry again. Last night she had dreamed that he had come to see her; Grandad Holmes had brought him. There they had stood at the bottom of her bed, Tittle Harry wagging his tail and Grandad smiling, then suddenly Grandad had taken off his cloth cap and waved goodbye, fading away into the darkness, leaving Tittle Harry to trot off all by himself, his lead trailing behind him. She would be glad to return home and make sure they were both safe.

It is said that no one can be completely happy for long. The saying was proved correct the moment the train drew into the station, for there on the platform Harry was waiting with the news that his father had passed away. The worn old lungs had refused to cope any longer and during a coughing spasm his heart had been unable to stand the strain. Jacqueline was the only one who didn't cry. She had seen her grandfather waving goodbye. He had been smiling then, and she had a feeling he was smiling still.

Grandad Holmes was laid out in the front room by a woman from the next row who specialised in bringing new babies into the world, and helping the bereaved when their loved ones went out of it. She would stay there every night until the day of the funeral, keeping the body company. If Grandma Holmes hadn't been in mourning she would probably have smiled. She could almost imagine her husband sitting up in his coffin and saying, 'What the bloody hell is she doing here?

Does she think I'm going to run away or summat?'

Nevertheless, the woman insisted on staying, and was made most comfortable in the easy chair with a bottle of sherry to fortify her through the night.

During the day a steady stream of visitors called at the house to pay their respects to the widow and her family, and the teapot was no sooner emptied than filled again. Some of the callers would pop in for a last look at their old friend; others would reminisce and attempt to cheer up the family by relating some amusing incident which had happened years before, but almost all would need to wipe away a tear or two at the passing of a dear friend and neighbour.

The women were kept busy preparing for the funeral tea. A ham had been put on to boil and fruit cakes and bread were baked non-stop on the day before the burial. Grandma Holmes left the girls to it, knowing Margaret, her youngest, had taken it the hardest and needed to be kept busy. The children, who had never experienced death before, were constantly under their feet and instructed to go out and play.

'Why can't we go in the front room, Una?' Jacqueline was filled with curiosity about what all the visitors were going to look at.

'Because Grandad's in there.'

'But Grandad's dead. I thought they'd taken him to the graveyard.'

'Not until tomorrow.'

'Let's go and see him,' Jacqueline whispered. 'I've never seen a dead person before.'

'Get lost!' Una cringed. 'You're not getting me

in there.'

Alan circled the yard on his red tricycle chanting, 'Grandad Holmes is deaded, Grandad Holmes is deaded.'

'Well, I'm going to see him anyway.' Jacqueline ignored her brother.

'You daren't.' It was the wrong thing to say. Una should have known better than to dare her cousin to do anything.

'Oh yes I dare,' Jacqueline said, and went towards the house. The kitchen was filled with yet more visitors. The under-manager from the pit and his wife had brought money which had been collected from the workers. Because these were posher visitors than normal everybody was giving them their full attention, and Jacqueline simply sidled in between the table and the dresser and through the kitchen door unnoticed. Her step faltered as she opened the front room door and the strong scent filled her nostrils.

She saw the flowers first, some arranged in a large glass vase, others placed on the table, large bunches tied with ribbons and covered with cellophane. And then she saw the box, something like Grandma Roberts's blanket box only longer. There it was perched on the table amongst the flowers, too high for her to see inside. She moved a chair towards the table, cringing as the complete silence was shattered by its scraping on the lino'd floor. For the first time she experienced fear as she wondered what a dead body looked like. She forced herself to climb up and peep into the coffin.

'Oh, Grandad,' she whispered. 'You do look nice and clean.'

His normally wispy hair had been flattened and his lined old face seemed to have been smoothed and the wrinkles ironed out. He looked to be almost in a sitting position, probably because his hunched back wouldn't allow for lying straight out, and Jacqueline could have sworn he was wearing a smile. She reached out and touched the white garment he was wearing and then her heart almost missed a beat as she gently touched his cheek. Suddenly she felt happy. She was glad she'd seen a dead body; there was nothing to be frightened of. She jumped down off the chair and lifted it back to its place by the window, then slipped out closing the door behind her.

'Well,' Una said, 'I'll bet you didn't go in.'

'I did,' Jacqueline said. 'And I wasn't scared at all. I saw him and I wasn't frightened even a little bit.'

'What're you on about?' asked the boy from the end house.

'She's been to see our grandad who's dead.'

'My grandad's deaded,' said Alan. 'He's gone to Jesus.'

'No he hasn't. I've seen him. He's going to Heaven tomorrow.'

'What did he look like?' Una enquired, rather wishing she'd been brave enough to go with her cousin.

Jacqueline shrugged. 'Just like Grandad,' she said, 'only different.'

'Can I go and 'ave a look?' the boy asked.

'No.'

'Oh, go on, just a peep.'

'No.'

'I'll give yer tuppence,' he said, knowing how he would rise in status with the gang if he could boast about seeing a dead body. 'Go on, Jacqui. I liked yer grandad. Let me 'ave a look.'

'It's not worth it, not for twopence.' Jacqueline had her eye on a jar on the window sill. 'What's in there?' she asked.

'A butterfly, a Red Admiral, go on let's 'ave a look.' By now it had almost become an obsession. 'I'll mek it threepence,' he said.

'Well perhaps just a little look, but only if you give me the butterfly.'

His face fell, he opened his mouth to protest and Jacqueline turned to walk away.

'OK, you can 'ave the butterfly,' he said.

'Come on then, but you'll have to be quiet, and wait until they aren't looking.' Grandma Holmes suddenly came out and went across the yard to the lavatory. Jacqueline looked into the kitchen. Her mother was on her knees in front of the fire, polishing the brass fender, and Auntie Margaret was nowhere in sight. The cellar door was open; she was probably down there.

'Come on,' she whispered, and the pair tiptoed behind the table unseen.

Once in the room Jacqueline watched proudly as the boy, taller than herself, peered over the side of the coffin. His face whitened and he turned and crept out, Jacqueline making sure the coast was clear before they made their way back through the kitchen.

'Blooming 'eck,' he said. 'I don't 'alf feel funny. I thought I were going to roll over in there.'

'I'm glad you didn't or I wouldn't half have been in trouble,' Jacqueline said. 'Now can I have my butterfly?'

Reluctantly he parted with the jar. Eeh, but it would be worth it when he told all the gang what he had seen. She was all right that Jacqueline Holmes, a right good sport. He would stick up for her in future.

Jacqueline studied the perfection of the fragile wings, memorising every colourful detail for future reference. She would paint a butterfly picture tonight when she got home. She unscrewed the pierced lid, walked up to the top of the yard where the banking began and released the trembling butterfly. It fluttered uncertainly, then made its escape to rest amongst the moonpennies and clover. She heard the boy from the end house utter a swear word worse than any Grandad Holmes had ever used, but she didn't care so long as the butterfly was free. Besides, just because he swore it didn't mean she didn't like him. He had liked her grandad enough to go and look at him when he was dead, and any friend of Grandad Holmes could be her friend too.

She ran down the yard and joined the queue for hopscotch.

'You can have my best piece of slate if you like,' she said to her new friend.

'Wow, thanks, Jacqui,' he said, and threw the heavy grey slate across to where it landed with a slight slither in number eight square. He grinned at the slightly built girl with the large brown eyes and the lovely smile. 'I like yer 'air,' he said.

She blushed to the roots of it, and a close

implausible friendship was sealed; between the scruffy ragamuffin Freddie Cartwright, the youngest of a family of ten, and the immaculately dressed Jacqueline.

Freddie grinned, wiped his nose on the bit of sleeve which was still minus a hole, and set off with a hop from one square to the next, intent on showing off to his new friend.

Chapter Twenty-One

Pepper nuzzled his nose into Jacqueline's hair as she brushed his mane perched on an old chair bottom which she had found in the shed. She was tempted to mount the docile old horse and trot along the lane, but Grandma Roberts had forbidden her to ride without a companion and she must wait for Douglas Downing. Douglas had taken over from his brother Cyril who had recently started work in the steel works in Millington. She was sorry for Cyril, who like his father was more suited to farm-work, but he had decided a steel worker's pay was more adequate to his needs. No one except Jacqueline knew his ambition was to own a farm of his own one day, and he had confided not so much in the girl as in the horse, whom he conversed with as if it was human.

'One day I'll be grooming a horse or two of my own, just like you, owd boy,' he had said. 'And on me own farm and all.' Then he had become all serious and sad. 'But until that day comes I'll 'ave to put up with it over yonder in't sweatshop.'

Jacqueline had missed Cyril a lot until Douglas had begun to help at Moorland House. He seemed to be there every weekend and after school each day and had proved to be every bit as industrious as his brothers before him. Now being hay-making time and the school holidays he was working all day alongside his father, and Jacqueline would just have to be patient until he arrived. She wished he would hurry; she really liked Doug. She decided to climb the rocks above the house and walk even higher on the moor. The heather was purple and sweet and she trod the bracken into a path. As she walked she searched for insects, large lazy moths and scarlet ladybirds. She could hear the grouse calling, and worried when shots on the distant hill could be heard. She knew that each gunshot probably meant the death of another bird. Some of the boys from the village would be working as beaters, disturbing the bracken to send the birds fleeing into the air and almost certain death. Jacqueline knew none of the Downings would entertain such sport and that Douglas would be up here as soon as he could. She picked a handful of bilberries, large, juicy and almost black. She wondered if Grandma Roberts would use them to make a crumble for tea, but by the time she had slid down to the house again most of them had either been eaten or squashed into a purple pulp, so she finished off the rest of them and wiped her hands on the grass. She went in through the back, into the glass lean-to where the pungent heady scent of chrysanthemums tickled her nose, causing her to sneeze. Grandma

Roberts was humming to herself and Jacqueline wondered if she would allow her to play the piano. 'Can I practise my lessons, Grandma?' she asked.

'Of course, love.' Gladys came from the kitchen, bringing her mending with her. 'When you've washed your hands.' Jacqueline did so, then followed Gladys into the lounge and sat on the velvet-topped piano stool. Gladys placed the music book on the rest, and Jacqueline opened it to the page on which the music started.

Gladys had led her through the first exercises and Jacqueline had already mastered the simplest pieces. She began the first one, saying to herself as she played, 'Thumb two two thumb two two, one four four one two one,' and so on until she finished the tune.

Gladys clapped and said, 'Bravo,' and the little girl flushed with pleasure. She began the second piece, and faltered as a breeze wafted in through the open window, mingling and enhancing the fragrance of flowers and Mansion polish.

'Now now,' said Gladys. 'You're losing your concentration.'

'I couldn't help it. I was just wondering.'

'Wondering about what?' Gladys knew that Jacqueline's active mind was always wondering about one thing or another.

'Well, Una says that in Heaven there are many mansions. I was wondering if they all have to be cleaned with Mansion polish.'

Gladys stifled a smile. 'I shouldn't be at all surprised,' she said.

Jacqueline sighed contentedly, and thought that if Heaven was half as peaceful as Moorland

House, Grandad Holmes must be a very happy man. In fact she wished she could live here for ever.

The school seemed eerie and unfamiliar without the bustle of normal everyday activities, and Jacqueline's leather soles seemed to echo on the long marble corridor. She stopped at a door marked *Examination Room* and went in. The desks, which were normally placed together in rows, had been set apart so that a large space separated each from the next. Some early arrivals were already seated, most wearing expressions of extreme anxiety, others simply waiting for the day to end, knowing that even if they were lucky enough to pass it was unlikely their parents would be able to afford new uniforms and other grammar school essentials.

Jacqueline found a vacant place near the window, where she could look out at the tree tops and the clouds which were gathering, low and dark as though a storm was brewing. She hoped it wasn't a bad omen. Not that she had any qualms about passing the County Minor. She had found the attainment tests easy, and had no doubt she would end up at grammar school rather than moving up to the senior section. The only thing worrying her was that Pam might not pass, and it was inconceivable that she and her best friend should be parted.

The papers were placed face downwards on the desks and the signal was given to begin. Remembering Grandad Roberts's advice she glanced through the papers from beginning to end, so that

238

any problem she was unsure of could be left until last. Satisfied that she was capable of completing the lot she began at the beginning, finishing with time to spare. Jacqueline looked across to where Pam was crouched over the paper, her arm circling her work, her face set in concentration. If she didn't pass it would be the English paper which let her down, and Jacqueline willed her to complete the paper successfully. She was growing restless waiting for the finishing time and began composing a poem about the scene outside. She could hear a blackbird's song echoing, as though rain was on its way, which gave her inspiration. The problem was that after a few lines she had forgotten the beginning. If only she could jot it down.

'Time's up.' The man's voice startled her, and the shuffling of papers began. 'Now you may go home,' he said, after carefully collecting the exam papers, and the candidates hurried thankfully out into the corridor.

It wasn't until they had descended the stairs and reached the playground that Jacqueline asked Pam, 'Well, how did it go?'

Pam rolled her eyes. 'Don't ask,' she groaned.

'Oh, come on, it wasn't all that bad, was it?'

'I don't suppose so, except for the second part of the English paper.'

'Ah, the part about adverbs. I was uncertain about that at first.'

'Really? Well, there isn't much hope for me then, is there?'

'What answers did you give?' Jacqueline asked.

'I can't even remember the question now.'

'We had to name three adverbs of time.'

'Oh, yes. Now, Then and Yesterday, and I'm sure they're wrong.'

'Well, if your answers are wrong mine must be too.'

Pam cheered up. 'Why, what did you put down?'

'Soon, Then and Tomorrow.'

'Do you think we were right, then?'

'We'll just have to wait and see, but I think so.'

'Well that's a relief.'

The friends linked arms and skipped down the school drive.

'Shall we go to the flicks tonight?' Pam asked.

'I'm not sure I can. My mam is measuring Una and me for our bridesmaid dresses.'

'Not another wedding. You've already been bridesmaids once, lucky things.'

'Our Una's been one twice already, and you know what they say, three times a bridesmaid, never a bride. Though I can't see her being left an old maid somehow.'

'Me neither. She's certainly a beauty, your cousin.'

'She's thinking of entering the Miss Millington competition, though my mam seems to think she's heading for trouble, and she might be right. I saw her down by the air-raid shelter the other night whilst I was walking Tittle Harry, and she was with a man. He looked ever so old, twenty at least, and you'll never guess what he was doing.'

Pam was all ears. 'What?'

Jacqueline whispered confidentially, 'He had his hand inside her brassiere.'

Pam gasped. 'What happened then?'

'Why, she buttoned up her blouse immediately

240

she saw me, of course.'

Pam giggled. 'What did you do?'

'Pretended I hadn't noticed, but it made me feel all hot, like ... well, like when I see Gregory Peck on the pictures.'

'I know what you mean. The new teacher has the same effect on me. Though I would never let anyone touch me,' she hastened to add, 'not even him.' She climbed on to the low wall and balanced her way along its narrow surface, jumping the gates as she came to them. 'Anyway, who's getting married this time?'

'Auntie Margaret. She's only known him a few weeks but he's lovely, almost as lovely as Gregory Peck. My mam says she's never seen her so happy. It's a case of love at first sight, she says. Oh, and you're being invited, she's promised.'

'Really?' Pam jumped down. 'I've never been to a wedding.'

'Never?' Jacqueline was shocked. 'If I'd known you could have come to Uncle Harry's. Oh, that was a lovely wedding. Auntie Sally looked absolutely beautiful. She's having a baby, though I'm not supposed to know, only Una told me.'

'She'll be having a baby herself if she keeps letting men put their hands inside her brassiere,' Pam said knowingly.

The two friends paused when they reached the top of Pam's street and Pam said, 'It seems strange being home from school so early.'

'Yes. We should have an exam every day,' Jacqueline replied.

'Oh, give over. It's OK for you being the brainy one but I haven't slept properly for ages.'

241

'I'm sure you've passed. Anyway, if you haven't I'm not going either.'

'Oh yes you are. You know how determined you are to be a teacher. Grammar school is the only way you'll make it.'

'No it isn't. We can both sit for the tech next year.'

'Hmm, and what if I fail that too? No, you must go, you know you've set your heart on it. Besides, your mother'll have a fit if you don't.'

'Well then, we'll just pray we've both passed.'

'Let's go to the flicks. Can't your mum measure you now? After all, we are home earlier than usual. I'll bet if Gregory Peck was on you'd make the effort.'

Jacqueline giggled. 'Well, I'll try. If I can I'll call for you at five. I quite like Dana Andrews too.'

Pam grinned. 'I'll keep my fingers crossed then.'

'Ta-ra then. I hope to see you later,' Jacqueline called as the friends went their separate ways, one dreaming of having been lucky enough to scrape through the County Minor, the other to ponder on the attractions of Dana Andrews in comparison to those of Gregory Peck.

Chapter Twenty-Two

In September Jacqueline and Pam began the new term at the grammar school several miles away. Pam's parents had gratefully accepted the offer from Mary Holmes to run up school blouses and gym tunics free of charge, an enormous saving to a family whose income was small in comparison to a miner's.

Grandma Roberts had treated the friends to new leather satchels as rewards for passing, and given Jacqueline a lecture on the theme of the harder she worked now, the easier she would find the road to university. But that seemed too far in the future to be important now. Nevertheless, the girl was naturally conscientious and seemed determined to do her best.

For Pam it was a different matter and she was to find the going much more difficult. Without her friend's help and encouragement she would no doubt have been left trailing behind.

It was soon after this that Bill Bacon heard the rumours about Una. He had worried for some time about the change in his daughter. The amiable outgoing girl had suddenly become sullen and secretive. She had also taken to wearing scarlet lipstick and rouge, which according to Marjory made her look like a tart.

It was the landlord at the Rising Sun who had

put Bill in the picture. 'You ought to do summat about yon lass of yours, Bill lad,' he said, as Bill had his tankard refilled during a darts match.

'Our Una? Why, I didn't know you knew her,' Bill said, surprised.

'I don't, but there isn't much that goes on as I don't hear about over the bar.'

'You mean they've been talking about my lass in here?'

'I'm sorry to say they have, and it isn't nice what they've been saying, especially a well brought up young lass like yours.'

'Well, what are they saying? Out with it, man.'

'Well, it's a bit embarrassing like, seeing as she's only sixteen, and 'im a married man.'

'What?' Bill made a grab at the man's shirt front.

''Ere, 'old on, lad, it's nought to do with me.'

'I'm sorry.' Bill let the man go. 'Just tell me what you've heard, that's all. Just tell me his name.'

'Con Shaunessy, I think that's the name he's known as. Lodging down in't prefabs by what I've heard.'

Bill downed his drink in one go, slammed a handful of change on the bar and left. He could hear the landlord calling, 'Now don't go mentioning my name, I've me business to consider.' But he was on his way. He knew quite a few folks from the prefabs. They were mostly young married couples on the list for a council house, and eager to escape from in-laws. The prefabs were not the ideal accommodation but at least they meant privacy and were a step towards something better.

He guessed the lodger would be with one of the

older occupants so that whittled down the search. The stench of stewing cabbage greeted him as he made his way down the rough track which served as a road. He knew Big Bessie lived at the far end, and she was the most likely to take in lodgers.

Big Bessie was built like a house side, as broad as she was long, but Bill always wondered if it was because of her size that she had been so named or because of her big-heartedness. After he knocked, the doorway was suddenly filled with an outsized wraparound pinafore housing a gigantic bosom, and Big Bessie let out a squeal of delight at the sight of Bill. Then she drew him into arms which would have been the pride of any male wrestler and cushioned him to her breast. 'Why, if it isn't me owd love Bill Bacon.' She gave him a wet slobbery kiss and pulled him inside. 'Don't stand on the doorstep like a stone statue. Bring yerself in, lad,' she said.

'I'd better before you either swallow me or smother me.' Bill laughed, forgetting for the moment the reason he was here.

'Well this is a surprise. Why, lad, I don't think I've seen you since the day yer owd mother was buried, God rest her soul. Eeh but we had some good owd chinwags, yer mother an' me. Fifty years we lived next door and never 'ad a wrong word, not that we allus saw eye to eye, and we 'ad some right grand argumentations at times. Eeh, but we allus enjoyed 'em, and we was allus there when we was needed. Did she ever tell yer?'

Bill knew that once Bessie got going about the old days she would carry on for hours, and he decided to interrupt. 'Bessie love, I'd love to stay and listen but I'm in a bit of a hurry and it's getting late.'

'Well then, lad, if you 'aven't come for a bit of a chinwag an' a pot of tea, what 'ave yer come for?'

'I came to ask, have you a lodger here by the name of Shaunessy?'

'Two of 'em. Depends if you want Cornelius or Patrick?'

'Oh.' Bill was taken aback. 'Well, I guess it'll be Cornelius if he's known as Con.'

'That's 'im, the youngest: good-looking feller. Now if I was only forty years younger... Mind you, I think 'e's kissed the Blarney stone, talk about gift of the gab. I'll bet 'is wife was glad of a bit of peace when 'e left.'

Bill could feel his temper rising. 'Is he a married man then?'

'Oh aye, an' according to Paddy 'e's a couple of kids an' all, though it doesn't stop 'im sowing a few wild oats over 'ere by all accounts. I could 'ear 'em last weekend, 'aving a right argument-ation they were. Yer see, Paddy doesn't agree wi' all the carryings-on.'

'Where is he, Bessie, do you know?'

'At work, lad. On'y comes 'ome on a Friday, goes back on a Monday morning. Works on a new road somewhere or other. Now, did yer mother ever tell yer about when our owd men went to build the reservoir? They–'

'Yes, I think she did, Bessie love. Anyway, I'll have to be going.'

'Aye well, come again, lad, and don't be so long next time.'

246

She followed Bill to the door, still chattering fifty to the dozen. Bill wondered which of them managed to get the most words in, Bessie or the one who had kissed the Blarney stone. Once again he was clutched to Bessie's cushiony bosom, and slobbered on in the way Tittle Harry used to welcome visitors.

'I'll show yer round me prefab next time yer come. Mind you, it's only temp'ry until the owd folks' bungalows are ready, but it saves me poor legs going up an' down stairs.'

Bill made his farewell for the umpteenth time and thought it was perhaps a good thing the Irish navvies were away. It wouldn't be fair to upset Bessie by causing an upheaval. No, he would bide his time till the weekend. In the meantime he would see what Una had to say for herself, and if she gave him any of the cheek he had been getting lately she had better watch out. He had never laid a finger on her yet but by God it wasn't too late to start.

'Where's our Una?' Bill asked when he got home.

'Over at Jean's. They've got a new radiogram and they're practising a new dance or something.'

'I'll make her dance when I've done with her.'

Amazed at her husband's uncharacteristic outburst, Marjory switched off the radio. 'Why, what's wrong?'

'She's only carrying on with a married man, and an Irish one at that.'

'What? Oh, Bill, she can't be, she must not know.'

'I expect that'll be her excuse, but she's sixteen,

247

Marje – she must know he's too old for her. Besides, she's so bloody secretive. We should have known something was in the wind.'

Marjory started to cry.

'It's no use crying, it's too late for that. She's been spoilt, I've always said so. Everything she asked for, you made sure she got it, and she never lifted a finger for you in return. You've made a right mess of bringing up your daughter.'

'Oh yes, blame me.' Marjory sobbed. 'You never complained when she was receiving applause in the school play, or when she landed a reception-ist's job, even though none of the other girls got set on. She was your darling daughter then; now the first time she puts a foot wrong, she's mine.'

Neither of them heard the door open. Una, looking apprehensive at the raised voices, walked over to the radio and turned the knob to Radio Luxembourg.

'Switch that off,' Bill roared.

'Why? I always listen to it.'

'Sit down.'

Una sat down with a flop in the nearest chair.

'How long has it been going on, then?'

'What? I don't know what you mean.'

'Don't you? Well then you must be the only one in Millington who doesn't.' Una paled as her father came up to her. 'Con Shaunessy, that's who I'm on about. A married man with two youngsters back in Ireland, that's who I'm on about.'

Una began to cry. 'He isn't – married, I mean. He would have told me. He's nice.'

'Oh, yes, he's nice all right. Any bugger'd be nice if they thought they'd a chance of getting a

248

young lass's knickers off.'

'He hasn't.' Una looked at her mother. 'Honest, Mam, I wouldn't let him.'

'Oh, so you admit he's tried, then,' Bill said more quietly.

'He loves me, he said so,' Una sobbed, then added quickly, 'but I didn't let him, I wouldn't.'

Marjory put an arm round her daughter. 'Well, that's something to be thankful for, I suppose.'

Una wept in her mother's arms and Bill sank dejectedly on to a kitchen chair.

'How old do you think he is, love?' he asked, more subdued now.

'He told me, he's twenty-two.'

'Do you think that's likely, love, if he's got a wife and two kids?'

Una broke into more sobs, a trail of mascara making its way down her rouged cheeks.

'I didn't know, Dad, honest. He said he loved me and could get me a job in the theatre in Leeds. He says he has a brother who's a well-known actor.'

'It's him who's an actor – a bloody good one too by the sound of it.'

Marjory lifted the kettle from the hob and made a pot of tea. 'Don't you see, love, he was just telling you that to get what he wanted. Anyway, I thought you were happy as a receptionist.'

'I am, Mam, but I still want to act, or be a dancer, anything on the stage. I've set my heart on it.'

'Well, we'll see, but you won't get what you want through men like him. All you'll get is either an unwanted baby, or a ruined reputation.'

Una began to cry again. 'What will people think? I won't dare go out – they'll all be talking about me.'

Marjory poured the tea. 'Well, you'll just have to face up to it, love, and let it be a lesson for the future.'

Una sipped the sweet hot tea. 'What will I say to him when I see him?'

'Oh, I doubt you'll need worry about that. Big Bessie'll be breaking her neck to tell him I'm on the look-out for him. I wouldn't be at all surprised if he doesn't do a moonlight at the news.' Bill smiled, relieved that no harm had come to his daughter. 'But I'll tell you one thing, Una. If I ever hear the slightest bit of scandal concerning you again, I'll break your bloody neck.' He took a gulp of tea. 'And another thing,' he said.

'What?'

'Wash that muck off your face, you look like a bloody clown. And don't let me see you with it on again.'

Una rushed to the sink. 'I won't, Dad,' she said, relieved to have been let off so lightly. She would keep the make-up for the stage in future. She was going on the stage, no matter what happened – she was determined about that.

The children's window at Miss Judith McCall's looked a picture, and Ada Banwell was unable to decide which dress to buy for her daughter. The child herself was pretty as a picture too, with a mass of almost white curls falling about her face. She was a happy child and most people would pause to admire her.

Ada herself had never been happier or more content with life. Her daughter loved her, and since the child was born a change had taken place in her husband. He never missed an opportunity now to come home to his wife and daughter, and was even talking about coming out of the Navy for good, so as to be with them all the time.

Ada opened the shop door and the little girl ran into the shop and beamed at the lady behind the counter.

'Hello,' she said. 'I've come to choose a new dress.'

Mary smiled down at the beautiful child before realising who she was. 'Well then, we'll have to find you something nice, won't we?'

'Where's Miss McCall?' Ada asked, taken aback at the sight of Mary Holmes.

'She's on holiday. I hope you don't mind putting up with me instead.'

Ada shrugged. She had nothing against the woman; come to think of it she had nothing against her brother-in-law either. In fact she would never cease to be grateful to Harry Holmes. After coming to see her after the birth of their daughter he had done as Ada requested and left them alone. He had brought with him an envelope full of banknotes and placed it on the bed.

'That's for the baby, Ada,' he had said. 'I'm sorry it isn't more but I'm not all that flush at the moment, what with being off work all these months.' He had looked pale and drawn and Ada had been sorry to see the normally cocky young man looking so down.

'Put your money away, Harry.' She had given

251

him back the envelope unopened. 'I don't need it. My daughter's dad has bought her everything she needs, and more. He'll be a good father so long as he thinks he is the father. I hope I can count on you to keep quiet.'

'Well, if that's how you want it, Ada.'

'That's how I want it. Besides, I reckon it's cost you enough in lost wages and ruined health. I didn't want that to happen, Harry. There was no need for it. Violence never solved anything.'

'Oh, I expect there was a need. I asked for all I got – I'm not complaining.'

Ada smiled. 'Nor am I, Harry. In fact I shall never be out of your debt. Every time I look at her I shall thank you under my breath.'

Harry had looked at the baby. 'By, but she's beautiful, Ada. I shall find it difficult to ignore my own child, but if you think it's how it should be...' Harry had kissed Ada on the cheek and told her if ever there was anything she wanted, anything ever at all either of them needed, she must let him know.

'All I need is right here in the cot, and anything she needs her dad will see she gets,' Ada had said. 'And now go, Harry. The neighbours are being good. I'm just earning their respect and I don't want to spoil things.'

'No hard feelings then, Ada?'

'No hard feelings, Harry, and thanks for coming. I appreciate that.'

'You're welcome.'

'And this one will look lovely with her fair curls,' Mary Holmes was holding a red velvet dress in front of the little girl, who reminded her of Una when she was her age.

Ada realised the counter was stacked with dresses in her daughter's size as her thoughts returned to the present.

'They're all lovely.' She picked one up, feeling the crisp cotton, and noticed the label inside the collar.

Mary Holmes
Cutie Wear

'Do you mean to tell me you made this?' She picked up another and inspected the label inside. 'And this?'

Mary blushed. 'I made them all,' she said.

'You're missing your way. You should be in Paris.' Ada laughed.

'Oh, I shall be more than satisfied to get my hands on this. You know Miss McCall's retiring? Well, I'm hoping to buy the shop, that's if the loan comes through.'

'Should be a good buy,' Ada said. 'Not much competition in Millington, and certainly nothing of a quality to compare with these.'

'Thank you,' Mary said. 'Now, let's just try some of these on and see which you like best.'

'I like the red one. Can I have the red one, Mummy?'

'Oh, I don't know. It's not the type of thing you can wear for school.'

'Oh, please, Mummy, I'll keep it for Sundays and when Daddy comes home, I promise.'

'It certainly looks lovely,' Ada enthused.

Mary laughed. 'Anything would look lovely on ... what's your name, love?'

'Yvonne.'

'Well, Yvonne, if ever I want a model I shall know where to come.'

Ada flushed with pleasure. 'We'll take it. Her dad's buying it, anyway. She can twist him round her little finger for anything.'

'They're all alike.' Mary placed the dress in a bag. 'And let me see if I can find a hair ribbon to match.' She cut a yard of red satin ribbon and placed it in with the dress. 'There, that's a present for my most beautiful customer today.'

Ada thanked her and paid for the dress.

'Bye-bye, Yvonne,' Mary said, and to Ada, 'Thanks for your custom. I hope to see you again.'

'I suppose you will, sooner or later.' Ada smiled as they left the shop.

'I like that lady, Mummy, she's nice.'

'Aye, she's nice, love.' Ada almost added, 'They're all nice, the Holmeses, and you'll probably grow up to be just like them.'

Chapter Twenty-Three

The treacle tin clattered as Alan kicked it along the main road, then he picked it up and hid it behind his back as Constable Jones walked towards him.

'Hello, Alan,' he said. 'You're looking a bit miserable, lad. What's to do?'

'Nothing. I'm just f-f-fed up, that's all,' Alan replied.

The constable was always friendly, but even so, Alan always made sure he was on his best behaviour when in his company. He knew the policeman had been known to give kids a walloping on occasions and didn't want the same thing to happen to him.

'I thought you'd be up at Barker's giving Charlie a hand?'

'I can't. He's in bed. He's got mumps, so I've got to keep away from him.'

'Quite right too. They can be funny things can mumps in lads.'

'Oh.' Alan didn't know what was meant by that, but thought he'd better not be cheeky and ask.

'Well, I'll be on my way then, lad. Give my regards to yer mam and dad, and yer sister.' At the mention of Jacqueline the policeman began to chuckle to himself as he walked on.

Alan didn't know what to do with himself. He didn't want to go home to the shop. His mother would be either serving customers or stitching away on the machine in the kitchen, where she had placed a mirror so that she could see the shop door in case anybody came in. She was always working these days. Even on a Wednesday afternoon, when it was half-day closing, she would be either cutting out or stitching up. Even his dad looked miserable, but if he said anything his mother would start on about having to work extra hard to pay off the mortgage, complaining that if he had let her accept the money Gladys had offered to give them it wouldn't have been necessary. His dad always got mad at that and said if she wasn't satisfied with the money he was bringing in to keep his family, without accepting charity, it was just too bad. He also accused his mother of being greedy, because she expected to make a profit at the same time as paying off the mortgage.

Something his dad had said had sounded to Alan as if the mortgage could have been paid over a period of ten or twenty years, but his mother had chosen to pay it back in five. He hoped they wouldn't be arguing for the next five years. It was bad enough living behind the shop instead of on Barker's Row. Only Jacqueline seemed unaffected by the move, but then she was always too busy with homework or some project or other to notice where she lived.

The house itself was quite nice, with a modern kitchen and a large comfortable living room behind the shop, and even Dad admitted it was convenient having electricity. Upstairs there were three large bedrooms and a bathroom with constant hot water. Mother said she had room now to invite the family to stay, and Dad mumbled something about how would she possibly find the time.

Alan liked having a bedroom of his own, despite missing the chats he used to have with Jacqueline late into the night. It was only when he looked out of the window that a sense of doom seemed to descend on him. Instead of meadows, and the tranquillity of Barker's Farm, and the treetops of the Donkey Wood, all that could be seen was factory roofs and tall sooty black chimneys, belching out smoke for twenty-four hours of the day.

Even the small patch of grassland in the

distance was a dirty brown instead of green, and the fumes from the coke ovens seemed to seep through any open door or window. Round the back was a sheer drop down into the works and there was nowhere for Tittle Harry to wander in safety, but nobody, not even Jacqueline, had apparently considered him. The only spare piece of ground was between their shop and the shoe shop, and on this stood the car. That was the only good thing to come out of the move. Grandad Roberts had bought a new car, and handed over the Morris to his dad.

'You really do need a car if you're starting in business, what with buying in and delivering out.'

His dad could take them over to Longfield now on Sundays, though his mother usually made the excuse of being too busy. This had also caused arguments, with his dad pointing out that Grandad Roberts had obviously given them the car to make visiting easier instead of rarer, but his mother seemed oblivious of everything except her work.

Alan found himself wandering up the hill in the direction of Grandma Holmes's. He always seemed to make for there when he was feeling miserable. She always had time to listen to his problems and was the only one to understand why he didn't want to go to grammar school.

'No point, my duck, if you're not book-minded,' she always said. 'You've made up yer mind to become a mechanic, and I for one can't ever see you doing anything else. Why, you've tinkered with owt that moves since the day you could crawl, taking wheels off, putting other things on.

No, lad, I don't think the grammar is the place for you. If you can get an apprenticeship at one of the garages I reckon you'll do all right.'

Grandma Holmes didn't think he was too big for a cuddle, either. 'Come over here, my duck, and give yer owd grandma a bit of a hug. She's badly in need of one today.' She had the knack of letting Alan think he was doing her a favour, when all the time she would be curing some sort of sadness on Alan's part. He had a feeling he was Grandma's favourite. She seemed to have replaced Grandad Holmes with her only grandson, at the same time fulfilling a need in Alan as well.

Alan passed St Catherine's and wondered how long it was since his mother had attended church, or insisted on Jacqueline's and his attending either, not that he cared. It was bad enough going to school, what with his best mate falling out with him because he hadn't passed for the grammar, and some of the others laughing at him because of his stammer. That was another thing that seemed to have happened since the move. He had never stammered at Barker's Row.

Oh, he was fed up. He thought he might run away and live with Grandad Roberts, who would take him fishing down at the reservoir where his troubles always seemed to float away in the water. When he grew up and had his own filling station he would buy a house in the country, next to a river, with no shops or sewing machines to disturb his peace.

He turned the corner of the top row, and there was Freddie Cartwright down on his knees, his bike on its side across the pavement.

'Hiya,' he said to Alan.

'Hiya,' Alan said slowly, which sometimes prevented him from stammering.

'Your Jacqui says you're a wizard at mending things,' Freddie said.

'Oh, s-s-sometimes.'

'Know owt about punctures?'

'A bit.' Alan knelt down by Freddie's side.

'I can't find the blooming thing,' Freddie grumbled.

'Y-y-yer need a bucket of water. If you get me one I'll mend it f-f-for yer.'

Freddie disappeared into the house and came out with a bowl filled to the brim, which must have slurped all over the kitchen floor judging by the language following in its wake.

Alan set to work and the wheel was soon replaced. He also fixed a broken pedal.

'How long 'ave yer been stuttering?' Freddie enquired. 'I used to stutter after I was scalded.'

Alan was all ears. 'Did you? You don't now, do you?'

'Oh no, it went off after a bit. I've still got me scars, though – do yer want to look at 'em?'

'Ooh, yes,' Alan said, fully appreciating the honour.

Freddie opened his shirt neck, and there stretching from his Adam's apple was a deep red scar about six inches long.

'Ooh, I'll bet that hurt.' Alan was impressed.

'Not 'alf,' Freddie said proudly. 'I pulled a pot of dripping over me. Me mam wasn't 'alf mad. We 'ad no dripping for us supper all week.'

'How long did the stammering last?' Alan asked

without stammering at all.

'A few months, I think. Don't worry. If yer stop thinking about it it'll stop.'

'I try not to, but it's the lads at school, they make fun of me.'

'What lads?'

'Some of the ones going to grammar school.'

'Oh, well, yer'll soon be rid of them then. I'll tell yer what, when yer come up to't seniors do yer want to be in my gang?'

Alan couldn't believe his ears. Freddie Cartwright's gang was the best gang in all the school. They had the best side at football, and the best bicycle races up on the common on Saturday mornings.

'Can I? Be in your gang? Are you sure?'

'Course yer can. We could do with a good mechanic to look after us bikes.'

'Oh, I'll enjoy that. And can I join in the races?'

'Course yer can. And when yer in my gang nobody'll laugh at yer stuttering or we'll bash 'em.'

Alan grinned. 'Do you want to come and see my grandma with me? She'll have been baking and she'll give you a bun.'

Freddie propped the repaired bike up against the wall. 'Come on then.' He shouted to his mam through the open door, 'Mam, I'm just going wi' me mate to see 'is grandma.'

Alan heard a voice shout after them, 'Bugger off then, and behave thisen or tha'll gerra good hiding.'

As they set off along the row Alan thought how lucky he was to have a nice clean house and a mother who never swore at him. Oh, and he was looking forward to going to the seniors. As he opened Grandma's door he hoped she wouldn't want to kiss and cuddle him today. He was far too old now for all that baby stuff.

Una went to the cloakroom yet again to check on her hair. She was glad now that her mother had persuaded her against having the DA cut. She had styled it instead by curling the hair round her finger and securing it with hair grips. Now it was brushed out so that it hung in natural waves to her shoulders, setting off the halter neckline to perfection. She touched up her lips with a soft peachy lipstick and checked the seams of her stockings were straight, then dabbed a little Evening in Paris behind her ears and tried to still her quickening heartbeat before returning to the dance hall. The band's vocalist was singing 'The Tennessee Waltz' and the dancers were crowded on the floor.

Una was glad the office staff had been given the day off; it had given her time to manicure her nails and soak in the bath, in front of the fire in the kitchen. She had been invited by Mrs Davenport to a coffee afternoon for charity, along with her mother and all the neighbours, but had preferred to be alone. She had tried on the dress Auntie Mary had made at least three times, once to check her bra didn't slip, as it was the first strapless one she had ever owned; a second time to make sure her shoes looked right; and yet again for no reason at all, except that she felt like a queen in the turquoise taffeta dress, with the nipped-in waist and the swirling circular skirt.

She could sense the heads turning as she glided, even taller than usual in her high heels, across the floor to where her friends were gathered.

'Only five minutes to go to the contest,' Jean remarked. 'You're bound to win, Una. You look smashing.'

'Oh, I don't know.' Una could see an older girl who looked far more sophisticated, in a clingy black dress and lots of gold chains about her neck and wrists. She began to wish she had worn more jewellery herself, only Auntie Mary had said it was unnecessary.

'If you think she's the main competition you can forget it,' Jean said, following her friend's doubtful gaze. 'She looks as common as muck, and that's an understatement.'

Una giggled as the band finished with a roll of drums. The MC's voice came over the microphone requesting the contestants for the 1954 Miss Millington contest to please line up in front of the stage.

Una joined about a dozen other girls, suddenly wishing she had chosen to wear lower heels as she towered over the girl in front. They were each given a number and asked to parade around the dance floor twice, before ascending the steps to the stage.

The girl in front stumbled nervously but Una's acting experience came to the fore and she smiled confidently, held her head high and revelled in the admiring glances that followed her as she circled the floor.

She could see her mother and father, accompanied by Auntie Mary and Uncle Jack. She could make out the pregnant shape of Auntie Margaret, and Uncle Harry saluted her as she glanced his way. She was glad they had all made the effort to come. Even Auntie Sally had found a babysitter.

The girls lined up on the stage where the judges were seated at either end, mostly councillors and local tradespeople. The MC began to interview each girl in turn, asking questions relating to their jobs, hobbies and ambitions. Una cringed as the high-pitched voice of the second contestant came over the microphone. 'My ambition is to get married and have at least four children,' she squeaked.

'Well,' said the MC, 'I'm sure number two will have no problem achieving her aim.'

Una remembered the drama teacher's advice when she had played Juliet last year, and she lowered her voice as she answered the questions.

'I work as a receptionist at present, but I would really like to take up acting, dancing or singing.'

'Well, I'm sure we all wish number six good luck in the future; in the meantime I wouldn't mind having her as my receptionist.' The crowd applauded loudly, and the man beamed as though he had made an extremely amusing remark, before moving on to number seven.

The time had come for the judges to decide, and the voting slips were handed to the MC.

'I will announce the winners in reverse order,' he said, with the air of a vicar from the pulpit. 'In third place, number nine.' The crowd applauded and a section of them broke into cheers. 'In second place, number seven.' Una's heart skipped a beat as she thought he was about to say six, and then she felt deflated. The girl in black was sure to win.

'And in first place, Miss Millington 1954, contestant number six, Miss Una Bacon.'

The crowd went wild. The judges rose to their feet to congratulate the winner, and the MC took advantage of his position by drawing Una towards him and kissing her far more intimately than was necessary.

'There's a dirty old man if ever I saw one,' Bill whispered to Marjory.

A female councillor then placed a satin sash over Una's head. 'Here is a cheque for ten pounds, my dear.' She handed an envelope to Una. 'And good luck with your ambitions.' Una glowed as she thanked the woman, who then proceeded to present the other prizes.

Bill Bacon was proud as a homing pigeon as one person after another congratulated Marjory and himself. His wife turned to him with a smile. 'I suppose she's your daughter tonight,' she said.

'No, love, she's ours. You've made a right grand job of bringing her up, I must admit. Mind you, I'm glad about one thing.'

'What?'

'I'm glad Big Bessie opened her mouth and frightened the living daylights out of that Shaunessy bloke.'

'So am I.' Marjory pulled her husband on to the dance floor. 'Listen, they're playing our song. Come on, let's dance.'

Bill wasn't much of a dancer but it provided a

good excuse to snuggle up to Marjory and that was an opportunity not to turn down.

The band leader came down to congratulate Una. 'What's this about you wanting to be a singer, love?' he enquired.

'Oh, I don't suppose I ever shall,' she said, embarrassed now by all the attention she was receiving.

'Well, can you sing? That's the main thing.'

'A bit. I've sung solo at school sometimes.'

'How about giving us a song tonight? The audience'd love it, and the press would have a ball. Think of the headlines in the *Star:* Miss Millington 1954 sings with the Tony Tanner Sound.'

Una laughed. 'I knew there was a catch in it. You're just after some free publicity.'

'No, really, will you give us a song? Please.'

'Well, I don't know. I mean, what will I have to sing?' Her heart was already pounding with excitement.

'What do you know?'

'"Too Young", I could sing that. I've sung it to the record.'

'Smashing.' He took the steps two at a time, and waved the band to silence.

'Ladies and gentlemen, we've a young lady here tonight, the most beautiful young lady here tonight without a doubt, who's given us all an enormous amount of pleasure. Now in return we're going to make her dream come true. Ladies and gentlemen, the Tony Tanner Sound with Miss Millington 1954, Miss Una Bacon.'

The band struck up the introduction and then the clear melodious voice joined in with the popular love song. The dancers took to the floor, swaying together to the romantic melody, entranced as the young girl made her first appearance with a live band.

Una Bacon's dream was becoming reality, she was Miss Millington 1954. But much more important, she was on her way to becoming a singer.

Chapter Twenty-Four

Jacqueline hated London, finding it difficult to breathe in the thick city air. Nor did she like the way college was changing her individual style, but most of all she was missing her family. She realised the variations in her practical work were a necessary discipline, but thought most of it, for her at least, was a waste of time. The modern abstract designs meant nothing to her and were rumoured to be drug-induced by the beatnik element amongst her colleagues. Gradually she learned to steer clear of the dubious characters and made a small number of friends with whom she had at least a few interests in common, such as a love of nature, music and the galleries. These were a source of quiet solitude where she could browse, or sit alone, contented with her thoughts and her books.

It was on one of these visits that she met Barney Ross, a rather shabby young man, with hair about the colour of her mother's and a beard to match. She had been enthralled in a painting by Camille

Pissaro, one of the Impressionists on whom she was writing a thesis. She was endeavouring to fathom out why he should spoil the beautiful *View From My Window* by adding the crude red, instead of toning down the roof.

'What do you think of it?' he asked over her shoulder.

She shrugged. 'Mixed feelings, but I do admire his work.'

'I prefer his *Hoar Frost* myself.'

'I haven't seen it, except in a book, and it's not the same.'

'You should visit Paris.'

Jacqueline smiled. 'Chance would be a fine thing.'

'It's a must for a student of art.'

'How do you know I'm a student?' Jacqueline queried.

'I was sitting behind you at the lecture on the history on the Arts and Craft movement.'

'Did you find it a waste of time too?'

Barney laughed. 'Oh, I don't know. I quite agree with the revolt against the pettiness of academic art.'

'I'm beginning to see what you mean. All I want to do is teach kids to create works of art, and I fail to see how William Morris's medievalism or John Ruskin's eccentricities enter into it.'

'Perhaps a cup of coffee would help us see things more clearly.'

Jacqueline knew she should carry on with her work but the blue eyes seemed to challenge her into acceptance. She gathered her books together and he held her bag while she packed them away, then slung it over his shoulder.

'There's a café round the corner, and it's cheap,' he stressed.

Jacqueline wondered if she should offer to pay. He certainly looked rather poverty-stricken in his faded cords and washed-up jumper. There was something about him, though, that attracted her. His eyes. He had beautiful eyes. She smiled to herself as she wondered what her mother would make of him.

'I'll tell you what,' she said, 'I'll let you buy the coffee if you let me buy the beans on toast.'

He looked uncertain and then nodded. 'OK.'

He held out a chair for her and as they waited for their order he questioned her about her studies. 'Well, how are you finding it? College, I mean?'

'Not at all what I expected.' Jacqueline frowned.

'Well, what did you expect?'

'I don't really know. I don't suppose I'd really thought about it, I was just so pleased at being accepted. How about you?'

'Well for a start it's a great opportunity to meet pretty chicks like yourself, and secondly I didn't dig the idea of following on in the family firm.'

'Oh? What type of business is that?' Jacqueline had never been likened to a chick before.

'Footwear. Now could you just bear to manufacture shoes for the rest of your existence?'

Jacqueline giggled. 'Sounds like my mother. All she ever discusses these days is the quality of dress material, or the price of cotton to sew it up with.'

'It makes you wonder what it is they have between their ears. I mean, who needs shoes anyway? Or clothes, come to that?'

As she didn't relish the idea of going barefoot, or starkers, Jacqueline didn't answer, and took a mouthful of beans instead.

'So I thought, get out of the rat race at the first opportunity, man. Make your mark on the world by all means, but at your own pace. So I'm here to create, do my own thing, not imitate the work of the normal run of the mill artist.'

'What did your family have to say about that?'

He laughed. 'Oh, they consoled themselves by believing I'm here to get it all out of my system. Besides, they reckon I'll go back with new ideas for the designer's department.'

'Well, it should help. I've designed quite a few patterns for my mother.'

'But I'm not going back. Now I have my own pad I can do what I like. There's no way I'm joining those squares again. Anyway, that's enough about them. Let's talk about you.'

Jacqueline wondered where the money was coming from to pay for the pad, suspecting that the squares he held in such contempt were probably the benefactors.

'What's your title?' he asked.

'What?'

'Your name?'

'Jacqueline Holmes. What's yours?'

'Barney Ross.'

'You've a slight accent similar to my grand-parents'. Are you from the north?'

'Scotland originally, we've still a factory up there, but we moved down to Derby when I was so high.' He indicated a height of about three feet with his hand. 'Started up a second firm there.'

Jacqueline thought they must be a very wealthy family.

'What do your folks do apart from make useless garments?'

'My father's a miner,' Jacqueline said.

He shook his head in disbelief. 'How can a man follow such an incredible path?'

'I don't think he had any option. He needed a job,' Jacqueline pointed out.

Barney didn't seem to have an answer to that, and they finished their lunch.

'I'll have to go,' she said. 'I've a class at two.'

He rose and picked up her bag, taking her arm as they walked round the corner in the direction of the college annexe. 'What do you do Saturdays?' he asked.

'Not a lot. Go to the park if it's fine, do some studying.'

'I'll go with you. Meet me here at eleven,' he demanded. 'So long, chick, I'll see you.'

She wouldn't go, she told herself. Nobody was going to tell Jacqueline Holmes what to do. But she knew she would. The blue eyes seemed to be still piercing deep into hers, even though the man himself had already disappeared from view, and she knew she would be unable to resist the chance of seeing Barney Ross again.

Jacqueline did see Barney Ross again, and the more she saw of him the more he fascinated her. It was only after a couple of months that the doubts set in, although Avril, her room-mate, mistrusted him from the start.

'There's something about him I can't fathom,

and he's definitely not your type,' she said on first meeting Barney Ross. Jacqueline knew deep down her friend was right. He wasn't her type, but that didn't prevent her from becoming infatuated by him. The situation was made more difficult by Jacqueline's lack of experience, and the man wasted no time in taking advantage of her naivety.

She had been back to his flat on a number of occasions and, unable to stand the mess, had given the place a thorough going over. It was during the cleaning that she came across a white powder in a small transparent packet, and though she had never seen anything like it before she was suspicious. However, she said nothing and kept the knowledge of its whereabouts to herself. That was Jacqueline's first mistake. She should have forgotten about Barney there and then.

Her second mistake was to fall in love. Barney was charming most of the time, but on other occasions he seemed to care nothing for anything or anybody. Jacqueline brooded on the problem and believed she had only to offer Barney her undying love in order to bring out the best in him. Avril had no such illusions and tried to warn her friend against becoming further involved, but it was already too late.

Barney Ross knew nothing about love. His main aim was to pleasure himself with as many conquests as possible, and Jacqueline Holmes, although a pretty little thing, was just another challenge. True, she was not as easy as the rest of them, but that just increased his determination to add her to the list.

Jacqueline knew she could not resist Barney for

271

much longer. When he slipped off her clothes and ran his hands over her smooth young body the desire was almost too much to bear, and she had decided Saturday was to be the day, the red-letter day when she would give Barney the precious gift of her virginity. It seemed to Jacqueline she was always giving something to Barney, but never receiving anything in return. It was she who gave up her evenings to launder his shirts and cook him a hot meal, with groceries bought from her meagre allowance, sent each month by her father and Grandad Roberts. It was supposed to be for nylons and other essentials like sanitary pads and books, and it was proving difficult to make ends meet. But Barney never seemed to pay for anything whilst in her company.

Yet because she loved him none of this mattered, and now she had decided to give him the ultimate gift, which once given could never be taken back. She was convinced that then Barney would be different, more loving somehow.

When Saturday came Jacqueline dressed herself with extra care. The circular stitched bra she usually wore was replaced by a satin and lace creation with briefs and suspender belt to match; she could see the triangular shape of dark hair through the lace inset on the briefs and a flood of desire threatened to drown her as she thought of the evening ahead.

The place as usual was a mess but Barney, lounging on the bed, seemed unaware of the squalor. The strong cloying smell from his cigarettes permeated the room, and Jacqueline frowned as she wondered what it was he rolled into them. She began to carry the dirty crockery to the kitchen.

'Leave them, chick,' he called, 'and come to bed.'

'It's like a tip in here. I don't know how you can live in it.'

'Leave it, it's my scene,' he drawled. 'Come to bed.'

Jacqueline went to sit on the edge of the bed.

'Come here,' he said. He reached out and pulled her by the hand until she was lying beside him. His eyes were bright blue in the dimmed light. He began to undo her blouse slowly, fumbling over her bra fastener so that she undid it herself. She slipped her skirt down so that she was wearing only stockings and briefs. Barney could sense the desire in Jacqueline, and wasted no time on gentleness or words of affection, although he guessed the girl was making love for the first time.

Uppermost in his mind was his own desire for fulfilment. Jacqueline had expected more pain, but she had also expected more pleasure and was surprised at the lack of both sensations. She felt suddenly deflated, and desperate for Barney's reassurance that it had been good, and that he loved her as she loved him. But Barney had collapsed in a heap beside her and it was she who caressed his wiry beard and murmured, 'Do you love me, Barney?'

He mumbled words that could have been any answer, oblivious of her yearning for reassurance that it was all right, that she was special to him. 'Make some coffee, chick,' was all she could

273

make out.

Jacqueline went to the kitchen, tears prickling her eyes, knowing deep down – in fact she had known all along really – that Barney didn't love her, and doubting he was capable of loving anyone. She poured water over the coffee essence, added milk and sugar and carried it automatically back to the bed, sitting down on the edge of it, her head down. She blinked hard, trying to still the threatening tears.

'Hey, come back to bed,' he said, clutching her arm.

She shook him away, the tears uncontrollable now.

'Shit,' he said. 'You're not another one of those chicks who turn on the vapours, are you? Nobody forced you, Jacqueline. Here, take a drag of this, it'll calm you down.' He held out the cigarette.

Jacqueline shrugged away from him and reached for her scattered clothing. She put on her blouse, fastening the buttons with trembling fingers, and stood up to step into her skirt. He watched her, a smug grin on his face. 'I'll say one thing in your favour, chick,' he drawled, 'you've a cute little arse on you if nothing else.'

Suddenly Jacqueline's tears of heartache changed to tears of rage, and a need to hurt Barney Ross as he had hurt her overwhelmed her. Unseeingly she picked up the nearest object, which happened to be the half-empty coffee mug, and flung it, hitting the half-drugged man straight between the eyes. Then she picked up her shoes and bag, and left Barney Ross for the last time.

It was not until the deluge of cold drenching rain cooled her temper that she realised her coat was back at Barney's flat, but there was no way she would ever return for it. She looked around for a place to shelter, surprised to find she had been walking for some time. Her clothes and hair were clinging to her skin, as if to thoroughly wash away the inner feeling of filth left there by Barney's lovemaking. She smiled wryly at the expression. How could it be called making love with someone who knew nothing of affection, let alone love?

She stopped suddenly at an open door. The interior looked warm and bright and the plate on the wall said *All Welcome N.U.S.C.* A small crowd was coming towards her and she found herself drawn in amongst them and almost carried in through the door with the laughing group.

The chairs were set in rows and she found one near the back. The service had already begun and the words 'Give Me Thine Ears' penetrated her numbed mind. She suddenly wondered what she was doing here in this place which would certainly be condemned by the Catholic Church. The words 'Hail Mary full of grace' came into her mind but were hastily dismissed, meaning no more to her than the words in the open hymn book before her. She wondered if she had ever been a true Catholic, and thought back to the morning assemblies at school, when she should have excused herself and gone straight to class with the other Catholic children. Instead she had stayed with Pat and joined in the prayers and singing of rousing hymns like 'Praise My Soul

The King Of Heaven'. Perhaps if her mother had been more steadfast in her faith, she and Alan might have joined the flock of St Catherine's, but the scepticism of her father, who was to Jacqueline the epitome of gentleness, kindness, and even perfection, proved to her that goodness was nothing to do with religion and one church no different from another. It was the people, and what was inside them, that mattered.

She picked up the hymn book and began to sing.

'Now we will join in prayers for all sick people everywhere. Please give out your love, and if it pleases God we will try to heal them with His help. Amongst the sick today are these members of our church.' The man then read out a list of names, and prayers were offered.

'Now we come to the clairvoyant part of the service when we will all try to relax, send out our thoughts of love, and open our minds so that our absent friends might inhabit them. And for the benefit of any members of the congregation who have never joined us before, I would like to assure them that our friends are not dead, but have merely passed into the world of Spirit and are no more than a thought away.'

Jacqueline could feel herself becoming drowsy and relaxed as she hadn't been for months. Her head lolled forward and she would have slept if the voice hadn't roused her.

'Can I come to you, miss, the young lady near the door? I have a gentleman here by the name of Bill, or Will. I can feel a weight on my body as though I am crushed, or trapped in a dark place,

a mine perhaps, or a tunnel.' Jacqueline remembered the story of her grandfather's brother, the
reason her mother gave for Grandad O'Connor's
heavy drinking when she was a little girl.

'Do you follow me?' the man was enquiring.

'Yes. Oh, yes,' Jacqueline said eagerly. 'He was
my great-uncle.'

'Well, he wants you to know he's happy now, no
darkness, and no suffering. I've also got another
gentleman ... wait a minute ... he says he's a
miner too.' The man suddenly laughed. 'Oh, I
don't think I can repeat that. This gentleman
likes to swear a bit. He says you're better off
without that selfish B, says you'll find love nearer
home. Do you understand?'

Jacqueline felt the tears rolling down her face.
It was as though Grandad Holmes was here in
person. 'Yes,' she said. 'It's my grandfather.'

'Well, he's certainly a character.' The man
continued. 'He says he'd never have believed he'd
ever come to church voluntarily, but he wants to
give you his love, and tell Lizzie to keep her
pecker up.'

Jacqueline felt a comfortable warmth envelop
her, and vaguely heard the man addressing another member of the congregation. She looked
round the church, which was badly in need of
repairs and redecorating. She joined in the closing
prayer and for the moment was at peace with the
world.

Afterwards a woman came to her. 'Will you join
us for a cup of tea, dear?' she said. 'Thomas
would like to have a word with you before you go.'

Jacqueline was reluctant to leave and welcomed

the invitation, joining the others in a side room which turned out to be the living quarters of the woman who had approached her and her husband Thomas. He brought her tea and an arrowroot biscuit. 'Welcome to our church,' he said.

'Thank you.' Jacqueline was suddenly overcome by guilt. 'I ought to confess, I really came in out of the rain.'

'I guessed so,' he said. 'But, you know, you ought to come here more often. I do believe you're quite psychic.'

Jacqueline blushed, embarrassed, yet for some reason the news came as no surprise.

'You really ought to develop your gift; it's rare and should be treasured. Tell me, have you experienced anything unusual at any time?'

'I had a visit from my grandfather on the night he died, although I was miles away at the time.' She laughed, 'That's the one who swears a bit.'

He smiled. 'Look, I shall have to circulate, but will you come again? Preferably to the open circle on Wednesday evenings, about seven. I do think it's important to you, and we always welcome new members.' He shook Jacqueline's hand warmly and moved on through the remaining groups.

Jacqueline was calmer when she left the church. She knew now how stupid she had been, thinking that Barney had cared for her. The past few months seemed unreal now as she attempted to analyse her feelings for him. She had liked the look of him, certainly. He was one of the most handsome men she knew, but it wasn't just that. There had been something else. He had been rebelling against his parents. He had told her

278

about how much the business mattered to them and how they had imagined money could make up for not spending time with him. How he had been sent away to boarding school.

Jacqueline thought now that it might have been pity she had felt for him. He had been like a small boy and in a funny sort of way she had felt the same. Perhaps she had been rebelling against her mother by falling for someone she knew her mother would have disapproved of – if not hated. Maybe it had been a protest about all the hours Mary had been too busy for them. Too busy for Alan, too busy to visit her family in Newcastle, despite numerous invitations. Too busy to spend time with the Robertses, who cared for her like a daughter. Worst of all, her mother had been too busy to enjoy time with her father.

Jacqueline had never realised how much she resented the hours her mother spent at that bloody sewing machine until Barney Ross had brought it to her attention. She hoped to God that after tonight she wasn't pregnant. Her mother would never stand the shame of it. Besides, it might lose her a few customers and that would never do. Jacqueline sighed. How she wished she was back home. Not at the shop, though, in her present frame of mind. She wished she was at Longfield, with Grandma and Grandad Roberts. With the Downings, who despite the farm always made time for her and Alan. Back with Doug. He would never treat a girl as she had just been treated. She had seen how gentle he was with the animals, appreciated the way he had taken time to talk to her – even though he was four or five years older. There was no comparison between someone like Doug Downing and Barney Ross. If only she had realised it before tonight.

As Jacqueline walked back to her room she braced herself for Avril's 'I told you so', but her friend had herself been the victim of one or two broken affairs and knew how deep the pain could be. She was actually relieved now Barney Ross was out of Jacqueline's life, and so provided the proverbial shoulder to cry on. She knew better than to criticise the weak useless layabout; her friend would already be aware of his shortcomings. But the knowledge didn't help heal the heartache; only time could do that. In the meantime, if Jacqueline needed her she would be there.

Jacqueline did need her friend, more than she had ever needed anyone. Her recovery from the Barney Ross affair seemed to be taking far too long, and Avril was extremely worried about the way her room-mate was surviving on endless cups of tea and very little food. Jacqueline's normally slim figure now looked like nothing more than skin-covered bones, and it needed nothing more than a letter from home or a word of kindness to reduce her to tears. Now the Christmas cards had begun to arrive it was even worse.

Jacqueline opened yet another one and Avril couldn't help feeling a pang of envy as the pile increased.

'Who's it from today?' she asked.

'My cousin Una.'

'Is that the pretty one?'

'Yes.' She unfolded a sheet of blue paper and

scanned the enclosed letter, her face becoming animated as she read. 'Oh, guess what, she's appearing in pantomime at the Lyceum. Only in the chorus, but that's really something. It's one of the best theatres in the country. I always knew she'd make it. Oh, I wish I was home so I could go and see her performing.'

'You should go home for Christmas, it's just what you need. Besides, you know how disappointed everyone will be if you don't.'

'I've told you, I'm not going to leave you alone at this time of year. What sort of friend do you think I am?'

Avril didn't try to argue. They had been through it all so many times, and Jacqueline was right: she would be lonely during the festive season. She experienced another wave of homesickness and wished her parents were here in England. Though she loved them dearly she did wish they had waited for her to complete her education before her mother had left for South Africa.

Her father had emigrated a few years ago and was now enjoying success as a builder. He had developed the firm and was now employing a number of men. Initially the arrangement had been for his wife and daughter to follow when Avril finished college. However, her mother, both impatient and lonely for her husband, had decided to join him, leaving Avril to follow later. Now Christmas was close she couldn't help feeling abandoned, and missed her parents dreadfully. Though not, Jacqueline suspected, half as much as she herself missed Millington, her parents and her brother. Dear Alan who had grown so tall and strong and broad of shoulder, his arms always waiting to surround her with their comforting warmth. Grandma Holmes, always there in her old rocking chair, and Grandma and Grandad Roberts, who would be missing her more than any of the others. Oh, what she would give to be with them at Moorland House. The warmth of the kitchen, the piano, the view over the reservoir, stark and beautiful in the weak winter sunshine. Suddenly she made up her mind. 'We're going home,' she said.

'We?'

'Yes.' Jacqueline looked her old self for the first time in months. 'You're coming with me.'

'I can't possibly. I haven't been invited.'

'Yes you have. I'm inviting you now.'

Avril didn't know what to say. 'Well, I don't know. You'll have to ask your parents.'

'No I won't. You'll be welcome any time – everyone's made welcome by my family. You're coming with me, so we'll hear no more about it.'

She went to the kitchen cabinet and brought out the pot containing their joint housekeeping money, and emptied it on the table. Together they counted out a couple of pound notes, then the ten shilling ones. 'Lucky we've been saving hard for Christmas extras,' she said. 'We have enough for the tickets and a bit besides.'

'Then we'd better buy your parents something nice,' Avril said.

Jacqueline laughed for the first time in ages. 'The sight of us walking into the shop will be the only present my parents need.'

Avril began to feel excited. 'Well, if you're sure?'

'I'm sure, and don't think you'll be getting away scot-free. When my mother discovers you're going in for interior design she'll be roping you in to do the window displays, just you wait and see.' Now Jacqueline had got all the resentment out of her system she couldn't wait to see her mother again.

With only five days to Christmas, Sheffield was swarming with shoppers, and by the time Jacqueline and Avril had made their way from the station into Bridge Street, laden down with luggage, they were already in high spirits and looking forward to a real family Christmas.

Normally Jacqueline would have crossed Snig Hill to scrutinise the window displays at Winstons for the latest designs in blouses, looking for ideas to pass on to her mother, but today, weighed down with bags and presents, she and her friend boarded the first available bus for Millington.

They had worked hard during the past few days, Jacqueline finishing a series of watercolours and her friend framing them. There was a picture of Moorland House for Grandma and Grandad Roberts, and a moorland scene complete with Tittle Harry for her parents. Another one, a portrait of Grandad Holmes, turned out to be Jacqueline's favourite and was intended for Grandma Holmes. She had one of Pepper grazing in the field along the lane for Alan. Jacqueline experienced the familiar pang of sadness as she thought of the day Doug Downing had discovered the old horse dead in the stable. He and Jacqueline had comforted each other, huddled together as Doug had broken the news. But since she had started attending the open circle evenings at the Spiritual Church she no longer visualized the old carcass being burned, but instead imagined Pepper galloping contentedly in a green and pleasant place.

She had found it easy to paint the pictures from memory, surprised at the amount of detail she could remember, and sometimes she fancied an unseen force was planting the images in her mind's eye. Now she was concentrating on completing the journey without breaking the frames. Avril had insisted on stopping outside the sheaf market to buy a bunch of chrysanthemums for Jacqueline's mother, and a bag of roasted chestnuts which they were now munching as they jolted on the upper deck of the bus. Bare tree branches brushed against the windows, and Jacqueline wanted to cry out with pleasure as they travelled the familiar countryside.

'I think I'm going to like Sheffield,' Avril decided.

Jacqueline laughed. 'You haven't seen much of it yet.'

'No, but after London I can't believe the difference in the air.'

'Oh, I'll grant you that. I'll guarantee you'll sleep well after a few days in the pure Yorkshire air.' She frowned. 'Not that it's all that pure where we live now, but just wait till you see Longfield.'

'If it's half as beautiful as your paintings I can't wait.'

'It's even better,' said Jacqueline. 'Looks like we are here. We'd better gather our luggage together.'

Avril found her stomach churning nervously. She hoped it would be acceptable her being here.

She wished her friend had warned her family of her coming, but Jacqueline had insisted on their visit being a surprise.

A surprise it was too, for Jacqueline as well as her parents. She had expected her mother to come running at the sound of the shop bell, but instead a pretty assistant dressed in an elegant black dress addressed the pair as they entered.

'Can I help you, madam?' She smiled from one to the other.

'Shh,' Jacqueline whispered, placing a finger to her lips. 'Is my mother about? Oh, sorry – you don't know me. I'm Jacqueline.'

The girl blushed. 'Oh, I'm sorry, I didn't know. I'm Yvonne Banwell. I've only been here a few months. Your mother's in the living room doing the tree.'

Jacqueline knew better than to dump her bags in the shop. It had been almost a mortal sin in her mother's eyes for as much as a duster to be left in view of the customers. She trundled through to the kitchen, her friend following uncertainly.

She tiptoed up behind her mother, placed her luggage silently down and pressed her hands over the busy woman's eyes. Mary jumped. 'What? Who – come on, stop messing about.' Her daughter let go, eager to witness her mother's surprise. Mary was more in shock than surprised, then she and her daughter were crying and laughing in each other's arms.

'This is Avril, Mother. I hope you don't mind me bringing her, only I couldn't leave her alone at Christmas.'

'Mind? Of course I don't mind. Oh, what a

Christmas this is going to be. Take your things off, Avril, and make yourself at home. Oh, I can't wait to see your father's face.'

'When will he be home?'

'He's on two to ten, but our Alan'll be home about half past six.'

Jacqueline sank into an easy chair, and Mary rushed to the kitchen to make tea.

'I didn't know you had an assistant in the shop, Mother.'

'Oh, didn't I mention it? I always forget half the things I mean to say when I write.'

'She looks efficient,' Jacqueline said. 'And pretty.'

Avril smiled. 'I think that's an understatement. I'd say she was beautiful.'

Mary came back with the tea tray. 'You're right. I held a fashion show last week in aid of a children's hospital appeal, and Yvonne was the main model. I can't believe the orders that came pouring in. Not only that, but the customers love her. Besides, I can concentrate now on the sewing part knowing the shop is in good hands. She's paying her own wages over and over again.'

'What did Dad say?'

'Well, actually it was his suggestion. He threatened he would leave if I didn't cut my working hours. I ignored him for too long, I'm afraid, not realising I was really neglecting him. Luckily I took his threat seriously in the end.'

Jacqueline looked worried. 'I'm glad you did. I wouldn't have liked a divorce on my hands.'

Mary giggled. 'You know your father better than that. Besides, I think he rather fancies Yvonne. He says she makes him feel twenty again.'

'Where did you find her?' Jacqueline enquired.

'She's been a customer since she was in frilly dresses and ankle socks. I knew she was leaving school next year so she was the obvious choice. At present she's coming in after school, on Saturdays, and full time in the holidays, like now.' Mary didn't add that being a member of the Holmes family the girl was worthy of a little consideration. She wasn't supposed to know. The truth had only been revealed when she tried dresses on the little girl. The tiny birthmark exactly between the shoulder blades was identical to the one on both Jacqueline and Una.

Yvonne's parentage had been confirmed to Mary by the look on Harry's face when he first saw his daughter behind the counter, but nothing had been said and Mary intended to keep the knowledge to herself, realising she had landed herself with a bargain in Yvonne. Besides, the girl obviously idolised Mr and Mrs Banwell, and they her.

The shop was closed and the bags unpacked by the time Alan arrived home in the old banger. They heard him long before he arrived outside the shop, and before coming in he lifted up the bonnet and shone a torch inside to begin adjusting something or other.

'Oh, no,' Mary moaned. 'Don't tell me he's brought home another heap of someone else's rubbish. I don't know what people will think. That's the third time this week he's brought his work home to clutter up the road.'

287

'Well, at least he hasn't changed much. I can't remember a time when he wasn't tinkering with some motor or another.' Jacqueline was growing impatient and eventually she knocked on the shop window. Alan looked up and his grease-smeared face blossomed into a huge grin. Dropping the spanner he almost ran into the shop, and gathered his sister against his greasy overalls.

'How long have you been home?'

'Hours and hours. Well, it seems like it waiting for you to arrive, and then as usual someone's old engine is given priority.' They laughed happily together as they entered the kitchen.

Avril stood up as Jacqueline introduced her brother to her. She had seen photographs and heard a lot about Alan, but nothing had prepared her for the sight of the tall handsome man with the fair hair and the laughing eyes. She gulped and managed a hello.

'Nice to see you, Avril.' He smiled. 'Looks like being an exciting Christmas after all, and I must say you've achieved a miracle already: you've drawn my mother's attention from that damned sewing machine.'

Mary laughed. 'Wrong,' she said. 'I'd already decided to call it a day. All the orders are completed, and if we haven't enough stock made up they'll just have to wait until the new year.' She went to the kitchen to lay the table, calling out, 'I couldn't decide whether to close the shop for two or three days, but our Jacqueline's arrival helped me make up my mind. I'm giving Yvonne a whole week off – with pay, of course. I'll see how things go and if there doesn't look to be much doing I'll take a week off myself too.'

Alan sank into a chair in a mock faint. 'Oh, God, we'll be bankrupt,' he groaned.

Laughing, Jacqueline warned, 'You'll not only be bankrupt, you'll be thrown out if she sees you on the furniture in those overalls.'

Alan jumped up. 'Oh, I forgot. I'd better go and shower.'

'Shower?' Jacqueline shrieked. 'Are we turning all posh?'

'My Christmas present to Mum and Dad, all fitted and working,' Alan boasted.

Mary popped her head round the door. 'Aye, and we'll all know whose fault it is when one of us ends up scalded,' she warned.

Alan laughed and disappeared upstairs. Avril looked at Jacqueline and smiled wistfully, saying softly, 'Oh, Jacqueline, you don't know how lucky you are, having such a caring family.'

'Well, I don't know about that. I reckon they're all a bit dotty sometimes, and you haven't met half of them yet. Wait until Christmas Day when we all get together – you'll think you're in a madhouse.'

Avril didn't answer. She could already see the transformation in Jacqueline, and she reckoned she could stop worrying about her friend, for the next several days at least.

'Come on, dinner's ready,' Mary called. 'I'd have done something special if I'd known you were coming.'

'Well this looks special enough to me,' Avril said, beginning to tuck in to the large plate of meat and potato pie and mushy peas. 'You were right, Jacqueline – I am going to like it here. I'll never be able to thank you enough for having me, Mrs Holmes.'

'No thanks necessary, love,' Mary said, glancing at her daughter. Something had happened: she didn't know what and did not intend to pry, but was grateful that Jacqueline had had a friend like Avril to see her through the trauma. Oh well, she hoped that whatever it was it was over, and for the next few days she intended to concentrate on feeding up the pair of scrawny figures. 'Come on, eat up,' she said. 'There's baked apples and custard to follow.'

Initially Jack had invited Gladys and Rowland to spend the whole of Christmas with them, but on hearing of the arrival of his daughter Gladys had changed their plans slightly, knowing from her letters how much Jacqueline missed Moorland House. So it was arranged that the whole family would spend Christmas Day at Millington and then, weather permitting, visit Moorland House on Boxing Day. Gladys hoped to persuade Jacqueline to stay overnight and show her friend the beauties of Longfield the next day.

Jack had been shocked at his daughter's appearance. 'I don't believe they are feeding themselves properly,' he said. 'Either that, or she's unhappy at college. I'll not have her staying down there if she's miserable.'

'She's enjoying college,' Mary assured him.

'Mary, can't you see she looks drawn – older, somehow? Surely being her mother you can see the change in her.'

'I can see,' Mary insisted. 'But I don't think it's anything to do with college, or the way they eat.' She paused. 'I think the girl's probably had love troubles.' She didn't add that she was seeing herself all over again after Tom Downing's death.

'Well, I only hope nobody did the dirty on her. If anybody harms my lass I'll swing for 'em, I'm telling you, Mary.'

'Jack, she's not a little girl any more. She's twenty tomorrow and we can't protect her from life. She needs to learn from her own mistakes like anyone else.'

'Aye well, we'll see. If she's miserable down there she's not going back, I'm telling you.'

'Yes, and I'm telling you, a week at home and she'll be back to her old self, just you see.'

As it happened it didn't take a week to transform Jacqueline. It happened quite unexpectedly on her birthday.

It was during the afternoon that the shop bell rang and Yvonne came through to the back. 'There's someone asking for you, Jacqueline. A man.'

'A man? Well, he'd better come in.' Jacqueline looked at Avril in confusion.

Douglas Downing looked ill at ease. It was the first time Jacqueline had seen him dressed up and he had obviously taken pains with his appearance.

'Doug! Come in. It's been ages – how are you?' She didn't wait for Doug's reply. 'This is my friend Avril, she's staying over Christmas.'

Doug shook the girl's hand, even more embarrassed. It had taken some courage to visit one girl, and now there were two.

Avril realised she was in the way. 'Shall I put the kettle on, Jacqueline?' she asked.

Her friend nodded, smiling at Doug. She went towards him. 'Oh, it's lovely to see you. I am glad you've come.'

'Aye, it's been a long time.' A hell of a long time, he thought. He stared at Jacqueline, noticing the shadows beneath her eyes, but they only seemed to emphasise the depths of those eyes' warm beauty.

Jacqueline was overcome by an urge to run into the strong waiting arms, to feel them circle her body and draw her towards the hard muscular chest, just as they had on the day Pepper had died. She could hear Billy Fury on the radio. The words 'so near yet so far away' filled her with confusion, and she stopped within arm's length of her friend.

Doug wanted to gather her to him, had wanted to since she was hardly more than a child, but then he had told himself that he was too old. He had been then, but now the six years' difference seemed irrelevant.

'I brought you your cards. I happened to be coming into Millington so they asked me to call.' It was only a slight white lie, he could have filled up the tank of the van in Longfield, but he had jumped at the opportunity when his mother had mentioned forgetting to post the cards for Jacqueline's birthday. 'It wouldn't have mattered much if she hadn't been home,' Mrs Downing had said, 'but we really ought to have made sure they arrived on the right day.' Bessie had volunteered to deliver them after finishing work but Doug had already picked them up and popped them in his pocket.

'I've to go into Millington this afternoon,' he had said. 'I'll pop them in at the shop.'

Now he was here and he was standing like a dope, unable to think of anything to say and staring at Jacqueline as though she was made of bone china, wanting to touch her and not daring.

'Your mum never forgets our birthdays.' Jacqueline smiled at Doug.

Mary had been upstairs, but now she walked into the sitting room and stopped dead in her tracks, going cold with shock. Except for the stylish haircut and the Slim Jim tie the dark-haired man in the navy suit could have been Tom Downing himself. She was confused at first, not sure if it was Cyril or Douglas. It was a long time since she had seen either of them.

'Doug's brought me my birthday cards, Mam,' Jacqueline said. Mary noticed the sparkle in her daughter's eyes, and the way she had lapsed in her speech and come out with Mam instead of Mother. She smiled at Doug. 'Well, sit down and tell us all the news. How are your mother and father?'

'Fine.' He grinned and sat on the edge of the settee.

'Lucy calls in occasionally,' Mary volunteered. 'But I see more of her daughter nowadays. She's just at the age to be buying new clothes every week.'

'Have you seen our Bessie lately?'

293

'Not for some months. Not married yet, I gather?'

Doug laughed. 'That'll be the day. She's too fond of a good time is our Bessie, popping off to Spain for holidays two or three times a year.'

'The last time I saw her she looked well on it.'

Doug chuckled. 'Well, I reckon she's put on a couple of stone over the last year.' His tone became more serious. 'I think there may be wedding bells soon, actually. Her friend Sam isn't too well and she's spending more and more time at his place. I reckon she's about ready for settling down.'

'And how's Cyril?' Jacqueline enquired.

'Working till he drops most of the time, saving up for a place of his own. He's courting a girl from the other side Sheffield.'

Avril brought in the tea and Jacqueline opened her cards. There was one from Mrs Downing, another signed Bessie and Sam, though Jacqueline had never seen Bessie's man friend, and a beautiful scented one with cut-out red roses. She opened it slowly and read the words written in a neat hand: 'To Jacqueline from your loving friend Doug.'

By the look in Jacqueline's eyes it might have been a romantic love poem of at least ten verses. 'Oh, it's beautiful.' She smiled radiantly at Doug and his face turned crimson.

'Well,' he mumbled, 'I'd better be off. Thanks for the tea, Mary.'

The way he pronounced her name caused a stirring in Mary's stomach; he reminded her so much of his brother, it seemed almost like yesterday.

She pulled herself together as he asked Jacqueline, 'Will you be at the house over Christmas?'

'Boxing Day, all being well,' she answered quickly.

He grinned. 'I'll probably be seeing you again then before you go back.'

'I suppose so.' She smiled.

'I, er, I don't suppose you'll be at the dance on Christmas Eve?'

Jacqueline looked towards Avril. 'Shall we? Do you feel like shaking a leg?'

Avril shrugged. 'Sure, that would be lovely.'

Her friend followed Doug out into the shop, and then out on to the pavement, both reluctant to say goodbye.

'Oh-oh,' Avril said, 'I think Jacqueline's in love again.'

Mary picked up the word quickly. 'Again?'

'Oh, dear – you weren't supposed to know. Anyway, it's over – has been for a while.'

'I would say it's certainly over, and it looks like another has begun.' Mary smiled at Avril as Jacqueline walked nonchalantly back into the room.

'Now where can I make room for some more cards?'

Every surface in the room was filled with either Christmas or birthday cards, but Jacqueline managed to find room for three more, with the one from Doug noticeably given pride of place.

She wondered why she hadn't realised before how much she liked Doug. Well, more than liked, actually. And this time she had a notion that the feeling was mutual.

When they entered the dance hall on Christmas Eve Jacqueline, Avril and Pam were already in high spirits after Jack had insisted on treating the friends to a drink at the Working Men's Club. Unused to alcohol, the trio had needed no more than a couple of gin and oranges to go off into a fit of giggles, and Uncle Harry and Alan hadn't helped by insisting on telling a string of jokes. Most of them were absolutely awful, but the friends were so happy to be together that they found it easy to laugh at anything.

Avril was surprised at the size of the hall and the quality of the music. The floor was throbbing as dancers let down their hair and gyrated to a rousing version of 'Summertime Blues', oblivious of the fact that it was midwinter.

Suddenly, her attention caught, Jacqueline peered across the dimly lit room to where a large ungainly figure was twisting away to the music. It couldn't be, yet she was sure it was Charlie Barker.

'Pam, am I seeing things?' she asked her friend, 'or is that Charlie over there?'

'It's Charlie all right.' Pam laughed. 'Didn't Alan tell you? He never misses a dance these days. It's completely transformed his life since Alan and his mates took him under their wing.'

Suddenly Charlie spotted Jacqueline and started across the floor towards her, elbowing everybody out of the way in an effort to reach his long-lost friend. With a grin as big as a teacup he grabbed her, gesticulating wildly as he attempted to make himself understood. Although it was more than a year since she had last seen him, she had no difficulty gathering he was trying to ask her to dance.

'Oh, no.' Pam winced. 'You'll be black and blue. If ever anyone had two left feet it's Charlie. Do the same as everyone else and ignore him. He's quite happy jigging about on his own.'

But Jacqueline was so delighted to see her childhood friend enjoying a normal lifestyle that she was oblivious of Pam's warning. Besides, the gin had given her extra confidence, enough to make a spectacle of herself without caring. So she said, 'OK, Charlie, come on,' and pulled him on to the dance floor.

Charlie was wearing a gaudily checked sports jacket, but then he always had been one for bright colours, and he had now apparently found a new love in his life: dance music. The band suddenly hushed as the drummer began a solo, and the dancers paused to listen and to watch the manoeuvres of the musician. But Charlie had no intention of standing still, and continued his clumsy gyrations. Jacqueline tried to calm him, but for once he realised he was being watched, and so twisted and turned even more violently, lifting his partner off her feet and spinning her round until she began to feel quite giddy. As the beat of the drums reached its finale, he threw himself onto the floor, kicking his legs in the air, and Jacqueline slunk away in the direction of her friends. Then, as the music finished and the crowd applauded and screamed for more, Charlie, believing the applause was for him alone, stood up and bowed, grinning widely, without a doubt the proudest man in the room.

'You can't say I didn't warn you.' Pam laughed.

'I know.' Jacqueline chuckled. 'Come on, let's escape to the refreshment room before he comes over again.'

Alan turned up just as they were finishing their tea and biscuits.

'Well, you might have come a bit sooner and rescued me from Charlie,' Jacqueline said.

Alan chuckled. 'Why? I've just been told how much you enjoyed yourself.'

'Oh, Lord, they're talking about me already. Anyway, how long has Charlie been part of the human race?'

'Oh, it began when I cadged a potato picking job for Freddie Cartwright up at Barker's. Freddie might be a tough nut but he's a soft streak about him when it comes to helping the underdog. He became quite upset when he found out what a lonely life Charlie was leading.'

'Oh! How is Freddie? Is he here tonight? I do write to him sometimes but he never replies.'

'Too busy courting.' Alan laughed. 'Anyway, Freddie thought we should get Charlie to come out with us. Mind you, I think he had a notion that Charlie might make a good goalie, but that didn't work out.' Alan laughed. 'Charlie kept wandering off and we couldn't make him understand he was supposed to stop the ball going into the net. Anyway, with Freddie and the gang for protection Charlie followed us about like a shadow. It was then we found out how much he liked music. When we told his father he went out and bought him a record player. Since then Charlie's never looked back. The only sufferers are his poor old parents. He's driving them mad playing "Sweet

Nothings" over and over again. Seems he's fallen for Brenda Lee.' Alan laughed and then looked serious. 'It is puzzling, though.' He hesitated thoughtfully.

'What is?' Pam asked.

'Well, we all know Charlie can't read, but yet he can pick out his favourite record from all the rest.'

'It's probably the colour of the label,' volunteered Avril.

'Not so. We've tried mixing it up with a whole lot of other Brunswick labels, but he still picks it out with no trouble at all.' He looked in Avril's teacup. 'If you've finished, would you like to dance?' As Avril rose to her feet Alan said to Jacqueline, 'Oh, I almost forgot, Doug asked me if I'd seen you. He's over by the stage.'

Jacqueline's heart skipped a beat. 'Are you ready, Pam? Shall we go back in? I think it's almost time for the cabaret.'

Pam followed her friend into the crowded hall, just as a velvety male voice began to sing 'It's Now Or Never'. She hoped Doug Downing wasn't about to steal Jacqueline away. She saw little enough of her friend as it was, and they had so much news to catch up on and so little time.

Pam had achieved a lot considering she had left school at sixteen, unable to face striving for more exams. She had taken a job on a switchboard at a wholesalers in town and had worked hard, been noticed by the manager and landed promotion. Luck had been with her when his private secretary had married and moved away, and Pam had been given the job. Though it was a demanding position she seemed to thrive on the challenge, and would have been ecstatic if only Jacqueline was living at home. The pair had never needed to be part of a crowd and since her friend had left for London Pam had found it difficult to make new friends. Now Jacqueline seemed to be close to Avril, and though she was nice Pam couldn't quite control a feeling of jealousy.

She watched as her friend circled the floor with Doug Downing. His dark head was bent towards Jacqueline's and they were smiling and chatting. He was holding her close, his hand slipping every so often from her waist down to her bottom, and though she took his hand and returned it to where it should be Jacqueline didn't look the least bit offended. In fact, Pam couldn't help thinking how right they looked together, he in his dark well-cut suit, and she in a pencil slim cocktail dress of kingfisher blue jersey wool. Oh well, it looked as if her friend was lost to her even though she was at home.

'Want to dance, Pam?' The voice startled her and she smiled up at the ginger-haired foreman. He had fancied her for a while, and frankly she quite fancied him too. Perhaps it was time to stop playing hard to get.

'OK.' They walked with his arm circling her waist until they found an empty space on the floor, and then he drew her towards him.

'I'd been looking for you, then I spotted your hair,' he said.

Pam's hair, once held back with slides, now hung sleek and shimmering to her waist. She laughed. 'Well, with hair the colour of ours, we should stand out a mile. Funny – when I was little I hated it, and now it seems everyone is dying theirs auburn, so we're in fashion at last, just when I was thinking of changing the colour.'

'Don't you dare. I like you just the way you are.' He hugged her closer, and the cabaret singer, who sounded remarkably like Connie Francis, broke into her thoughts. 'Hey, that's Una Bacon.'

'Hmm. I think she's for the big time, that girl. She's certainly talented.'

'And lovely.'

'So are you,' he whispered, and Pam snuggled closer. Una sang on, her voice ideally suited to romantic numbers.

Jacqueline and Doug made their way across the room towards them. 'Are you going to introduce us?' Jacqueline asked, still a little tipsy from the earlier gins.

'Sure.' Her friend stopped dancing. 'This is Brian. He works at Congleton's too. Brian, this is my best friend Jacqueline, and Doug Downing.'

'Happy Christmas.' Brian grinned.

'And the same to you, Brian.' Doug shook Brian's hand warmly.

'Happy Christmas, Pam.' Jacqueline hugged her friend to her and planted a kiss on her cheek.

Pam blinked away the tears that sprang to her eyes. No matter what happened, nobody would spoil their friendship. It was the kind which would survive anything, though she had a feeling it was about to come up against some strong competition, in the forms of Brian and Doug Downing.

Una began to sing 'Silent Night' and the dancing couples swayed together, as the spirit of

Christmas filled the room. Doug Downing kissed Jacqueline for the first time, a kiss which lasted through two whole verses of the carol, and then he whispered, 'I love you, Jacqueline Holmes.'

'I know,' Jacqueline murmured. 'And I love you too.'

Avril caught a glimpse of her friend across the smoke-hazed room and smiled. Jacqueline's hurt was certainly healed. She snuggled closer to Alan. It was going to be an absolutely fabulous Christmas.

It had been a hectic Christmas Day, with Grandma Holmes revelling in being surrounded by sons, daughters and grandchildren, the two youngest – Harry's son Barry and Margaret's Anthony – being at the boisterous stage, when to sit still for more than five minutes proved an impossibility. Balloons, crackers and chocolates were soon disposed of, and organised games swiftly turned into wrestling matches with fathers and uncles joining in. Only when the large fairy-lit tree was in danger of being overturned did Mary put a stop to the mayhem. Gladys had felt rather sad at one point to think their nephew had not even bothered to send a card this year. Oh, well – this was her family now.

Nevertheless, everyone had a wonderful time and it was early next morning when the guests began to disperse. Despite the festivities, though, Jacqueline couldn't help wondering if something was worrying her father. Since she had arrived home he had seemed to be unusually preoccupied, though making a heroic effort to hide the fact, using Tittle Harry as an excuse.

'I'm afraid it's time the poor old thing was put out of his misery,' he said when Jacqueline questioned him as to what was on his mind. It was true that Tittle Harry was only just managing to soldier on, crippled according to the vet by rheumatism. The poor old dog had all on now to drag his tired old body across the room, and though he usually completed the shuffle to where Jacqueline happened to be sitting, it was proving more and more of an effort before he finally collapsed with his head on her feet, and a sad tired expression on his face. Once or twice, too, Mary had found a pool when he had been unable to reach the door in time to be let out. This distressed the old dog and they all knew it would be kinder to let Tittle Harry go. Yet Jacqueline thought there was something more on her father's mind, and wondered why nobody else seemed to notice.

Una had also been rather quiet, anticipating the opening of the pantomime on the following day. After rehearsing a part in the chorus for many weeks she had suddenly been promoted to a more prominent role, and had spent Christmas Day suffering from last minute nerves. No one else doubted her ability, and she knew she was fortunate not only to have landed the part, but to have been given leave of absence by her employers. Though Una planned to attend an audition soon in Scarborough for one of the summer shows, she realised how lucky she was to have her receptionist's job kept open for her should she need to return to it.

On Boxing Day the calm and beauty of Moorland House was a soothing balm to Mary's nerves, and Jacqueline almost ran from the car in her eagerness, feeling somewhat guilty at feeling more at home here than she did at the shop.

Avril couldn't decide which was the more beautiful, the exterior view of the house surrounded by evergreens, and slightly shrouded by a storm-laden wintry sky, or the warm welcoming interior, heavily garlanded with holly and ivy from the garden.

Oh, what a house! She had sometimes wished Jacqueline would stop harping on about the place, but now she understood completely. It was not only the house, but the atmosphere within it which seemed to cushion one in a cloak of welcome. Not for the first time she felt a pang of envy at the thought of her friend's good fortune at being surrounded by such a large and loving family. Then she reminded herself that she too was lucky, to be here sharing their hospitality. She glanced to where Alan was arranging chairs round the large, exquisitely dressed table. He caught and held her glance for rather longer than necessary, sending a blush rising embarrassingly to her face. She hoped she hadn't encouraged him, she couldn't remember doing so, but when he had suddenly kissed her outside the dance hall it had seemed natural and right, and the sensation he had caused in her body had been reciprocated; she had sensed his arousal and drawn away. He was a year her junior, and it wouldn't be fair to take advantage, not after all the hospitality the family had shown her.

She told herself it would be a casual flirtation, nothing more than a fleeting holiday friendship to be forgotten on her return to London, and what could be the harm in that? But she knew it couldn't be dismissed so easily, and she would not wish it to be. Besides, he didn't seem young. He had a maturity about him, a sense of responsibility, despite his air of merriment.

'A penny for your thoughts, dear.' Grandad Roberts caught her eye. She blushed, and he smiled, knowing without her answering in which direction the wind was blowing. He had noticed yesterday that when Alan had held a twig of mistletoe over each of the ladies in turn, joking that this was the best part of Christmas, it was this young friend of Jacqueline's who had received the longest kiss. He sighed. He had always been a romantic at heart, and he had done well for himself in that respect, Gladys being just as warm and affectionate as himself. Come to think of it he had been lucky in other ways too. A career he loved, though sometimes he wondered if he should consider retirement, make way for a younger doctor. He supposed it would have to happen some time in the near future, possibly within the next year, what with his darned blood pressure, and the angina. If Gladys knew about that, he would be pensioned off here and now, and he couldn't hide the symptoms from her for ever.

Oh, yes, Rowland was a fortunate man. Who would have dreamed he would be surrounded with family like this? Well, not actual family, but as good as. He blessed the day he had offered

305

Mary O'Connor a home; these were his family all right. He frowned. Far more so than actual blood relatives. How long was it now since Ruth and Richard had been in touch? Rowland tried to remember and was shocked when he realised the number of years that had passed since their last visit.

It had been different when his nephew had been younger; the boy had almost lived here then. Rowland had paid for his education, bought him his first car and given him numerous other expensive gifts. Now, when a visit from the family would have so delighted Gladys, they were always too busy. He sighed, then cheered up again as he looked towards his wife and Jacqueline admiring a table decoration, or something or other, the girl's dark curls falling over her face. Such an alive, animated face it was, so like her father in looks, yet with the same vibrant energy Mary had possessed when she first arrived at Moorland House, despite the TB glands. Oh, yes, he was a fortunate man. Perhaps, he had not been blessed with a family of his own, but this family sitting down at the table today meant more to him than his blood relatives ever could.

'Are you coming to the table or are you going to carry on musing until the soup's gone cold?' Gladys broke into his thoughts.

In the afternoon Jacqueline decided to take Avril for a walk along the lane and down by the reservoir, and no one was surprised when Alan decided to tag along, leaving the house quiet except for the gentle snores of Jack and the doctor. Nor was it any surprise to Alan and Avril when

306

Jacqueline suggested calling in at the Downings', knowing the elderly couple were always delighted to receive visitors. On this occasion, however, it was Douglas who welcomed them with the greatest enthusiasm, keen to show them the many improvements he had made to the farm.

The yard was uncluttered and clean and one of the outbuildings had been turned into a huge greenhouse with a sign on the door inviting walkers and other passers-by to go in and look round. As Doug opened the door the scent of hyacinths greeted them, their heady perfume causing Avril to sneeze. On long wooden tables seed boxes of pansies and pots of crocus and daffodil bulbs were spread in rows, each one labelled with a name and a colour. Hanging from the ceiling artistic arrangements of holly and greenery tied with red ribbons added a festive air.

'You should have seen it a month ago,' Doug said. 'The place looked a picture. I didn't know if I was doing the right thing venturing into the gardening side, but as you can see we've nearly been cleared out for Christmas.'

Jacqueline wanted to hug Doug. She had had no idea he had turned his talents in this direction, but it shouldn't really have surprised her. After all, he had always taken a great interest in the garden at Moorland House.

'Come on,' he said, 'I'll show you the trees.' He laughed. 'What's left of them that is.'

They walked out and round the corner in the direction of the five acre field, where Mr Downing had opened the gate for the cattle to amble through, heavy and ready for milking. At the top of the second field rows of fir trees stood to attention, graded in size, the little ones at the front. The back row and half the next were missing.

'It's unbelievable how many I've sold.' Doug grinned. 'And the man from the market's already placed an order for next year.'

'I can't believe it.' Jacqueline gazed around her. 'It all looks so organised.'

Doug began to laugh. 'Go on, say what you're thinking, that it all used to be such a mess. I know, and I can't say my dad's quite used to the idea, but I think he's gradually coming round to my way of thinking. As I told him, there's no fortune to be made in just working the fields any more, not enough to keep two men in wages, any road.'

'But Cyril wants to carry on farming,' Jacqueline pointed out.

'Aye, but he has his heart set on a larger outfit. Otherwise he should have had this place by rights, him being the eldest like. But don't worry about our Cyril. He'll be back on the land before long – that's all he's slaving for over at the works. I'm telling you, he'll end up one of those gentlemen farmers before he's done.' His eyes travelled over the fields. 'Like the rest of us Downings, it's in the blood.' He laughed. 'And the rate I'm going I'll not be far behind.'

'Well, I think it's lovely.' Avril gazed round. 'And the view, I've never seen anything like it.'

'So you like country living then?' Alan asked hopefully.

'Oh, yes. I don't know about Jacqueline but I'm dreading going back to London.'

'Well, it won't be for long. Besides, I've heard it's beautiful in South Africa. Ask Grandad Roberts – he has a friend who came from there.'

'South Africa?' Alan looked puzzled.

'Avril's parents are there, waiting for her to join them after college.'

'Oh.' Alan's face fell.

'Well, I'm not sure yet. I know I ought, but it depends on the work situation here.' She smiled. 'After all, I might land on my feet in a top job. One never knows.'

'Well, let's hope so.' Alan's gloom seemed to lift a little.

'We'd better go in. You know what my mother's like, she'll have the best china and tablecloth out,' said Doug.

'And the best mince pies we've ever tasted,' Jacqueline added.

'I don't think I can eat another thing after that dinner.' Avril patted her stomach.

'I can.' Alan led the way into the kitchen in anticipation of Mrs Downing's baking.

'Oh, I almost forgot, you've been invited to tea at Moorland House,' Jacqueline told Doug.

'I'd better get ready then. Won't be long.' He hurried upstairs, and was changed and spruced up in no time at all.

'Bring yerselves in out of the cold, an' pull yer chairs up to the fire.' Mrs Downing brewed the tea and cut a spiced cake, which she placed on a fine cut-glass stand with the mince pies. 'Eeh, but it doesn't seem two minutes since yer mam was sitting there, and no older than you are now,' she said.

Her husband knew without being told what his wife was thinking. Time might be a great healer, but it would never erase the hurt of a lost son, or dim the memories. It would have been nice if this young lass and lad had belonged to their Tom. Oh well, there was plenty of time for some more grandchildren. Granddaughters were all very well but the farm needed a grandson.

Mr Downing leaned back in his chair and closed his eyes, searching in his mind's eye for a picture of his Tom, afraid that one day he might not be able to visualise the handsome young soldier. He shook himself. He had only to look across the table at his youngest, the spitting image of his brother. Oh, why did he always have to get all melancholy at Christmas? He'd be glad when the new year came round and they were all back to normal.

After Mary had helped Gladys clear the tea things away, and Jacqueline, unable to resist renewing her musical skills, had entertained them to a couple of pieces on the piano, the warm cosy atmosphere and the cherry brandy seemed to have a calming effect on the assembled party.

With Jacqueline and Doug squeezed into one large leather chair and Alan and Avril sitting on the hearthrug, the scene was set for stories of the old days, when Gladys began work as a seamstress at the age of ten at the turn of the century. It was only then that Jacqueline realised how old Grandma Roberts really was. She had always seemed so youthful somehow, and smart; and as for Grandad Roberts, why he should have retired years ago.

Alan received a good-natured reprimand from Jacqueline when he related an incident which occurred one day when he had given Charlie Barker a lift to the dentist. Freddie Cartwright's mother had been making brawn from a sheep's head, and Freddie had slipped the largest sheep's tooth he could find into Charlie's hand.

'Cor, Charlie,' he had said, 'that must be a record. I've never seen a tooth so big in my life.'

Poor Charlie had gone round for weeks showing everyone the tooth, as proud as Punch, thinking it was his own.

'You shouldn't tease him,' Jacqueline said, at the same time laughing with the others.

'Why not? He loves to be the centre of attraction.'

'Well, he certainly seems happy enough,' Doug said.

After that the conversation turned to who could tell the best ghost story. Jack began by describing his fear whilst cycling to work one morning in the blackout. As he neared the loneliness of the wood leading to the pit yard, with the hooting of an owl and the wind moaning in the trees, a white figure suddenly loomed in front of him. 'I've never been so close to soiling my underpants,' he said, 'and I was in a cold sweat by the time I reached the pit yard. It wasn't until I was going home in the daylight that I found out what it was: a white sheet which had blown from somebody's clothes line.'

'Oh, Dad.' Jacqueline laughed. 'That wasn't a real ghost.'

'Course it wasn't. There's no such thing,' mocked Alan.

'Oh, now, don't be too certain of that,' Dr Roberts said. 'There have been all kinds of strange sightings at the Royal Hospital.'

'I'm not surprised. The place gives me the shudders, especially the corridors.' Gladys shivered.

'What kinds of sightings?' Mary asked.

'Well, on one occasion a young nurse was in charge of a ward on night shift, sitting calmly at her desk, when suddenly a figure rose up from one of the beds and disappeared through the wall. The poor girl ran trembling and locked herself in the lavatory. When she and another nurse went to investigate they found the patient had passed away.'

'Probably a figment of her imagination,' said Doug.

'No,' Jacqueline said. 'I saw Grandad Holmes the night he died. He came to say goodbye.'

Alan laughed nervously. 'But we were on holiday, miles away.'

'What difference would that make? Ghosts don't have to travel by train.'

'You never told us,' Mary said. 'About Grandad Holmes.'

'You'd only have laughed. Besides, I didn't think it was anything unusual at the time.' She hesitated, unsure whether to continue. 'I've seen other people too.'

'Caroline,' Alan drawled.

'Yes, but not just Caroline. I've seen a soldier, but I thought it was because I had Douglas on my mind. Oh, I know he isn't a soldier, but the one I saw looked just like him. I couldn't quite believe it, but then he came through to the medium too.'

Mary had turned quite pale. 'What medium?'

'At the church. Oh, I know you won't approve, but I can't help that. They've been so kind, helping me after–' She broke off, wishing she had never begun.

Avril came to her rescue. 'It's just a church we go to sometimes. They're a nice crowd, there's nothing weird about them.'

'Thomas got Grandad Holmes, too. There couldn't have been any doubt it was him, he was swearing like a trooper.'

'That was our old man all right.' Jack laughed.

'And your Uncle Willie, the one who was killed, he came through too, Mam, so now you know. I know you won't like it.'

'Why not?' Jack asked. 'Your mam's been to a church with Auntie Madge, so she can't very well object, and she was disappointed when no message came for her.'

Alan looked at Mary in wonder. 'You didn't, Mother? Oh, this is too much.' He laughed. 'Two weirdos in one family is just too much.'

'You can laugh.' Jacqueline blushed. 'But you'll find out one of these days.'

'What about the soldier?' Mary asked, glancing at Jack. 'I mean, did you get a message?'

'Yes.' Jacqueline couldn't quite remember. 'Oh, yes. He said something about Christmas and Mary and the stable and how he was at peace. Oh yes, and he said he was thankful for the joy of Christmas Day. I think it must have been something to do with the nativity. There was such a feeling of peace coming through, it was wonderful.'

Mary rose on the pretext of collecting the empty glasses and went to the kitchen. Gladys followed her out and found her in tears.

'It's all right, love,' she said. 'Jacqueline didn't know, though, did she?' She closed the door. 'About Tom, I mean.'

'No. No, I never mentioned it, I'm sure of it.'

'Well, then, it sounds as though he was a contented man.'

Mary splashed her eyes with cold water. 'I'm all right,' she said, smiling. 'I'm fine. Perhaps now I can forgive myself.'

Gladys tutted. 'After all these years, I should jolly well hope so. Look, I don't know what happened the Christmas before Tom was killed, but I can hazard a guess and I'm sure in the circumstances, I mean the war and everything, there was really no reason to feel guilty.'

'I couldn't help it. I got it into my head that Tom's death was God's way of punishing us.' She hesitated. 'For making love.'

Gladys sighed. 'There was a lot of punishment handed out during the war but it was committed by man, not God.' She uncovered the plate of cold meat sandwiches. 'You bring in the cakes, love,' she said. 'I dare say the youngsters are starving – they usually are.'

'You know something?' Mary said. 'I might just pay a visit to Darnall again. Perhaps our Jacqueline'll come with me.'

'Oh, and what will Jack say?'

'He won't mind. He's never been jealous of Tom.'

314

'You know something, you're a lucky woman having a man like Jack.'

'I know. I haven't always appreciated him, but I know.'

'Then tell him so. He's been looking a little bit neglected lately.'

Mary stopped and looked at Gladys. 'You don't miss much, do you?'

'Not much, not when it affects my nearest and dearest, and Jack is as dear to me as you are. So I don't think you should go raking up the past. Jack may not complain but he could be hurt.'

Mary smiled. 'I'm sure you're right. You usually are. I'm lucky not only in my choice of a husband, but in having you as a friend. Though I've been so wrapped up in the shop that sometimes I've forgotten that too.'

'Well, as long as you know.'

Then they carried the supper into the sitting room to feed their nearest and dearest.

It had been a lovely Christmas, the best for years.

Especially for Mary, who could at last consider the Christmas sin forgiven.

Chapter Twenty-Five

The churning began in Jack's stomach, and a cloud, heavy and grey, seemed to enshroud him, so that sleep was impossible. He would be glad to get back to work and hear the worst; it would be better than this uncertainty.

Harry with his usual optimism considered the rumour to be too daft for words.

'Why the devil should they consider closing the pit with all the rich seams still to be worked out?' he queried. 'Besides, it's only four years since they forked out eighty thousand pounds for the pit head baths.'

But Bill, who was in close contact with the under-manager, didn't hold out much hope.

'It'll be the closure of the coke ovens that'll see the end for us. Ninety per cent of the output serves the steel works, as you well know, and with the billet and rod mills turning over to gas producers, I can't see much chance of the pit staying open, can you?'

Jack was in a better financial position than most. The shop was paid for and was bringing in a tidy though irregular profit, but that was Mary's domain. It was his place to keep the house ticking over, and then there were the rates, not cheap for a decent-sized business property on a prime main road position. Not only that, but the nest egg he had managed to accumulate in the early years of their marriage had been sunk into building up the business. Still, financial considerations couldn't account for the depression which seemed to have enveloped him since he heard the news.

He had at least got the car, if the worst happened and he couldn't find a job locally. And he wasn't in debt like some of the young family men who would have their rents to find and young families to support. No, the worst part would be breaking the news to Mary. Oh, she wouldn't have hysterics or turn on the tears. In her normal matter of fact way she would say, 'Don't worry, we've got the shop.' That was the trouble. No normal man would want to sit by and let his wife keep him in idleness. Oh, no, he wouldn't do that. He would strike while the iron was hot: he would go job-seeking now instead of waiting. He'd have no chance of competing with the thirty-year-olds if he waited for the closure. No, he would find another job now and tell Mary later. No point in worrying her at this stage.

The panicky feeling was coming on again, the heat rising from his stomach, surging into his head and arms. He threw down the thick blankets and stood up gingerly, feeling a slight dizziness as he rose to his feet and walked to the coldness of the bathroom.

He had had a couple too many last night. There was something about Moorland House and Rowland's company that made you forget about work the morning after. He heard the wall clock in the sitting room strike five. It wasn't worth getting back into bed for another ten minutes, so he slipped quietly back to the bedroom, dressed in his work clothes and pressed down the button on the alarm clock. Then he bent and kissed Mary lightly on the forehead and tucked the bedclothes in round her neck.

He could feel the phlegm rising in his chest and hurried downstairs before the usual early morning coughing bout woke up the whole household. He could hear his old man's voice now. 'The bloody rotten coal dust'll see us all off in the end. Get out now before it's too late.'

Jack smiled ironically. If Jacqueline's story about the medium was true, her grandad would soon be seeing his ambition fulfilled, that no lad of his would work down the bloody pit. He felt his depression lift. Maybe it would be for the best; at least his old man would be able to rest content.

Tittle Harry whimpered at his feet and slunk past him as he opened the door, did what he had to do and returned to the warmth of the kitchen fire.

Jack picked up his snap tin and water bottle and prayed that the car wouldn't be too cold to start. It was enough to freeze the– He laughed to himself as he locked the door. He was getting to be as bad as his old man. Well, he supposed he could do a lot worse than that.

Considering it was the first shift back after a holiday, the normal bantering and exchange of gossip was scarce and the atmosphere strained. Jack guessed the rumours had circulated, and whether the result was anxiety about the threatened closure, or the effort to increase output and add to the bonus whilst the opportunity still existed, was hard to tell. Only young Freddie Cartwright voiced his fears, and Jack could offer him no consolation, knowing the rough and ready young man would be one of the hardest hit, what with a dependent mother and an ailing sister to support.

'I'm thinking of going over to Donstone Main,' Freddie volunteered. 'I've heard they might be setting on over there.'

'They're allus setting on over there. I hope you realise what you'll be letting yourself in for, lad. I've heard the safety standards are non-existent, and what with it being a non-union pit an' all.' Jack coughed and spat out a dollop of chewed twist. 'Besides, how will yer get there?'

'Oh, I should be able to cadge a lift on me mate's bike, until I get one of me own. I'm popping down to Grey's next week to see what the asking price is.'

'Going to treat yersen, are yer, lad?'

'Aye. I've been saving long enough. Besides, it'll be essential if I 'ave to travel to work.'

'What are yer looking for, second hand?'

'Not likely. I've worked like a bloody horse, an' I reckon it's time I spent a bit on mesen. I'm after an AJS, I think.'

'Aye, I reckon yer deserve a treat, lad,' Jack agreed.

Freddie went on to extol the virtues of the AJS, ending with, 'An' anyway, I've always got your Al to give us a hand if owt goes wrong.'

'Aye well, so long as yer don't go putting ideas into his head about buying a motor bike. My life wouldn't be worth living with his mother whittling every time he was five minutes late home.'

Freddie grinned and peered around in the darkness for a place to use as a lavatory. He wondered what it would be like to have a mother who worried about him, instead of one who was all grab. One of these days his mam would realise how well off she was, but he knew that wouldn't be until he left home and he couldn't see that happening for a long time, especially if they closed the rotten pit.

The men carried on in silence, each wrapped up in his own private thoughts, even more exhausted than usual after a couple of days' respite. Both wondered what would be round the next corner, dreaming of a future away from the damp, depressing darkness of pit life but unable to visualise anything better.

The pit closure was announced officially on New Year's Day.

'A bleeding good start to a new year, I must say,' Freddie ranted. 'New year and no job.'

Jack was more fortunate. He was all set to begin work at the brickworks, where he would be earning only about two-thirds of his present wages in return for a sixty-hour week. The twelve-hour shifts were supposed to be alternate weeks on days and nights but soon turned into mostly nights at the insistence of his partner. Admittedly the work was almost non-existent, consisting mainly of watching a series of meters and clocks which recorded the temperature of the kilns.

Jack, who was used to manual graft, could not adjust to the boredom and the lack of camaraderie he had always been used to. Mary considered the move a godsend, pointing out the benefits of working in a clean healthy atmosphere. She even went out to the Co-op and bought him a radio to keep him company, in an effort to cheer him up, and couldn't seem to understand it was the men he missed.

Jack was also missing his daughter. On her return to college the light seemed to have been extinguished from his life, and each time he entered the shop and noticed the windows he was reminded of Jacqueline and her friend.

Before leaving, Avril had insisted on dressing the windows, passing on her imaginative ideas to Yvonne, who was eager and delighted to learn.

In one window she had formed a tableau of a spring wedding, the bride in an ivory silk dress and a short frothy veil, a new line Mary had begun to meet demand from the customers for whom she made wedding and bridesmaid dresses to measure. Avril also dressed a window model in a chic navy Alexon suit with ivory accessories, and a tiny one in pink taffeta with a navy muff and Juliet cap.

In the other window a display of handbags, hats and gloves surrounded a central model in an oyster-coloured slinky negligee, making an eye-catching change from the normal run of the mill dresses and blouses. Mary, who had had misgivings at first, considering it far too early for a spring display, was now reaping the benefit of orders for Easter weddings, and working harder than ever before, serving all day in the shop and sewing well into the night after Jack left for work at six.

Eventually it was Alan who drew her attention to Jack's unhealthy and haunted look.

'I think Dad should see a doctor, Mother,' he said one evening when his father had passed within yards of him without noticing his son, got into his car and driven off in a most erratic manner.

Mary looked up from the zip she was inserting. 'Why? He hasn't complained of feeling ill.' She sounded unconcerned.

'He doesn't need to. You've only to look at him to see he isn't right. I'm not talking about physical illness. He's a bag of nerves, surely you can see that.'

'He hasn't adjusted to his new job, that's all,' Mary said.

'I don't think it's just that. Besides, I noticed before he left the pit. Even our Jacqueline was concerned about him when she was home, and she's worrying now she's gone back, she said in her letter.'

'He was upset about Tittle Harry. Having to take the poor old thing to be put down didn't help.'

'I know, but I still think he should see a doctor, or at least you should have a word with Grandad Roberts. My dad's never been volatile, but now we can't talk to him without him flying off the handle.'

'Well, he was never exactly on top of the world on night shift.'

'Exactly, and now he's just about on permanent nights, and twelve hours at that.'

Mary was exasperated. 'Surely you're not suggesting he was better off as a miner,' she snapped. 'He's not exactly overworked, and admits he can get his head down at the works for a couple of hours.'

'But it's not doing him any good, Mother, working in solitary for hours on end. He's in need of some companionship. God knows he doesn't get much from you.'

The colour soared in Mary's face as she jumped to her feet, dropping the almost completed garment to the floor. 'And what exactly do you mean by that?' she demanded.

'I mean it's time you showed Dad a bit of consideration for a change, rather than your customers.'

'Your father should be grateful, especially with his cut in wages. At least he needn't worry financially.'

Alan's voice rose uncharacteristically. 'Oh, that's great. Don't you realise what it must feel like to be told you don't have your job any more, and to know your wife is earning more than you are? My father needs to be given back his confidence, not to be made to feel inferior to you.'

Mary resumed her sewing. 'I'm sure you're exaggerating. Anyway, how come you presume to know so much about how your father feels?'

'I know, because Freddie Cartwright told me how my father was looked up to by his workmates, respected as one of the best workers, and the kindest. I know, because when Freddie was upset at losing his job I took time to listen. How long is it since you listened to Dad? That's if you ever did.' Alan picked up his coat and stormed out, letting the door slam behind him, leaving Mary reflecting on her son's words.

Maybe he was right and she had been a little inconsiderate, but it had been a busy time, what with Christmas and now Easter coming up. Once she caught up with her orders she would have more time to spend with Jack, she promised herself. In the meantime she would keep her eye on her husband's health, though she was sure there was nothing to worry about.

She plugged in the iron to finish the completed garment.

Jack had cleaned down the panels with paraffin waste, washed down the table and even gone over the floor with an old dried-up mop which he guessed hadn't seen the light of day for years. Now there was nothing left to do except be there in case anything sent the clocks out of action, and make sure he adjusted the temperatures accordingly.

He could hear the men from the brick yard as they changed shifts. Although the dust they worked in was every bit as harmful as coal dust, he would have given anything to be amongst them doing a proper job. He went outside, hoping to engage one of them in a bit of conversation, but the afternoon shift were eager to be home to beds and wives, some of them shouldering bags of coaloids, a coke-like perk which saved them quite a bit when mixed with coal. Others entering the yard were in a hurry to clock on at the last minute and had only time for a hiya or goodnight.

He returned to the stark loneliness of the kiln room, silent except for the monotonous drone of the mechanism. Eight more hours to go.

He switched on the radio and settled down, picking up a magazine left by the man he had taken off earlier. He thumbed through the pages of scantily dressed pin-ups. At the pit he would have passed it round to an eager audience, amongst laughter and ribald remarks. Now he didn't even have any interest. What was the use of looking when his sex life was non-existent and had been for weeks, apart from once at Christmas, and even that had been a half-hearted attempt on Mary's part.

Suddenly Jack's heart began to pound, the thudding filling his head and beating on the back of his chair. He felt the dizziness wash over him again, and the sweat cold and clammy on the back of his neck. He made his way shakily to the door on quaking legs, and gulped in the fresh night air. The feeling of panic began to subside but Jack was afraid, and a weakness drained his body of energy.

He resumed his place in front of the meter panel, distressed at the thought of making a major mistake. Suddenly he began to cry, in deep harrowing sobs, drowned in a feeling of self-pity. It was as though there was nothing for him any more except a job he loathed, a wife who seemed indifferent to anything but her work, and all the joys of the former years disappearing in a haze of gloom. Jacqueline, his little girl, had made the transition to woman, and would soon belong to some other man. Tittle Harry, his trusting old friend, gone now, cold and limp in the arms of the vet; and his father, distressed and dying and he hadn't been there, but in some bloody caravan many miles away.

The tears began to subside, leaving Jack staring fixedly at the clocks on the panel, a broken man, whose feelings were shattered into a thousand fragments. His watch said two o'clock.

Four more hours to go, but that wouldn't be the end, only the beginning of another nightmare day.

It was Joe Johnson who found Jack when he came in for the morning shift. He was still sitting, transfixed and trembling, before the monitors.

'Come on, Jack, it's time yer were off, man – 'asn't tha been 'ere long enough?' But there was no response from Jack. Joe switched off the radio, not knowing which to do first, check the temperatures or see to Jack. In the end he hurried to the telephone and called Dr Sellers.

By the time Jack was escorted home Alan was up and ready for work, and it came as no surprise to see the condition his father was in. He explained to the doctor how his father had seemed. 'It's been brewing for some time,' he finished.

'He should have come to see me before he reached this stage. I'm afraid it will be a long haul back now. Luckily, he hasn't broken completely.'

Alan was almost as sorry for his mother as for Jack, and regretted his outburst of the previous day. All she could do was keep repeating 'I didn't realise, I didn't realise' as she helped her son get Jack upstairs and into bed.

'You mustn't distress yourself,' Dr Sellers tried to reassure her. 'It isn't always obvious until it's too late.'

'But I should have known,' Mary said.

'Has he had any worries recently? More than

usual, I mean.'

'He lost his job, and the dog had to be put down, that upset him a lot,' Alan said. 'And he's been depressed for some time.'

'I believe it's overstress rather than depression,' said the doctor.

'What's the difference?'

'With stress or anxiety the patient has to be taught how to relax and become calm again. In a depressed state the patient needs to be shocked into becoming interested in normal everyday activities. If not they automatically withdraw into themselves.'

'So how can my father be treated?'

'By helping him voice his anxieties, talk about what's in his mind, and above all by getting him to relax.'

'Isn't there any medication?' Mary suddenly seemed aware of what was being discussed.

'Oh, yes. I'll make out a prescription. The pills will calm him for the time being, but in the long term he needs to unwind, and be protected from pressure and anxiety. He also needs to know he has your love and support – which I'm sure he does,' Dr Sellers hastened to add.

When Jack's trembling had ceased, he apologised for the third time for causing such an upheaval. Mary looked at his pale haggard face and wondered how she could have failed to notice the stress her husband must have been suffering. Jack knew he should be getting up and doing the usual chores of fetching in the coal and letting down the canopies over the shop windows, but his body seemed drained of all energy. Besides, if he moved the panic might return, terrifying in its intensity. So he offered no resistance when Alan insisted he stay in bed.

Mary, filled with remorse, brought him strong sweet tea and toast which he left untouched, and tried to fathom what must be done in the future. She knew her son was right when he said his father could no longer work at the brickworks, and deeply regretted not realising sooner the effect the job was having on her husband.

She glanced at the clock. The shop should have been open some time ago, but she remained by Jack's side, aching inside as his dark-rimmed eyes searched her face, appealing for reassurance. She drew him towards her, enclosing him in her arms, protective as a mother towards her child. And there they stayed, unheeding of time, pressed together, as Mary prayed for the first time in years. For her husband's sanity and her own peace of mind.

Three months had gone by since Rowland Roberts had taken Jack under his wing and offered him the sanctity of Moorland House. Now the daffodils were at their fullest, pale golden trumpets playing in the breeze, in time to the ripples on the reservoir.

Jack paused to rest on the green grassy bank and skimmed a stone across the water. Catkins trembled above his head and he was at peace in the solitude. The last time he had come to this place he had stood on the rock close to the water's edge and considered throwing himself down into the cold mesmeric depths. At the time it seemed easier than striving to find a reason for living. Now, looking back, he cringed at his weakness, ashamed that he could even have considered such an action, and wondered if he had been sane at the time.

It was Rowland who had brought him back from the abyss with his calm reassurance and his gentle persuasion, Rowland who in the beginning had encouraged him to leave his bed, and then the shop, wheedling him into taking his first steps out of the door and into the car, calming him as yet another panic attack threatened to send him cowering back into the safety of his familiar armchair and Mary's protection.

When Alan had rung Rowland on the day of his father's breakdown it had been for the doctor's advice, but Rowland, only just semi-retired, had taken over the care of Jack completely, releasing Mary so she could continue running the shop, which would be essential if Jack was to be unemployed. It had given Rowland an objective just when he had been at a loss as to how to fill his extra leisure time, and Alan had willingly handed over his father into Grandad Roberts's capable hands.

It had been Rowland who had sat up for hours at a stretch trying to still the trembling and the jerking limbs, guiding Jack through the desperation as he struggled to breathe. Calming him with words of reassurance and praising him after each small achievement, such as shaving himself or making the early morning tea.

It had been Rowland who had taken him into the garden, leading him by the hand like a child, through the gate and on to the lane, each day a few yards further until they had reached this place, where the tranquillity had acted like a healing salve on Jack's shattered nerves.

It had been Rowland who had followed at a distance, anxiously watching, the first time Jack had come here by himself, hoping he was sufficiently recovered to cope with yet another hurdle. His heart had raced when he saw Jack pause beside the deepest part of the reservoir, but he had trusted his own judgement that Jack was over the worst and strong enough to resist the call of the cold grey waters. He had been right.

Now Jack looked around him, listened to a blackbird's song and marvelled at the marble effect of the vast blue-white skyscape. He knew it was time to go home, not for an afternoon visit but back to the activities of a normal working day. Back to Mary, not as an invalid to be cosseted, but as a husband and lover.

He frowned as he wondered what he would do, how he would cope with finding a job, but he breathed in the pure country air, relaxing as Rowland had taught him to do, and flung the worry aside. He had already glimpsed the horrors of Hell and had no wish to see more. He turned and retraced his steps in the direction of Moorland House.

Rowland, watching from the window, marvelled at the improvement in the appearance of his young friend. The dejection seemed to have disappeared and his shoulders to have lifted. He knew Jack had some way to go before he was back to his normal self, but the breakthrough had been made. Rowland didn't profess to be an expert in psychiatry, indeed he knew very little on the subject, but he did know enough to realise that Jack had needed to talk. Gradually he had wheedled out his fears and anxieties, most of which Rowland had already been aware.

The losses of father, job, pet and daughter had obviously gnawed away at Jack's nerves, but a far deeper worry, of which even Jack himself had been unaware, had turned out to be the culprit: the fear that Mary had never loved him, that she regarded him as second best. That it was Tom Downing who still held the special place in her heart.

Mary had been shocked when Rowland had revealed Jack's anxiety.

'Why, that's ridiculous.'

'It may be to you, but it isn't to Jack.'

'But how could he think such a thing?' she cried. 'Oh, I loved Tom, but in a totally different way. I never loved him as I love Jack – I could never love anyone as I love Jack.'

'Then tell him so,' Rowland had advised.

After that, Jack's recovery had begun.

Jack had been home three weeks and showed no desire to seek employment, and Mary was so thankful at his improvement that she had no intention of setting him back by mentioning it. Instead she encouraged him to catch up on any odd jobs around the house, taking Rowland's advice and praising him for even the slightest achievement. Jack found peace of mind and a great satisfaction in turning to his old hobby of working with wood, and set about replacing pan-

331

try shelves and putting up extra shelves in the shop. After that he fixed a picture rail on the wall of the sitting room, and hung the pictures Jacqueline had given them for Christmas. He found he was somewhat comforted by the picture of Tittle Harry gambolling across the purple-heathered moor.

He spent quite a bit of time next door at the shoe shop. Old Will Whitaker had owned the lock-up premises for as long as most people could re-member. He was a good businessman and a gentleman, always immaculately dressed in white stiff-collared shirt and dark pinstriped suit, com-plete with gold watch and chain. Before opening the shop, and sometimes in the evenings, he would take off his jacket, don a long hessian apron and work on repairing the shoes and boots. Jack had never had much to do with him apart from passing the time of day, but Mr Whitaker had been the first to offer Mary his support on hearing of her husband's illness.

'If I can be of any assistance whatsoever, you have only to ask,' he had said.

He had followed up the offer by bringing first a basket of fruit for Jack, and then a bottle of Win-carnis, the finest tonic for nervous disorders in his opinion. When Jack came home he had called to offer Mr Whitaker his thanks, over a cup of tea and an interesting and stimulating conversation. After that Jack had taken to calling in at the shoe shop each morning, and a firm friendship had developed between the two men.

Jack realised that the old man was finding the business too much for him in his declining years, and often took over some small task such as sorting the wellingtons into sizes, or checking the shoes on delivery day for faults like varying shades or imperfect inner soles. He also designed a new footstool for the shop to replace the one which must have been in use for at least sixty years and, although sturdy, looked extremely shabby owing to the leather's being worn away in parts.

After a few weeks Mr Whitaker asked Jack, 'I don't suppose you know anything about cobbling, lad?'

'Well, I've fixed a few clog irons in my time.' Jack laughed.

'Did you make a fair job of it?'

'Fair enough for the pit,' Jack answered, wondering what Mr Whitaker was getting at.

'What would you say to a bit of training? In cobbling, I mean.'

'What, fixing clog irons?'

'Well yes, if needs be, though there's not so much call for clogs these days, what with the pit closure. No, what I meant was soling and heeling.'

'Well.' Jack was taken aback. 'Would I be able to, seeing as I've never tried? I don't really know.'

'Oh.' The old man brushed away Jack's doubts. 'There's nothing to it. The hardest part about it is squatting down on the floor, and that's what's beating me, I'm afraid. My poor old legs won't stand it for much longer, not to mention my back. So I thought with you being out of work, if you don't mind my mentioning it, you might like to learn the trade, sort of. Of course, you would be paid for any repairs you did. I do hope you'll consider my suggestion. I wouldn't like to discontinue the repairing side of the business. Apart from disappointing my regular clientele, it would be quite catastrophic to let it go, in case I decide to put the shop up for sale in the future.'

Jack didn't need to consider Mr Whitaker's offer. 'I'd love to. Learn the trade, I mean. It always used to fascinate me watching my old man when I was little. There he would sit with the old cobbling foot and a piece of leather, cutting and shaping, while I passed him the nails.'

Mr Whitaker's face broke into a thousand creases as he grinned. 'Put on my apron, then. There's no time like the present for beginning something new,' he said, and so began Jack's first lesson.

Mary was delighted, not only that Jack had something new to interest him, but that he was about to begin earning again. Not that they were desperate for cash, the shop was busier than ever, but Mary had learned her lesson and decided to cut her working hours and devote more time to Jack.

Accordingly, she had begun to stock more high-quality ready-made garments, and was surprised to find that trade hadn't been affected in the slightest. There were still a few discerning customers who insisted on Mary Holmes wear, and she continued to make all her own bridal gowns, taking pride in knowing that each dress was an exclusive design.

No, it wasn't the thought of extra cash which pleased Mary, it was the knowledge that Jack would feel independent once more, which would be another step towards his recovery. She was also relieved that he had at last been able to cease taking his medication. At first he had suffered sleepless nights and the tension had seemed to build up again, but with Rowland's constant support and Mr Whitaker's friendship the withdrawal symptoms had been overcome. Now, with yet another interest, she hoped her husband's recovery would soon be complete.

After about a week of being supervised by Mr Whitaker, Jack was quite confident to be left to work on his own, calling on the older man for advice if he needed it, and becoming more proficient every day. He had been given back his self-respect, and was far less stressed now he had been relieved of the need to think about seeking employment. By the time Jacqueline brought Avril home for the summer holidays her father was almost back to his old self; indeed he looked fitter than his daughter could ever remember seeing him, and had taken over the shoe repairing completely from Mr Whitaker. The family were astounded at the amount of work it entailed, and some weeks Jack was earning almost as much as the wretched job at the brickworks had paid.

After the first few days Jacqueline spent little time at home during the day, and her friendship with Doug Downing seemed to go from strength to strength. On the pretext of painting a selection of nature studies she was off to Longfield each morning, wheedling a lift out of Alan before he left for work. Then, weather permitting, she would paint for a couple of hours, visit Grandma and Grandad Roberts for lunch, and spend the afternoon working alongside Doug in the greenhouse, recently named Gardener's Rest. Jacqueline had painted the name on a sign and hung it by the roadside, and now she was busy learning the names of the various plants, and how to pot out the cuttings. Her artistic talents were put to good use in the arrangement of hanging baskets, and she took over the customer sales so that Doug could attend to the farm work.

Some days Avril would accompany her friend, but in general she much preferred to make herself useful in Mary's shop, intent upon repaying the Holmeses' kindness in inviting her to stay, and enjoying the company of Yvonne, who was now employed full time.

Jacqueline completed her set of pictures, a selection of seven by ten watercolours in various floral designs. One was of tall purple foxgloves, rising like sentinels against the blue of the summer sky; another depicted the meadow at Downing's Farm, the wild flowers nestled against silvery shimmering grasses. Her favourite was a study of a wild rose, pale and fragile against a mossy green drystone wall.

Originally she had intended sending the finished pictures to a greetings card publisher for appraisal, but Doug persuaded her to exhibit them in Gardener's Rest instead, and within a week Jacqueline was accepting commissions for her work.

'I can't believe how popular they are,' she told Avril, completely astounded by her success.

'People recognise a good thing when they see it,' Avril pointed out. 'I don't think you realise the amount of minute detail you put into your work. I hope you're charging their true worth,' she added as an afterthought.

'Well, I didn't really know what price to put on them, so I left it to Doug. I was sure he had over-priced them but he insisted if people wanted them they'd be willing to pay, and he was right.'

'Good for him.'

Jacqueline looked thoughtful. 'Why don't you do some? Pictures to sell, I mean?'

Avril stared at her friend. 'Me? Why, who'd want to buy anything of mine? You know my style is nothing like yours; everyone says I'm way ahead of my time.'

'Well, I know they're rather way out, but you never know, they might catch on. A lot of people are going for abstracts at the moment.'

'Maybe in London, but can you honestly see them selling in Longfield? Now, be honest. Can you see one of my designs hanging on the wall amongst the polished copper saucepans in the Downings' kitchen?'

Jacqueline began to giggle. 'Well put like that, no, but some of the city dwellers might well be tempted. Doug's getting a fair amount of after-noon car trade, some of it from select areas like Dore and Millhouses. They're quite sophisti-cated, wanting shrubs and plants I've never even heard of.'

'Maybe, but I'll stick to dressing the windows for your mother if you don't mind. Besides, I'm supposed to be on holiday. Unlike you I'm happy to see the back of my drawing equipment for a few weeks.'

'You've made a very good job of the windows,' Jacqueline said.

'Mr Whitaker must think so. He's asked me to do his shoe displays.'

'Really? Have you agreed?'

'Oh, yes. It's all experience for the future. Besides, I've always been fascinated by shoes. My dream is to have a pair of shoes to match every outfit. Not that I've all that many outfits at the moment.' She dimpled.

'I hope your dream comes true one day.' Jacqueline smiled.

'It will,' Avril said. 'I'm not slaving my guts out at college for nothing. Just you wait – in a few years' time I shall be planning the decor at Buckingham Palace.'

'Oh, and what about South Africa?'

Avril blushed. 'I've decided I'm not going after all.'

'Oh, and why not? I don't suppose my brother has anything to do with your decision?'

'Of course not,' Avril said, but the look in her eyes and the indignant tilt of her chin gave a different answer.

'You can tell me, you know. After all, I've bored you solid with details of my love life in the past.'

'There's nothing to tell.' Avril turned away from her friend and began clearing the table.

'Oh, so I must be imagining the way you look at each other, and the way you seem to spring to life the moment he walks in the room. And I'm not so dumb that I don't notice the way you sneak downstairs the moment you think we're all asleep. I'm not condemning you, Avril. In fact, I think it's great – I just wish you weren't so secretive. After all, I am supposed to be your best friend, aren't I?'

'OK, I'm sorry. I just didn't think you'd approve; besides, I never thought things would turn out as they have. I thought we could just be friends. It was Alan's fault. If he hadn't been so damned attractive, and warm, and–' Avril suddenly burst into tears. 'Oh, Jacqueline, I'm sorry. I'd have given anything not to have fallen for your brother, but it just happened. It was sort of love at first sight, or at least that's how Alan described it. I should have told you. I'm sorry.'

Jacqueline placed an arm round her friend and drew her towards her. 'So, what's all the weeping about? I think it's marvellous. You could do a lot worse than fall for my brother, and he could do worse too.'

'But he's younger than I am.'

Jacqueline laughed. 'So what? By how much? Eighteen months at the most. Oh, come on, what difference does age make? Look at the difference between Doug and me, but it doesn't stop me loving him. I would love him if he was twenty years older – I don't know why I didn't realise it sooner.'

Avril cheered up. 'So you're in love too. I thought as much but you never said.'

'Well, it looks like it's confession time.' They both began to laugh, happy to have confided in each other, relieved now their secrets were at last disclosed.

Avril was in her element. The floor of the shoe shop resembled a bomb site, but the windows were so eye-catching that passing shoppers wondered if the place was under new management, and paused to admire the new displays.

Gone were the monotonous rows of footwear, placed like soldiers standing to attention, all facing the front in pairs, and instead of segregating the men's, women's and children's in their own windows she had intermixed them, dressing each window by theme rather than age and gender. One displayed sandals, plimsolls and beach bags; she had even popped out to the Co-op and purchased a bucket and spade to use as a centrepiece. Another window was ultra-smart with high-heeled courts with matching handbags or evening purses, placed in colour groups of half a dozen, with only the outsides of each shoe facing the window, and the men's styles similarly displayed, complemented by leather wallets. School shoes were set off by satchels, and toddlers' by one of Jacqueline's teddy bears.

The window in the centre was given over completely to such things as carpet slippers, wellies, football boots and sundries like stockings, inner soles and leather belts. Mr Whitaker almost had a seizure when he realised the pairs had been separated, wondering how on earth he would find the odd shoe in a hurry, but Avril had come up with the ingenious idea of sticking a red spot on the end of each shoe box containing only one shoe.

'You'll know immediately that one of the shoes is in the window,' Avril pointed out. 'And as I've

340

only used the less popular size threes in ladies' and sixes in men's you're not likely to have to disturb the displays very often.'

Mr Whitaker had to agree that the difference was remarkable, and spent a good ten minutes admiring his windows from the pavement. He even called Jack from his work to give his opinion. Jack was full of admiration. 'It just goes to show what a bit of young blood can do,' he said. But he couldn't help wondering what would happen when the windows needed cleaning and the displays rearranging, although he decided not to voice his doubts.

Mr Whitaker offered to pay Avril for her work but she refused emphatically. 'I enjoyed every moment,' she said. 'I love shoes so it was a pleasure to work with them.'

'Then you must choose a pair. No, don't argue, I insist.' Mr Whitaker's face resembled a walnut as it broke into smiles, and Avril didn't argue. All day she had been admiring a pair of soft kid sandals with tiny straps and a high slim heel. She knew they were the kind of frivolous footwear she would never consider buying, but if Mr Whitaker was giving her a pair they were the ones she would choose.

'You have excellent taste,' the old man told her. 'They'll feel like gloves, I can assure you.'

Avril tried on the pale grey sandals and walked to the mirror. They really were comfortable and she couldn't help noticing how slim her ankles looked, and the way her calves seemed more shapely. She would wear them with the new pencil slim skirt Jacqueline's mother had made

341

her for helping in the shop. Swirling in front of the mirror she wondered if Alan would notice and experienced a warm glow at the thought.

One day, Avril told herself, she would wear shoes like these all the time. She sighed as she looked round at the cluttered shop floor. Clearly, that day had not yet arrived. She changed her lovely new sandals for her old flat shoes and began to clear away the piles of tissue paper, sticky tape and shoe boxes, in order to leave the shop as she had found it. It had been a busy day, but it would be worth it to wear the lovely new sandals for Alan. She packed them carefully in their box and thanked Mr Whitaker once again.

'Don't mention it, my dear,' he said. 'You've more than earned them.'

'That was a large sigh,' Jack told Mr Whitaker after Avril had left.

'Ah, yes,' the old gentleman said. 'It's just that she reminds me so much of my dear late wife. She had the same imaginative streak about her. I'm afraid I've neglected such things as window displays of late.'

'Well, it doesn't seem to worry the customers.' Jack grinned.

Mr Whitaker sighed again, even more deeply. 'What year are we in now, Jack lad?'

'Nineteen sixty-two. Why?' Jack hoped the old man wasn't losing his memory.

'Ah, I think it's all getting too much for me. Perhaps it is time I went into retirement.'

Jack frowned and began to worry as a panic attack threatened for the first time in weeks. He wondered what would happen if the shop changed hands, and a cloud seemed to enshroud him, though he tried his best to brush it aside. The two men carried on with their work in silence. Jack remembered the days when his old man could never have afforded a cobbler's prices. He would come home from a hard shift at the pit and set to mending shoes and clogs. Jack couldn't imagine Mary coping with hardship the way his mother had. He loved her dearly but sometimes she made him feel so inferior. He had an idea Alan felt the same. It was as though she had to prove something to herself. Make amends for something in the past. Still, she had been different lately, and hadn't she proved her devotion to him throughout his illness?

Both men were deep in thought, each wondering what the future would bring.

Chapter Twenty-Six

It had been a hectic afternoon and Doug had finally closed the shop for the day. He had also completed the milking so as to give his father an early Sunday finish. Now it was time to change from work clothes to Sunday best in order to look smart for Jacqueline.

She had decided to take a day off from helping Doug in order to spend some time at Moorland House. She and Avril had worked all day in the garden, cutting back the dead flowers, weeding, and gathering raspberries and gooseberries in readiness for Grandma Roberts's annual jam making.

Although Gladys now employed a woman to come in for a few hours a day, Jacqueline still worried that the house and grounds were becoming too much for the doctor and his wife. The young friends had brought over a selection of holiday brochures, hoping to persuade the couple to take a well-earned holiday.

'You should treat yourselves as a retirement present,' Jacqueline suggested. 'How long is it since you last had a holiday?'

'Twenty-odd years at least,' Grandad Roberts mumbled from behind the Sunday paper. 'That was when we went to Ruth and Richard's wedding.'

'Twenty-odd years?' Jacqueline shrieked. 'Why, you're worse than my mam and dad. At least they used to take us to the caravan.'

'What do we need with holidays? Living here is one permanent holiday.' Grandma Roberts stood by the open window. 'Now you just tell me a place more glorious than this, or where the air is half as pure.'

'I know that, but you need a change of scene just the same, and a rest from the housework. If you went now Avril and I could look after the house.'

'I agree.' Grandad Roberts suddenly sprang to life. 'We haven't had a proper holiday since our honeymoon. Now let's have a look at those brochures.' He picked one off the pile, placing it immediately to one side. 'I don't think Spain is quite us, do you, dear?'

'Goodness me, no. What would I look like amongst all those bikini-clad girls? No, I don't fancy a beach holiday at all.'

'I'm sure you'd look every bit as glamorous as everyone else,' Rowland said, glancing at his wife. 'But no, I prefer more scenic surroundings.'

'Italy, then.' Jacqueline waved a brochure enthusiastically in Rowland's direction. 'Florence, Venice, Rome, Sorrento.'

'Or Amalfi,' Avril volunteered. 'I knew someone once who had served in the forces, a friend of my father's, and he said the Amalfi coast was the most beautiful place on earth.'

'This is the most beautiful place on earth,' Gladys said.

'Yugoslavia.' Rowland scanned through a leaflet. 'Professor Jones visited Yugoslavia. Now what was the name of the place? Something to do with surgery, I'm sure. I know one of the nurses made a joke about its name. Something to do with blood.'

'Goodness.' Avril scowled. 'I wouldn't bother.'

'Said it was like the Garden of Eden,' Rowland mused. 'Look, here it is – Bled. Lake Bled.'

Gladys left her position at the window reluctantly to look and was pleasantly surprised. 'Oh, yes,' she said. 'Almost as nice as Longfield.'

Jacqueline giggled. 'It's even better than Longfield,' she said.

'But we don't have passports.' Gladys at last seemed to take an interest.

'That's a point.' Rowland frowned.

'Oh, but surely that can be arranged? Surely you know someone who can hurry them through?' Jacqueline was used to Grandad Roberts knowing

345

a man who knew another man who could arrange anything.

'Well, not today, seeing as it's the Sabbath, but we'll see.'

Jacqueline thumbed through the leaflet. 'Wow, just look at this hotel – it's out of this world. It even has a swimming pool fed by thermal springs, and a glorious view of the lake and mountains.'

'Then we shall go there,' Rowland announced.

Gladys read the details. 'Have you seen the prices?'

'No, and I don't care. If we're going at all we're going in style.' Rowland turned down the corner of the page and hoped the wretched pain in his chest wouldn't be aggravated by the flight.

'Goodness, Doug'll be here soon.' Jacqueline hurried up to the bathroom, collecting her cosmetic bag on the way.

'And Alan,' Avril said. 'He promised to come straight from the garage.'

They had arranged to walk along the moor and back down towards the reservoir, calling in at the pub for a drink on the way. The heather was just at its best, and with the sun golden on the bracken, the moors were a delight to behold.

'Grandma Roberts is right,' Jacqueline said, as the four of them set off on their evening stroll. 'This is one of the most beautiful places on earth.' The distant crags were pale sunlit grey in contrast to the deep silhouettes of the pine trees, and a strange silence surrounded the young friends.

Avril paused to pluck a spray of heather and Alan perched himself on a rock to wait. Jacqueline turned and shouted, 'We'll see you later at the pub,' and Doug placed an arm round her waist, quickening his step as he envisaged getting her on her own for a while.

'I think they're trying to lose us,' Alan said, catching Avril's hand and pulling her down beside him on the flat surface of the rock.

'Well, you don't seem too upset about it.' Avril smiled.

Alan didn't reply, but instead caught her to him with a kiss which filled them both with yearning. Avril knew she should resist before the feeling became uncontrollable, but it was already too late. The caresses they enjoyed in the living room when the household was asleep were becoming more than the lovers could bear, and they knew that this time they would only be satisfied by making love completely.

The sun sank lower and the evening air turned cool, but Avril and Alan, in the way of all young lovers, were consumed with a burning desire for fulfilment.

Mr Whitaker waited until he had cashed up for the night before divulging his plan to Jack. He hoped it wouldn't cause Jack to have a setback just when he was doing so well. All day he had been rehearsing in his mind how to put it, and had decided to come straight out with it.

'I'm selling the shop, Jack lad,' he said. 'I've no alternative considering my age. I don't suppose you'd consider becoming the next owner?'

Jack had been expecting it, but the news still came as a shock. What he hadn't expected was the suggestion that he might buy the business himself.

The idea whirled round in his head for some time, causing him to remain speechless. At last he replied, 'I couldn't afford it. I've sunk all my savings in next door.'

'I expected you to say that, but it's a good investment, and there's such a thing as a bank loan, as you well know.'

'Aye, I know, but to borrow that amount ... besides, I know nothing about the shoe trade. I'm just a working man at heart – the cobbling's more in my line.'

'I wouldn't rob you, lad. I'd like you to have it, and as for not knowing the trade, I dare say you'd soon pick it up. I'd give you time to get the hang of it, show you the ropes before I left.'

'But you've admitted it needs one to sell and one for the repairs.'

'Then employ somebody. I'm telling you, lad, it's a good business. I think you'll be surprised at the turnover.'

Jack jumped as he cut himself trimming off a leather sole. He sucked the blood from his thumb and decided to call it a day, unable to concentrate with the proposition whirring round in his mind.

'I'll need to discuss it with Mary, but I don't know what her reaction will be.'

'Of course. It isn't a decision to be taken lightly. It's your whole future at stake.'

'Aye,' Jack agreed, and wondered what the alternative would be. Another mind-destroying job like the last one? Oh, no, he couldn't bear that.

He took off his apron and placed it on the nail

behind the door. 'I'll say goodnight to you, then,' he said.

Mr Whitaker opened the door to let him through. 'I'll see you in the morning.'

Jack turned on the step. 'Oh, and thanks for the offer,' he said.

'You're welcome, lad. Goodnight.'

'You're early.' Mary smiled. 'It's nice to have you home before the tea gets cold.'

Jack glanced at the clock. 'It's half past five, the normal closing time, though I admit it's usually nearer to six.' He hesitated. 'I've had a bit of a shock.'

Mary looked alarmed. 'Not a bad one, I hope.'

'I don't know. It depends on what we decide to do, I suppose.'

'Why, what happened?'

'Is our Alan at home?'

'Not yet. Why?'

'Sit down, then, love, and let's talk.'

Mary sat down, perplexed by Jack's sense of urgency.

'How do you feel about owning a shoe shop?'

'What?'

'Mr Whitaker's selling, and he's giving us first option.'

'But we don't know anything about the shoe trade. And I wouldn't be able to help much – I've all on to cope with my own shop.'

'That's what I told him, but he seems to think I could manage if I employed an assistant. After all, he and his wife ran the place for years. In fact he was managing on his own before I took over

349

the repairing side of it, though I don't know how.'

'How much?'

'What?'

'How much is he asking?'

'I don't know – I never thought to ask. That just goes to show I'm no businessman. We'd better forget it.'

'No, we'll consider it. I was no businesswoman either but I've made a go of it, and so can you. We'll wait and see what he's asking before we decide.' She glanced at her husband, worrying she was bossing him into something he didn't want, afraid of sending him back into his state of anxiety. 'Of course, it's up to you. You must have some idea by now.'

'But that's not the point, Mary. Of course I'd like it. I feel at home amongst the shoes and boots and I get on well with the customers, but you know how I feel about getting into debt. I can never rest if I'm owing. It would be different if we had a decent deposit to put down.'

'How do you know we haven't?'

'Well, I know my savings aren't all that rosy at the moment.'

'You don't know, you're just surmising. How long is it since you last went to the bank, or had anything to do with the accounts?'

'Well, I suppose I have neglected the financial side of things since my illness. Come to think of it, I never had much to do with it before.' He grinned shyly. 'I always did prefer to bring home the money, pay the bills and keep straight. The shop I always left to you, I want none of that. You've worked hard for what you've got, and it's yours.'

'Ours.' Mary got up from the table and went to the bureau in the corner. She unlocked the bottom cupboard and took out a green hard-backed book. She brought it to the table and opened it at the last page. Jack started to read and the figures suddenly began to make sense. Income, expenditure, the columns neatly laid out. He blinked and wondered if the amounts were registering correctly. He looked up at Mary, who was waiting expectantly for his reaction.

'Well?' she asked. 'What do you think? Will we have enough for a decent deposit or not?'

'More than enough, but, as I said, it's all yours. I'm having none of it.'

'Jack Holmes, if you say that one more time I'll crown you with this accounts book and knock some sense into that head of yours. Who do you think has kept me and the kids all these years? You have, working down that goddamned pit, and then in a job which almost put you six feet under, and now the first time you've the chance to do something you would enjoy you're talking about turning it down. Well, I won't stand by and let you do it. Of course, if you don't think you're up to the challenge that's a different matter entirely.'

'Of course I'm up to it,' he retaliated. 'Well, I think I am. I won't know until I try.'

Mary grinned. 'So what do you say? Shall we give it a go?'

Jack was still wary, but Mary knew she was winning. 'Well, it all depends on what he's asking, and we'd have to think about who to set on in the shop.'

'We'll cross that bridge when we come to it, but I already have someone in mind. Of course, you're the manager. It would be up to you.'

'Who?'

'How about Sally? I know Harry's new job isn't bringing in as much as the pit, and she's on the list for a job back in the Co-op.'

Jack grinned. 'And she'd be experienced, too. In fact I'll bet she'd be able to teach me a thing or two about shop work. Oh, Mary, do you think we should take the plunge? I'd pay you back every penny once we were established.'

Mary lifted up the green book, high above Jack's head. 'I warned you,' she said, then they burst into laughter as he took his wife in his arms. 'Our Alan's working over,' she said, and led Jack from the room and up the stairs. 'That means we've a full hour in which to celebrate.'

By the time they reached the bed, they were half undressed and the celebrations were about to begin.

A white swan sidled out of the water, pausing a couple of feet in front of Gladys. He stretched his neck gracefully and gazed into her eyes. She wanted to take his picture, but dare not move in case he became aggressive.

'Honk,' he murmured and arced his wings, posing beautifully.

She'd always thought swans were mute creatures, but still, in a magical place like Bled, she supposed anything was possible. She remained motionless, swallowing nervously.

He arced his wings again so that she could no

longer resist reaching out, opening the brown leather case and carefully composing the picture in her viewfinder.

The camera clicked, causing the swan to spread his wings and fly majestically over the edge and into the lake. Gladys slid down the grassy bank and dangled her toes in the water. A fat orange snail sailed by on a broken lily-pad boat, and a fragile butterfly settled beside her amongst daisies and clover. She breathed deeply, filling her lungs with pure alpine air, and looked out across the lake. 'I got a picture of the swan, Rowland,' she called, but Rowland was snoring gently beneath his old panama hat.

On the island the white church nestled amongst lush greenery, mystical in a haze of heat. Sometimes its tall spire glistened in the sun; now it was hidden by a descended cloud. Behind it the magnificent Mount Triglav changed colour continuously, from lilac to greyish gold and back again.

She gathered her belongings: camera, sun cream, towel, insect repellent and the romantic novel of the year she had bought at the airport. Romance, that's what a place like this was made for, and romance she had got. Lovemaking didn't happen very often nowadays – they could hardly expect it at their age – but Bled seemed to be acting like an aphrodisiac, for Rowland had wakened each morning with the desire to make love, not the hot torrid act of passion they had known in younger days, but a warm, tender, more fulfilling experience.

The holiday had indeed been like a second

honeymoon. They had walked through green meadows, abloom with wild primroses, scarlet poppies and buttercups. Other unfamiliar flowers and herbs she had identified with the help of a handbook. They had waved to smiling farmers' wives as they gathered plump peas and beans, and fruit from orchards. They had watched brown swarthy men replenishing wood stocks in readiness for the harsh winter, which would freeze the lake and prepare the ski slopes for winter visitors.

Another day they had followed the road to the wooded valley and the gushing river of Vingtar Gorge, where the towering rocks shut out the sunlight, and icy droplets fell to the shimmering water below.

They had taken a boat to the island in the centre of the lake where a concert in the chapel had delighted Rowland, the local choir being just as enthusiastic as his own back home.

They had ridden in a horse-drawn dray to the centuries-old castle and watched the celebration of a local wedding. Now it was almost time to leave, and it was more than Gladys could bear to leave this magical place.

She clambered back up the bank and shook Rowland gently. 'Come on,' she said, 'it's time we were changing for dinner.'

Rowland grunted and roused himself from the seat. 'I must have dozed off,' he said, unaware that he had slept solidly for at least an hour.

Gladys smiled, gratified by the sight of her husband's suntanned arms and face. 'You look so much better, dear,' she said. 'I hope you feel as well as you look.'

'Haven't I proved it?' he asked with a proud grin. Gladys chuckled.

'We must go on holiday more often,' she said.

They set off in the direction of the hotel, past the flower beds and fountains, wondering what delicacies would be on the menu this evening.

'Oh well, I expect we shall have to begin packing after dinner.' Gladys sighed.

'I suppose so.' Rowland sounded miserable at the prospect. 'What time do we leave for Ljubljana?'

'Straight after breakfast.'

'So we won't really have time to do much in the morning.'

'Well, we could take a last walk round the village if we rise early.'

'I think I prefer to visit the church again, just for five minutes. I think it is the most peaceful place I have ever had the good fortune to visit.'

'Oh, I agree,' Gladys said. 'And so beautiful.' She turned and looked back along the lakeside, to where the white church nestled at the foot of the castle. Reluctantly she tore her eyes away, and they walked back to the hotel hand in hand like a couple of teenagers.

'Jacqueline certainly had the right idea, persuading us to take a holiday,' Gladys said. 'But then, she always was one for coming up with bright ideas.'

'Ah yes,' Rowland agreed, 'except that this time it was my bright idea, Jacqueline just supplied the brochures.'

Gladys looked confused. 'You mean it was you who planned it all the time?'

'Well,' Rowland's eyes gleamed, 'you never did take much notice of anything I suggested, so I called on the young ones for assistance.'

'You old schemer.' Gladys began to laugh, and then paused to plant a kiss on her husband's cheek. 'But a lovely old schemer all the same. Thank you, dear, for a perfect holiday, and for being a perfect husband.'

They left the warmth of the afternoon for the cool of the hotel, the wide staircase highlighted by chandeliers glistening in the sun from the tall windows.

'I shall never forget this place as long as I live,' Gladys whispered.

They entered the lift chuckling like a pair of mischievous children, causing the uniformed lift attendant to wonder if they were in their second childhood. He understood quite a bit of English and joined in their merriment, hoping they would come back to Bled. He liked the English, especially this lady and gentleman who were always so courteous and generous. Rowland gave the attendant a handful of dinars and doffed his hat, and then they made their way to their room where the balcony overlooked the lake and the island.

'Oh, well, I suppose we'd better change for dinner, our last one. Oh, I am going to miss this view, and the dancing, I've so enjoyed the dancing.'

'And I shall miss the Riesling,' Rowland moaned. 'And the fishing.'

'Even so,' Gladys gave a mischievous grin, 'I still think Moorland House is the most beautiful place on earth.'

Chapter Twenty-Seven

Great Yarmouth was a far cry from Bled. Nevertheless, a week later a charabanc party left Millington for a weekend at the resort with no less enthusiasm. The party mostly consisted of the Holmeses and the Bacons, with any vacancies filled by friends and neighbours, all eager to be in the audience for Una Bacon's theatrical performance.

Una was appearing in a musical Monday to Friday in Scarborough, but had been singled out by her agent for a special Saturday night tour of all the major resorts, as a member of the backing trio to the top vocalist Billy Flame.

The tour was a sell-out and Yarmouth was the only place Una had managed to secure advance bookings for a whole coachload. The success of the tour had been assured from the beginning with a host of famous celebrities appearing on the bill. Even Jack was enthusiastic about the trip in order to see his favourite country and western group. Mary had left Yvonne in charge of the shop, and Madge had volunteered to look after the house, enabling her dearest friend to take a well-earned weekend break.

Jacqueline was thrilled at the prospect of seeing her cousin for the first time in ages, but disappointed that Doug couldn't possibly manage to get away. The pair were particularly disappointed as this was the last weekend before the girls were due to return to college, which meant they would have to part again after only a few more days. Avril consoled her friend by pointing out that absence makes the heart grow fonder, but was relieved that Alan had decided to take a weekend off so he could join the party.

Bill had stocked up the bus with crates of beer, and soft drinks for the women and children, and the atmosphere was one of jollity from the moment they left Millington. Grandma Holmes was in her glory surrounded by her family, and was looking forward to seeing her oldest grand-child appearing on stage. Harry brought her a bottle of brown ale and she was soon leading the party in a good old-fashioned sing-song. The youngsters in the back seat, including Anthony and Barry, giggled uncontrollably as the men sang 'Roll Me Over In The Clover' and other such bawdy songs, and the journey was an altogether enjoyable one for all concerned.

The hotel in Apsley Road was taken over completely by the guests from Millington, and immediately the luggage was unpacked everyone made for the beach. Una was waiting to greet them, having escaped from rehearsals earlier than usual. Bronzed by the sun, her long slim legs shown off to perfection by a pair of skimpy shorts, she was a vision of loveliness.

Grandma Holmes was a little shocked by the sight of all the exposed flesh and wondered if Una would ever settle down and marry. She worried about her oldest granddaughter, not trusting show-business people at all, what with all the scandals she kept reading about in the Sunday newspapers, but nevertheless she couldn't help feeling proud of her. Especially when Una said, 'I hope you don't mind, Gran, but I've decided to use your name for the stage.'

'My name? Nay, lass, whatever sort of name is Lizzie Holmes? It might be all right back in Millington, but never on the stage.'

Una smiled. 'No, Gran, I mean your maiden name. I've often thought how nice it sounded when Mum talked about her Grandma Gayle, so I thought I'd borrow it. Oh, I'll still be Una Bacon really, but Mr Power – that's my agent – doesn't think it would look too good on the billboards.'

Bill laughed. 'I think he's right, love. You'd be bound to get some smart Alec adding *eggs and tomatoes* to the posters.'

'So you don't mind then, Dad?' Una looked relieved. She had worried her father might be disappointed.

'Mind? Now why should I mind? You'll always be my lovely daughter, whatever you decide to call yourself. Besides, it sounds right somehow. Una Gayle. Aye, I quite like it.'

That settled, Grandma Holmes made her way towards the sea. 'Come on,' she said. 'My poor feet could do with a bit of a paddle.' And off they went, splashing and laughing amongst the waves.

At last it was time for the party to make their way to the theatre, full of fish and chips, or pie and peas from the market, and armed with even more goodies in the form of popcorn and choco-lates. Everyone had changed into their very best suits and dresses, making certain Una had no reason to be ashamed of her family and friends.

Marjory could hardly contain herself as the orchestra began to tune up and the lights were dimmed, and she clung nervously to her husband's hand as the curtain was raised. When the dancers began their high-kicking routine she could hear whispers of 'Where's our Una?' and 'I can see their knickers' from Barry and Anthony, and she would have loved to have shouted for all the theatre to hear that her daughter would not be on until the main act.

Instead she settled down to enjoy the variety of talent leading up to the interval. Then it was time for the compère to make the announcement. 'Ladies and gentlemen, boys and girls, I know you are all waiting for Billy Flame and the Fireflies ... well, I am sorry to disappoint you, but the fire brigade's put them out.'

The mass of teenagers, unsure if the comedian was joking or not, began to boo, clap and scream, almost deafening the Holmes party who were taking up most of the front seats. Then the lights were lowered and the spotlight fixed on centre stage where the group was revealed.

'Ladies and gentlemen, Billy Flame and the Fireflies.'

The compère's voice was drowned by screams and the sound of the musicians leading the singer into his first number, which was obviously one of the audience's favourites.

'Oh, Bill, look – there's our daughter.' Marjory almost choked over the words, and Bill was too overcome to answer.

Una and the other two girls were dressed in skin-tight sequined dresses which sent myriad shimmering stars darting round the stage. The trio harmonised perfectly and enhanced the singer to perfection.

After each number Billy Flame turned and acknowledged the band and the trio, then at the end of his performance he gave each a small solo spot announcing each by name. Una was introduced as a new and glamorous addition to the Fireflies. Then he said that as tonight was a very special one for Una, because her parents and grandmother were in the audience, she would sing one of her own compositions.

The spotlight suddenly came down on Marjory and Bill and then settled on Grandma Holmes, who wasn't sure whether to laugh or cry when the crowd applauded.

Una was led forward to centre stage by Billy Flame and the band began to play. Una's voice suddenly filled the theatre.

'Night after night I dream I'm near you,
Night after night, I seem to hear you.
Close to me, dear, whispering near,
Sweet words of love I long to hear.
But when I wake, I find I'm lonely,
Though my arms ache just for you only.
Your every caress is my happiness,
And I am yours, to love and possess.
Night after night, my dreams remind me,
I try to hide, but still they find me,
Stay by me I pray, when dreams fade away,
Day after day, night after night.'

Suddenly Billy Flame came towards the microphone and Una. He placed an arm round Una's waist, and as they looked deep into each other's eyes he joined her in another verse.

'Night after night, you keep returning,
Kindling the flame, keeping it burning.
Making me blue. I long for you.
Soon you'll be breaking my heart in two.
I hear your lies, your laughing and taunting,
And yet your eyes keep right on haunting
I can't regret how our lips met,
But now it's over, why can't I forget?
Maybe like you, I'll find a new love,
But till I do, I still need you, love.
I'll still hope and pray, still dream this way,
Day after day, night after night.'

The audience went wild, and hysterical Billy Flame fans rushed to the stage, waving their arms in an effort to touch their idol. Older, staider members of the crowd clapped, and gave a standing ovation to the lovely girl who had sung so well, in words easily understood, after all the deafening, undecipherable lyrics performed previously by Billy Flame.

Marjory Bacon couldn't control the tears of pride and happiness at her daughter's success. Only Grandma Holmes was slightly uneasy, having noticed the look which had passed between Una and that Billy Flame character. Not that she judged people on their appearance, but what with all the make-up and the garish outfit he was wearing, she didn't think he was suitable at all for her granddaughter. Besides, she didn't trust pop singers, or whatever their name was. She didn't trust show business folk at all.

It never occurred to her that Una was now part of that scene. In fact, if she could only have seen into the future, her granddaughter was destined to become one of the greatest of them all.

And when the recording of 'Night After Night' hit the music shops in time for Christmas, it was not Billy Flame whose name was on the label, but Una Gayle. She had made the big time, just as she always promised herself she would. And nobody, according to the people of Millington, was more deserving of her success.

By the time Mr Whitaker retired, both Jack and Sally Holmes had been given the benefit of his whole working life's experience. They had been taught how to do the books, how to take stock, and where the finest-quality footwear and sundries could be obtained.

'I know you can buy cheaper,' he said. 'But I haven't built up my reputation by selling shoes which fall apart after a couple of wearings, or socks which shrink in the first washing. No, Jack lad, you buy from the reputable firms I've recommended and you won't go far wrong.'

Mr Whitaker was quite overcome when the day came for him to leave, especially when Jack presented him with a book on house plants, and a beautiful *Camellia japonica* in a white china pot, specially chosen from Gardener's Rest. Jack had thought long and hard about a leaving gift, realising the old gentleman would need an interest to keep him occupied during his well-earned leisure time. He hoped the book would encourage him to develop an interest in plants. He also gave Mr Whitaker an open invitation to return to the shop at any time, knowing how he would miss the company, and Mary invited him to tea on the following Sunday.

Jack also received quite a few tips from Sally, which she had picked up during her years at the Co-op, and immediately Mr Whitaker had left she set about re-arranging the shelves, so that the style numbers and sizes were in order, and the colours in their own sections. This meant that she could see at a glance which size and colour of each style had been sold. Before long Sally was fully competent at running the shop, leaving Jack to concentrate on the repairs. After a few weeks he decided to begin a home delivery service, so that repairs left at the shop would be returned the following day. He also began replacing zips in bags and boots, and was even requested to reupholster an office chair, surprising himself when he made an excellent job of it. Only once had he almost relapsed into ill health, when the sum the bank repayments would amount to was revealed. But Mary had calmed him down again and after a few weeks the shop takings convinced him he had absolutely no reason to worry.

Jack was now putting on his lost weight and had never looked better. He enjoyed working with a cheerful girl like Sally and was so pleased with her efforts that he gave her an increase in salary after the first month. Sally accepted it gratefully, intending to spend it on guitar lessons for Barry, who was doing his best to make some kind of sense out of Harry's Christmas present. The money Sally earned was helping to get them back on their feet again, for Harry's new job as a crane driver in the steel works had meant a cut in wages and they hadn't quite recovered from the weeks he had been between jobs. Now they were starting to be able to afford a few luxuries again, and Sally intended to work hard at the job she enjoyed so much.

Owning two shops also meant that hosiery, gloves and leather goods could be bought in larger quantities at a bigger discount, so bringing in more profit for Jack and Mary, and by the time Easter arrived a well-organised routine was in progress.

It was Easter when Jacqueline managed to persuade Avril to unburden herself of her worries.

'You must see a doctor,' she told her friend. 'If you aren't pregnant then there's something seriously wrong with you. You've been sick now for months.'

'All right,' Avril revealed in desperation, 'I admit I'm pregnant, so now what happens?'

'Oh, Avril, I know it's too late now, but I did warn you when we went home for Christmas to be careful.'

'We were. I know you won't believe me, but we did use something. It wasn't our fault the bloody thing leaked.' Avril burst into tears, partly out of frustration and partly from relief that she had at last confided in her friend.

'So,' Jacqueline said, her mind struggling to puzzle out what needed to be done. 'The first thing to do is see a doctor.'

'I can't. I don't want anyone to find out. I've worked out that I can at least finish my training, but I couldn't if the news got out.'

'The news needn't get out, but you must see a doctor, make sure everything's OK. What did our Alan say?'

'He doesn't know and he isn't about to find out. He isn't going to be forced into marriage just because I'm pregnant.'

'I can't believe this. You mean you've known for three months and you haven't told him? Oh, but you're so wrong, Avril. He's the father: he's a right to know. Besides, he loves you – you must marry him. I don't want to be auntie to an illegitimate child.'

'No, I've made up my mind. I'll go to the doctor for my baby's sake, but I won't tell Alan.'

Jacqueline argued all day and well into the early hours of the next, but it was like throwing dandelion seeds to the wind, and she finally gave up and slept fitfully, no nearer a solution to the problem. It was only after Avril had had the pregnancy confirmed by a doctor some distance away that Jacqueline wrote to her brother with the news. She only hoped she was doing the right thing.

Two days later she came home to find him waiting on the step, pale and heavy-eyed with anguish. Jacqueline knew she had made the right decision the moment his eyes met Avril's and they ended up in each other's arms, Avril sobbing uncontrollably and Alan strong and gentle as ever.

Jacqueline disappeared inside to make tea. She

had done her bit; now it was up to them. But she wouldn't like to be in Alan's shoes when Mary was told.

Alan told his mother as soon as he returned home. He had tried to persuade Avril to come home with him and arrange the wedding, but knew it made sense for her to stay on at college until her training was finished.

Mary was like someone demented, accusing Alan of bringing shame to the Holmes family, and the O'Connors, not to mention Avril's parents. Once she thought fleetingly of her friend Joyce Bailey, and how her mother had looked down on the girl, but that was different. This was her son, who had been brought up in a respectable household, and now she wouldn't be able to hold her head up in the shop. She wouldn't be at all surprised if the news didn't turn away some of the customers. And what did they intend to live on, and where?

Alan waited until his mother had finished her outburst. 'Mother, I love Avril. Surely you've noticed?'

'But not enough to respect her until you were married.'

'Of course I respect her, otherwise I wouldn't love her. It was an accident; we didn't mean it to happen.'

Mary was uncharacteristically in tears, which made Alan feel even worse.

Jack reacted in an altogether different manner. 'So. You're not the first, son, and you won't be the last, and so long as you love each other, and I think you do, what are yer going to do about it?'

367

'We'll get married, of course. I'm going down to arrange things for Whit week. After that she'll finish her training and come home.'

'Can't you get married up here, have a proper wedding with all the family and everything?'

Alan was prevented from answering by his mother's breaking into another torrent of anger. 'Oh, that'll be lovely, won't it, everyone in Millington turning up to look at the bride, only for her to disappear again. I can just imagine them saying it's a marriage of convenience and nothing else.'

Alan paled. 'I don't care what people say. It's up to Avril and me, nobody else.'

'We'll remind you of that when you've nowhere to live. I suppose it will be up to your father and me then to provide you and a wife and child with a home.'

Alan said calmly, 'No, Mother, I wouldn't expect any favours. I don't think you could bear the shame of it. We'll manage somehow.' Then he went upstairs, found a suitcase and opened his wardrobe, calmly packed his clothes, went to the bathroom, collected his toiletries and fastened the case, then walked silently downstairs. He looked round the sitting room and lifted down the picture Jacqueline had painted for him.

'Where do you think you're going?' Mary snapped.

'To someone I know who won't be ashamed of me.' Alan looked at his father, afraid of what the shock might do to him. 'Don't worry, Dad, I'll be OK. I'm sorry. I wouldn't have upset you for the world.'

'Don't go, son,' Jack pleaded. 'Your mother didn't mean half the things she said. You know what she's like.'

'Oh, I know what she's like all right: she who can do no wrong. Well, I'm sorry, I'm no paragon. I can't live up to her expectations.'

His eyes swept the room, then he turned and walked out. He wanted to cry, but he was a grown man, soon to be a father. Besides, he would feel better when he reached Grandma Holmes's. He knew she would understand. Alan had no doubt she would welcome him with open arms, and his wife and child too when the time came.

He had climbed the hill and passed the clock before he remembered he had left the car parked near the shoe shop. He couldn't go back now; it would only upset his father again. Better to wait until after dark. He continued up to the top row and past the well-scrubbed doorsteps of the lowly terraced houses. He had the feeling that after a long time away he was finally coming home.

Grandma Holmes was in her normal place near the fire, with her swollen feet soaking in a bowl of salt water, and Alan couldn't help smiling as she almost tipped it over in her eagerness to towel them dry and hobble on her bare feet to fill the kettle and make tea.

'So what have I done to deserve a visit from my favourite grandson?' she enquired, uneasy at the sight of a suitcase and a pale haggard face.

'You say that to all of us. You call us all your favourite.' He pulled out a chair and sat at the table. 'I've come to ask you a favour, Gran. Do

369

you think I could stay with you for a while? It doesn't matter if you say no, I'm sure Uncle Harry'll have me. I can pay my way.'

'I've told you before and I'll say it again, so long as my house has a door on it'll be open to my own flesh and blood, or to many another if needs be. Though I'd like to know what's been going on for you to leave your own home, before I say yes.'

'Avril's having a baby, my mother's going mad, and we've both said things we shouldn't, so I've walked out.'

Grandma Holmes stared into the fire and continued rocking for what seemed ages before asking Alan, 'And what does your father have to say?'

'My dad's on my side, says I mustn't take any notice, but I won't give her the satisfaction of going back. It'll look as though I'm grovelling. Oh, Gran, you know what my mother is like. She's set such high standards for us all. It was the same when I went to the garage – she thought it wasn't good enough. She seems to have forgotten how poor they were in Newcastle.'

'But you've got to admit she's got on and done well for you all. You can't knock her for that.'

'I'm not. She just seems so hard at times, as though she's turning her back on her roots.'

He got up and poured water into the teapot. 'It's as though she's afraid of slipping off her pedestal because of what her customers might think. Well I'm sorry but she's set her standards too high. I'm only human and I love Avril. I don't feel as though I've committed a crime by loving her, and I'll not have my mother finding me guilty.'

Grandma Holmes went to the cellar head and came back with a cake tin. She lifted out a fruit cake and cut two portions before answering. 'Well then, you'd better pour us a cup of tea and then we'll see about getting the back bed aired.'

'I can stay then?'

'Well, I don't suppose yer mother'll like it, but so long as yer planning on doing the right thing by yon little lass...'

'Gran, she's twenty-one,' Alan pointed out.

'Aye well, when yer get to my age anybody under thirty seems like a little lass. Besides, I like her. She doesn't sit by and let other folks do all the work. I've noticed how she gets on with the pot washing without being asked. And when I've gone up the bottoms to the market I've seen what a good job she's made of them shop winders. Aye, I reckon she'll make a good little mother. In fact she reminds me of yer own mother when I first knew her.' Grandma Holmes looked at Alan and he noticed she was smiling from one side of her mouth. He couldn't help smiling with her. 'Oh, Gran,' he said, 'I knew you'd make me feel better. You always do.'

'Aye well,' she said, 'I do me best and neither man nor woman can do more.'

Alan looked thoughtful. 'How long do you think we would have to wait for a council house, Gran?'

'Maybe seven or eight years.'

'Then I'd better start saving for a deposit. I can't expect you to give us a home for that long.'

'Yer welcome here for as long as yer like, lad, providing yer married and not living in sin.'

371

'We'll be married, I promise you that, and I'll work my fingers to the bone to get a home together.'

'That's exactly what yer dad said when he married yer mother.'

'He did, too.'

'Aye, but yer mother was a worker as well.' Suddenly she burst out laughing.

'What's so funny?'

'I can just imagine yer mother's face when she hears yer on the list for a council house. Eeh, no, lad, I think you'd best stay here until you've saved up that deposit. We don't want yer mother having to come down off that pedestal, do we?'

Elizabeth Ann Holmes was born on 19 September, as fair and placid as her father, and the apple of his eye. Mary had long since made her peace with Alan, apologising for losing her temper, though it had taken some persuasion on Jack's part before she would do so.

Alan had accepted her apologies graciously, but refused to move back to the shop. Avril didn't interfere, leaving the decision to Alan. Though she got on well with her mother-in-law she wasn't sure if she could cope with her for twenty-four hours a day, and was rather relieved when Alan chose to stay in the calm, easy-going atmosphere of Grandma Holmes's rather than return to the shop with its lack of privacy.

After her daughter's birth Avril decided to repay the old lady for her kindness, by scraping off the old patterned wallpaper room by room and replacing it with a plain paper which could be

Walpamured, and made the house seem much lighter. She also burned off the chocolate-coloured varnish from the woodwork and painted it all magnolia. Grandma Holmes hated the mess and inconvenience but was delighted with the result, and invited all the neighbours in to admire Avril's handiwork.

The outcome was a number of requests for Avril to use her skills and decorate their houses too. If Jack took her to the wholesaler's she found she could make quite a reasonable profit on the materials alone, apart from being paid for her labour.

One young couple who had bought a house called on Avril for an estimate for the job of decorating the walls and choosing a colour scheme for carpets and curtains. Keeping the cost as low as possible she still managed to make a decent profit, and the couple were highly delighted with the finished result.

Baby Elizabeth seemed to thrive on being surrounded by stepladders and wallpaper, and if she did have a bad day occasionally Grandma Holmes was delighted to be given the chance to spoil her first great-granddaughter, and would wheel her down to the memorial gardens, where the rhododendrons grew in profusion round the lawns.

When spring came she would take an old mackintosh and spread it on the grass, so that the baby could lie and kick to her heart's content. It was here she began to crawl and try to eat the daisies, whilst her great-grandmother gossiped to her neighbours about the good old days, and watched the little girl with pride.

There was no doubt that Elizabeth was the best-dressed child in Millington, if not in the whole of Yorkshire. Alan refused to accept a penny from his parents but could hardly refuse gifts for the baby, and Mary kept her granddaughter supplied with Cutie Wear dresses, frilly underskirts and best-quality baby shoes and socks.

Avril was grateful to her in-laws, pointing out to Alan that the less they had to spend on Elizabeth the more they could save towards a house in the future.

Grandma Holmes dreaded the time they decided to leave. She had hated living alone and the house had become alive again over the past year. The help she gave Avril occasionally by looking after Elizabeth was far surpassed by their just being there. Besides, the money they gave her for their board more than covered the expenses and went a long way towards paying the bills.

Jack was relieved things were working out for the couple. He thought the world of Avril and idolised his granddaughter.

Chapter Twenty-Eight

After Avril finished college Jacqueline missed her friend terribly, but knuckled down to her final year in order to fill the void, and graduate with first-class results. By the time her training finished in the summer her little niece was toddling round by holding on to the furniture, and looked like following in Una's footsteps and developing into another Holmes enchantress.

Jacqueline wondered why, apart from her father, she was the only dark one in the Holmes family, and the plainest, but as she had never been vain by nature she didn't let it trouble her. Besides, Doug must consider her attractive, otherwise he would never have proposed.

He had waited until she finished college before buying the ring, and the engagement had taken place the week after her homecoming, on the understanding that they would wait until she was settled in her new job before arranging the wedding.

She considered herself fortunate to have secured a teaching position at the newly built junior school in Millington. She found the children on the whole friendly, intelligent and thirsty for knowledge. She had the knack of making lessons interesting and lively while at the same time managing to keep discipline without appearing heavy-handed. Before long she had the majority of children eating out of her hand.

Yet for some reason she didn't find teaching as satisfying as she had expected. After analysing her feelings, she came to the conclusion that it was because she was unable to use her talents to the full. Most of the day's timetable was made up of other subjects, and her artistic flair was only brought to the fore on two or three half-hourly periods a week. As a result, she became more and more frustrated and couldn't wait to leave her tutoring behind, and escape to a place where she could nurture her gift in the floral surroundings of Gardener's Rest.

Once, she applied for the headmistress's permission to take her class on a nature expedition. They set off in the morning armed with drawing equipment, exercise books and a packed lunch. On their arrival at the farm Doug explained how the seeds and cuttings were planted and the best way of caring for the many different species.

After he had answered the questions the children were encouraged to ask, they were allowed to draw or paint any of the beautiful and colourful hothouse plants, or were free to wander in the meadows and paint pictures of the animals or the countryside. Jacqueline was impressed by the variety of talent displayed, and the day was voted an outstanding success, especially when Doug gave each child a small pot plant to take home, with instructions on how to care for it.

During the weekends, Jacqueline became more and more familiar with the gardening scene. She studied the books, memorising the names of the different species. She created bottle gardens and hanging baskets, and most of all she painted: pictures of beautiful double begonias, scarlet bush roses, and later on, in time for Christmas, red-breasted robins and snow-clad hills, with fir trees in silhouette against the sunset.

Doug had extended the display area to include an old stable, and this was taken over by Jacqueline for use as a gallery to display her work. It was also used as a hideaway for the couple to make love, usually on a Sunday morning before the visitors began to arrive. Doug was becoming impatient to be married, so that their lovemaking could be more frequent and leisurely, but Jacqueline was content for the time being and needed space to think things out.

'We need to be practical,' she told him. 'We haven't thought about where we're going to live, for a start.'

'I thought that was decided,' he said in surprise. 'The farm's plenty large enough for us to live here.'

'But it wouldn't be our own place.'

'I know that, but we can have the front room, my mother's said so.'

Jacqueline had already thought about it, and decided against it. 'But I want our own place.'

'Well, so do I, but it wouldn't really be practical, would it? I mean, we'd be here, on the spot, to keep an eye on things.'

Jacqueline didn't enjoy arguing, but she knew she couldn't give in on so important an issue. 'But it wouldn't be fair, Doug. What about Cyril and Bessie? It's their home too. I can't just intrude on them. Besides, there isn't really all that much room. If we had a family the house would be overcrowded. And what if Lucy and her husband wanted to come and stay?'

'Well, our Bessie's never at home. She's always at Sam's. And Cyril'll be off for good in the near future.'

Jacqueline looked worried. 'But that's another thing. Even if Cyril goes the farm wouldn't be ours. If anything happened to your parents it would have to be shared. They've all a right to a part share.'

Doug frowned. 'Not if I'd done all the work around the place. They wouldn't be so mean as to put a claim in.'

'You can't know that. Besides, it wouldn't be meanness, it would be their right.' Jacqueline hated to have to hurt Doug. She came closer and touched his hand, saying gently, 'I love you, Doug, and I want to be with you all the time, every moment of the day, but when we marry I want our own home. We can still run Gardener's Rest, but independently from the farm. You can still help run the farm with your father – you couldn't desert him now at his age – but I don't want to live with them. I wouldn't feel secure knowing our home might have to be sold at any time.'

Doug shovelled compost into brown paper bags and dumped them on the scales. He knew Jacqueline was talking sense, but couldn't think of an alternative.

'What do you suggest we do then, live over the brush? There are certainly no houses going in Longfield. Nobody ever leaves once they've lived here.'

'Well, they wouldn't, not if they'd any sense. We'll think about it – there isn't any hurry.'

'Maybe not for you, but I'm not completely happy with a roll in the hay on a Sunday morning. I want us to be able to make love when we feel like it, and in a bed.'

'And do you think I don't? Look, I'll tell you what, we'll go away for the weekend. We can close up early next Saturday and be away by six at the latest. I'll book us in somewhere nice, not too far away, and we can be back to open up by eleven on Sunday. There's never much doing before then.'

Doug cheered up. 'And what will your mother

have to say about that?'

'Who cares? I'm over the age of consent and even if I weren't it's you and me who matter.'

Doug grinned. 'I'd better buy myself a pair of silk pyjamas, then,' he joked.

'I wouldn't bother.' Jacqueline pulled a face. 'They'd only be a waste of money. I prefer nice silky flesh myself.'

The dispute was put to one side for the time being, but a solution would have to be found, and soon. Especially after a night at the Rutland Arms in Bakewell, for instead of satisfying their desires all the night of lovemaking did was whet their appetite for more.

As trade in the shoe shop increased and the bank account looked more healthy Jack couldn't understand why he continued to feel ill at ease. The house just hadn't seemed the same since Alan walked out, and though he and Avril visited often there still seemed to be a barrier between the two families. Jack wished his son would accept a monetary gift, or even a loan to start them off in a home of their own, but Alan wouldn't hear of it.

'We're almost there,' he said when Jack renewed the offer. 'Besides, we haven't found anywhere suitable yet.'

It was true that the young couple were well on their way to being able to take on a mortgage, but Alan didn't confide in his father his fears that the garage was about to be sold.

Avril wasn't worried. Alan was good at his job and if he lost his existing one she was confident he would find another. 'Besides,' she said, 'I could take on more decorating jobs if you were home to see to Elizabeth.'

'Oh, no.' Alan refused to listen to such suggestions. 'Elizabeth needs you, at least until she starts school.'

'Yes, you're right,' Avril agreed. 'And I need to be with her. She'll grow up far too quickly and I don't intend missing out on her progress.'

Avril could have taken on more work. Grandma Holmes was always delighted to be left in charge of Elizabeth, but Avril knew what a handful her daughter could be and only left her on rare occasions. Anyway, the landlord had recently divided the large bedroom and installed a bathroom so she was busy decorating, tiling and making curtains. It meant that she and Alan had been forced to move up into the attic, leaving their daughter in the smaller room. The arrangement was not ideal and they stepped up their search for a suitable house within their means.

Alan usually worked late, so the night he arrived home on time Avril knew something had happened. Grandma Holmes saw the worried expression on her face when the car drew up outside, and tactful as ever decided it was time to visit one of her neighbours, asking permission to take Elizabeth with her. After they had gone, the little girl toddling happily along holding on to the old lady's hand, Alan came in, wearing a smile which laid to rest any worries Avril had harboured.

'You're early,' she said. 'Has the garage burned down?'

'Not on your life!' Alan grabbed Avril round the

380

waist and danced her round the kitchen table. 'How does it feel to be dancing with the new manager of Hillside Garage?' He stood away from her so he could see her face, the face he had loved from the first moment he had ever set eyes on it. Now it was a picture of smiling astonishment.

'What?'

'You're looking at the new manager of Hillside as from today.'

'But I thought it was to be sold. Has the new owner employed you or something?'

'They've changed their minds. They're still moving to Derbyshire as planned, but they're keeping Hillside too, and I've been put in overall charge. Colin's decided if I'm half the business-man my parents are I'll have no problem.'

'I'm sure he's right.'

'And that's not all. Colin's house is up for sale. What do you think?'

'Oh, we couldn't, Alan. They'll be asking a fortune – we can't possibly afford it.'

'But I haven't told you the best part. I shall be given a substantial rise in salary, enough to enable us to take the chance.' He hugged Avril to him. 'We'll show my mother I can keep my wife and child without any help from anybody.'

'You've already done that. I do wish you'd let bygones be bygones and stop harping on past differences. You only upset your father by being so stubborn.'

'OK, OK, I promise, but only if you agree to consider buying Colin's house.'

'All right. We'll make some enquiries, I promise.'

Looking down into the gentle grey eyes, Alan ran his fingers through her tousled shoulder-length hair and was suddenly overwhelmed with a desire to kiss her. It was at that moment that Grandma Holmes chose to walk in the door.

'Dada,' Elizabeth said. 'Dada.'

Alan grinned and lifted his daughter high, planting a kiss on her turned-up nose. The only shadow on Alan's happiness at that moment was the thought of having to break to his grandmother the news that they would soon be leaving.

It was Jacqueline's birthday, and Mary wasn't very pleased that her daughter had arranged to join the other teachers at her school for their annual dinner dance. Husbands and boyfriends were invited and a coach was to take them to the Angler's Rest in the village of Bamford. 'It's been arranged for ages,' Jacqueline said. 'They just added my name to the list automatically. No one knew it was my birthday. Besides, I would have gone anyway.'

'But we've always had the family to tea on your birthday,' Mary moaned.

'I know, and I'm sorry, but I'm not a little girl any more, Mam. It's not as though I'm going to miss the jelly and cream buns. And we shall be having all the usual Christmas get-togethers in a few days.'

Jack admired his daughter's ability to stand up to her mother, and wished he'd done the same years ago. Not that he didn't love Mary dearly, but she did tend to boss everybody around given half a chance, though she had mellowed a little after the set to with Alan.

That evening Jacqueline wore a royal blue cocktail dress with rhinestones adorning its low scooped neckline. She was also wearing a diamante necklace, a birthday present from Doug, and a pair of silver earrings from Grandma and Grandad Roberts.

'You look a sight for sore eyes, sweetheart,' Jack said when she came downstairs. 'Here's a little bit of something from yer dad.' Jack always found himself embarrassed when handing out presents and he shyly gave Jacqueline a parcel wrapped in rose-patterned paper.

Jacqueline tore open the paper eagerly to find a jewel box in polished wood. When she opened the lid a ballerina began a pirouette and the tune 'Fascination' began to play.

'Oh, Dad, it's absolutely beautiful, and I adore the tune. Thank you.' She hugged her father and left the box open so she could continue to listen. Mary watched her daughter with pride.

'You look a million dollars, love,' she said.

'Thanks to you, Mam.' Jacqueline gave a twirl. 'The dress is really smashing. I bet everyone at the dinner dance'll be queueing outside the shop for one just like it next week.'

'Well they won't get one.' Mary brushed a dark hair from Jacqueline's shoulder. 'Anything I make for my daughter is exclusive, and no one else will ever have one the same.'

'Well, thanks, both of you. You're making me feel guilty now for going out. I tell you what, Doug and I will make amends by taking you out for a meal tomorrow. How's that?'

'Don't be daft.' Jack laughed. 'Go and enjoy

yerselves. Make yer memories, you and Doug, now while you're young. When you get to our age they're the most precious things you can have, memories.'

Mary looked at her husband thoughtfully as Jacqueline ran out to the coach. 'That was a lovely thing to say, Jack, about the memories.'

Jack coloured slightly. 'Well it's true, isn't it? Don't you ever look back – you know, when you're sewing away all on yer own? I know I do. I might be sitting there hammering nails into someone's old shoe, surrounded by the smell of leather, and all the time I'm miles away, barn dancing in the old school at Longfield or eating a picnic among the heather, with a freckle-faced auburn-haired beauty.'

Mary felt tears prickle her eyes. 'Oh, Jack, I wonder where she's gone, the girl of your memories.'

Jack grinned. 'She's still here, love, alongside a virile dark-haired youth. Though sometimes he's hard to recognise these days.'

'Oh, Jack, you're still the same – still virile, if only I encouraged you more.' Mary walked over to where her husband was sitting and perched on his knee. 'It's just that we seem to have lost sight of each other amongst all the turmoil of raising a family and running the shops, though I don't think we've made too bad a job of it all, do you?'

'We've made a damn good job of it when you look at the kids.'

'There's just one thing though, Jack – they aren't kids any more. We need to let them go, and I'm finding that hard to come to terms with.'

Jack placed an arm round his wife and kissed her. 'Aye, love, and another thing is it's time we started making more memories.'

'Come on, then, show me some of that virility you've been bragging about.' Mary undid her blouse and slipped it off. 'We paid good money for this sheepskin rug; what do you say we try it out for comfort?' Jack joined her on the rug. They were in their prime, and it was indeed time to make more memories.

Chapter Twenty-Nine

'It's been a lovely party, as usual,' Gladys remarked as she fastened her beaver lamb coat. 'You must be exhausted, Mary, after all the catering and organising.'

'I am, but it's worth it for all the family to get together. After all, it's only Christmas once a year.'

'It looks like you'll have to throw Rowland out, otherwise he'll never go.'

'There's no need for you to go. You can have Alan's bed. Jack's mother is in Jacqueline's bed and Doug won't mind the settee.'

'No, we wouldn't think of imposing further. Besides, if you're all coming to dinner tomorrow I'll need to make an early start.'

'Imposing? After you've been like parents to me for all those years? Look, I know I haven't visited Newcastle as often as I should but I love my parents very much and I'm going to make up for that in the new year. But I love you just as much. We all do. The children have never considered you anything but their grandparents, so don't ever mention imposing again. Besides, Jacqueline's coming over with Doug in the morning. You must let her do the donkey work.'

'I will. Don't you worry about me, you know how I enjoy having you all.' Gladys walked back into the sitting room where Rowland, Jack and Doug were sprawled out discussing the boring subject of taxes. Gladys sighed. 'Don't tell me you're still on about finances. Can't you give it a rest, seeing as it's Christmas?'

Rowland dragged himself reluctantly to his feet. 'Looks like my wife's all ready to go,' he said. 'Oh well, it's been a lovely day, and that was an excellent brandy. We must continue where we left off tomorrow.'

Jack accompanied the departing guests to the door. 'Take care,' he said. 'There may be some ground frost by the looks of it.'

'We will, don't worry. You know I never do more than thirty even in daylight.'

Jacqueline giggled. 'Yes, we know. You're nothing but an old slow coach. Did you know, Dad, Doug's herd of cattle moves faster than Grandad's car?'

'And quite right too,' Mary said. Rowland cleared the windows and started the engine amidst a good deal of jesting and much waving.

'Gosh, it's cold,' Mary said, closing the door and locking up for the night. 'I'm going to bed, I don't know about anyone else.'

'Oh aye, I expect I shall have a pair of cold feet to contend with,' Jack remarked, and they went upstairs, leaving the young couple to their privacy.

'I thought they'd never go,' Doug sighed, taking Jacqueline into his arms.

'Me too.'

He undid the buttons of her silk blouse and slid his hand inside her bra, feeling her nipple harden. When her hand unzipped his trousers he was immediately erect and ready to make love, but he undressed her slowly, running his lips over her body until she was almost crying out for him to enter her. Still he caressed her, sensuously, almost driving her mad with desire. Only then did he take her by the hand and lead her silently up the stairs and into Alan's room, where they finally came together, locked in a powerful and exquisite climax.

'I don't want to leave you,' she whispered.

'Then stay,' he said. Then he changed his mind. 'Except that we don't want your mother having kittens, especially on Boxing Day.'

Jacqueline giggled and slid out of bed, crept quietly out of the room and slipped into bed beside Grandma Holmes. She lay awake for some time wondering what the year ahead would bring, and decided that if nothing turned up she would consent to live at the farm. If it was the only way to be with Doug she really had no option; their love was too powerful a force to be denied. She couldn't help comparing the tender lovemaking she had just enjoyed with Doug to the clumsy grappling of Barney Ross. What a lucky escape she had had.

Suddenly Jacqueline sat bolt upright in bed. She was drenched in perspiration despite the coldness of the room. She wondered if it had been a dream, yet knew deep down that she had been awake, that the vision had been perceived whilst she was in the hazy, half-awake state. She had witnessed it perfectly clearly, like a scene from a play, only the setting had been Moorland House and the characters had been Grandma and Grandad Roberts standing on the steps to the front door. They had waved and smiled, then disappeared in a haze. Jacqueline felt a wave of nausea wash over her as she remembered the visitation of Grandad Holmes on the night he died.

She wanted to confide her fears, to seek reassurance, but knew she mustn't wake the family so early in the morning. Besides, they would scoff at her fears – except for her mother. Jacqueline slipped out of bed and tiptoed across the landing to her parents' room, where they were sleeping like a pair of spoons, one in the other.

She shook her mother gently and Mary unlocked herself from Jack's embrace.

'What is it?' she whispered, following her daughter from the room. Jacqueline was trembling and Mary led her downstairs to the fire.

'What is it, love? Are you ill?' Mary prodded the fire with the poker, inciting a blaze, then filled the kettle before sitting beside her daughter.

'I'm frightened, Mam.' Jacqueline shivered.

'Frightened? Of what?'

'I don't know. It's just that I've had another queer vision, like the one of Grandad Holmes,

388

only this time it was Grandma and Grandad Roberts!'

Mary felt a shiver run down her spine. 'You were probably dreaming. Or maybe it was the wine – you did drink quite a bit.'

'Oh, I do hope so, Mam. I couldn't bear it if anything happened to them.'

'I'm sure it won't, but you know, love, they aren't getting any younger. We all have to go sooner or later.'

'I know, and I'm not afraid of death, I know there's a far better life beyond this one, but I'd miss them so much.' Jacqueline wiped the tears from her cheeks but her eyes continued to stream.

'Come on, love, you'll make yourself ill. I know how much you love them, so do I, but I'm sure you've no cause to worry. I'm sure it was just a dream.' Mary made the tea and poured two cups. 'Just you see, they'll be waiting for you to help with the dinner as usual in the morning.'

Jacqueline managed a smile. 'It's morning already. I'm sorry to have woken you so early.'

'It doesn't matter. I wasn't asleep anyway,' Mary fibbed. 'Come on, let's go back to bed. It isn't often we get a chance to lie in.'

They did have a lie-in, but at ten o'clock the knock on the shop door sent a shiver of fear down Jacqueline's spine. It was Jack who opened the door, expecting Alan and his family. He went cold at the sight of a policeman in uniform and another in plain clothes.

'I'm sorry to have to bother you, and on a Boxing Day too, but I've been given your name in connection with Dr Rowland Roberts and his wife Gladys. Is it correct that they were friends of yours?'

'Were?' Behind Jack Mary uttered the word in a whisper, her heart thumping in her chest.

'I'm sorry to inform you that there's been an accident. Their car swerved off the road between Cowholes and Lower Longfield and careered down the bank towards the river. I'm afraid they were killed instantly. Mrs Roberts was thrown from the car when it hit a boulder, and the doctor died from head injuries whilst still in the car. We think he might have had a heart attack initially.'

Jacqueline began to cry and Mary tried to comfort her, even through her own pain. Jack, white-faced, asked the necessary questions as though in a daze, and Doug, who had only just come downstairs, feared for the man who was not yet completely recovered from nervous illness.

'Sit down, Jack,' he ordered, and went for the brandy bottle, still on the table from last night's celebrations. 'Here, get this down you.' He gave a glass to Jack and a smaller one each to Mary and Jacqueline. The policemen refused, wanting to complete the nasty business as quickly as possible.

'Are you related to the deceased?'

'No. Oh, no, just friends, very close friends,' Jack said.

'Do you happen to know of any relatives we could contact, who might handle the arrangements?'

'There is a nephew ... my wife will probably know his whereabouts.'

Mary managed to take in what the policeman was saying. 'There is a nephew but they haven't been in contact for years.' Then she remembered. 'Gladys left some instructions in an envelope in a cash box.' Her voice broke.

'Take it easy, love,' Jack said.

'She told me once, showed me where to find it if anything happened. I think there's a copy of the will in there too. She wanted me to carry out the instructions in the letter.' Mary sobbed. 'I made a joke at the time, told her she was good for another forty years.'

'Ah well, so can we leave the arrangements in your hands? Of course there'll have to be a post-mortem. We'll be in touch with you later.'

'Where are they?' Jacqueline whispered. 'The bodies.'

'At the infirmary. We may require you to identify them later, though the doctors on duty at the time of admission have already done that informally. Seems they were colleagues of the doctor and almost as upset as you are.'

'At least he's been taken to a place he loved. It was his life, or an important part of it until he retired,' Mary said.

'If you can spare the time we'd appreciate it if you'd come to the house with us, to get the envelope you mentioned. We need to see that any arrangements are approved by their solicitor.'

'Of course. We'll come now.'

'There won't be much we can do today, being a holiday, but we need to make sure the house is made secure again, you understand.'

'I'll get our coats.' Mary followed Jack and the

policemen to the car.

'We'd better go and break the news to Alan,' Jacqueline said.

'Yes.'

'What about Grandma Holmes? It'll be a shock to her too.'

'I'd wait until we get back, if I were you. She'll need someone with her in case of shock at her age. I can hear her still pattering about in the bathroom.'

The couple went out with heavy hearts, Boxing Day celebrations forgotten. Jacqueline tried to revive the picture in her mind of the smiling couple waving from the steps of their beloved Moorland House. 'You know something,' she said, after the news had been broken to a sorrowful Alan and Avril, 'I'm so pleased they went together. I don't think either one could have survived without the other.'

'You're right,' Alan agreed. 'I've never known a couple so in love. They were like' – he searched for the right description – 'like a pair of shoes, one no good without the other.'

'Oh, I'm going to miss them so much.' Jacqueline broke into a fresh bout of weeping, and this time it was Alan whose arms enfolded her, but for once he wasn't strong: he cried just like his sister, his tears damping her dark curls. And they knew that without Grandad and Grandma Roberts life would never be quite the same again.

Despite the overwhelming heat of the car the hand clasped in Jack's was cold and lifeless. In other circumstances the low smooth hum of the engine might have lulled them into drowsiness. Through the mirror other cars could be seen following, like a trail of black shiny snails.

In the village Christmas trees twinkled in the windows of cottages, and a string of lights hung across Mrs Poppleton's shop.

Gladys would have enjoyed the glitter.

Occasionally an elderly person would stand cap in hand, paying their last respects to a well-loved lady and gentleman. Mary looked at the car in front, and another in front of that, the long wooden caskets, the rich autumn hues of chrysanthemums, cream, bronze, purple and gold. That's how she would remember them, knee deep in chrysanthemums, carrying in bunches from the garden, and other more magnificent blooms, filling the glass lean-to with their overpowering perfume.

She heard Richard in the seat in front comment on the size of the cortège and responded automatically. 'It's probably the largest funeral ever to take place at Longfield Church,' she said, and all the time she was thinking that if Rowland was there he would be chatting, cheering her up, joking her out of her misery. But he wasn't there, and neither was Gladys; they were gone, extinguished like a light, no bother to anyone, just the way they had always wanted to go.

'Life is for the living,' Rowland used to say. 'No use worrying about the dead.'

Mary supposed he was right, but even so there would always be an empty place in her heart for the dearest friends she had ever known.

The church was full to overflowing, people from

the surrounding villages and nuns from the convent mingling with doctors, nurses and professors of the highest standing. Father Flynn had made the long exhausting journey from Newcastle, and Rowland's choir was already assembled in the choir stalls, numbed by the loss of their beloved conductor.

Richard and Ruth had arrived in the morning, more for the purpose of finding the name of their uncle's solicitor than to mourn their dead. They were given front seats in the car as chief mourners. Dressed completely in black and putting on a pious look for the benefit of the undertaker who was unaware that the pair hadn't found time to visit their aunt and uncle for more years than anyone could remember, they looked at Mary with disdain.

'To them I'm just an ex-housemaid,' Mary whispered.

'You're probably richer than they'll ever be,' Jack replied. 'And richer certainly when it comes to peace of mind.'

Mary had left the choice of hymns to the choir, and they had chosen Rowland's favourite 'Abide With Me', and 'The Lord's My Shepherd' for Gladys. There were few dry eyes in the centuries-old church.

Afterwards, as they stood at the graveside, the words of Tom Downing came back to Mary: 'Doesn't the church stand well?' Thinking of Tom it would have been easy to blame the Christmas sin for this further tragedy, but remembering Jacqueline's experience at the Spiritual Church she wisely dismissed the thought from her mind.

She looked across the valley to where the tall rooftops of Moorland House rose proudly among the trees. It was fitting that her friends should be laid to rest within view of the house.

At the request of Richard the reading of the wills took place immediately after the funeral tea, on account of his having business to attend to and being in a hurry to leave.

Rowland's dear friend Ernest Sessions had been appointed executor and Mary would have given anything to spare the poor old man the pain of having to be here so soon after the burial of his friend.

The shock of the solicitor's reading was almost as traumatic as the news of the accident had been. In the first place only a small monetary bequest had been made to Richard and Ruth, on the grounds that they had been so busy succeeding in their chosen professions over the past ten years that a larger legacy would be unnecessary.

Jack almost smiled as the solicitor read the words. They were so clearly Rowland's own words, and he could almost imagine the doctor's hearty guffaw, booming round the room. Mary, however, felt sorry for the couple, whose crestfallen faces proved they had expected the bulk of the estate.

Gladys's jewellery and some other mementos had been left to Mary, and Rowland had left any car which he might own, his gold pocket watch and some other pieces to Jack. Fortunately, Jack valued the personal items far more than the car, which had been written off in the accident.

A bequest had also been made to the infirmary. But the shock came with the further announcement that all stocks, shares and money remaining after the funeral expenses and taxes had been paid was bequeathed to Alan, who couldn't quite believe what he was hearing. Jacqueline was so pleased for her brother she almost missed the last and most important part of the legacies: *I devise my freehold property known as Moorland House situated in Longfield in the County of York to Jacqueline Mary Holmes.*

Halfway through January Mary announced she had decided to go to Newcastle. Jack, who had been worried about his wife, who looked decidedly run down and pale, a reaction from the shock of the accident, pronounced the trip an excellent idea.

'It's so long since I saw my mother and father I feel almost as bad as Richard and Ruth,' Mary said.

'Oh, come on, it's not all that long, and they know they're welcome here any time.'

'I know, but losing Gladys and Rowland has made me realise how quickly things can happen, I couldn't live with myself if anything happened to my parents when I haven't seen them for over a year.'

'Is it really so long? Well then, we'll get things arranged as soon as possible. I'll get the tickets tomorrow.'

'You mean you'll come with me?' Mary's face brightened.

'I don't see why not. It's quiet at the moment except for wellingtons and boots – shoe sales won't really pick up till Easter. I'm sure Sally can manage for a week or even two – in fact she'll probably enjoy it. I'll put a notice up cancelling repairs until we get back. What about you?'

'I've already arranged it with Yvonne. She's eager enough if I pay her extra, and I'm sure Avril will help out. She and Alan might even move in here until we get back. If we go now we'll be back before they move to the new house.'

Avril enjoyed the change, and the company of Yvonne, who kept her up to date with what was happening amongst the young set. Yvonne's new boyfriend was a rocker; he called for her in the evenings wearing full leather motorcycle gear and a lot of facial hair. Avril had to admit he was well mannered, though, and it was hard to believe he was part of a group rumoured to have clashed with a gang of mods a few weeks previously.

Yvonne said it was untrue, and the culprits were from Barnsley way, and that the Millington rockers were more interested in spending Saturdays tinkering with their own bikes than smashing other people's scooters. Avril gave her the benefit of the doubt and helped her young friend create a high beehive hairstyle ready for the dance. She felt quite envious when the young couple went off hand in hand after the shop had closed for the weekend.

She still couldn't take it in about the legacy. Alan was astounded at the amount of money involved. He needn't worry about a mortgage at all, and would still be quite wealthy even after settling the undertaker's bill. He felt slightly guilty that the money had come to him instead of his parents, and decided to talk to his father about it. Jack explained it had been done for a reason.

'It should have been yours and Mother's by rights,' Alan insisted.

'Your mother and I have enough to last us till the end of our days so long as trade keeps as it is now. Enjoy it, son, but spend it wisely,' Jack advised.

Only Jack had known of Rowland's intentions. He had discussed his finances at length when Jack was recovering from his illness; in fact he had discussed everything he could think of to reawaken Jack's interest in the outside world. One day he had said to Jack, 'Gladys and I are about to make a new will. We're debating what to do with all our wealth, which is quite considerable.'

'I hope you're not going to die on us yet,' Jack had replied.

'I hope not too, but one never knows. Of course, when one of us dies it will all belong to the other. But after that we're uncertain of what to do for the best. You and Mary aren't the type to sit back in the lap of luxury, and anyway it wouldn't be good for you in your present state of health.'

'I'm not going to be ill for ever, but you're right: I need to be occupied.'

'So we're thinking of leaving it to the children.'

'Richard's boys?' Jack asked.

'Jacqueline and Alan,' Rowland answered, searching Jack's face for some reaction.

'That'd be nice. They'd appreciate a little nest egg.'

'It wouldn't be a nest egg, it would be the nest.

Moorland House, and all that goes with it.'

Jack hadn't taken it in at first, unsure what to say. 'What does Gladys think about it?'

'Her idea,' Rowland said. 'We think the world of Mary, and you of course; not having been blessed with children of our own, we kind of adopted her from the beginning. But with the children it was different – it was they who adopted us. From the first they accepted us as grandparents and they've brought us a great deal of joy.'

'I know,' Jack said. 'And I'm pleased.'

'It would be terrible to think Moorland House was to be sold to strangers after we'd gone, and I don't think Jacqueline would do that. She loves the house in the same way Gladys does, and my parents did before us. It's like some powerful obsession they have about the place.'

'She loves you and Gladys in the same way.'

'So you won't be offended then if it misses a generation?'

'Our kids mean everything to us, you know that, and I can't think of anything that'd make Mary and me happier than knowing they had security. Not that we'd ever see them short, but our Alan's so bloody independent.'

'And you know as well as I do who he takes after.' Rowland smiled. Jack had nodded and grinned, and the conversation had never been mentioned again.

'Well,' Alan was saying, 'if ever you and Mother need anything you know where to come.'

Jacqueline had said the same, offering them a home at Moorland House should they ever need it.

'What, and miss all the gossip and scandal of Millington?' Mary had scowled. 'No thanks, love. Your dad and me are more than happy where we are.'

Jacqueline walked the rooms of Moorland House in a daze, touching the porcelain figurines Gladys had collected over the years, the school photos of her and Alan, her parents' wedding photograph on the piano. Even the piano belonged to her, and she still couldn't take it in.

She walked upstairs into the bedroom used by Grandma and Grandad Roberts for half a century, and saw their clothes in the wardrobe, a nightdress just as Gladys had left it draped over the basket chair. She picked it up and buried her face in its softness, overcome by the scent still on the garment. She sat on the edge of the bed where she had bounced as if on a trampoline as a little girl, and suddenly she caught the pungent aroma of cigar smoke. She turned swiftly, expecting Grandad Roberts to be there in the room. She couldn't see him but she knew he was present. They were both present, and always would be. No matter how many generations passed through Moorland House, the Robertses would never leave.

She cheered at the thought, the sadness and melancholy of the past weeks draining from her body and leaving her refreshed, and ready for the future. This wasn't a house for sorrow. She would fill it once more with love, she and Doug together, for the next half-century with God's help.

She went to the window and opened it wide,

letting in the cold fresh air, savouring the glory of the view over Longfield. It was only then that the full impact hit her. This house was hers, all hers, and soon it would be Doug's too, as soon as the wedding could be arranged. She called out into the stillness of the room, 'Thank you for the house, thank you for your love and thank you for the memories, and Doug and I will add to them, just like Dad told us, just you see if we don't.'

Then she ran downstairs and out of the house, locking the door behind her. She had no time to lose. There was a wedding to be arranged.

Apart from organising the wedding Jacqueline threw herself wholeheartedly into her work. She wasn't certain she was suited to teaching. She adored the children and was happy with the school. She got on well with her colleagues but somehow she wasn't gaining the satisfaction from the job she had expected. She decided to give it everything she had until after the wedding and then make up her mind what to do.

She had an idea she would be happier running Gardener's Rest. Her mother wouldn't like it, would no doubt rant on about wasting all her education, but it couldn't be helped. Besides, her dad had told her to make memories and nothing could make better memories than being by Douglas Downing's side.

Chapter Thirty

The wedding ceremony took place at Longfield church, and the vicar was delighted to marry the new owners of Moorland House.

Jacqueline wondered what his thoughts would have been had he known she was regularly attending the Spiritual church in town. But the thought of Grandad and Grandma Roberts in the churchyard helped her decide on Longfield.

The congregation consisted of the whole O'Connor family, the Downings, the Holmeses, and half of Longfield. Father Flynn declined the invitation on the grounds that the journey was becoming too much for him, though Mary couldn't help wondering if he would have made the effort had the wedding been taking place at St Catherine's.

Pam, Yvonne and Lucy's daughter made beautiful bridesmaids in dresses of turquoise organdie designed by Mary, and little Elizabeth in white caused quite a stir. An awkward moment occurred when Yvonne was dressing the little girl and remarked on the birthmark on her back. The moment passed and Mary realised that unless anyone ever told her, there was no way Yvonne could know she possessed an identical one herself.

It was Jacqueline who stole the limelight, in an ivory gown of pure silk, with a train which seemed to go on for ever. Her hair had been tamed for once and piled high to form a dark crown of waves on which was set a coronet of pearls and orange blossom, which Avril had spent all morning trying to perfect.

Jack thought he would burst with pride and even considered refusing to give her away, so dear to him was his daughter. Freddie Cartwright made a handsome usher along with Charlie Barker, on whom Jacqueline insisted on bestowing the honour, despite protests from the family. Charlie was so proud he carried out his duties to perfection, just as Jacqueline had expected.

Jack had insisted on hiring the dance hall for the reception, a buffet affair for which Grandma Holmes thought he had paid through the nose. 'These posh dos are all very well,' she remarked to Mrs O'Connor, 'but you can't beat a good sit-down tea. With what this lot's costing we could have had ourselves a three-course meal.'

'I know what you mean. These pastry things with the fancy French names are not very filling,' Mary's mother replied. Mary pointed out that there were far too many guests for everyone to sit down, what with all the customers, most of the teaching staff and a class full of children invited. In fact Alan said he thought half of Millington had gatecrashed the dance which followed the meal.

Mick O'Connor wondered if there would be another fist fight before the night was out. He wouldn't be surprised with the number of teenagers writhing about on the dance floor. He looked round at his three strapping sons and his sons-in-law, at his grandson and now Jacqueline's new husband. If there was any trouble they were all big enough to sort it out. Oh, but he was a fortunate man – maybe not rich in money, but with his family all healthy and most of them settled close to the family home, he was richer in love than any millionaire.

Una looked a picture in a dusky pink linen two-piece, and Grandma Holmes thought her young man ever so handsome. He kept the old lady supplied with glasses of brown ale, and the more she drank the more she revealed to him of the family history. He said he couldn't wait to sample the home-made cakes which Una missed so much now she was working away all the time. Grandma Holmes invited him to tea, and thought how smart he looked in his dark suit and white shirt.

She told Una later, 'You want to look after your new young man. You could do a lot worse.' Then she whispered confidentially, 'He's much better than that Billy Flame character.'

Una smiled. 'I hope you haven't told him that.'

'Course I 'aven't,' her grandmother said.

'Grandma,' Una said, her eyes twinkling, 'my new young man, as you call him, is Billy Flame.'

Grandma Holmes's mouth sagged open.

'Minus the wig and the make-up. Surely you didn't think Billy was dressed in his normal everyday attire for the stage?'

'Eeh, well, would you believe it?' Mrs Holmes was lost for words. 'Eeh, just imagine, I've invited Billy Flame to tea.'

'Shush,' Una warned. 'Don't let anyone hear or

he'll have no peace for the rest of the night.'

Mrs Holmes sat there bemused, and only came round when Billy Flame dragged her on to the dance floor for the hokey-cokey.

'Eeh,' she said to herself. 'Fancy me dancing with one of them show business folk.' But she had to admit he did seem nice.

Harry was propping up the bar waiting for the drinks to be served. He stiffened as the voice beside him said, 'I'll pay for those.'

He hoped to God Eddie Banwell wasn't the worse for drink. He opened his mouth to protest, but Eddie didn't give him a chance. 'Go on. I reckon I owe you a drink, as a peace offering.'

'Nay, you don't owe me owt. I got what I deserved, no more no less. I don't need any peace offering. I'm not a man to bear malice, never was.'

'I'm glad about that.' Eddie paid for the drinks and told the bartender to keep the change. 'It's been a grand do.'

'Aye.' Harry was uncertain about Eddie Banwell. Surely he wasn't going to make trouble after all this time, and with his wife and daughter amongst the guests?

Eddie leaned against the bar. 'I reckon it's set your brother back a bob or two for this little lot.'

'Aye.' Harry smiled. 'He can afford it. He's done well for himself has our Jack.'

'No more than he deserves. They've been good to our Yvonne, giving her a job and that.'

'Oh, I don't know. According to Mary they couldn't have employed a better lass.'

Eddie glanced at Harry. 'Oh, she's a good lass

all right.'

'She's a little beauty.' Harry tried to sound casual. 'She made a lovely bridesmaid.'

'Hmm,' Eddie drawled. 'Yes, I reckon I owe you more than a pint, Harry.'

Harry looked at the man warily but Eddie only grinned. Then his face turned serious. 'You'll never know how much I owe you. My lass means everything to me, and she was the making of Ada too. She's been a good wife since Yvonne was born. But I'm not blind, and I'd have to be not to know she's yours.'

'Oh, come on, man...' Harry was silenced as Eddie put up his hand.

'No, no, hear me out. I'm not complaining. It's obvious I couldn't have kids – I reckon I'd have had one in every port I ever docked in if I'd been able. I was no angel, not by a long chalk. No, Harry, I love that lass more than life itself, but I know she's yours.' The man gave a weak smile but looked closer to tears. 'Ada doesn't know I know and she never will. But I didn't want the likes of you thinking you'd pulled the wool over my eyes.'

Harry didn't know what to say and just stood there shame-faced. Then he said quietly, 'I'm not proud of meself, Eddie. There hasn't been a day since when I haven't regretted what I did. Every time I walk in the shop, or see Yvonne on the street, I'm haunted by it.'

Eddie picked up the drinks. 'Don't be,' he said. 'Just keep yer bloody mouth shut, that's all I ask. I wouldn't like my daughter to find out, and she is my daughter, just remember that.'

'She won't find out from me,' Harry called, but Eddie had already gone, back to his wife and daughter.

Everybody agreed it was the best wedding ever to be celebrated in Millington, and Jacqueline shed a few tears when the time came to leave for their new home.

'We're off now, Mam,' she said. 'It's been a wonderful day thanks to you, and to you, Dad. We hope you don't mind if we slip off unnoticed – I'm going to cry and I don't want everyone watching me. Will you come to tea tomorrow? Bring Grandma and Grandad O'Connor – I'd like them to visit us before they go home.'

'They're staying a week so you'll be seeing them anyway, but yes, we'll come. That's if you want us to when you're honeymooning.'

'We want you.'

Doug saw the tears welling in the eyes of his wife and mother-in-law. He clasped Jacqueline's hand and they made their exit, leaving their many friends to enjoy the party for a few more hours.

'At last. I thought I'd never get you away.' Doug kissed her, a long passionate kiss. 'That's just to be going on with,' he promised, and then Jacqueline started the car and they were off on the journey into marriage.

When they'd made love, rested and made love again, Jacqueline looked at the ring her mother had slipped on her finger before they had left for the church.

'You didn't tell me my mother was once engaged to your brother.'

'I thought you already knew. Besides, I was only a nipper at the time; engagements meant nothing to me then. In fact, I can only just remember our Tom.'

'She's given me the ring. She wanted me to have it, says it belongs at Moorland House not in Millington.'

'She must have loved our Tom a lot to have kept it after her marriage.'

'Yes, she did, she told me. She also told me they'd made love, only once, the Christmas before he was killed, and how she'd blamed herself for the tragedy. Can you imagine anyone being influenced by the church so much so that they think God would punish them for making love?'

'Well, morals are a lot more lax nowadays,' Doug pointed out.

'Do you know, if I hadn't mentioned what happened at the Spiritual Church, I think she'd have carried on worrying for the rest of her days. The Christmas sin, that's how she thought of it. She says she must have been blind, not to see all the good things that happened at Christmases through the years. All my mother ever saw were the bad things.'

'And now she's finally over it?'

'Oh, yes. She's only sorry she made Dad miserable for all those years. Apparently he thought she was pining for her lost soldier, when all she was doing was trying to forgive herself.' Jacqueline twisted the ring on her right hand. 'I'm going to wear it all the time. I'm sure your brother would like that. He may even come through at church again and tell me so.'

Doug drew her into his arms. 'You're a strange girl,' he said. 'But I love you all the same.'

Jacqueline was all for making love again, but Doug suddenly drew away. 'I've got a surprise for you. Well, for us actually,' he said. He opened the drawer next to the bed and took out a large brown envelope.

'What is it?'

'Open it and see.' Jacqueline opened the envelope and took out a document. It was the deeds of his father's farm.

'What are you doing with these?' she asked.

'They're ours. The farm's ours. I know how worried you were about losing Gardener's Rest, so I put a proposition to the rest of them, gave them all a quarter of what the farm is worth and had a contract drawn up for my parents, to safeguard their future. They will be allowed to live there for the rest of their days.'

'But don't they mind? I mean, they're not making anything out of it.'

'My father's relieved, actually. I shall be responsible for any necessary repairs, and he knows the farm will stay in the family. If you read the deeds you'll find the place has belonged to the Downings since it was built a hundred and fifty years ago. It would have been sold and the money shared on the death of my parents. My father would have hated that.'

'But what about the others? Don't they mind?'

'Not at all. Our Bessie's already planning on taking Sam on a cruise. It looks like being a honeymoon too, and not before time. Our Lucy'll probably pay off their mortgage, and our Cyril thinks it's a godsend. He had his eye on a place he couldn't quite afford, and now he'll be able to.'

'You haven't said what your mother thought of it all.'

'So long as we're going to be close at hand my mother'll be content. She loves the hustle and bustle of Gardener's Rest and is talking about opening a teashop in the front room, selling her home-made cakes. I wouldn't put it past her, either.'

'Oh, Doug, it must have cost you a fortune.'

'It has, but no more than if I'd needed to provide us with a home. Besides, the business is going from strength to strength. We'll soon be on our feet again. Actually, it's an investment for the future, for our children. My father's counting on our having a son, to follow him on the farm.'

'We mustn't let him down, then.' Jacqueline decided it was time to resume their honeymoon and dived under the sheets.

Chapter Thirty-One

Mary went to draw the bedroom curtains and noticed the moonlight, and the tall chimneys casting shadows on the snow-topped hill.

'Oh, Jack, just look at the moon, and the snow on the hill.'

'I'd rather not. It should be spring by now. Who ever heard of snow in March, especially on our daughter's wedding day.'

'Well, it didn't actually snow today, that's one consolation, and where it's lingering on the hill it looks beautiful – weird with the chimneys, but beautiful all the same. Do come and look.'

Jack walked over and placed an arm round his wife's waist. 'You're right, it does look well. And I noticed the grass is growing now they've shut the coke ovens. It might even cover the hills in a few years' time. But I'm dead beat. Can't we go to bed? It's been a long day.'

'Yes, we'd better if I'm to be up early in the morning.'

'Up early? It's Sunday. Aren't we having a lie-in?'

'I thought I might go to church.'

'Church? What, St Catherine's?'

'Of course. Where else would I go?'

'Well I never know with this family. There's our Jacqueline born a Catholic, turns Spiritualist and then decides to get married at Longfield.'

'Ah, but the Downings have always worshipped at Longfield church, and you know our Jacqueline. She's a free spirit; no one will influence her.'

'Quite right too. Then there's our Avril, she's begun going to the chapel of all places, taking my mother with her too. And you, well, it's so long since you've been to St Catherine's I wondered what suddenly changed your mind.'

'I've been talking to Theresa tonight. Seems they have a new priest, she says he's like a breath of fresh air, caring and more modern in outlook than the old one. Besides, I feel as though I need to go. I've missed it these past years, and this time I won't be going out of duty or conscience, but because I want to.'

411

'Well, we'd better get some sleep then. I feel as if I haven't been to bed for weeks.'

'But it all went off splendidly, the wedding I mean.'

'Aye, but we're going to miss our Jacqueline,' Jack said.

'Just like we missed our Alan,' his wife added.

'It's going to be quiet without them, Mary.'

'Not for long.'

'No, I suppose there'll be one or the other popping in most days.'

'I didn't mean that.'

'Oh? What did you mean then?'

'I mean I'm pregnant again.'

'What?'

'Oh, Jack, I hope you don't mind. I know I should have worn my cap, but I just got carried away. Besides, it wasn't entirely my fault. After all, you were bragging about how young and virile you were on the night of our Jacqueline's birthday.'

'You mean you've known since Christmas and you've only just told me?'

'I had so much on my mind that I didn't realise at first, what with the funeral, and then our trip to Newcastle. Besides, at my age, it could have been the change, but it isn't. Dr Sellers says I'm definitely pregnant.'

'Oh, Mary, you will be all right, won't you?'

'I'm fine, never better. I've worked it out, and with Yvonne's help I should be able to carry on with the shop. I shall just cut down on my own designs for a while and do more buying. I know one thing: you and the baby are going to come

412

first from now on. You're sure you don't mind?'

'Mind? I can't wait. It might be a son to follow me in the business, and maybe if I steer clear of presents like engines and Dinky toys he won't grow up with a mania for motors. We'll buy him a tool set instead and give him a few hints on repairing shoes.' Jack laughed.

'He'll do as he likes, just the same as the others have,' Mary said.

'Aye I know, and we shall be just as proud of this one as we are of the others.'

'But it might be a girl,' Mary said eagerly.

'Maybe.' Jack grinned. 'But there's one thing for sure, I shan't be buying her a bloody sewing machine.'

'Oh, Jack, it will be lovely next Christmas, with a new baby in the house.'

'Aye. Better than the last, but looking back we've had some good Christmases.'

'Like the ones when our Jacqueline was born, and our Alan,' Mary reflected. 'Then our Alan met Avril, and our Elizabeth was conceived at Christmas if I'm not mistaken.' She sighed. 'It seems all the best things in our lives took place at Christmas.'

'The best thing in my life was when I met you, and don't you forget it. Oh, and by the way, I've got something for you.'

'For me?'

'Aye, for our anniversary. Don't forget we once had a wedding too.' He took a tiny velvet box from his pocket, opened it and lifted out a gold ring set with sparkling hearts. 'I never can remember the exact date but I know I've got the

413

month right.' He smiled shyly.

'Oh, Jack, it's beautiful.' She placed it on her finger. 'And now I feel awful. With all the wedding arrangements I haven't got you anything.' She couldn't tell him he was a month late.

'I've already got the greatest gift possible. I've got you.'

'Yes, Jack, you've got me. Even without an eternity ring you'd have been lumbered with me for ever, and Jack, I know I don't tell you very often, but I do love you.'

'I know, lass. We neither of us tell each other very often, but I know.'

'Perhaps we should tell each other more. Gladys said we should, and Rowland.'

'Aye, but Rowland was good with words and I'm not. What was it our old man used to say?'

'I don't know, but I wouldn't be surprised at anything your dad used to say.'

'"If you want fancy words, Lizzie lass, you'll have to look them up in a bloody dictionary." I suppose I must take after him.'

Mary switched out the light. 'Your father was a wise man, and a lovely one,' she said. 'I'm glad you take after him.'

Then they went towards the bed, hand in hand in the moonlight.

This Large Print Book for the partially sighted, who cannot read normal print, is published under the auspices of

THE ULVERSCROFT FOUNDATION